the NECESSARY HUNGER

a novel

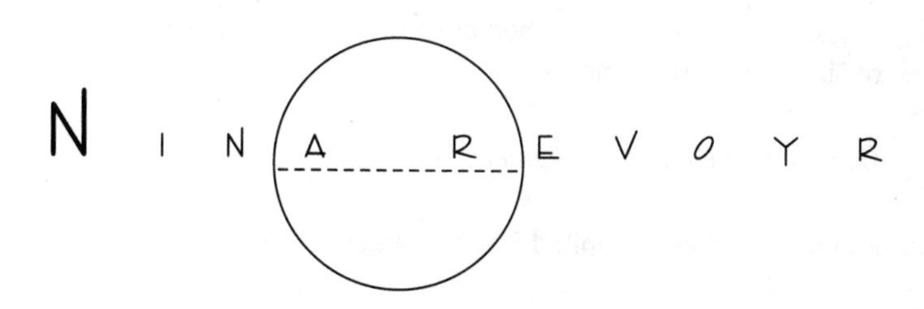

Simon & Schuster

SIMON & SCHUSTER
Rockefeller Center
1230 Avenue of the Americas
New York, NY 10020

This book is a work of fiction. Names, characters, places, and incidents either are products of the author's imagination or are used fictitiously. Any resemblance to actual events or locales or persons, living or dead, is entirely coincidental.

Designed by Elina D. Nudelman

Manufactured in the United States of America

10 9 8 7 6 5 4 3 2 1

Library of Congress Cataloging-in-Publication Data
Revoyr, Nina.
The necessary hunger : a novel / Nina Revoyr.
p. cm.
I. Title.
PS3568.E7964N4 1997
813'.54--dc20 96-32999
CIP

ISBN 0-684-83234-8

ACKNOWLEDGMENTS

I would like to thank the many people who helped me with this book: Donald Faulkner, for his support, his beer, and his patience when I was just starting out; Jane Dystel, my agent, for taking a chance on a young unknown; Ken McClane, for his energy, his faith, and his stories about Mr. Baldwin; Maureen McCoy, Lamar Herrin, Jason Brown, Karen Brown, Mike Chen, Julie Hilden, Kirsten Major, and Linda Myers, for their generosity and their criticism; Sarah Pinckney, my editor, for her advice, her prodding, and her enthusiastic conversations about books and basketball; Dan McCall, for his stubborn insistence that this story was really a novel; Alison Lurie, for the use of her office; and last but not least, special thanks to Stephanie Vaughn, for her eyebrows, and for never being satisfied.

I would also like to acknowledge my debt to the movie *Hoop Dreams,* and to Darcy Frey's brilliant nonfiction book, *The Last Shot.* Had it not been for these two works, and the interest and discussion they generated, my manuscript might have languished forever in the bottom of my desk drawer.

If I have forgotten to thank anyone, I apologize. I have been moved by the support and encouragement that people have given me, and I owe everyone a tremendous debt.

For my father

and

for Andrea

If you
train your ears
for what's
unstated
Beneath the congratulations(!)
That silence
is my story.

—Cornelius Eady,
"GRATITUDE"
from *The Gathering of My Name*

CHAPTER 1

In December of 1984, when Raina and I were sophomores, my high school held its first and last annual girls' winter basketball tournament, the Inglewood Christmas Classic. The next year, an hour before the first-round games were set to start, a light-fixture fell from the ceiling and left a six-foot hole in the floor, and the indignity of having to cancel the tournament once convinced my coach we shouldn't host it anymore. This was a shame, because the first Classic was the only tournament we ever actually won. It was also the place I met Raina. I was running the clock on the first day when my coach came over and told me that Raina Webber had just walked in, and that I should pay attention to her. He didn't add—he couldn't have known—that a few months later, our parents would meet and fall in love, and that eventually the four of us would live together. All he knew then was that Raina and I were two of the top sophomores in Los Angeles County. That day, when her game began, I sat and watched her in awe, so dazzled by the way she slashed through the other team's defense that I kept forgetting to add points to the scoreboard. Midway through the second quarter, Raina dove for a loose ball and landed smack on the scorers' table. She'd knocked the scoreboard control box into my lap, and she lay facedown, her head between my hands where the box had just been and her legs trailing onto the floor. Dazed, she looked up into my face for a moment. Then her eyes began to focus.

"Hey," she said, smiling. "You're Nancy, right? I'm Raina. That was a hella sweet pass you threw against Crenshaw yesterday, and I know their coach called you a hot dog 'cos you passed behind your back, but shit, there *was* a defender kinda standin in your way, and besides, if you got it, you should use it, don't you think?"

She stood up, pulled the box off my lap and placed it on the table, and then ran back onto the court before I had time to answer. To me, that first encounter would repeat itself in various forms through all the years I knew her—Raina would land in front of me, and I would flounder.

Basketball, for Raina and me, was more a calling than a sport; it was our sustenance; it underpinned our lives. Every Sunday morning, as I drove the twenty-eight miles from our house in Inglewood to a gym in Cerritos, I saw well-dressed people on their way to the churches, mosques, and synagogues that were scattered throughout Southern California. I was en route to my Junior Olympic team's weekend practice, but my intention wasn't really so different. That drive to Cerritos was my weekend ritual, but it made up just a fraction of the time I gave to my sport. I was reverent and devout. The only differences between my faith and theirs were that I wore workout clothes instead of my Sunday best and that I worshipped every day.

Los Angeles was a great place to live if you were a basketball fanatic, because the sport was all around you. Besides being the only city that had two NBA teams—the Lakers and the Clippers—it was the home of half a dozen major colleges. Better yet, the players were part of the scenery. In the mid-eighties, when I was in high school there, it wasn't unusual to run into Magic

Johnson at the mall; see Byron Scott drive through the neighborhood on his way to visit his mother; or spot Cheryl Miller, the great USC star, dancing up a storm at a local nightclub. Each August, Magic, Isiah Thomas, and other NBA stars would play pickup games at UCLA, and I'd go watch them as often as I could. The world was perfect on those summer afternoons. If Jesus himself had finally shown up, I wouldn't have noticed unless he'd worn sneakers and had a dangerous jump shot.

In our own small way, we high school players were celebrities, too. For one thing, we weren't subject to the same rules as other students. When my teammate Telisa got sent to the principal's office our junior year for calling her physics teacher an asshole (well, he *was* an asshole—he called Telisa a wench, because he referred to all women as wenches, and she finally got sick of it and told him off. All the girls in the class applauded when she did it, too), the principal just laughed and let her off without even listening to her side of the story. We were picked to win our league that year, and he refused to punish one of the people responsible for wresting glory away from the schools around us.

For another, we were always being recognized. This was especially true once our pictures started appearing regularly in the papers, and, in my case and in Raina's, after we'd been named third-team All-State our sophomore year and had begun to attract the attention of college scouts. I'd be shopping, or getting gas, or hanging out at the beach, and someone would come up and tell me that they'd seen me at such and such a place playing against this or that team, and that I'd scored however many points that day. Once, when I was with Raina at the movies our senior year, some little freshmen who'd seen her play in a tournament somewhere started screaming and asked for her autograph like she was a rock star.

The admiration was occasionally more ardent. I received a couple of suggestive fan letters, some players were given flowers or candy, and sometimes I even got phone calls from people who seemed impressed by things other than my skills on the court. After Raina moved in we got twice as many calls. She dealt with this better than I did. She talked to all her callers politely and said that she was sorry, but she already had someone and so it was impossible for her to meet them for a date. I, on the other hand, was not as composed—I always just got nervous and hung up.

If my teammates had ever heard me say I wasn't comfortable with being a big-time college recruit, they would have laughed long and hard, but it was true. As an only child, I lacked the social skills to shift easily into the role of semipublic figure, and I wasn't even gifted physically, except with height. Once, after a summer league game, I found a scouting report that a college coach had left in the bleachers, and so I discovered that the official word on me was this:

> Nancy Takahiro, Senior Forward—6′ 0″, 155 lbs. Doesn't have the best athletic ability, but a great scorer and effective rebounder. Smart, consistent, tremendously hardworking, and can be counted on to get the little things done.

I always wondered what my father would have thought about the "getting little things done" part, since his refrain throughout those years was that I never cleaned my room. Still, it was the textbook portrait of a type-A only child. Takahiro means "tall and wide."

It wasn't easy being big. It seemed to me that the world had a grudge against big people, especially Asian ones, like me, who were supposed to be small. A few houses down from us there lived an old widow named Mrs. Cooper, a lady whose skin was both the color and the texture of a walnut shell, and every time I passed her on the street she clutched her purse a little tighter, although we'd lived on the same block together for the past eleven years. Short adults glanced up at my face suspiciously, even when I was being polite. Babies looked at me and burst out crying.

Maybe that's why I was drawn to Raina, because she was compact, her body well-proportioned and economical. At 5′ 7″ she wasn't tiny, but she was still five inches shorter than me.

Tougher, too, or so I believed—and I felt qualified to say that because I watched her more closely than anyone else, with the possible exception of the scouts. The day she landed on the table and introduced herself, her team, which was seeded eighth, was going up against the number one seed. Raina was the shooting guard on that underdog team, and she was making all the other players look like they were standing still. She moved around the gym as if it had been built for her—not arrogantly, but with the casual assumption that everyone knew it was hers and wouldn't mind that she'd come there to claim it. She was always the first person up the court, always weaving through people like they were rooted to the floor, not because she was so much quicker than everyone else, but because it didn't seem to occur to her that she could fail. When she stood at the free throw line, she stared at the basket and held the ball at her waist as if she'd forgotten she had to shoot it, as if she could score the point just by concentrating hard enough. This attitude, I learned later, was typical Raina—she approached every aspect of the game as if it were a matter of will.

And who's to say it isn't? Over the years coaches and parents have encouraged kids to participate in sports on the grounds that sports build character. I've always thought it was more accurate to say that they *show* it. You live the way you play. A kid who blows an easy lay-up in the last few seconds of a close game is going to choke ten years later on the witness stand. A kid who can kick a field goal to win the state football championship could be trusted to land a plane in a tornado. If there is something to be known about a person, it will become evident on the court, or on the field. People with no experience in competitive sports don't understand how revealing they can be. Or how serious. Anyone who thinks traders on Wall Street are under pressure should try shooting a free throw in a packed gym with the game on the line.

When I saw Raina play that day, saw the way she stamped her foot against the floor in a stubborn refusal to give up, I knew my own devotion to basketball was just a shadow of what I was witnessing then. She played the game the way that it was meant to be played—as if her life depended on it. And she seemed driven by some need, or struggle, or fundamental resolve, that preceded the basketball and made it possible, and that I could never have accurately explained or described except to say that I myself didn't have it. The immediate effect of this resolve was that her team came back from ten points down that day to beat the top seed, which had finished second in the state the year before. Two days later, in the semifinals, her team would lose to the team *we* went on to beat for the championship, but that day, the day of the first-round games, was Raina's. As I sat at the scorers' table watching her team celebrate at midcourt, I wondered about the guts and will that had led to that improbable charge from behind. And later, when I noticed her strong, broad cheekbones, her suddenly hesitant step, the shy grin that flashed out of that smooth coffee-with-cream face, I wondered about the person who owned them.

Although Raina might have said I never made a fool of myself over her, I was a better judge, and I know that I did. I was fifteen when I met her, and at the beginning of an awkward phase that would last for roughly another decade, but I managed, somehow, to stumble my way into her life. We had some friends in common through summer league and the Amateur Athletic Union; through them I'd find out what game or party she planned to attend and then show up at it myself. My main source of information was Stacy Gatling—a high school teammate of Raina's who played on my spring league team that year. She was, like us, a lover of women, or as we put it, "in the family." Within a week of the beginning of spring league she informed me that Raina had a girlfriend, an older girl named Toni, and gave me her opinion of the calm, cool way I tried to deal with my attraction for her teammate.

"She knows you like her, Nance," Stacy told me in the middle of a game one day while we were both warming the bench. "It's fuckin obvious. You act like a fool around her."

"Shit," I answered. "Shit."

"Stop trippin, girl," she said. "It's all right. You know she don't want you, so just play it cool. She likes you, though, so don't mess the friendship up by actin all crazy and shit."

I hadn't known that Raina was spoken for, although I'd heard that she was gay. It was one of the great ironies of gossip that all the paranoid straight players who talked incessantly about who was gay actually did us the service of helping us find each other. That was how Stacy had heard about me, and I her. Anyway, Stacy went on to tell me that Raina's relationship with her girlfriend, Toni, was extremely rocky, or as she put it, "drop dead hella intense." This didn't surprise me, although I didn't say so. You live the way you play.

I would say that each love has a moment when it makes a mark on your poetic consciousness, when it rearranges the way you see both the love itself, and through it, your entire life. For me that mark was made the next July, when Raina and I, and a hundred other recruits, headed off to a nearby college to attend Blue Star. In theory Blue Star was a basketball camp, an instructional week, but in truth it was a glorified meat market—and it would become more so, in the next few years, as the popularity of women's basketball grew. That summer, two or three hundred vultures from colleges all over the country sat perched on one side of the stands and watched us, the main attraction, numbered and thrown onto the court like performing animals. Blue Star was big business, invitation only; we got free basketball shoes from Converse and a navy-and-red camp T-shirt that would unravel after the first time we washed it. Although we were all under great pressure to perform well and raise our stock with the scouts, the most important event of that week, for me, had nothing to do with basketball. On the second-to-last evening, after our afternoon games, Raina enlisted me to scoot back up to the dorms with her to beat the crowd for dinner. It was seven o'clock by then and still light outside, although the sun was low and muted. We took a shortcut and started through what looked like a little patch of woods, but after the initial clump of trees we stumbled into a clearing that wasn't visible from the road.

"Holy shit," said Raina softly, and I knew that all plans to be early for dinner were out the window. She walked off toward the little pond that was tucked into a corner of the clearing. Green and yellow stalks were shooting out of the water, and a few ducks sat communicating in the middle. All the greenery was darker than it might have been in broad daylight, as if the moisture from the insides of things had been pushed out to the surface, so that everything assumed a richer color. I followed Raina from maybe twenty feet behind, watching her steps get smaller as she got closer to the edge of the water. The grass extended halfway up her legs, and her thin shoulders rolled back as she turned her head to look at something.

"Nancy," she said without turning, "come here."

I worked my way towards her through the long yellow grass. A few feet in front of us were a bunch of ducklings, little brown balls of feather and fur. They were waddling around, bumping into each other, peeping, falling down. I turned to look at Raina and she was staring at them, eyes bright as if lit from within.

I felt, suddenly, that I was intruding on something, and backed away. She didn't seem to notice. She just kept standing in the grass, motionless, and as I stood there watching Raina watch the ducklings, it just hit me. Boom. I couldn't have explained what it was that moved me so much; all I knew was that the sight of Raina absorbed in something, oblivious to me and to everything else, touched off such a tangled surge of imagination, pain, and desire that I had to take a few steps away from her to keep from falling over. It was as if something had cracked in me, had opened up, suddenly, into some other place I knew nothing about.

So it was ironic, to say the least, when my father leaned forward at summer league the next week and asked about the gorgeous, straight-backed woman sitting in front of us in the bleachers. A few weeks later he asked Raina's mother out for dinner, and Claudia blinked a few times and said yes. I figured they'd go out once or twice maybe, and that would be it. It wasn't. Even after it became clear, though, that there was really something going on between them, it took a while to register with me. Part of it was that my dad had dated several women since my mother left when I was six, and I had learned not to have expectations. Also, I rarely saw them together—they tended not to spend much time at our place. And of course it was just too strange to consider the fact that my father was dating the mother of the girl I liked.

My father, Wendell, like me, was large. Twenty-three years before he'd been the only Asian named to the All-State high school football team, at linebacker. He got his optimism and sense of humor from *his* father, who was a shopkeeper before his internment during World War II, and a gardener after it. His size came from his unusually tall mother, and also from consuming—as he put it—"lotsa meat." Now he was a math teacher and assistant football coach at a high school a few miles from our house. My father was a popular teacher—kids came to talk to him about their problems, and he gave his players rough bear hugs when they did something good on the field. He was the kind of cheerfully macho big man who could get away with crying, which he did every year at his football banquet, and at home, during *Eight Is Enough.* He was thrilled to have an athlete for a daughter. The first time I beat him at one-on-one, the summer I turned twelve, he slapped me on the back and gave me a beer and moaned about getting old. Claudia said he was adorable. I didn't know about that. But when I looked at other people's fathers, or at least the few who were around, I knew that I was luckier than most.

I finally realized that his relationship with Claudia was serious when it occurred to me that he was almost never home. Normally, even when he was seeing someone, he wouldn't take her out very often. He blamed finances, claiming that it was too expensive to pay for a babysitter and then dinner for two; instead, he'd invite the woman over, cook dinner for her, and then all three of us would watch a rented movie. Occasionally, the woman would spend the night, and my father would look embarrassed in the morning. He'd never stay over at her place. The woman would eventually get tired of this arrangement, accusing my father of being cheap, antisocial, or completely unromantic. I didn't think that this was accurate or fair.

The truth was, he didn't want to leave me. I'd been his main companion since my parents got divorced, his sidekick, his second-in-command. When I was younger, we'd watch cartoons together—usually Bugs Bunny or the Road Runner—and if I left and went to a friend's house, he would watch them by himself. After I beat him at basketball, though, he started taking me to bars. We'd go to Gardena, a Japanese-American town, where it didn't matter that I was almost a decade from legal because the bartenders were all his friends. My father believed in the redemptive power of heartfelt talks with strangers. He taught me always to tip the bartender well, and never to drink cheap beer.

After he met Claudia, though, he started going out more, and leaving me at home by myself. From the way he'd behaved with past women, I'd expected him to make a big production out of presenting her to me, but he didn't; he was too far gone to care. He and Claudia went out to movies and dinner and basketball games, and he'd even spend the night at her apartment. I'd never been jealous of my father's girlfriends—his priorities had been so obvious—and I wasn't jealous of Claudia, either, but for an entirely different reason. I was sixteen by the time he met her, old enough to drive, and it was easier to have my own social life when my father wasn't around. With his attention taken up by Claudia, I could stay out later, have friends over, spend more time alone. Sometimes, though, he'd still go through the motions of asserting parental control. "You are *grounded,*" he'd say after I'd broken some household rule. Then he would leave for the weekend.

Raina didn't seem too rattled by our parents' relationship, either. We ran into each other at college games and high school tournaments throughout the fall and winter of our junior year, but we didn't often refer to our parents' romance and only acknowledged that it existed when one of us asked the other to give the corresponding parent a message. "Ask my dad to pick up some cereal on the way home tomorrow," I'd say, or, "Tell him his friend Kenneth called." The novelty of it, the irony, soon wore off for both of us, and their relationship faded quickly into everyday life. There was something I noticed about the way children of divorce dealt with their parents' postmarital love lives—we never got our hopes up about anyone new, but on the other hand, we were never surprised.

They moved in on the third Sunday of August 1986. Although my father and Claudia had taken Raina and me out to dinner a month before to tell us this was happening, I didn't really believe it until they showed up that morning with a U-Haul full of their stuff. I was both annoyed and thrilled about the move—drunk with the idea of seeing Raina more often, but unhappy about sharing the house. I had no idea what Raina thought; she didn't talk much, to me or to anyone else. When I'd seen her at parties, there'd always been people around her, but they'd kept a respectful distance. I intended to do the same, as much as possible. Raina seemed poised, mature, in control of herself—completely out of my league.

The day they moved in, Raina and I helped bring boxes in from the truck, while our yellow Lab, Ann (after Ann Meyers, the first woman to try out for an NBA team), stood ears-up on the driveway, supervising. Occasionally a neighbor would stop by to help, and look at Claudia and Raina curiously, interested in the spectacle of two black women moving into a Japanese household. There were a couple of people, too—not people we were close with—who glared at my father disapprovingly, but they were the same ones who had always looked at us with vague suspicion and disapproval, so I tried not to pay them any mind. My more immediate concern, after I'd accepted that they were really staying, was what Claudia and Raina thought of the house. It had always looked, to me, like a huge cardboard box—it was exactly the right color, and the crumbling stucco gave it a rough, unfinished feel. The garage faced the front, but we didn't use it for the car, because the door was cracked so dramatically, the fissures running from ground to roof, that you couldn't lift it without it breaking into pieces. Our driveway was a network of small, interwoven cracks, like a flat expanse of bone-dry earth. The two shrubs by the front door reached up toward the sun halfheartedly, as if uncertain that they wanted to grow. Claudia watched all of the moving activity from the chair my father had set up for her on the scraggly front lawn. He'd told her to "take it easy," although she was muscular and fit and could probably have lifted as much as we jock types. "No problem at all," he gasped from under a large box. He was still trying hard to impress her.

Our place was big for that section of Inglewood—two stories and three bedrooms, one of which my father had used as a study. It had been cheap when he'd bought it in the mid-seventies, a time when—as its first owner, a white man, had put it—the neighborhood was starting to "turn." We'd moved there right after my parents' divorce because he'd wanted to escape the white suburb where my mother had insisted we live—a place that I, too, had hated, because the kids there hated me—and go back to a place more familiar to him, more like the racially mixed, working-class neighborhood in Watts where he'd grown up in the fifties and sixties. My mother had stayed behind in Redondo Beach, eventually marrying a white lawyer whose bully son had beaten me up on a regular basis. She was horrified by my father's choice of neighborhood. Inglewood, when we moved there, was already quite poor, but things had gotten worse in the next ten years, after the economic benefits that Reagan had promised, instead of trickling down, trickled out. At first, our neighborhood had also been more mixed, but gradually, the whites, Asians, and Latinos had moved on to other places, leaving a bunch of black families, and us.

I didn't sleep much the week that Claudia and Raina moved

in. At night I lay rigid, eyes open, pondering the facts that there were two more people in the house, and that Raina was just on the other side of the wall. Daytime was awkward—we were all overly conscious of each other, and careful, especially my father, who ran around the house like a mad scientist tending to his wildest experiment. Raina, meanwhile, was friendly to my father and me, but distant, as if she were a temporary guest who had to be tolerant of us because we were putting her up for the night. My father didn't seem to notice because he had his hands full with Claudia. She often worked late at her job in the circulation department of the *Los Angeles Times,* but when she was home he floated around, grinning, as if he couldn't believe she was gracing our house with her royal presence. He'd bring her roses he'd bought from stoplight vendors, and serve her breakfast in bed in the morning. She indulged this behavior patiently, but she was obviously flattered. "I can't remember the last time a man spoiled me this way," she said. "I'm sure it won't last for long."

As for me, I moved around in a constant daze. I kept bumping into things, and was amazed to find that solid objects—tables, chairs, the dog—didn't dissolve right there in front of me. I tried to touch the image I saw in the mirror of a tall person with light brown skin and permed shoulder-length hair, and was surprised when my fingers encountered the cold, hard glass instead of that stranger's flesh. I sat down immediately upon entering the house and usually anchored myself in a chair for the rest of the night. That way, I knew, I couldn't hurt myself. People react to wonderful news and disastrous news in the same general manner—joy or sorrow does not immediately register on their faces; they are in such a state of shock that it takes them a while to absorb the information. Going through that first week with Raina in my house was like hearing a huge piece of dramatic news over and over again—the fact of it was constantly hitting me, but whether it was wonderful or disastrous I still didn't know.

And how did I act around our two new housemates? Like a

spectator, mostly. I realized that despite all the time I'd spent thinking about her over the last year and a half, I knew almost nothing about Raina and even less about her mother. I pictured Raina, vaguely, as a strong, intense person, but I had no idea who she really was. So I just watched her. She and Claudia didn't battle like most mothers and daughters I knew, nor did they have the amiable but nonintimate coexistence of my father and me. They seemed close, and according to Stacy, Claudia even knew that Raina was gay. This was inconceivable to me—I would sooner have become a cheerleader than talk to my father about my love life. But I realized Stacy was right, because Claudia obviously knew about Toni ("Are you going out with Toni tonight?" she'd ask, or, "What should I say if Toni calls?"). And it was a good thing she did, too, because it looked like Toni was causing some problems in her daughter's life.

One night about a week after they moved in, Raina went out with Toni and was late coming home for dinner. This was unlike her—she usually made it home in time to eat, and the one other time she'd been running late she'd called and told her mother beforehand. We waited for half an hour before finally sitting down at the table. My father loaded my plate with a small mountain of spaghetti, completing his creation with the minor eruption of tomato sauce he poured over the top. The dog watched the proceedings anxiously.

"You need carbohydrates," my father said. He was forty-one then, and still a bear of a man, large and strong but getting soft around the edges. His skin was the color of worn leather and his hair was still mostly black, although there were a few sprinkles of white in it, as if he'd just come in from the snow.

"I know, Dad," I said, imitating the sermons of my high school coach. "Because complex carbohydrates give you energy, and they burn off more easily than fat."

"Right. So you can eat as much as you want without worrying about putting on weight." He served himself a heap of spaghetti about twice the size of mine.

I laughed. "Sure. Like you, right?"

"Exactly."

"Oh, please," said Claudia. She reached over and poked his stomach, which hung out over his belt like a bag of sand.

"Hey," he said, batting her hand away. "See if *you* get any food tonight." He grinned savagely at her and she raised her eyebrows, smiling. I laughed, a bit uncomfortably. Before Claudia had moved in, I hadn't been around her and my father very often, and I wasn't used to seeing them interact. Claudia scared me a little. She was shorter than Raina, and slighter, but she had a way of putting her hand on her hip and lifting a skeptical eyebrow that made you instantly forget how small she was. Her face was free of wrinkles, her hair contained no gray, and she appeared younger than her forty years. She had the same serious and focused air as her daughter—even, I saw, when she was amused.

After much discussion about what he was going to do to her for implying that he was fat, my father finally served Claudia some spaghetti. She handed me the Parmesan cheese, then asked, "Would you like some more water?" with the careful politeness of someone who doesn't know you very well and who wishes not to offend. Just then, the front door slammed shut. Ann left her post beside the table and trotted out to the hallway, toenails clicking on the warped linoleum.

"Hello!" Claudia called out, lifting her face toward the doorway. Her skin looked as smooth as her daughter's, although her forehead was a little smaller and her cheeks not quite as broad.

Raina didn't answer, but came straight into the dining room and sat down so hard the dog jumped back in fright. She was wearing normal summer jock attire: Lakers T-shirt, baggy shorts, basketball shoes—an outfit identical to my own except for the print of the T-shirt (mine was a Magic Johnson). She didn't speak a word to any of us.

"Well, nice of you to show up," my father said, not angrily. He must not have looked at her very closely, though, because she was obviously in no mood for humor. Her brow was furrowed, but other than that her face was blank, like the deceptive still surface of deep water. Her entire body was rigid. The thing that struck me most, though, was her eyes—out of that expressionless face, they were burning. Raina's eyes were always alert; they never settled into that passive glaze that other people's did when they weren't focused on something. But just then they were even more alive than usual. Claudia must have noticed this, too, because when she spoke her voice was like a gentle hand reaching out to touch her daughter's arm.

"How was your day?" she asked.

"Perfect," Raina said. "Just great." She gripped her fork so tightly I thought the metal might cut into her hand.

"Have some spaghetti," my father said, piling some onto the plate he'd set out for her.

"Thanks," she said, although she didn't look at the food.

I kept my eyes on my half-eaten pasta, stealing glances at her now and then. I'd never seen her upset before, and I wasn't sure what to do—whether to act like I didn't notice and resume talking, or to just sit there and keep my mouth shut. Raina couldn't even pretend to be in a civil mood, and I remembered other times I'd seen her out of step with her surroundings—at a UCLA game the previous winter, where she'd stared at the court, completely absorbed, while Toni and Stacy talked over her head; at a party during the summer, where she'd danced by herself, eyes closed, unself-conscious, while people danced in couples all around her; the week before, in the house, when she'd suddenly started laughing, without trying to hide her amusement, or sharing the reason with anyone.

My father, however, still seemed not to notice that anything was wrong. "Your mother's been complaining about my belly," he said to Raina, "but I keep telling her that I'm a football coach and ex-football player and I'm *supposed* to have a belly."

No one said anything for several moments. My father wiggled his eyebrows at Raina, and I could tell he was trying to charm her. Claudia was always cautious and polite with me, as if she wanted to assure me that she wasn't a rival, but my father acted like Raina was the head of a committee that had yet to approve her mother's choice of partner.

"I'm going upstairs," said Raina, finally, and off she went so quickly that none of us had a chance to speak.

My father snorted. "Well, I didn't think my belly was *that* big."

I tried to smile at him but couldn't. Claudia looked after Raina like she wanted to go to her, but didn't move. The three of us ate the rest of our dinner in silence. I remember being very aware of the clink of the silverware against the plates.

After we'd finished, Claudia popped Raina's food into the microwave. "She needs to eat," she said, and then gave me the nuked spaghetti to take to Raina's room, since I was headed in that direction anyway. I mounted the stairs with plate in hand, the dog following close behind in case I dropped something. She found it entertaining that I blocked her when she tried to push past, so with every step I moved sideways to cut her off, taking my time to work my way up because I was in no hurry to get to Raina's room. I had no idea of what to say to her once I got there, beyond, "Hi," and, "Here's your food." Eventually, though, I made it to the top. I knocked lightly, questioningly, on Raina's door. I'd expected no answer, or at least a length of time before she gave one, but almost before I'd finished knocking she said, "Come in."

I pushed the door open and looked around apologetically. Just a week before, my father had graded his students' homework in this room, and lifted weights to old R & B albums. Now all traces of him had vanished, replaced by Raina and her things. There was a new Nerf hoop attached to the closet door, and a pair of basketball shoes in the corner. A line of trophies rose like golden spires from the top of the dresser. I took a step in, feeling self-conscious and strangely, stupidly, flattered to be allowed briefly into her territory. My breaths, I noticed, became short and shallow—the air, because it was inhabited by Raina, suddenly seemed too rich to ingest. Raina sat on her bed cross-legged, slapping a basketball back and forth between her hands.

"I brought you your food," I said, and put the plate down on the desk beside her bed.

"Thanks," she replied. The slapping got louder.

I stood there awkwardly, my eyes alighting everywhere except on her face. On the wall to my left there was a Nike poster of a bunch of women playing basketball in a gym somewhere, so I looked at that instead. All ten bodies were in motion. The two women on the wings were just starting to run, and several players were struggling for position in the middle of the key, while one figure rose up above them all and launched a beautiful arching shot toward the basket. Then the dog thumped her tail behind me. That brought me back, and I started to leave.

"Wait," Raina said, and I turned toward her. "Tell my mom I'm sorry I took off like that."

"O.K."

"Tell her I'll come down later."

"O.K." I hesitated. "I think she's worried about you."

"Yeah, well, you know parents."

With great effort, I lifted my eyes to her face. To me it was perfect—smooth and strong, as if sculpted out of some dark, luxurious wood. Her jaw was prominent and firm; her lips full and soft; her eyebrows were thick near the center of her face and then tapered toward the sides, as if someone had touched her forehead with a full brush of paint, which had thinned as she finished her stroke. Her skin was unblemished except for the scar, the width of a pencil line, that ran an inch along her rounded left cheek. Her jet black hair was combed straight back off her forehead into a single braid, and now, as she looked at me, her eyes continued to burn as they had at the table. I almost looked away, but made myself meet her gaze. "Is . . . everything O.K.?" I asked. It seemed an awfully brave question.

"Sure, everything's great," she said, "except that women suck." Her voice was strained and a little rough.

I nodded sympathetically. "I know."

She raised her eyebrows at me. "I *know* you know."

I smiled, but just for a moment, since she was so obviously unhappy. She'd heard I was gay, of course, through Stacy, but this was the first time we'd really acknowledged it. I wondered how she felt about living with someone who liked her, but that thought was too frightening, so I buried it. Instead, I repeated, "So women suck."

"Well, maybe not all women, but at least one of them does."

I looked down at my feet. There were rumors that Toni cheated on her, and I wondered if they—or the truth behind them—were the cause of Raina's distress.

"Fuckin shit," she said. "Goddamn fuckin shit." She shoved the ball away from her, and it made a huge crashing sound when it hit the closet door. I wanted to leave, but couldn't. Also, I wasn't sure what *she* wanted me to do—it seemed like she didn't want me to get too close, but still wanted me around; like she would never tell me what was wrong, but still needed me to ask. What I *was* sure of was that it made me uncomfortable to be there. I didn't know what exactly Toni had done to her that night, but I could see the results. Raina's fists were clenched on top of her thighs so tightly that the knuckles were purple. Her whole body was like one huge contracted muscle, or like a cocked rifle that might go off at any second.

We stayed there, unmoving, for what felt like an hour. Finally I heard the creak of the staircase, and then the sound of the dog padding out of the room to greet whoever was coming up. A few seconds later Claudia appeared in the doorway. Her hair was shoulder-length and loose, and she looked more relaxed, in her jeans and baggy T-shirt, than her daughter ever did. She glanced from Raina to me and back again. Because she was so thoughtful by nature, she always gave the impression of choosing her words carefully, even when they were perfectly ordinary. "Everything all right?" she asked now.

"Yeah, I guess so," Raina answered, her voice softer. She stood up and walked over to the closet door now, which had a round gray spot on it from the basketball, and pulled out a pair of shoes. "I'm gonna go run around the block a few times," she said, and then fixed a three-second gaze on Claudia, as if to tell her that everything was indeed under control, before pushing past her on her way downstairs.

"Be careful," Claudia said. She watched her daughter go, and then turned back to me. I shrugged my shoulders at her.

CHAPTER 2

In the first week of September, the school year began. I don't know about Raina, but I was even less enthusiastic than usual about the ending of my summer freedom. It was my senior year of high school, the last rung on a ladder where the next step had always been visible. After this final rung, though, I saw nothing, just a huge, frightening void. I knew I'd go to college, but where? I'd have to start thinking about it soon; the letters and phone calls I'd been receiving from coaches for the last two years were no longer just ego boosters, feathers in my cap. It was time to really consider the various cities and states; to start comparing the different programs and schools.

This future-planning was hard, though, with parents in the picture. Sometimes I'd catch my father looking at me when he thought I wasn't paying attention, and it was a look of sadness, and of resignation, like he was about to send me off to war. I began to notice something, too, in the downturned eyes and wistful smiles of adults when they talked about their youth, which I know now was a painful mixture of loss and regret. I think that, watching us, they remembered what it was like to have their whole lives in front of them. No one had ever fired us from jobs we needed to support ourselves and our families, nor forced us to humiliate ourselves in order to keep them. No one had ever shattered our hearts with the cruel, complicated methods that adults use in their attempts to destroy each other. We had fought in no war, we had voted in no election; we hadn't yet done anything irrevocable. And yet, they were almost *waiting* for us to do something irrevocable; they half-expected us to trip up and break their hearts somehow, as countless others had done before. There were so many mistakes we could make, so many ways to abort our futures—crime, pregnancy, gangs, drugs, or simply leaving school and giving up. Adolescence in L.A. was like Russian roulette, and the game would not be over until we were gone.

Raina went to the same school that year—Leuzinger—as she had for the previous three, although now she had to take a bus or hitch a ride with her mom every day. We had a chuckle about that, because so many players moved around, or pretended to, in order to go to schools with better basketball programs. If you played for a well-known team, that increased your chances of being seen by college scouts. And being seen was important. Some parents went so far as to move their whole families so that their daughters could play on teams that got lots of exposure. Most of the time, though, players just used someone's address—usually that of a relative real or created—in the city of the desired school, so that they could claim to live in that school's official district. Sometimes this practice was taken to extremes. None of the starting five for that year's third-ranked team in the state, for example, actually lived in the district of the school they played for. The California Interscholastic Federation, or CIF, occasionally investigated flagrant cases of creative address-listing, but for the most part, players did as they wanted. And now here was Raina—moving, but not to get to a new school, and illegally attending a school in whose district she no longer resided.

By the second week after Claudia and Raina moved in, my father and I had calmed down a little. I was no longer surprised to find Raina's shoes in the bathroom, where she always left them for some inexplicable reason; no longer startled by her quick, padded footsteps outside my door. I was no longer surprised by the velvet smell of Claudia's perfume, or by her presence in the kitchen at breakfast, which had caught me off-guard every morning for the first couple of weeks, as if she hadn't been in the exact same spot the day before. Raina and Claudia, for their part, had also settled down, although Claudia was still too polite to me, and Raina still didn't talk very much. They seemed comfortable, though, choosing the TV shows or raiding the refrigerator; several new paintings appeared on the walls; and Raina had taken such complete possession of her room that it was hard to remember it had once been my father's office. Raina always kept her door open, which I found strange; I always shut my door, even when I was home alone. She wasn't secretive, like me, but it was more than that—she was so centered, so self-contained, that there was always a sense of privacy about her, even in the presence of others.

The thing I remember most about those first few weeks is that I was constantly on edge. It wasn't so much that I was always thinking about Raina—it was that I *couldn't* think about her, because my thoughts of her were crowded out by her actual presence. When we were both at home, all of my energy was required to deal with the situation at hand, to recover from the last one, or to gear up for whatever was coming next. I was exhausted and overwhelmed, and the situation would have driven me crazy if I hadn't been infatuated with the main person who was invading my space. Still, I couldn't believe that she and Claudia were really there forever—it's hard to accept that any major change is permanent, even one that you're essentially happy about. When I got tense from having too many people around, I took the keys to my father's Mustang and went for a drive. This was usually at night, after dinner, when Raina's proximity (we each did our homework in our own rooms, divided only by that thin but insurmountable wall) made it hard for me to concentrate. I usually drove to the ocean and then up the coast for half an hour, putting a tape on the stereo and letting Marvin Gaye or Luther Vandross give voice to my longing. The sun would be setting as I headed north, and while I liked the pink clouds and orange hue of sunset, I liked the darkness better; I liked the sense of disappearing into something. Finally I parked near the Santa Monica pier and stared out at the blackness of the water. The rhythmic thunder of the ocean and the rough feel of the wind managed to calm what was left of my nerves. When I got back home, two hours after I'd left, nobody asked where I'd gone.

A few days after school started, my friend Telisa came over to do some homework. Our Trig teacher, Mr. Byers, had given us a long, comprehensive review assignment in order to test our basic algebra, and the entire class had groaned at being saddled—in the very first week of school—with such a heavy and dull load of work. He'd given us strict instructions to do the assignment alone, which Telisa and I were ignoring. We were teammates, we figured—she was our point guard—and teammates should stand together in times of trouble. Besides, I wanted the benefit of her superior skills in math.

Telisa Coles was my oldest friend. We had met when we were seven, about two months after I'd moved to Inglewood, at a time when I was getting into a lot of fights. Because I was the new kid, and Japanese on top of that, all of the local kids felt it was their duty to take a crack at me. I'd had years of practice defending myself against the white bullies in Redondo Beach, so I managed to hold my own; eventually, I won the kids' respect and they didn't bother me anymore. During one of the last of these fights, Telisa had stood to the side and watched as I'd fended off a couple of older girls. When they'd finally stumbled away from me, nursing their wounds, I'd touched the bruise on my cheek where the bigger girl had hit me, and then turned to get ready for Telisa. Instead of attacking me, though, she'd just looked me up and down. Then she'd yawned. And this reaction of sheer indifference, after all the hostility I'd faced, had made me feel grateful and relieved. "You all right, girl," she'd said, and then she'd asked if I wanted to get some ice cream. She had been my best friend ever since.

Telisa came over that night around six, carrying two chicken-and-bean burritos from the local take-out. No one else was at home, so we ate in the living room, beneath the eight-foot scroll of Japanese calligraphy my great-grandmother had painted, which was one of the few things that had survived her internment. I brought out a quart of Coke and we took turns drinking from the bottle. Telisa seemed subdued and distracted, though, so finally, between bites, I jiggled the box lid that held her burrito.

"What's wrong?"

"Oh, nothing," she said. "My mom's just trippin again."

"What happened this time?"

Telisa sighed. "She started yellin at me and shit when I was leaving. Said I shouldn't be runnin around like a wild woman all the time. I told her I was comin over here to study, but I don't think she believed me."

I nodded sympathetically, but Telisa was looking down and didn't see me. She picked up a tortilla chip, inspected it, and then stuffed it into her mouth. We both sat there in silence for a while, Telisa lost in her thoughts, me getting increasingly annoyed at her mother. I didn't know what gave Mrs. Coles the idea that Telisa was, in any way, wild—one glance at T's report card should have been enough to show her that her daughter had things under control. But Mrs. Coles was strange—frazzled and emotional, so that when you saw the two of them together, it seemed that she, and not Telisa, was the child.

I'd consumed my burrito in about two minutes—I was always a fast eater—so I watched my teammate as she finished with hers. Telisa was thin and short—5' 5" and maybe 110 pounds—but she moved through the air with broad, expansive motions, as if staking out her space; as if daring you to say she had no right to it. She was the color of dark chocolate with a little cinnamon sprinkled in; her features were angular and she had a dramatic wedge of short, thick hair. Some of these physical details—her color, her thin nose—she'd gotten from her mother, but I didn't know where her emotional makeup had come from. It could have been her father, but there was no proof one way or the other—he was out of the picture and she didn't remember him. But whatever the source, whether it was inherited or self-created, Telisa had this essential steadiness, this equilibrium, that seemed to increase in direct proportion to the craziness around her. These were good qualities, of course, in a point guard. But they may also have been the reason that her mother took so much out on her. Telisa's older brother, Earl, was an ex-gangbanger, and at twenty-three he'd already spent two years in juvenile detention and three years in Folsom State Prison. He had the same kind of brains and steadiness as Telisa, and they had helped make him a star with the Inglewood Family Bloods, but after he'd been shot three times in an ambush a couple of years before, he'd decided to leave the gang. Now he worked whenever he could, doing whatever was available, which wasn't much for a young guy with a record like his. Anyway, Mrs. Coles didn't bother with him—maybe she figured he was already beyond her grasp—but Telisa, her A student, her college-bound kid, had to deal with her fury every day.

There was another thing, too. Although they'd never acknowledged it, Mrs. Coles knew that her daughter was gay. She'd asked a family friend of theirs, a cool, laid-back high school counselor in whom Telisa had confided, and the friend, not wanting to lie, had told her the truth. The woman had warned Telisa, though, so Telisa was aware that her mother knew. She'd braced herself for a confrontation, but her mother never brought the subject up, and chose a more subtle way of conveying her disapproval. She started acting rude to Telisa's girlfriend, Shavon—being short with her on the phone, not acknowledging her in the house—and whenever someone female called, she refused to give her daughter the message.

"You know," I said, as Telisa wiped her mouth with a napkin, "I bet your mom thought you were goin out to meet Shavon." I dropped a chip on the floor and Ann, who'd been lying at my feet, immediately gobbled it up.

Telisa nodded and put her napkin down. "Yeah, that's what I thought, too," she said. "But I wouldn't *lie* to her, you know what I'm sayin? That's what pisses me off. And even if I *was* gonna meet Shavon, it'd be none of her fuckin business." She pushed her chair away from the table, tilted back in it, and patted her stomach. "But I don't wanna talk about that shit no more," she said. Then she smiled. "That was a damn good burrito."

We went upstairs to my bedroom, and spread our papers out all over the light green carpet. My room, in those days, looked somewhat schizophrenic. The dresser and bedside table were part of the white-and-blue furniture set my parents had bought me when I was five; the single bed had a dark wooden frame and headboard that had once belonged to my father's parents. There were two posters on the walls—one of Magic Johnson and the other of the 1984 women's Olympic basketball team, which had won the gold medal two years earlier just down the street from us at the Forum—and on my desk stood a framed picture of my father at nine or ten, sitting with his parents on the front porch of their house in Watts. Telisa insisted that she couldn't think without music, so we turned on the old radio my dad had bought at a garage sale and she did a little dance step before sitting down to work. Just then the phone rang. I got up and answered it.

"Is this Nancy?" asked the overly cheerful voice on the other end. It was one of the assistant coaches from UC Santa Barbara, who had called me several times already.

"Yeah, hi," I said, trying to sound as uninterested as possible. It wasn't that I minded talking to coaches on the phone—in fact, I usually enjoyed it. But this was not a man I particularly liked. He was pushy and often annoying; he'd once called at nine on a Saturday morning after I'd been out until three the night before.

I had no interest in Santa Barbara—too many rich kids for me—but it was still too early to close any doors behind me, so I couldn't tell him yet to leave me alone.

"Great!" he nearly shouted. "I'm just calling to wish you a happy Labor Day. I know it's Thursday already, but hey, better late than never, I always say."

I turned to the wall, embarrassed that Telisa had to hear this. "Uh, thanks. Listen, I'm tryin to do this big math assignment right now. Could you call back in like a couple of days?"

"Sure thing," he replied. "Just wanted to check in with you, anyway. Don't forget about us, Nancy, all right?"

"All right. Goodbye." I hung up the phone, sighed, and turned back to Telisa. "Now where the fuck were we?"

Telisa gestured with a bony finger toward a piece of scratch paper, where she'd already scrawled a bunch of numbers. "Nowhere much yet," she said, "but I did a couple of these questions while you were talking. Check it out."

She showed me the problems she'd finished, and then together we did the next six, Telisa stopping now and then to explain how she'd figured something out. At one point, frustrated by my lack of understanding, she dropped her pencil and shook her head.

"I thought Japanese people were supposed to be *good* at math," she said.

I smiled. "I think my dad kept all the math genes so he could *teach* this shit," I said. Then I pulled out the blanket explanation I used for all of my mother's crimes. "And whatever Japanese genes my mother has, she probably don't even want."

We'd just started on the seventh problem when the phone rang again. This time it was for Raina, the Michigan State coach. I took the number down and left it on the dresser.

"That reminds me," Telisa said when I got off the phone. "How things goin with Ms. Webber, anyway?"

Her question threw me off—I was sure I hadn't told her how I felt about Raina. It wasn't that I didn't trust her, or that she wouldn't understand—but I was terrified, then, of letting anyone in, of allowing anyone to know too much about me. After a moment, though, I realized that Telisa wasn't asking about my feelings at all; that she simply hadn't been over to visit since the recent population explosion in my house. "It's cool," I said. "She's cool. She's a trip, though."

"Is she as crazy-ass intense as she seems on the court?"

I started to say that I hadn't spent enough time with her to know yet, but then the phone rang again.

"Shit!" we both said, and I got up to answer it.

This time, it was someone I wanted to talk to—Vivian Stringer, the head coach from Iowa, which was one of the schools I was actually interested in. I moved to the downstairs extension, and talked to her for half an hour until I started to feel guilty about Telisa. I assured the coach that Iowa was one of my top choices, and she told me to call her if I had any more questions. Then I ran back upstairs to my room. Telisa was sitting on my bed and thumbing through the latest issue of *Sports Illustrated.*

"I'm sorry," I said. "I should of tried to get off sooner."

Telisa grinned. Her face was so narrow that her smile seemed to split both her cheeks. "That's O.K., homegirl. You a celebrity and shit. Is it like this around here every night?"

"It has been lately," I said. "Especially since Raina moved in."

"I'm just not gonna let you answer the phone no more, till we finish this stupid math."

Just then, as if on cue, the phone rang again. Telisa jumped up and grabbed it. "Chinese take-out."

I heard mumbling from the receiver, and then she laughed. "Sorry," she said into the phone. Then, turning in my direction, "It's for you."

I took the phone from her and said, "Hello?"

"Does that mean dinner's going to be served when I get home?" asked the voice on the other end.

I laughed. "Hey, Dad. Telisa and I were just doin some homework."

"Yeah, right," my father said. "You bums. Anyway, I'm still at school watching a tape of the team we're playing on Friday. I should be finished pretty soon, though. Is Claudia there?"

"No. I guess she's still at the office."

"That woman works too hard."

"Well, one-point-five million readers of the *L.A. Times* are depending on her for their news."

"Oh, stop it. When you talk like that, you make it sound like she's the Pony Express."

I grinned. "The Pony Express was mail, Dad."

"Whatever. Anyway, if she does get home in the next hour or so, tell her that the love of her life called."

"O.K. But do you want me to say that *you* called, too?"

"Ha, ha. Very funny. I'll see you when I get home."

"All right," I said. "Goodbye."

As I was hanging up the phone, I heard the front door open. "Shit," I said. "That's probably Claudia now." The dog, who had been sleeping on my bed, trampled all over our papers in her haste to get downstairs. When she got there, though, it wasn't Claudia's voice that greeted her.

"Hey, dog," I heard Raina say. "Don't jump."

She climbed the stairs, went into her room for a moment, and then came down the hallway and appeared at my door. Her presence moved through all my layers of self-protection, like a cold gust of wind through a jacket. "Hey, ladies," she said. She was wearing green shorts and a loose white tank top; her legs looked sleek and powerful. Just watching her made all the hair on my arms stand up, as if she were running her fingers along the back of my neck. There was a wide smile on her face, and she looked, for once, completely at ease.

"Hey," I replied. "Raina, you've met Telisa, right?"

"Yeah," she said, smiling at my teammate. "Wassup?"

"Nothin," Telisa answered. "Just doin some stupid homework."

"Really? You guys got homework already?"

"Yeah, that's fucked up, huh?" I could tell that Telisa liked

Raina—she was smiling, and nodding a bit, as if in approval. "So what *you* been up to tonight?"

"Oh, this and that," Raina answered noncommittally. I took this to mean that she'd been over at Toni's, and felt a sudden pang of jealousy.

"You know where you gonna sign yet?" Telisa asked. She never asked *me* this question anymore, because she knew I had no idea; she also knew me too well, after ten years of friendship, to think I might want to discuss it.

"Nope," Raina answered.

That reminded me of the message I was supposed to give her. "Hey," I said, looking up at her. "Michigan State called."

Raina straightened up immediately. "Really? When?"

"An hour ago, maybe. He left a number."

She looked at my clock, which read 9:37. "Shit. I guess it's too late to call now, huh?"

"Actually, he said you could call till midnight." I handed her the message, without meeting her eyes. I could never look at her face for very long; it was like staring straight into the sun.

Raina looked at the slip of paper as if it held the secret to her future. "What time is it there now? Are they three hours ahead of us?"

"No," Telisa answered. "Two."

Raina smiled hugely. "The Midwest," she said. "Wheat and corn. The Midwest is the kitchen of the country." Then she turned and practically ran down the stairs.

Telisa and I stared after her and laughed. Raina often said things, I was starting to notice, which didn't really make sense, or which adhered to their own strange logic. She didn't seem to care whether people followed her train of thought, or found her too intense, and that kind of confidence and self-possession was remarkable at an age when the rest of us were struggling hard to be cool.

Telisa turned to me and shook her head. "Nancy," she said. "That girl is *crazy* fine."

I smiled. "Yeah, I guess she do look pretty good."

"Pretty good!" Telisa exclaimed. *"Pretty* good! Shit, she's gorgeous. I guess I just never noticed before, 'cos I've only seen her in a basketball uniform."

"Get your eyes back in your head, girl," I said. "You got a woman already."

Telisa dismissed me with a wave of the hand. "Oh, I'm just lookin. You know I'm happy where I am."

And I did. She and Shavon were great together, still madly in love, neither of them having her head turned by all the attention that came from other quarters. They started seeing each other the first month of our sophomore year, around the same time I got together with a senior named Yolanda. Shavon and Yolanda both ran track and Telisa and I both played basketball; the four of us had often doubled together since only Yolanda had been old enough to drive. I think she got tired of chaperoning us, though—she broke up with me just after Thanksgiving vacation, saying it was her last year of high school and she wanted to be free. I was heartbroken at the time, but soon realized that there'd been nothing more to our relationship than a strong, mutual lust; if I'd run into her during my senior year, we would have had nothing to say to each other. There was one other girl I'd dated, Lisa. She was a basketball player from New Mexico I met at an AAU tournament in Virginia; we'd continued our affair throughout the summer at camps and tournaments all over the country. But that was before Yolanda, and there'd been no one in the two years since, because then Raina had come into my life.

"So," said Telisa, flipping some pages in her math book. "Your pops realize he's now got *two* gay kids in the house?"

"Hell, no," I said. "He doesn't even know he's got one."

Telisa raised an eyebrow at me. "Oh, yeah?"

"Yeah," I said, feeling the blood beat against the side of my neck. "Why, you aware of something I'm not?"

She shrugged. "I just think he's probably figured it out. Your pops ain't stupid, you know. And you were trippin so hard over

Yolanda that time that I can't believe he wouldn't of known what was up."

I felt a little thrill of fear, then, listening to this, because I knew my friend was probably right. But I had no idea what I would do with the subject of my love life if my father ever brought it up. Not that he would—he didn't like to talk about anything too personal or potentially difficult. Both he and his parents had always been silent, for example, about their internment during World War II, their history, their culture, their past. I wouldn't have known anything about my parents—about how my mother was head cheerleader the year my father was team captain; how they were always the best dancers at the socials held at the Japanese Baptist Church; how my father had wanted more children—if it hadn't been for my grandparents on *her* side. A few years earlier, he used to joke about what would happen once I started dating boys, but then, when the boys hadn't materialized, when time after time I'd turned down requests for dates, he'd finally stopped kidding about it.

"I don't know," I said finally. "Maybe you're right."

We still had homework to contend with, and I wanted to change the subject, so we cut our discussion short and got back to work. We decided to split up the remaining problems and then exchange our answers at the end. I had a hard time concentrating—I kept thinking of how Raina had looked standing in the doorway, how her face had lit up when I'd given her the message. Still, I managed to finish my part in a reasonable amount of time, and then presented my answers to Telisa, who was already done. We copied each other's work as fast as we could. It was after eleven by the time we finally wrapped things up.

"I'm tired, girl," Telisa said as she gathered her books and put them into her backpack.

"Me, too," I said. "But think how long this would of taken if we did it by ourselves."

Telisa snorted. "Probably half the time."

"Yeah, but this way was a lot more fun."

She rolled her eyes and smiled. "Fun for *you,* maybe. Shit. Who you think did all the work?"

We went downstairs to say hi to my father and Claudia, who had both come home while we were still doing our assignment. They were drinking beer and watching a rerun of *Taxi.* Telisa and Claudia hadn't met, so I introduced them; we all made small talk for a while, and then I saw my friend to the door.

"Your dad and Raina's mom seem real happy," she said.

I turned to her. "For real?"

She looked surprised. "Yeah, don't you think so? Your dad seems calmer, or something. I mean, he seems, like *giddy* and everything, but at the same time more relaxed. So what's Raina's mom like, anyway?"

"I don't really know," I said truthfully. "Nice. Real serious. She doesn't smile that much."

Telisa nodded thoughtfully. "I can see that. She's not as intense as Raina, though. Maybe she has less to prove."

"Maybe," I said. "But I'll be able to tell you more in a couple of months." I opened the door. "Hey, thanks for the burrito."

"Anytime, homegirl," she answered, and I watched her walk out to her car. As she started up the engine and drove away, I thought about what she'd said. She was right. My father *was* more relaxed—less frantic, less talkative, more at ease with himself. But I hadn't really noticed these things until she'd brought them up. Because I'd never seen my father in a good relationship before, I had no way of recognizing that he'd finally found one. And besides that, I was feeling a bit removed—after the first couple of weeks of rubbing up against the other members of the household, I'd shrunk back into myself, and watched them from a distance. This, I understood, had something to do with why it wasn't harder for me to adjust to the new living situation. I felt safe in this position, in control of myself, hidden where no one could find me.

CHAPTER 3

A couple of days later, I arrived home from school to hear the chatter of the television coming out of the living room. I was carrying recruiting letters that had come in the day's mail—it seemed that the college coaches, without being told, had immediately caught on that Raina had moved, while her high school was still in the dark. By senior year, I barely glanced at most of the letters that arrived, but two years before, when I'd first started receiving them, I'd rushed home every afternoon to check the mailbox. I'd loved getting letters; and later, getting phone calls; and knowing that the unsmiling, note-taking scouts in the stands were usually there to watch *me.* It had been like winning the lottery, or being discovered: it was the closest I could get to being a movie star. Soon I, like many other recruits, had bought a cheap cardboard file box to keep track of my mail. I'd alphabetized the file and looked through its contents every week. Bright, multicolored school mascots appeared on some of the envelopes; on others there was just the university's name, printed in black or blue ink. The paper of both the envelopes and the letters was thick, textured, usually white or beige. It was the highest quality paper I'd ever touched or even seen, and it reeked of prestige and importance. Recruits were special, and we knew it. Other kids applied to the colleges they wanted to attend. But colleges applied to us.

On that particular afternoon there were three letters for Raina and two for me. I separated them and walked into the living room, where I found Raina parked in front of the TV set with her high-tops and socks in a sweaty pile on the carpet. She was massaging her right thigh, and I watched the motion of her hands, which were gathering the flesh, and kneading it, like dough. Her knees were bruised and scarred from years of falling on pavement. To me they were like an intricate map of mysterious ridges and valleys, a geographical testimony to her devotion.

"Hey," she said, looking up at me, her mouth full of cookies.

"Hey. How was practice?" The season hadn't officially started yet, but both of our teams had been playing informally during sixth-period PE.

"Good," she said, turning back to Oprah. "We talked about you today."

"About me?"

"Well, actually, about your whole team. But especially you. About how we'd shut you down if we ever had to play you." She grinned wickedly, encouraging me, I knew, to brag about how thoroughly we'd kick their asses. They were in a different league, though, so there wasn't much chance we'd face them, unless we met them in a tournament, or in the playoffs.

"Well, if you ever did end up playing us, would you be the one to guard me?"

"Sure, why not? It worked O.K. that one time in summer league."

I laughed. "Ouch. Bitch. Tell your coach you got no business guarding me. I'm a forward."

"No way," she said. "'Course, the best way for us to take you out the game would be to fix it so that *you* guard *me*."

I smiled and tossed the letters at her, ignoring her references to the one time we'd played each other, in a summer league game—a contest in which I'd held her to only ten points, but had been so intent on stopping her that I'd only scored four myself. I was feeling good. This pseudo-arrogant banter reflected a sense of ease I was glad we could simulate if not really feel. Raina had been talking to me more in the last few days—not because she was giving me any special attention, but simply because she was friendly, and I was there. I wasn't entirely happy about not having the house to myself; the hours between when I got home from school and when my father did had always been my favorite part of the day. But losing some alone time in exchange for spending afternoons with Raina now seemed like a pretty fair trade. I didn't know what *she* thought about being there—after all, she was now sleeping a room away from someone who wanted her, and whom she didn't want. Besides, she was an only child, too, and attached to her privacy. But maybe it was all right for her. Maybe she'd created such a space around herself that it protected her wherever she went.

After we'd rested a while, we left for the park. Raina wanted to take the roundabout way; we'd been going on dribbling tours of Inglewood so she could familiarize herself with the area. That day we reached Victoria and headed north, the opposite direction from where we needed to go. I didn't mind this little detour; we could have walked through the most boring stretch of desert together and it would have been fine with me. The weather was beautiful that afternoon—there were a few high tufts of cloud that looked like rows of stretched-out cotton, and the sun felt good against my skin. Every once in a while there was a strong breeze from the east, and the palm trees that lined the sidewalk all bent toward the west, as if bowing to the ocean. All down the block, women sat on doorsteps and watched children play in balding front yards. It was September, the first month after another long, rainless Los Angeles summer, and what little grass there was in these yards was brown, dry, and coarse.

Raina and I exchanged hellos with the mothers and walked slowly in the cooling air. Ahead of us a garbage truck positioned itself in front of a large blue trash bin, which was overflowing with stained paper bags and crushed beer and soda cans. The truck extended its two metal arms, hooked onto the bin, and reverse slam-dunked the garbage into the trash compactor behind the driver's cabin. "Two points," said Raina, nodding. She was wearing a new USC shirt that Toni had given her, minus the sleeves she'd ripped off, and those long, baggy shorts made popular by a third-year guard for the Chicago Bulls named Michael Jordan. I was wearing the orange shirt I'd gotten for being named to the all-camp team a month earlier at Blue Star. We were both dribbling basketballs—mine an old outdoor ball brown and smooth from years of constant use, hers a still orange and shiny indoor ball, "borrowed" from a camp, that she was in the process of destroying by subjecting it to concrete. Her shoes she was more careful about. We'd both changed into outdoor pairs, so designated not because they were made for that purpose, but because we'd come to use them as such. It didn't matter that the bottoms of these particular pairs had been worn smooth as glass and were no longer suitable for indoor use, because basketball shoes, at least for us recruit types, were in no short supply. We were bombarded with them; we received them from camps, from leagues, on AAU teams, and even sometimes as awards. Not including the ones I'd given away, I had nine pairs myself: my practice pair, my outdoor pair, my home game pair, my away game pair, even a pair I wore as boots on rainy days (basketball shoes make great rain boots because they're so high and thick and insulated). After Raina moved in we took our combined supply of shoes and formed a huge, haphazard white mountain of them in the hall closet. Sometimes it took us five or ten minutes to find a matching pair.

As we reached the first corner, Raina hit me on the shoulder with the back of her hand. "Yo, Nance, check out that house," she said, gesturing in front of us and grinning. She stepped off the curb and I grabbed her by the arm, pulling her out of the path of an oncoming car. "Check it out," she said again, barely seeming to notice.

I looked up and saw the house she was referring to, which was unabashedly hot pink, and hard to look at. I'd passed it so often that I didn't notice it anymore, but now, through Raina's eyes, and with the help of the summer sunlight, I was struck once again by its glory. "It's beautiful, don't you think?" I said. "I wish *our* house was that color."

Raina nodded. "If the Ku Klux Klan wore sheets that color, we'd all be a lot better off."

I turned to look at her. "Why?"

"If they had to wear hot pink instead of white, they'd be too embarrassed to come outside."

I stopped dribbling and shook my head. She saw the look on my face and laughed out loud, her eyes turning up toward the sky. This didn't surprise me—when Raina laughed, she always looked away. Other people, myself included, made eye contact with people when they laughed—either to show their appreciation of the funny thing that was said, or simply to enjoy the moment with someone. With Raina, though, it was different—almost like she could only enjoy the moment if she *didn't* share it with anyone else. She threw her head back and laughed as loudly as the next person, but with her face turned, her eyes averted. As if everything were meant to be experienced alone.

We kept walking, Raina commenting now and then upon a peculiar house, an interesting car, the smog-tinged view of downtown. The neighborhood was still new to her, and the interest with which she viewed it made me see things I hadn't noticed in years. Our block, and the several blocks around it, looked roughly the same. Most of the houses were one-story and small, but there were a few two-story houses scattered here and there, and several four- or six-unit apartments. All of the buildings were stuccoed in deceptively cheerful colors, but if you looked closely, you could see spots where the paint was flaking off like dead skin, and an occasional gaping white hole in the walls. Many of the houses sat behind short chain-link fences, and a few of them had red Spanish-style roofs. Their doors and windows were covered with bars, most of which were black, but some of which were white and decorated with metal flowers, as if design could disguise their function. Several of the properties had "For Sale" signs on their lawns; the signs usually stayed there for a year or two before the landlord or the family who lived there gave up and finally took them down. A generation earlier, those properties would have sold in a matter of weeks, and there were still suggestions of what the neighborhood had once been—a pleasantly lower-middle-class community with no frills and no wasted expenditure. Now, though, it showed the effects of twenty years of deterioration—like many of the people who lived in it, the 'hood seemed to have let itself go, to have given up. It hurt me to see this—it was like living with a friend whose health was failing right before my eyes. But the same thing was happening, in varying degrees, all over the city. The old, majestic Victorian houses of the Westlake district now seemed stooped over, like withered old men. In Watts, where my father had grown up, the half-demolished stores and collapsing houses made the area look like it had been bombed.

"Hey," Raina said suddenly. "Y'all ever been robbed or anything?"

I nodded. "My dad's car got stolen once a couple years ago. That's why he's driving the Mustang now—he thinks it's less tempting than the Toyota he had before."

"But no one's ever, like, broken into your house?"

"Nope," I said, bouncing the ball between my legs. "But it happens pretty often, though. You gotta be careful. One time a couple years ago, the same guys broke into three different houses by crawling into the second-floor bathrooms. That's why my dad put bars on all the upstairs windows. Used to be we just had 'em downstairs."

"Our apartment got broken into twice," Raina said. Her old neighborhood, in Hawthorne, was similar to ours. "I think maybe that's why my mom wanted us to move in with you guys."

I turned to face her. "You mean it wasn't because of her burning need to be near my dad all the time?"

"Oh, well, yeah," Raina said, smiling. "That, too." She bounced her ball, looked thoughtful. "You know, I like your dad. I was kinda suspicious of him at first, but he's all right."

"Why were you suspicious?"

"I'm suspicious of *all* men who wanna get close to my mom."

"I'm suspicious of all women who wanna get close to my dad, too. But I like your mom. She's nice."

Raina shook her head distractedly. "Yeah, your dad's a trip, man. He's pretty damn funny sometimes."

I nodded, feeling strangely jealous. Suddenly I wasn't worried that Raina thought badly of my father, but instead, that she found me boring in comparison.

We continued along Victoria, picking up our basketballs as the street began to slope downhill. At Florence Avenue, which ran east and west, we waited for a clump of traffic to pass before jaywalking to the other side. The land leveled off there, and we resumed our dribble, walking along in silence for a block and a half.

"Check out that car," Raina finally said, pointing toward an old Buick that was parked on a lawn. There were a lot of cars parked on lawns here, behind chain-link fences; most of them were old and American, and they looked like big dogs cooped up in people's front yards. A couple of elementary school kids were sitting in the front seat of the Buick; Raina waved at them, and nodded. "It'd be better than a playground," she said. "Except that parents ain't gonna come outside and drive a playground to the store."

I nodded, but didn't say anything. I pictured a playground pulling free from the earth, sprouting wheels, and driving away.

"Although you never know," she continued. "When the Big One hits, all *kinds* of stuff is gonna come loose. It'll be great. We could bring Griffith Park closer to Inglewood, you know, and put the Sports Arena in the parking lot right next to the Forum."

I smiled. "What about the beach?"

She looked thoughtful. "The beach'll still be there. And we'll have another one, to the east of us, probably around Blythe or something. 'Cos you know, when the Big One hits, California'll be all right, but the rest of the country's gonna fall into the ocean."

"You," I said, laughing, "are strange." And she *was,* I was finding—strange, and not eager to hide it. I liked the way her mind worked, though—she put disparate elements together; she envisioned things that other people would never come up with. This was part of why, I realized, she was so much fun to spend time with. It probably also accounted for some of her success on the court, since Raina saw possibilities where a less creative player would have seen nothing. Her oddness surprised me, but also, somehow, made me feel closer to her; I thought that by sharing it with me, she was revealing something, even though it must have been there all along.

We were in the Hyde Park section of Los Angeles now, just a few blocks away from our house, but the difference between the two areas was obvious. The cars here were older and sputtered more loudly. The houses stood closer together. The pavement was more brittle and cracked, and the oil stains seemed fresher and larger; there was garbage all over the street and sidewalk. Graffiti seemed to cover every inch of the walls—the graffiti in our 'hood was much more sparse—and all of the houses, garages, and apartment buildings were more dilapidated, broken-looking, crumbled. Old metal objects—bikes, broken fans, scratched-up card tables and chairs—sat rusting on crooked front porches. People hung their clothes outside to dry, and on that day, which was so warm and beautiful, with just a bit of a breeze, it seemed like every other house had clothes and linens draped over the fences, as if their residents were waving white flags at the world.

As we walked, an ice cream truck rolled by us, playing a loud, cheerful tune; its sides and back were covered with graffiti. Several small children passed us and chased it down the street, and finally it pulled over to the curb. We turned the corner, still smiling at the kids and their ice cream, and almost bumped into a young couple who were arguing on the sidewalk. The guy was wearing baggy shorts like Raina's and a Lakers cap turned backwards. He was gesturing widely with his hands, and the girl, who was wearing a yellow tank top and white Bermuda shorts, wagged a finger in his face with one hand and held a baby with the other. Despite the expansiveness of their movements, they kept their voices low, not wanting the neighborhood to know their business. They stopped talking for a moment as we walked past them, and I looked into their faces, nodded, saw that they were younger than we.

"Young love," Raina said when we were out of earshot. I turned back to look at them, and they were hugging now, the boy enveloping the girl and the child in his long arms. Raina had seen them, too, and she seemed happy with this conclusion. I loved watching Raina as she noticed things. She took a genuine delight in the world around her; she engaged it and entered it without hesitation, in a way that I could only imagine. She simply went with whatever happened to catch her eye or her mind, and sometimes this resulted in her doing something dangerous or out of context—like introducing herself to me in the middle of a close game, or wandering out in front of a car.

At Crenshaw, we turned right and headed south toward the park. A few minutes later we reached Manchester Boulevard. Inglewood High School—my base of operations—was on Manchester, as was the Forum, a half a mile to the east. Whenever there were Laker games, the boulevard swelled with the fancy cars of people who were headed toward the Forum, people talking on their car phones to feel connected to the outside world, driving east from the 405 freeway, or west from the 110. The Forum, which was the home of the Lakers and the Kings and which also hosted the occasional concert, was like a big magnet that pulled white people into Inglewood. As soon as the event was over, though, the magnet's power wore off, and they got out of there as fast as they could.

There was a 7-Eleven on the far corner, right next to the check-cashing place, and Raina and I decided to go in and get some candy. Although this was a normal stop for me, I felt a bit nervous that day. The night before, my father and Claudia had gone in to buy some toilet paper, and had run into two men who had cursed at my father for being with one of "their" women, and then had told Claudia that she should be ashamed. I didn't know what I expected to happen now; of course the men would be long gone. Ty, the young basketball fanatic who worked on weekday afternoons, raised a hand in greeting when he saw us come in.

"Yo, Nance," he said, pulling his short, stocky body out of his chair. "What you gonna average this year? Thirty-five a game? Forty?"

I picked out a pack of gum, set it down on the counter, and shook my head. "Eighty," I said. "Naw, maybe seventy-five. Gotta get my teammates in on the scoring action, too."

He took the dollar I held out and then gave me my change, silver coins gleaming in his earthy brown hand. "Culver City's gonna be pretty tough this year," he said. "You think you can beat 'em?"

"No problem," I said. "They got no size, so they can't handle our big people."

Then Raina came up to the counter and set her candy bar down. She was standing only an inch or two away from me, and I could feel the electricity of her presence, as tactile as any touch. My heart began to beat so loudly that I was afraid she'd be able to hear it. I took a deep breath to compose myself, and cocked a thumb at her. "Ty, this is Raina Webber," I said.

Ty put a hand on top of his head, his splayed-out fingers palming his skull like a basketball. "Raina Webber!" he exclaimed. "Damn! I *thought* you looked familiar! I saw you play against Carson last year in the playoffs!" He shook his head and whistled. "You cleaned *up,* girl! You *schooled* those mother-fuckas!"

"Yeah," I said, smiling. "She's the shit."

Raina shoved me on the shoulder. "Naw, *you* the shit."

Ty put his hands up, as if to stop us. "Y'all are *both* the shit. Damn. Couldn't get me on the court with either one of y'all if you paid me a thousand bucks."

We laughed. Raina looked slightly embarrassed, but also pleased. "Well, it's nice to meet you," she said to Ty. "I'm stayin with Nancy and her pops now, so I guess I'll be in here a lot."

"Naaaw . . ." he said, looking at her cockeyed. "For real?"

"Yeah," we both said, and I grinned, happy about it all over again.

"Well, that's cool," Ty said, nodding. "I'll be seein you then. Y'all keep each other out of trouble, now."

When we went back outside, Raina stuck the candy bar into her waistband and bounced her ball. "That dude seems really cool," she said. "You go in there a lot?"

"Yeah," I said, "either there or to the liquor store by our house." This was true. Because there were no supermarkets for miles around, we often went to the 7-Eleven, or to Mr. Wilson's liquor store, when we needed some basic necessity. We also went to the 7-Eleven to use the ATM machine—there were no banks nearby—although if we didn't get there by the time the machine shut down at seven, we had to go all the way to Hawthorne to get cash.

Raina and I stopped just around the corner from the store so I could open my pack of gum. I handed her a piece, and unwrapped a piece for myself, while she considered the graffiti on the side of the building. I looked at it, too. "IF" was written several times, in various sizes, all across the wall. There were "IF's" painted everywhere in the neighborhood, occasionally even on the door of our garage.

"Inglewood Family Bloods," Raina said thoughtfully, naming the huge set which controlled our part of the city. We saw the names Baby Loc, Crazy De, and some others we couldn't decipher. Some of the names had been crossed out by rival gangs. "Smiley R.I.P.," it said on the upper right corner, and "Kill Crabs" at chest level to the left. All the writing was black and spindly, and painted at sharp angles; it looked like a jungle gym had been splashed against the wall.

We walked west on Manchester, and then turned left on 12th Avenue, back into a residential section. I'd made this walk almost every day for the past eight years—to get to the park, of course, and then, during my sophomore year, because I was going to see Yolanda, my ex-girlfriend. A few minutes later we encountered the crack lady. She was an extremely skinny woman of indeterminate age whose joints and limbs all seemed to fold in on themselves, as if she were a collapsible structure. She always wore a dirty black bandanna and a black Members Only jacket, and she could be found wandering the streets and mumbling to herself at any time of the day or night. I'd been seeing her around for the last couple of years, ever since crack had come into the 'hood. Now, she walked toward us, completely oblivious; she would have walked right into us if we hadn't parted to let her through.

On the next block we passed a pair of junior high school girls who were walking home from school. One of them nudged the other and said, "Girl, that's Nancy Takahiro!" I ignored the two girls, and tried to put on a serious expression befitting an important local hero, but I don't think it worked, because Raina laughed.

"You goofball," she said. "You know you love it."

I gave her a shove, and said, "Fuck you." She was right, though. I *did* love it—not just the attention of the kids, but the kids themselves, the 'hood and everyone in it. I was the great-grandchild of immigrants, in love with America—and the Inglewood of the 1980s was America to me.

Raina lost her balance for a second as a result of my shove, and then resumed her stride. She walked slowly, breaking off once in a while to bounce the ball against the side of a building, or to bend over and dribble circles around me. I loved watching her move—she was fluid, but there were a few small breaks in her movement, as if she were a river interrupted by rocks. She could dribble low, behind her back, through her legs, do a perfect crossover, but it wasn't the fancy stuff that made her such an effective guard. It was that the ball seemed drawn to her hand, as if by some invisible force, always returning to it no matter what direction the rest of her body was going. When Raina dribbled, her wrist didn't move, but her fingers ebbed up and down on the ball, like waves. And although she wasn't skinny, she had narrow, quick-moving hips, which she swung one way or the other to avoid the people who were blocking her path.

We stopped because Raina had to tie her shoe, and as she crouched down I picked up her ball. I started dribbling both her ball and mine, making them hit the ground at the same time, and then alternating the dribble so that one bounced while the other was in my hand. Then one of the balls hit a corner that jutted up from the sidewalk, and rolled off into the street.

"Give it up, girl," Raina said, laughing. "You forwards can't take care of the ball."

"It bounced off that piece of cement there," I protested, pointing in the general direction of the sidewalk as I stepped down off the curb.

"Yeah, right," said Raina, standing again. "Just leave the ball-handling to me—and the babies."

I turned around and looked at her. "Huh?"

She smiled. "You know how good babies can dribble."

I brought the ball back, came right up in front of her and looked down into her face. "Yo, why you tryin to dis?" I said. "You know you can't stop me. Just see what happens when I post you up, you fuckin little shrimp. I'll just step on you and crush you like an empty Coke can."

We grinned at each other savagely, and I noted her wide forehead, the tiny mole on her right cheek, the soft, lovely skin just beneath her shining eyes, which was slightly lighter than the rest of her face.

Just then, we became aware of a low thumping sound, the vibrations reaching our feet through the pavement before the sound actually came to our ears. We both looked up, and saw that a car had turned the corner—a bright red Honda, sparkling new, with tinted windows and a tremendous sound system. I had seen this car before; it usually made its rounds about that time. It rolled down the street slowly, the pulse of the music entering my feet and my legs, running all the way through my body until it seemed to replace the beating of my heart. As the car got closer, we saw some of its other extras—shiny, elaborate rims, a lion ornament on the hood, a front grille that might have been lifted from a racing car. The driver's window was rolled down a few inches, but all we could see was the top half of a man's face, and a pair of black shades. It was clear that he was looking for someone, and I feared for the person he sought. When he pulled up level with us, he slowed the car down even more, and then stopped, right in front of what looked like a bloodstain. Through the crack in the window, I could see him considering us, and I felt an icicle of fear in my chest. I hoped we hadn't caught him in the middle of a bad day. Raina stood up straight and held her ground beside me; I had the presence of mind to do the same. I wanted to say something to her, but the music was so loud that it seemed to have absorbed all other sound. The window inched down a little further, and I half-expected to see the muzzle of a gun slip out over the glass. There was a very long moment when nothing happened. Then the man put his hand to his mouth, drew it away, and blew us a kiss. He rolled his window back up and drove down the street.

When he had turned the corner, I collapsed against the nearest palm tree and laughed in relief. "I was *scared,* girl!" I said. "Shit, I can't *believe* I was so scared! I mean, I've *seen* that guy before, he usually don't bother no one but his buyers, but damn, I was gettin ready to piss my *pants.*"

Raina shook her head and squatted down on the pavement. "I was scared for a second there, too."

"People around here don't usually mess with me," I said, my heart still beating fast. "And they won't mess with you, either, once they know who you are." I paused and shook my head. "Shit, a little group of the Inglewood Families used to come to our games last year, and they were some of the best fans we had."

We were both quiet for another few moments, and I could hear some kids shouting at each other in a yard a little further up the street. I took a deep breath, and the air smelled like late summer in L.A.—dead grass and a bit of dust. After another minute, I stood up straight again, and looked at the tree I'd just been leaning against. The bark was peeling off of it in inch-long curly strips. There were a couple of "IF's" carved into one side.

"Come on, girl," Raina said, standing up. "Get away from that tree and let's go to the park before you get hit on the head by a coconut."

I turned my eyes up toward the spreading circle of fronds; it was like looking up someone's skirt. "There's no nuts in this tree," I noted seriously.

"Maybe not," Raina said, smiling now. "But there's a hella big one under it."

We continued down 12th Avenue, talking and laughing, our heart rates gradually returning to normal. After waiting for a few minutes to cross 90th Street, we squeezed through the back entrance of Darby Park. There were people playing tennis to the left of us, although without the net, which had been stolen the year before. Beyond them, we saw two baseball diamonds, the walking path, and in the distance, the southwestern part of Inglewood. The land level dropped dramatically just west of the park, so that when you stood on the grass, you could see the Forum and Hollywood Park, and look down at planes descending toward the airport.

As we passed the tennis players, the park's two basketball courts came into view. They were slightly undersized, with huge cracks that caused the ball to bounce crazily if you dribbled on them. The chain nets were mostly rusted, but whenever you scored a basket, they made an emphatic and satisfying "clink!," like a handful of pennies all hitting concrete at once. The taped red squares on the backboards had fallen off, leaving only faint shadows, and half the lines on the pavement were worn away. One of the rims had been bent by someone hanging on to it after a dunk.

I smiled as soon as I saw the courts—I'd grown up here; I'd been playing at the park for almost ten years by then. When I first developed a halfway decent shot, the summer I turned nine, I was suddenly a lot more liked. It was as if I had learned the secret handshake for membership in the 'hood. With the people I met at the park, and eventually, with the players I met through school, spring leagues, and AAU, I felt, for the first time in my life, something close to a sense of belonging.

The first few members of the usual afternoon pickup crowd were already there. Ordinarily a few stray high school boys showed up, some middle-aged men who either worked at night or not at all, and the occasional younger kid who risked life and limb for the privilege of playing with the big people. Sometimes, but not often, there'd be some girls from Morningside, the other public high school in Inglewood. And later, after five, a whole new influx of players would arrive, men and sometimes women getting off of work, people ready to run or shove or hit out the frustration that had built up throughout the course of the day.

The way pickup games started was so universal at courts across the city that someone might have issued official instructions on the subject. When it was early, and there were only one or two people, they just shot around by themselves. Sometimes with two people, but more often with three, a game of Twenty-one was proposed: each player for him or herself against the other two. If a fourth showed up, or if there were two groups of two, a game of two-on-two would be suggested. As time passed and more players appeared, this expanded to three-on-three, four-on-four, and finally, to five-on-five full court. People chose teammates on the logical basis of height and visible physical condition, but also on the basis of the air a player might have, or his race, or the brand of his basketball shoes. Eventually there would be a backup of people waiting on the sidelines to play the winner. Usually the games went to eleven or fifteen. You didn't want to lose, because if you did, you might have to wait half an hour before seeing the court again. If you continued to win, you could keep the court all night.

We surveyed the situation as we approached. On one court a lone high school kid was shooting semi-accurately—not a varsity player, because all the varsity boys were playing at the school that afternoon. On the other were two men who looked like they were in their mid- to late-thirties. The taller one, who was about my height, was a dark brown-skinned man with a protruding potbelly so large that it might have been grafted onto his otherwise slender frame. The shorter one was light-skinned, with inch-long hair that was almost straight, and bright hazel eyes. We watched for a few minutes. The guys' shots were reasonably accurate, but their technique was terrible. Both of them depended on their off-hands so much that they seemed to be shooting two-handed. They had no follow-through, and the taller one took a step sideways as he released the ball. Raina gave me a nod and we headed over to their side of the court. They obviously played for fun, were not serious players. Easy prey.

"Hey, guys," Raina said as we approached. "How 'bout a game?"

They stopped and looked us over, and I could read the thought that flitted across both sets of eyes—*girls.* I also saw that they didn't know what to make of me in particular, an Asian kid in a predominantly black town. All of the people in the 'hood, including the regulars at the park, were used to me by then, but strangers still did double takes when they saw me.

"O.K., sure," said the potbelly. His voice was low and solid, and I might have liked him if he'd had the sense to take us seriously. "Maybe you two want to split up, though."

"Naw, it's cool," Raina said. "We'll play together."

"You wanna shoot around a little to warm up?"

"Naw, we don't need to. We just played somewhere else." This was true—we'd left our respective practices about an hour before. And of course at that time, in high school, it seemed we had always "just played somewhere else."

Raina shot the ball for outs, and made the free throw with a commanding clink! of the chain net. The taller man raised his eyebrows. She took the ball back behind the key a few feet, and bounced it to the shorter one to check. I lined myself up to the left of the key. Raina passed me the ball to start the game, I passed it back, and she took four quick dribbles to her right. I made a jab step with my left foot and got my man going in that direction; then I cut right sharply and burst into the lane, where Raina hit me with a perfect pass. I went in for the easy lay-up and scored. On the next point, Raina passed to me, I passed right back to her, and she took a long-range jumper from about three feet in back of the key. Swish—or rather, clink. The shorter man swore. Raina grinned. Beads of sweat gleamed like diamonds on her forehead.

On the next point we took a little longer to try a shot, poking here and prodding there, trying to figure out which part of their defense was most likely to give. Finally I took a pass on the left wing, faked right, then drove hard to the baseline and shot a power lay-up from the left side of the basket. On a power lay-up you take off with both feet, making a wall of your body and shooting with the ball way out in front of you so that your shot can't be blocked from behind. People still try to block it, unless they've been taught better, and this guy came down on my shoulder so hard that I had a bruise there for more than a week. I scored anyway. Basket and foul. On the next point, Raina, in a rare lapse of concentration, threw a soft floating pass that the shorter guy picked off. It was their turn.

There is a rule about men playing pickup ball against women: the women almost always win, because the men, most of whom are just average, nonskilled guys who show up at the park for fun, believe that they have already won the game simply by virtue of their being male, while the few women who play the parks are usually serious players, college caliber or better, and for them these men are no competition. Men who are real players are of course a different story, and can usually beat most women. But these real players are far outnumbered by the other type, the average guys, who only come to the parks occasionally, and who see basketball as nothing more than a fun way to get some exercise. These guys can't imagine the possibility of a woman—any woman—being better players than they. The regulars, however, know better.

There's a great story about Cheryl Miller and her brother Reggie. When they were in high school and junior high school respectively, Reggie would approach men at the park while Cheryl hid in the bushes, and tell them that he and his sister would play them for money. I can imagine what the guys must have thought—here's this skinny young kid barely sprouting his first body hairs, and he's going to challenge us with *who?* His *sister?* Sure, buddy (wink, wink). Bring her on. So they'd agree and then out would pop Cheryl—6' 2", agile and unstoppable. She and Reggie would then proceed, of course, to devastate their opponents, and make enough pocket money in the process to buy their dinner. I almost feel sorry for their victims. Almost. Little did they know that they'd bet on a game with the future star of the Indiana Pacers, and the greatest women's basketball player of all time.

The guys who lose in the most spectacular fashion are the boys who play during the summers. Teenage boys migrate to outdoor courts in packs once June rolls around—because they're out of school and the weather is nice, but also, more importantly, because in the summer hordes of girls come to watch them play. More crushes are developed during one summer pickup game than at a year's worth of high school dances. These T-shirted Romeos aren't stupid; they know that the best way to dazzle a young lady they're trying to talk to is to show her a good game of basketball. So every day they come to the park in twos and threes, streamlined and beautiful, sporting new Nike shoes, fade haircuts, and much-practiced gangster limps. They never look at the girls on the sidelines but are always aware of their presence. They make breathtaking, graceful, impossible moves, bending like willows as they change directions in midair, triple-pumping, double-reversing—and missing their shots. They shout loudly, gesture dramatically, give each other high fives so hard that the slaps can be heard across the park. The girls point and preen and giggle. They know that everything the boys do is intended to impress them, and it doesn't matter that the boys are so busy showing off their moves that they often fail to deposit the ball into the basket. During the summer, my high school teammates and I would go about these games as usual, scoring quietly and trying not to get too caught up in the excitement. But occasionally I'd make a twisting move pretty enough to warrant a squeal from the girls on the sidelines. I, of course, was trying to impress them, too.

That day at the park, though, Raina and I weren't trying to impress anyone. We were just playing regular pickup ball, for the love of the sport itself. We beat the guys eleven to six in the first game, and then, having had that warm-up, eleven to three in the second. The guys swore and complained, and by the fourth point of the second game they were yelling at each other instead of at us, a sure sign that they were frustrated.

As for Raina and me, we were silent except for necessary court talk, yelling "behind you" when the other was tied up with the ball, or "you got help" to let the other know that we were backing her up on defense. We complemented each other well—she had more smoothness and I had more power; she was fluid and fast while I was slower but explosive; she had greater range on her jump shot but I could muscle the ball inside—but we were just starting to get used to each other's games. Occasionally, when we made a good play, we allowed ourselves a nod or a congratulatory high five, and each time she grabbed my arm or slid her fingers around the back of my neck, I felt the ghost of her touch after her hand was gone; I felt the place where her fingers had met my skin.

By the time we'd finished our second game, enough people had arrived from the after-five crowd for us to start going full court. A group of the Inglewood Families had gathered, too, sitting atop the nearby picnic tables and drinking forty-ounce brews, keeping half an eye on the game. Raina and I split up and guarded each other. Full-court pickup games are notorious for their lack of passing, and neither of us saw the ball very much. It didn't matter, though—scoring is just one part of basketball, and so we focused our personal contest elsewhere. We sprinted shoulder to shoulder down the court while everyone else lagged behind; we shoved against each other for rebounds, pushing with backs, hips, and arms even after someone else had recovered the ball; we shadowed each other on defense so tightly that there was no way someone could have gotten a pass to us, even if they had been so inclined. Defense takes discipline, concentration, and pride. Pride is by far the most important of these factors, and Raina and I both had a lot of it.

Whenever anyone on either team did something impressive—a pretty finger roll, a heads-up steal, a behind-the-back pass—Raina would smile widely, delighted. She took such joy in the game that she was happy when anyone played it well, as if each good play was a flower that someone had laid on her doorstep. My appreciation was not as pure. I wanted to win, to outdo people, and I begrudged my opponents' successes. At the end of the third game I got cramps in my calves, and after rolling around in pain for a while I had to drag myself off the court. Raina helped me over to the sideline, then laughed as I swore at my mutinous legs. We were done for the day. She ran her fingers along her thigh, and they left five blurred trails through the sheen of perspiration, like paths spreading in the wake of ships. The muscles of her arms seemed more defined than usual, and her shoulders looked both solid, cut from pure, polished stone, and also delicate, soft to the touch. I dragged a towel across my arms and legs while Raina pulled the bottom of her T-shirt up and used it to wipe her face. This left a six-inch strip of her torso exposed, and I saw her slightly rounded belly, the sweat that pooled in her navel, the smooth line of soft hair that disappeared into her shorts. One of her hip bones jutted toward me, her waistband riding just below it. I imagined touching those hips and pressing my face against the curves of her stomach; I wanted to feel her flesh rise to meet my hands.

CHAPTER 4

The next day, Wednesday, three of Claudia's friends came over for dinner. They met for meals, according to Raina, about twice a month, rotating the location and cooking duties. When Raina and I got in from the park, they were just sitting down around a beautiful, steaming lasagna that Claudia had labored over for much of the previous night. Having all these strangers in our dining room made me slightly uncomfortable. It seemed odd that Claudia, who'd only been in the house for a few weeks, was playing hostess as if she'd lived there for several years. At the same time, though, I was curious to see how she acted with her friends. As we walked into the dining room, a tall, stately woman, who was sitting to Claudia's left, spotted us coming, and smiled.

"Hi, Raina," she said. "Girl, you getting so pretty. Come on over here, now, and hug your aunt Rochelle."

Raina looked sheepish, but obeyed. Rochelle regarded her with the glowing approval that mothers bestow only on young girls they think suitable for their sons.

"You looking skinny, girl," said the woman to Claudia's right, who'd had her back to us. She was a small, dark-skinned woman with chipmunk cheeks and straight, shiny, ear-length hair. "Why don't you come on by the restaurant and I'll fatten you up?"

The third friend, a thin, honey-colored woman with flashing green eyes and wavy hair, smiled and shook her head. "Kim, leave the poor child alone. You think everyone's skinny who's not at least twenty-five pounds overweight, and you're always trying to shove food down people's throats."

"Excuse me?" said Raina, grinning. "Look who's talking, Paula. Every single time I go over to *your* place, I leave about ten pounds heavier."

Paula smiled back at her, happy to be teased. "That's not because I *feed* you, though. It's 'cos you *eat* every damn thing in the house."

I stood a little outside of their circle, trying to attach names and faces with the stories Raina had told me on the way home from the park. Rochelle, the woman who'd hugged her, was a buyer for Robinson's and the mother of a teenage son. Kim, the woman who'd offered to feed her, owned and managed—along with her husband—Barry's Chicken & Waffles on Century; they had two junior-high-school-age girls who played basketball. The third woman, Paula, ran a real estate office in Hawthorne. She had no children of her own, so she indulged her friends' children; the San Francisco T-shirt that Raina was wearing had been a gift from her. Claudia had known Rochelle since they were in high school together; she'd met Kim and Paula through the Black Businesswomen's Alliance, which they'd all been members of since its inception ten years before.

"Now, who's this?" asked Rochelle, finally noticing me. She was a classic big woman—not fat, but tall and solid; she would have made a wonderful center.

Claudia gestured for me to come over, and put a hand on my arm. "This is Wendell's daughter, Nancy," she said. "She's a basketball player, too."

"Hi," I said uncertainly.

"Hi," they all said in unison.

"So you play basketball," said Kim. "Are you as good as Raina?"

"Well, I, uh . . ." I glanced at Raina, who was still standing next to Rochelle. She shook her head at me and rolled her eyes, apologizing that I had to be subjected to this—but also, obviously, enjoying the attention.

"Oh, Kim," said Rochelle. "Don't put the poor child on the spot like that." She considered me thoughtfully. "You know, you look just like your daddy."

"Really?" I said. I didn't know whether to be flattered or annoyed, so I bent down to pet the dog, who ignored me and stared at the lasagna.

Raina shook her head and said, "No, she doesn't."

Claudia laughed. "She is *so* much like Wendell. Not just in looks, either. Although neither of them know it, of course." She turned toward me, and I was surprised by the affection in her voice. I hadn't thought she'd paid much attention to me.

"Well, I'm a big basketball fan," said Rochelle. She patted her hair, which enclosed her head like a bicycle helmet. "And so's Paula. We go with Claudia sometimes to watch Raina's games. Maybe we'll come to see *you* play, too. What high school do you play for?"

"The green and white," I said proudly. "Inglewood."

Paula, who'd been playing with her napkin, crossed her arms now and looked at me. "Really," she said. And there was something in her voice—the bluntness of it, the way she ended her word on a down note, like the British—that made me a bit uneasy. I didn't have time to think about it, though, because Kim came at me with another question.

"Does your father teach there, too?"

"No," I said, "he teaches at Hawthorne."

Claudia leaned forward, smiling. "Yes. Wendell's annoyed because Hawthorne's colors are maroon and gold—like USC, you know, and he's a UCLA man."

Just then, as if on cue, my father came into the dining room. The dog, her trance broken, ran over to greet him. "I heard my name. Are you all saying scandalous things about me?"

"The worst," said Rochelle. She smiled, lowered her chin, and looked at him coyly; I was startled by the realization that she found him attractive.

"That's fine," he said, resting a hand on Claudia's shoulder. "Just as long as they're all true." She turned toward him, and they smiled at each other.

"You're looking good, Wendell," said Rochelle. Kim rolled her eyes theatrically and said, "Oh, Lord." Claudia and Raina laughed.

"Thanks," my father said. "So are you, ladies. How you all doing tonight?"

"Great," said Kim. "Except our food's getting cold. You sure you don't want to join us?"

"No, thanks. I got places to go." He turned to Paula, who seemed to be examining the design on the tablecloth. "How you doing tonight, Paula?"

She looked up at him briefly, then back down at the table. "Fine."

There was a moment of silence, during which Rochelle shot Paula a dirty look.

"Hey, Dad," I said finally. "Where you goin?"

He looked at me, then smiled down at Claudia. "Claudia's forcing me to spend the evening elsewhere, so I'm meeting one of my colleagues and her husband for dinner. Since you and Raina aren't being kicked out, though, I guess it's just me that the ladies object to."

"We're *working,*" insisted Claudia. We have to talk about this conference the BBA is having in February. Besides, you could always stick around if you really wanted to."

My father shook his head. "And listen to you all gossip? No thanks."

He left, after a round of goodbyes, and I watched him walk

away. I couldn't understand what women saw in him. He didn't seem particularly handsome to me, but he was athletic, and big, and good-natured. Sometimes, when I was lucky, or when he'd had too much to drink, he'd tell me stories about his childhood, about going with my grandfather on gardening jobs. My father would mow the grass while *his* father did the tasks that required greater precision, like weeding, and trimming the bushes. He told me how good it felt to push himself, to sweat in the summer sun, and how sweet and cold the water tasted afterward; it was then, on the gardening jobs that began when he was twelve, that he knew he would be an athlete.

After Claudia carved out pieces of lasagna for all of us, Raina and I took our plates and went upstairs. Before we left, though, Rochelle grabbed Raina again, spoke in a hushed voice that all of us could hear. "Now you and your mother should come over to eat sometime before Curtis leaves for college next week." She leaned in closer. "Girl, Curtis is a real good cook."

Kim and Paula laughed loudly, and Claudia just a little; Raina freed herself and we both went up the stairs.

"I guess she don't know about you, huh?" I said.

Raina shook her head. "I guess not."

The phone rang, and Raina went into her room to answer it; from the way her voice softened and her body cradled the phone, I knew that it was Toni. Since I had nothing better to do—and since I wanted to see what Claudia was like away from my father—I tiptoed back down the stairs and into the living room, just out of the range of sight from the table. I got there just in time to hear Rochelle say, "Girl, that Wendell is one good-looking man."

Claudia laughed. "Thanks for the stamp of approval."

"I've got to admit," said Kim, "he's grown on me. Not *that* way," she said when Rochelle laughed. "He's not my type at all, you know that. I mean, I just like him better now. He's done right by you, Claudia, and this house is a hell of a lot nicer than that place you were staying before."

"Yeah, you got yourself a good one," said Rochelle, sounding like her mouth was full of food. "And Kim, you do, too—you and Don are about the only happy married people I know. How long's it been now, twenty years?"

"Eighteen," Kim replied. "And it's been hell sometimes, honey. But between the restaurant and the kids, we're just too busy to have problems between us."

"Damn," Rochelle said softly, and I heard silverware clink. "It's been too damn long since I had a steady man. Almost three years since Christopher. And Paula, hasn't it been almost that long for you?"

"Two years since Alex," she said. She sounded much more at ease now that the rest of us were gone. "And you're right, girl, it's been *too* damn long."

"Well, do either of you have any candidates?" asked Claudia.

Rochelle cleared her throat. "Well, there was this fine lawyer that Paula and I met at the barbecue on the Fourth of July. . ."

Paula finished. ". . . but the line for *that* brother was about a mile and a half long."

Kim laughed. "Rochelle, what about that banker you tried to set Claudia up with before she met Wendell? He was all right, Claudia, wasn't he? Good-looking? Steady income? Smart?"

Claudia snorted. "Yes, he was perfectly nice," she said. "But Rochelle neglected to mention to me the minor fact that he was married."

"Oh, shit, girl," said Paula, laughing. "You didn't tell me that."

"Well, so what?" Rochelle said. "Most marriages end. Except for you, Kim, we can all attest to that."

"Mm-hmm," agreed Claudia. "But I don't want to be responsible for speeding up the process." She sounded different away from us kids, I noticed—less careful, more relaxed. She wasn't a parent now, but just a woman hanging out with her friends. "And speaking of divorced people, what happened to that detective y'all met at Sandra's party last month?"

"Well, *I* thought he was cute," said Rochelle, "but he only had eyes for Paula."

"He was all right," Paula said. "But I wasn't interested. I'm suspicious of any brother who's a cop."

"Do you have anyone we could meet, Kim?" asked Rochelle. "Shit, you probably see more black men in a single night than the rest of us see in a year."

Kim laughed. "Sure, we got a *lot* of brothers coming into the restaurant, take your pick. As long as you don't mind that they're real young, and that a lot of them dress in blue—*Crip* blue."

They all laughed. "Well, I guess I'll just keep trying my luck in the professional world," said Rochelle. "Hey, do you think there'll be any men at the conference?"

Paula laughed. "Well, considering it's called 'Black Women in the Workplace,' I can't see them showing up en masse." She paused, and when she spoke again, her voice sounded serious. "One thing I know, though. Whoever I finally end up with, you can be sure he's going to be black."

Rochelle made a noise somewhere between agreement and protest. "Well, I'm looking too, honey, but there ain't that many black men our age who aren't married or nasty or gay."

"I know," Paula said. "But I still think it's better to hold out for a brother than to settle for something else."

There was a silence, and even from where I stood, I could feel the mood in the dining room shift.

"Are you trying to tell me something, Paula?" asked Claudia quietly.

There was another silence. Then Paula said, in a hesitant voice, "I don't know. I guess I am. It's nothing against Wendell personally."

"Girl, you being a fool," said Rochelle. "I've been alone for so damn long I'd take any man who treated me well."

"No, I know what she's saying," Kim put in. "And I agree with you, Paula. To a point. I didn't really approve of Wendell, either." She paused. "But look at him—he's got a good job, he treats Claudia right, and he's raised a child by himself. Wendell's a *man,* Paula, and there ain't a whole lot of men *around* anymore, in black or in any other color."

"I know that," said Paula. "I do. But I'm still not comfortable with him."

I heard Claudia put her silverware down, and sigh. "Paula, I can't believe this. I mean, what do you want me to say? You're my friend, and I shouldn't have to explain myself to you."

"That's right, girl," said Rochelle. "Shit, the only thing you *should* explain is why you stayed with that damn fool Carl for so long. If I'd been married to him, *I* might've given up on black men, too."

"I'm not . . ." Claudia began, sounding frustrated. "I didn't 'give up' on black men. If you remember, Paula, all of the men I've dated before now have been black. Wendell just happened, and I fell for him. Is that so hard to understand?"

Upstairs, I heard a door slam shut; it was Raina, going into the bathroom. Claudia and her friends must have heard it, too; there was silence, and then a couple of sighs.

"Anyway," said Kim finally, sounding like the mother she was. "The food's getting cold. Let's figure out what's happening with the conference."

Slowly, awkwardly, they managed to switch gears; they left the talk of men behind, and moved on to the conference. I picked up that it was a weekend event in February sometime, and that their organization was inviting black women from all over the county. I wasn't sure what the purpose of the conference was, and I didn't stick around long enough to find out. Instead, I retreated up the stairs and into my room, thinking about what I had heard. It upset me that Claudia's friend didn't approve of my father. I was angry with Paula—she didn't even know him, who was *she* to judge whether he was good for Claudia?—but what confused me, what kept me up that night, staring at the ceiling, was that part of me understood.

• • •

In the next several weeks, our house became a showroom. The coaching staffs of about twenty different colleges came through our door, and Raina and I had each turned down requests from dozens of others. The first set of coaches appeared on September fifteenth, just after Claudia and Raina finally finished unpacking.

"I feel like we're about to be bombarded with traveling salesmen," complained Claudia, as we straightened up the house in preparation. Raina was vacuuming, I was dusting, and the parents were breaking down boxes from the move.

"Hey! What's wrong with recruiters?" my father asked, pretending to be hurt. "You just don't like coaches, do you?"

"No, dear," said Claudia, patting him on the head like a sad puppy. "I love coaches. I might even consider going out with one." She smiled. "I just don't want to sacrifice all my nights for the next two weeks."

My father scratched his chin. "Well maybe we should have a housewarming party and invite all of them to come at once."

"Fine," Claudia said. "As long as you do the cleaning up."

As we tried to make the house more presentable for the influx of coaches, I was suddenly very conscious of the way it looked. Our couch and our love seat didn't match—the former was a light tan, and the latter sky blue—and both of them dated from my babyhood, their cushions nearly threadbare in the middle. There was a green chair against the wall, which my father and I called the dog chair, because Ann had slept in it every day as a pup and had chewed one arm into a gnarled lump. An old, white piano missing two of its keys sat cringing in the corner by the window. There were two stains on the light green carpet, where Ann had vomited, and an oval-shaped stain on the coffee table where I had once spilled a bottle of beer. My great-grandmother's scroll dominated the wall behind the love seat, but other than that, the only decorations were the framed pictures of Raina and me which my father had placed on top of the television. I spent fifteen minutes being terrified that the coaches would hate our house. Then it occurred to me that they'd seen places in far worse condition, and I managed to relax a little.

While our parents may not have been excited about the home visit process, Raina and I were looking forward to it. For one thing, it meant a narrowing down of choices—from here on out, we would only seriously consider the schools that made home visits. I was still nowhere near to making a decision, but it was a lot less overwhelming to hold twelve or fifteen schools in mind than the hundred-plus from whom I'd gotten letters. For another, it was mind-boggling to consider that all of these coaches—all of these folks I'd seen on TV and read about and watched from the stands—were going to be sitting there in the flesh, on our sofa. And I knew they'd be nicer now, while they were courting us, than any of them would ever be if we decided to play for them.

The first visit was from USC, for Raina. Coach Linda Sharp and her assistants came right at seven, and Claudia showed them all into the living room. I'd been in the kitchen washing dishes, but then I went through the living room on my way upstairs, just as my father was giving the coaches the choice of coffee or Japanese tea. Coach Sharp turned as I passed.

"Hi, Nancy," she said. "Good to see you. I'm sorry we don't need a forward for next year, or I'd want to talk to you tonight, too."

What she'd said was not exactly true—if she could claim now that they didn't need a forward, it was because they already had a verbal commitment from one of the top three high school forwards in the country. Still, I said, "No problem. Good to see you, too."

She turned back to Raina, and I was forgotten.

I climbed the stairs, went to my room, and shut the door loudly while I stood in the hallway. Then I crept back over to the top of the staircase and sat down. The only thing I could see from there, besides the carpet and the back of the sofa, was the dog's butt. Coach Sharp was just beginning her pitch.

"Well, Raina," she said, "I know you've been a USC fan for a long time. And in the last five years, you've had a lot to be excited about. I don't need to tell you about our two national championships, and of course you know about Cheryl."

I stifled a laugh. For most recruits, Coach Sharp could have stopped right there. Who wouldn't want to sign with such a powerhouse team, and wear the same uniform as the greatest and most dynamic player in history? Watching Cheryl Miller play had been like seeing joy in motion. When she got the ball at the high post to start the USC offense, the entire crowd would hold its breath, waiting for her to jump high in the air and hang for a moment before sinking the shot; or swoop by her multiple defenders and invent a new way to make a lay-up; or see three moves ahead, like a chess player, and throw a pass to what looked like an empty space until her teammate magically appeared to catch the ball. Whether Cheryl was hurtling down the court, or diving six rows into the bleachers to make a save, or leaping high off the floor to block an ill-advised shot, everyone in the building, including her opponents, would watch her like a phenomenon of nature. I had worshipped her since she was in high school, where she'd once scored 105 points in a game. I had clipped articles about her from papers and magazines, gone to as many USC games as I could. I'd taped the Grammy Awards when she'd appeared onstage and dunked while Donna Summer sang, "She Works Hard for the Money." She played with such energy, style, and passion that it was impossible to tear your eyes away from her, and every young player I knew, as she shot around in her driveway, or in the park, or in her high school gym, dreamed that she could be like Cheryl Miller.

Coach Sharp knew this, and it helped her tremendously in terms of recruiting. But I knew something that Coach Sharp didn't—that Raina wanted to get out of Los Angeles. She had no intention of signing with SC, and while she was still flattered enough by their interest to agree to a home visit, she'd scheduled them first, as kind of a practice run, precisely because there was nothing at stake. While I was a bit jealous that they wanted Raina and not me, it didn't bother me as much as I expected—I knew I would never have wanted to play in the obliterating shadow of Cheryl. Besides, if I went to USC, it would change my feelings about the place. It would somehow taint Cheryl and my admiration for her; it would make her, and SC, less special. Eight years later, Cheryl Miller herself would be making these home visits as the head coach for USC, and to *those* recruits, who'd never seen her in action, she was simply another former player turned coach. I'd want to shake them out of their ignorance—this was *Cheryl,* the greatest ever, and none of them would be fit to carry her shoelaces—but by then, in the nineties, she was already old news; she was just a name in the history books, and Reggie Miller's older sister.

"Now," Coach Sharp continued, "*you* can become a part of our great tradition. Cheryl graduated last spring, but we have some terrific young players coming up right behind her, and with you and another player or two of your caliber, we're sure to reach the Final Four again." She paused, maybe to take a sip of the coffee my father had brought her. "But let me put the basketball talk aside for a moment and tell you about our school. USC is a great learning institution, and it is one of the most famous universities on the West Coast. We have a wonderful faculty and a diverse, international student body, and no matter what your field of interest is, you'll find plenty of resources and a lot of support. Do you know what you're interested in studying, Raina?"

"Not really," Raina answered, sounding small. She cleared her throat. "Maybe, um, history, or like, sociology or something. So I can figure things out."

I smiled, knowing that the coaching staff would have no idea what she was talking about. What she meant was that she wanted to figure out why people acted like they did; why things turned out the way they had; why everything in our city and country and world was the way it was.

"Fine," Coach Sharp said, after a moment of silence. "But

whatever you decide to pursue, you should know that at USC you are a student first. Remember, 'student' is the first half of 'student-athlete.'"

I just knew Claudia would jump in here, and she did. "What are the graduation rates for your . . . student-athletes?"

That was a good question. There were a whole lot of jocks at USC, I knew, who never got their degrees.

"I don't have the exact figures," Coach Sharp answered, "but I can assure you that the graduation rates for women's basketball players are comparable to those for the university at large. And some of our players have outstanding academic records. Cheryl Miller, for example, did very well."

Just then a helicopter passed overhead. Its propeller whirred so loudly that conversation was impossible. When it became clear that it was circling and wasn't going to leave right away, my father got up and replenished everyone's drink. A few minutes later it moved on and headed south, toward 7-Eleven, toward the park.

"What do you do to make sure that the players keep up with their schoolwork?" Claudia asked when things had finally quieted down. I could almost see her sitting with her elbow in her palm and three fingers pressed to the back of her jaw, which was the position she always assumed when she was skeptical of what she was hearing.

"We have an academic advisor for the team," Coach Sharp said. "And, if necessary, we set the players up with private tutors."

The academic talk went on for another fifteen minutes or so, with Claudia asking all of the questions. There was no way she was going to let Raina play for a school that wasn't strong on academics. Claudia had only gone to college for two years before her parents' money had run out; she'd then started taking classes at night while holding a full-time job. After she'd married Raina's father, though, and Raina had come along, she no longer had the time to go to school. Claudia had wanted to be a reporter, but without a degree, the closest she could get to the news was circulation. She had a lot of responsibility within her department—from what I heard, she practically ran the place—but because she hadn't received a BA, there was only so far they'd promote her. And since she'd never finished college, the idea of Raina getting a degree was very important to her; she wanted to ensure that her daughter started out at a place which cared about whether she finished. This was why she was giving the USC coaches the third degree that night—she'd do this to all the coaches who came through the house.

When the academic talk was over, one of the assistants played a videotape, and at one point I recognized the TV broadcast of SC's second national championship game. I'd gone to that game with some AAU friends—it had been at UCLA's Pauley Pavilion—and now, as I sat in the hallway, it took a big effort to keep from running downstairs to watch. After the tape ended, the coaches talked a little more and then asked Raina if she had any questions. It occurred to me that she had only spoken once throughout the entire presentation, and then only because she'd been addressed. Now, she had just one question. "When do I have to let you know?"

They told her as soon as possible, please—that night would be great. She said she couldn't do that, and Coach Sharp said fine, let us know when you're ready, just remember that most top players sign as soon as they can and that your spot might be grabbed by someone else. Everyone stood up and shook hands all around; then Raina showed the coaches to the door.

The next night, it was my turn, with UCLA. Like Raina, I'd scheduled my first visit with a school I wasn't thrilled about. Two years before I'd felt differently—I'd gone to all the Bruins' home games, and had idolized Jackie Joyner, the future Olympic heptathlete who'd been a forward on that team. It seemed back then like UCLA was the place I'd end up, especially since they'd signed Stephanie Uchida, the great guard from North Torrance who was two years older than me, and who I'd played with in the Gardena Japanese league when we were both in junior high. I was often compared to her, even though she was a guard, because we were the only blue-chip Japanese-American players that anyone could remember. But now I had two AAU friends at UCLA who were very disillusioned, and they'd warned me to stay away. By the time I'd agreed to let coach Billie Moore and her staff come argue their case, it was almost as if I were doing it for old times' sake; it was as if I were saying yes to someone I no longer desired simply because I'd once wanted her so much.

If anyone was excited about the visit, it was my father, who'd been a student at UCLA when John Wooden was the coach and the Bruins ruled the NCAA. He asked more questions of Coach Moore than I did, and also recounted, in great detail, some of the games he'd seen in the sixties. He beamed when she said she'd been following my career for three years, and mentioned that he'd seen her assistant coach at a couple of my games. I did not enjoy his performance. The only thing that saved me from utter embarrassment was that the visit was not important to me. I wasn't trying to impress the coaches, and so I just sat back and took in what they said. Coach Moore talked in more specific terms than Coach Sharp had, and seemed much more intense about her pitch. This made sense—her program was good, but had a lot less to show for its efforts; UCLA hadn't won a national championship since Ann Meyers was there in the seventies. I could see, though, that Claudia preferred Coach Moore to Coach Sharp. Billie Moore was a direct, no-nonsense type of person while Coach Sharp had been smoother, and UCLA was a better school. Both Claudia and my father were impressed, too, when the coaches talked about what some of their recent graduates were doing. A couple of them were playing pro ball in Europe and Japan, several were in graduate school, and the rest of the former Bruins seemed to have good, secure jobs. I listened to all of this patiently, but it didn't sway me. Just before they left, Coach Moore invited me to make an official campus visit over one of the upcoming weekends, and I told her I'd get back to her on that. We were only allowed five of those campus visits and I wanted to choose my schools carefully.

When they were gone, I went upstairs and found Raina sitting at the top of the staircase, in the exact same spot I'd been the night before. It was strange to think about her spying on me; I felt like a photographer who'd been dragged out from behind the camera and suddenly thrust in front of it. She smiled up at me without a trace of guilt.

"What you doin up here?" I asked.

She scratched her neck and as I followed the movement of her hand, my eyes fell upon her right earlobe. I imagined slipping it into my mouth and rolling it on my tongue, like a smooth piece of butterscotch candy. "Same thing you were doin last night," she said. "Hey, maybe if *you* don't wanna sign with UCLA, they'll take your dad instead."

I laughed. "I know, huh? He really wants me to go."

"Well, maybe he could pass as you if he shaved more often and curled his hair. Y'all do have similar faces, I guess, although he's not as good-looking as you."

I didn't answer—my tongue was stuck, even though I knew she hadn't meant anything. She'd been matter-of-fact, the way that people are when they're indifferent and have nothing at stake. I wondered if she was upset that UCLA wasn't recruiting her anymore—they'd already gotten a verbal commitment from an All-State guard—but she didn't seem troubled by their visit.

"But where do *you* wanna go?" she asked now.

I looked down at Ann, who was at my feet, so that I wouldn't have to look at Raina. "I don't know, girl. And I don't wanna think about it."

Now it was Raina's turn to laugh. "Yeah, well these coaches sure want you to think about it. They want you to think about it all the time."

She wasn't kidding. In the next two weeks, I saw, among others, Oregon, Berkeley, Georgia, Old Dominion, Tennessee, UNLV, and Arizona. All of these coaches promised that their schools were the place for me, that I'd get plenty of playing time, that they were going to win the national championship. All of them were very eager to get their points across, and it gave me a new appreciation for the relatively low-key approaches of Coach Sharp and Coach Moore—both local coaches who realized that no matter what their programs' faults or merits might be, at least we already knew a lot about them. Some of these other coaches had styles which disoriented me. There was the one who placed a letter of intent on the table before he'd even introduced himself, as if just seeing it would make me trip all over myself in my haste to sign; and the one who said I shouldn't have to hear any more about her school than I wanted to and then proceeded to sit silently until I asked her some questions. Several coaches did mental double takes when they laid eyes on our parents—you could see their eyebrows begin to lift, and then reverse themselves, as the coaches realized it wouldn't help their cause to express surprise at the couple in front of them. But the essential message from all of them was the same—come play for us, we'll make you happy, you'll leave us not just a star athlete but a well-rounded person who will go out and succeed in the world.

Raina was hearing the same crap. One night, while entertaining the coaches of a school she was no longer interested in, she came into the kitchen to get some coffee. I was standing at the counter making a peanut butter and jelly sandwich, and although my back was to the door, I could feel her presence. I was always conscious of where Raina was, as if she were an energy source which gave off light and heat. When I turned around, she looked tired and impatient.

"So what's he telling you?" I asked about the evening's coach, who looked, I thought, like Governor Deukmejian.

She sighed. "That I'll start for them and we'll win the NCAA next year. That all of his players are outstanding, motivated, brilliant people who are gonna go on and win the Nobel Prize."

"Yeah, but can they do *this?*" I asked, and stuffed the entire sandwich into my mouth.

Raina laughed. "Probably not," she said. "Maybe if you go

and show the coaches that, they'll decide they wanna sign you, too."

There were some schools that needed both a shooting guard, which was Raina's position, and a forward, which was mine, and those coaches met with both of us at once. These were all good places—Iowa, Connecticut, Washington, and Virginia—but not one of the head coaches made it through the evening without making a joke about killing two birds with one stone. We didn't really mind, though—especially me. I liked being there with Raina, and I wanted to get a sense of whether she was interested in any of the schools. As we sat on the couch together, I wondered if these coaches, these strangers, could see what I saw—the intensity in her face, the anxiousness, the way she always leaned forward slightly, whether standing or sitting, as if she needed to get going somewhere. There were some awkward moments, though. There was the coach who told my father and Claudia that they were fortunate to have two preseason All-America picks in their house, as if our parents were supposed to feel lucky to have the honor of supporting us (besides, we were only Honorable Mentions). There was the coach who asked, "Who wins when the two of you play one-on-one?"—to which Raina and I hemmed and hawed, and didn't look at each other, and answered truthfully that we'd never done it. There was the coach who remarked that he hadn't realized Japanese kids could be so tough, and then congratulated me on uplifting the race. And there was the coach who was clearly uncomfortable in our neighborhood and who asked what we did when we heard gunshots nearby, to which Raina answered, wryly, "We duck." Otherwise, though, the coaches were tactful, and didn't give one of us more attention than the other—which was good, because I definitely paid attention. I was glad that Raina and I played different positions—even if some of these schools later focused their efforts on one or the other of us, at least we weren't competing for the same spot.

By the end of the whole process, the four of us were exhausted. We were sick of the parade of coaches coming through the house; we were sick of the similar messages. The visits had completely consumed our lives for two weeks, making it almost impossible for Raina and me to do our homework, and there'd been days when we'd had more than one. Despite this bombardment, though, my thoughts about the future still weren't any more clear. The early signing period was in mid-November, and I knew I wouldn't be prepared to choose a school by then—I didn't even want to visit them yet. All I wanted by the end of the home visit process was to be left the hell alone.

The last home visit was on a Thursday, and it was Long Beach State, for Raina. Since she was as tired of the visits as I was, I figured she'd want to let loose and celebrate once she'd been released from this final appointment. I waited for her in my room, eschewing the staircase—I'd heard the spiel too many times, by then, to want to eavesdrop on another variation. The coaches were done with her a little before eight, and as soon as they were out the door, I hustled downstairs. I was going to ask Raina if she wanted to do something before she had a chance to make other plans. Everyone was in the kitchen and so I started to go there, but then, as I was passing through the living room, the doorbell rang. I figured that one of the coaches had forgotten something, and wondered if I should wait for Raina to come answer the door. Then I decided that was stupid and, without looking through the peephole, unlocked the door and answered it myself. But it wasn't a Long Beach State coach I found waiting on the doorstep. It was Raina's girlfriend, Toni.

I don't think she'd ever been to the house before, but when I opened the door, she raised her eyebrows as if it were me who was out of place.

"Wassup?" she said, and it sounded like a challenge. "You're Nancy, right?"

"Yeah," I said. "You're Toni."

"I've heard a lot about you," Toni said.

I wondered if this was true. "Oh, yeah?"

We stood there sizing each other up. I'd seen her around—at tournaments, at college games with Raina—but I'd never been this close to her before. I didn't particularly like the view. Toni was a little shorter than me, but her swaggering ego seemed to make up the difference. She was not especially attractive—her dark skin was a little blotchy, her features too small for her face—but she had an air of knowledge about her, and a barely restrained aggressiveness, that made people stop and take a closer look. Although I thought, of course, that Raina was too good for her, I knew this air was part of what she saw in her, and I understood why she liked it. Toni exuded danger, and this made her sexy. She just had, as they say, a way with women.

Raina arrived in the living room as we were conducting our little stare-down, and when I moved aside so she could see who was at the door, her face lit up like a child's. A ball of jealousy formed in my stomach. Toni glanced at me as she passed, and there was no mistaking her look—I wasn't worthy of being considered a rival, it said; she'd dismissed me as no possible threat.

"Hey," she said to Raina. "Ready to go?"

Raina was still smiling. "No. Long Beach just left a minute ago. I feel kinda slimy from all the coaches I've talked to, so let me go change my clothes."

As she ran up the stairs, taking two at a time, Claudia and my father came into the living room to finish cleaning up. Ann trailed along right after them. She trotted over to Toni, wagging her tail cheerfully, and I realized that our wonderful watchdog had failed to bark at my mortal enemy.

"Nice dog," Toni said, petting her, and I cringed. I did not want her touching my dog. I wanted my dog to bite her hand off.

"Hello, Toni," Claudia said, sticking her chin out a bit, and there was a definite coolness in her manner. I wasn't sure what this was about—whether Claudia disapproved of Raina's having a girlfriend, or whether she objected to this particular choice. Since Claudia was understanding, I knew, about Raina's love for women, it was conceivable that it was the latter. Toni was no great prize. She was two years older than us and neither worked nor went to school, yet from what I could tell, she seemed busier than we were. No one knew what she did with all of her time, but none of her activities seemed directed toward any foreseeable end. Toni floated. A couple of years earlier she'd been a decent high school player with two or three scholarship offers, which she'd turned down because she didn't want to have to be so serious about basketball. Knowing a little about her, this didn't surprise me. You play the way you live.

"Hey," Toni said to Claudia now, crossing her arms, not sounding particularly friendly herself. "Bet you tired of coaches by now, huh?"

"Yes. We are," said Claudia. That was all.

Now Toni turned toward my father, who was picking up two coffee cups from the table. "How you doin?" she asked.

"All right. All right," my father replied, not looking at her. "And you?"

As they were having this exchange, it occurred to me that my father had met Toni before—probably at Claudia and Raina's place, before they'd moved in with us. Suddenly I wondered if he knew about Raina, knew what significance Toni had in her life. I wondered, too, if he and Claudia ever talked about Raina's love life, but it was conceivable that they didn't. Silence on personal matters was one of the fundamental rules of our house.

I had no desire to stick around, so I went into the kitchen and hid. Claudia and my father made polite conversation with Toni, whose short, terse answers made it clear she was uncomfortable. I liked that. Soon Raina came back downstairs and said goodbye to the parents, assuring her mother that she'd be home by eleven, and then she and her girlfriend were gone.

I stood in the kitchen for a moment, until the parents came in carrying dishes and discussing the promises of the Long Beach State coach. The dog was mauling one of her squeaky toys in the living room, so I went and played with her for a few minutes until she ran into the kitchen to receive a bone. After she was gone, I lay flat on my back on the floor, staring straight up at the ceiling and feeling jealousy move through me like a large piece of hot, jagged metal. Then I did the only thing that one can do in a situation like that. I went outside and shot some baskets.

CHAPTER 5

The next day, Friday, I went home after school and took a nap. When I woke up around seven, there was no one else in the house—Claudia and my father were at his team's football game, and Raina, who must have come in while I was sleeping, had left a note saying she'd gone out to a movie with Toni. I decided not to call anybody—it was so rare that I had the house to myself that I wanted to make the most of it. I fed the dog, who looked injured because I served her dinner late, and then made myself a bowl of Top Ramen. The two of us took a quick walk up and down the street, and then I stood in the shower for twenty minutes and let the heat coax the soreness from my muscles. When I went into my room to get dressed, the big pile of brochures, folders, and media guides I'd collected over the last two weeks seemed to shout at me from its place on my dresser, so I went downstairs to escape it. There, on the couch, I nodded off in front of *Miami Vice,* until I heard my father's voice, loud and animated, as he and Claudia approached the door. Ann heard it, too. She jumped up with a start and beat my dad to the door, wagging tail thumping the wall.

The key turned in the lock, and then Claudia and my father were in the hallway. "Hello there, sweet puppy dog!" my father said, as Ann jumped up and licked him on the chin. "Hello, delinquent daughter!" he called out to me. Then he extricated himself from the dog, set down his bag, and grabbed Claudia by the shoulder and arm. He sang some tune I didn't recognize, spun her around the living room with exaggerated dance steps, dipped her low while she shrieked with laughter. The dog backed out of the room, ears cocked.

"Are you guys all right?" I asked, pressing the mute button on the remote control. I had seen my father act happy after a football victory—he'd been coaching for ten years—but never before had the outcome of a game warranted a full Fred Astaire imitation.

"We're fine," my father said, letting go of Claudia and smiling at me. "We're wonderful."

"I take it you won," I said.

Claudia smiled at my father, and pushed the hair from her eyes. "In several different ways."

"What are you talking about?" I asked.

My dad came over and sat down on the love seat. He was wearing a thin black tie, slightly loosened, which made his already broad chest seem broader. "Well, you know how Larry's son, Eric, is the starting quarterback?"

Larry was Larry Henderson, the head coach of my father's team, and the brother of Julie Henderson, who was one of the members of the Hawthorne City Council. Eric Henderson was his son, a big bulky kid with a squarish body and crew-cut sandy hair; he looked less like a quarterback than a linebacker from an earlier era.

"Yeah," I said. "What about him? Did he do something awesome?"

"No, no," my father said, sounding impatient, as he loosened his tie even more. "Eric never does anything awesome. About the most awesome thing he's ever done is get the flu this week, which kept him at home throwing up for the last three days."

Claudia sat down next to him on the love seat, resting her hand on his thick forearm. "And so one of your father's little protégés stepped in and—"

"Hey," my father said. "Let *me* tell the story." He grinned at her, then turned back to me. "So the backup quarterback is this kid named Eddie Nuñez. Real good kid. His mom's a maid, she doesn't speak much English, and she always comes to all the games even though Eddie hardly ever gets to play. The thing is, though, he *should* be playing. Eric was definitely the better player when they were both freshmen, and Eddie actually played JV. But then Eddie made varsity last year, and improved a lot, and I think he surpassed Eric around the end of the season. In practice, Eddie just *schools* Eric Henderson now. He takes that boy to *town.*" He paused for a moment, and shook his head. "But Larry still insists on starting his son. I don't know. I guess fielding the best team possible is not his number-one priority."

Claudia pressed a hand to her cheek and gave an exaggerated gasp. "Are you saying that Eric might be the starting quarterback just because his father's the coach?"

My father placed a hand over his heart and smiled. "I would never say such a thing."

"O.K., O.K.," I said, laughing. "What happened?"

My father turned to me. "So anyway, Eric Henderson's at home barfing his guts out."

Claudia bent over and did a fake retch.

"Right," he said, laughing. "And Eddie Nuñez has to start at quarterback. And we're playing the defending league champions, who we haven't beaten in about three or four hundred years, and who supposedly have this unstoppable defense. And Eddie just tears it *apart.*"

Claudia jumped up off the couch, pranced around, pretended to throw a football. I had never seen her act so silly; my father was clearly having a terrible effect on her. Ann, who'd just reentered the room with one of my father's shoes in her mouth, dropped it and stared in amazement.

"Four touchdowns, he had," my father said, leaning forward and pounding his knee. "Three passing and one rushing. We won 28–20, and the kids were the most pumped I'd ever seen them." He straightened up again, and nodded in satisfaction. "You know the last time Eric Henderson was responsible for four touchdowns? Probably in some wet dream he had when he was twelve."

"Dad!"

"I'm sorry, I'm sorry. Anyway, the point is, Eddie Nuñez should be the starting quarterback. And I've thought so since last year, but Larry's been determined to play Eric." He smiled. "Maybe after tonight he'll reconsider."

Claudia sat down next to him again. "Are you going to talk to him about it?"

"Yeah," my father answered. "Yeah, I am." He paused for a moment, shook his head in disgust. "And while I'm at it, maybe I should also talk to him about his son's attitude. Eric's in my fourth-period Trig class, you know, and all he does is sit there and preen like a goddamned king."

"Is he a senior?" I asked.

"No. He's a junior. And so's Eddie, which is why I'm so concerned. I mean, Eddie might actually be good enough to get a scholarship somewhere, but if Larry keeps starting Eric, no one's ever going to get to see him play."

Claudia shook her head. "Poor kid." She looked at my father thoughtfully. "How do you think Larry's going to react to all of this?"

My father sighed. "I don't know. I'd like to think he'll be reasonable about it. Larry's not a bad guy, you know, he just has a blind spot when it comes to his son. But even so, he *has* to realize that Eddie's the better quarterback. Larry's a coach, and part of being a coach is doing what's best for your team. I'm sure that he'll eventually come around."

• • •

But when my father came home from school the next Tuesday, he was so grim and distracted that he didn't even bother to pet the dog. He went straight to his room, and didn't emerge again until Claudia got in at eight. I was at the table just outside of the kitchen, doing my math; Raina was over at Stacy's.

"I'm hungry," I heard Claudia say to no one in particular. She came directly into the kitchen, stepped out of her heels, and put three big steaks on the broiler. Then my father finally appeared in the doorway, looking drained. He allowed Claudia to kiss him, and then opened the refrigerator and pulled out a bottle of Sapporo.

"Tough day?" Claudia asked, as he sat down across from me at the table. There was a small pass-through between the kitchen and the little nook where the table was, and a thirteen-inch television took up most of the space. Claudia had to bend down in order to see him.

He took a long, slow drink from his beer, and then set the bottle on the table. "Tough practice," he said. "But I guess I should have expected it. Eric was out sick again yesterday, and the kids were still riding high from Friday's win. Eddie was the quarterback in all the drills we ran, and the players all seemed to like it. In fact, a bunch of them came in this morning to tell me that they thought Eddie was the better player and that they were more comfortable with him on the field. They wanted me to talk to Larry about it, and I told them I would." He paused. "But then Eric came back today. And Larry immediately put him back into the starting squad, which means that Eddie's with the second string again."

Claudia looked at me and gestured toward the table, which was her way of telling me that I should set out the plates and silverware. Then she turned toward my father. "Well, *did* you get a chance to talk to Larry?"

My father sighed, and shook his head, and kept his eyes on the table. He ran his fingers through his hair and then rested his hand on the back of his neck. "Yes. We went back to the coaches' office after practice today, and I asked him if he'd consider making Eddie the starter. And he gave me a whole list of reasons of why he wouldn't."

I got the plates out of the cupboard and set them down on the table, clinking one accidentally against my father's beer bottle. Claudia put three potatoes in the microwave, set the timer, and looked at my father. "Like what?"

"Like Eddie's too short, which I don't agree with. He's five-ten, which doesn't make him the tallest guy in the world, but we're not talking the NFL here. And besides, the five extra inches that Eric has on him sure haven't helped the strength of his arm. Anyway, that's one thing. Larry also said that Eddie doesn't have enough experience, which is stupid, because how the hell's he supposed to *get* experience if we don't let him play? Larry also thinks it's a problem that his first language is Spanish, but that's bullshit. Half the kids speak Spanish anyway, and it's not like they don't also speak English. Besides, it's not just the Mexican kids who're pushing for Eddie. All the black kids are in his corner, too."

Claudia poured a bag of frozen vegetables into a pot, and turned the gas on high. Ann sat right beside her, wet nose pointed up toward the broiler.

"Somehow, none of this surprises me," Claudia said, looking over her shoulder at my father.

"Well, *I* think Eric's weak," I offered as I set out the forks and knives. I'd only seen him play in one game, and he hadn't been particularly awful, but it seemed like an appropriate thing to say.

My dad laughed now, and pressed his bottle against his knee. "He's not terrible, actually, but he's certainly not the player his father thinks he is. Or the player *he* thinks he is, even—you wouldn't believe all the bragging he does. I have to hear him every day in my class."

Claudia peeked in on the meat and stirred the vegetables. "How is he as a student?"

My father shook his head. "Bad. He's got this attitude, this self-importance, that's really obnoxious, although I don't know if his father can even see it. He sure as hell can't see it in himself." My father looked down and sighed. "You know what Larry said when I went in there today? He said that I should never question him about a coaching decision again, that I should mind my own business, and that I didn't know what I was talking about. After ten years of coaching together, he told me I should mind my own business and that I didn't know what I was talking about."

Claudia put down the big bowl she'd just pulled from the cupboard. She came over to the side of his chair, touched his head, and put her arms around his shoulders. "Oh, Wendell," she said. "I'm sorry."

They stayed like that for a few seconds, and I tried not to look. Finally Claudia stood up straight again, and my father gave a dry laugh. "At least I never coached *you,* Nancy," he said, looking at me. "I'm sure I would've messed up any team you were on. There's obviously something about being a coaching parent that gives you the delusion that your child is the shit."

I looked at him seriously. "Yes, but I *am* the shit."

He rolled his eyes, and Claudia laughed.

"Just eat your damn dinner," he said.

Claudia took the steaks out of the broiler, using a fork to stab each piece of meat and put it onto a plate. I dealt out the potatoes and vegetables. My dad asked for another beer, which I brought for him, along with water for Claudia and Coke for myself. We all sat down to eat and my father continued to talk about his team; about how he wasn't sure what to do from there, or what to tell Eddie Nuñez. Claudia offered an occasional comment, but I said nothing. I chewed my steak and felt lucky that I didn't play football.

Like Claudia, I wasn't surprised by what was happening, or by how disappointed my father seemed to be. He was—in contrast to my own coach or Larry Henderson—deeply invested in his players and their lives. They came to him with problems about family or school; he gave them advice about job interviews or college. He'd counseled a couple of players who'd gotten their girlfriends pregnant, and let kids from bad home situations spend the night on our couch. His attachment to Eddie Nuñez made sense to me. Eric Henderson already had a hundred things going for him, even without his father's giving him a spot he hadn't earned—his family, one of the few white families still living in Hawthorne, seemed to control the entire city. But Eddie Nuñez was an underdog, and my father always rooted for the underdog; he had always been an underdog himself.

That Saturday, after Eric Henderson threw two interceptions and no touchdowns on the way to a tie with the last-place team in their league, I received a call from my friend Natalie. Natalie was one of my AAU teammates and an All-State center for Compton. I hung out with her a lot in the summertime, because she lived only two blocks away from Compton College, which was where our summer league games were held. She was calling me that night because her boyfriend, Charles, was a tackle on my father's team, and because she'd seen their poor performance the previous night.

"What's up with that coach, girl?" she asked. "Can't he see that his son ain't shit?"

"I don't know," I said. "I don't know what he's thinking."

"Well, Charles say the guys don't even like that coach's boy, and they think that skinny kid Eddie should be the quarterback."

"Yeah, he's supposed to be pretty good," I said noncommittally. I didn't want to give my father's position away, although I was glad to hear that the team agreed with him. Charles was one of its leaders, so his opinion was important. He was gruff and quiet and generally calm, a good counterpart to Natalie's high emotions. For the three years we'd played on AAU teams together, Natalie's unpredictable outbursts of anger or joy had been like a sixth player on the court. She was volatile, and fiercely loyal, and never hesitated to say what she thought. I had always liked her immensely.

"He is," Natalie said now. "I seen him play last week, and

Charles and them been talkin about him all season. They don't know what to do now, though. They don't trust Coach Henderson, and he ain't gonna pull his son just 'cos the players think he should." She paused. "I think they kinda hopin your pops'll say something. A few of the guys went and talked to him already."

I was lying on my bedroom floor, and now I put my hand on my forehead. "I don't think my dad has any say in that, Natalie."

"I know, I know," she said, although I wasn't sure she did. "I think the guys just wanna know that there's someone on their side."

He *was* on their side, but it didn't result in anything. All through October, my father came in distracted on weeknights, and it usually took him an hour or so to snap out of his little funk. And each Friday, after a game in which Eric Henderson had made some costly error or had simply failed to be effective, he came home with his brow furrowed and a grimace on his face, and would hardly talk to me before he went to bed. I heard from Natalie that when the players realized that Eric would never be benched, they began to pull their blocks once or twice each game and let him get hit by the other team. They meant to send Eric and Larry a message, and maybe they even half-hoped that Eric would sustain some kind of injury, but Larry wasn't listening, and Eric did not get hurt. Natalie was of the opinion that they should go all out, and keep letting the defense hit Eric until he finally *did* get hurt, but the players didn't like that idea—they were trained to do their best, and they didn't want to end up blowing a game just to get a point across. Unless Larry Henderson underwent a miraculous change of heart, they were going to be stuck with Eric for the rest of the season.

In November, I had a team party at my house, parent-sanctioned, to celebrate our opening scrimmage, which—although you weren't supposed to keep score at these things—we had easily won. We'd played Mira Costa, a school we despised—it was wealthy and almost totally white. Teams like Mira Costa often had a difficult time when they played schools from the inner city. Whenever Mira Costa came to Inglewood, for example, they faced not only my teammates and me, but also an overwhelmingly hostile crowd. While we destroyed them with our play, the kids in the bleachers would cheer when they committed a turnover, laugh when they missed a free throw, yell out that maybe they should drive their Beamers back home and eat caviar in the hot tubs of their mansions. My teammates and I didn't participate in this taunting—we made our statement on the court—but on the other hand, we didn't disapprove. The scrimmage that afternoon had been at Mira Costa, and we'd been amazed, as we always were, at the beauty of their campus—there were no fences around it, the buildings looked new, the grounds were well-kept and pristine. And although most of Mira Costa's players had seemed perfectly nice, there were two girls we'd all disliked—their center, who'd hit us all in the face repeatedly with her ponytail, and their point guard, who'd asked Telisa how much money her father made. Even though it was just a scrimmage, we all felt vindicated after we won. "*That* kind of shit," said Telisa, referring to the point guard's talk, "is why they haven't *beat* us in ten years."

Around eight o'clock that night, eleven girls showed up at my house, with sleeping bags, wine coolers, music, food, and various present and potential boyfriends. It was the first team party I'd had since the end of my sophomore year. I had used to have them frequently during the season, about every other weekend. My father had allowed us to drink because he reasoned that since we were going to do it anyway, we might as well have a place to spend the night so that at least no one would have to drive home. But then one Saturday morning he'd come back early from a conference to find empty wine cooler bottles, cheese-crusted pizza boxes, and *Playgirl* magazines all over the floor, not to mention the five water-filled condoms—which we'd prepared to launch at the mailman—he then discovered in his bathroom sink. I think that, given the presence of condoms in the house, he was afraid—or maybe hopeful—that I was sleeping with a boy; he didn't notice, or want to notice, that

Yolanda was always the last one to leave. Anyway, that put an end to the parties for a while, at least until Claudia and Raina moved in. He finally lifted his ban after they'd been there for a couple of months—because it was my senior year, and also because he and Claudia often spent weekends with her parents in San Diego. Her parents had left L.A. and moved into a small house down there when her father had retired, and while they'd found a nice community of black senior citizens, they still felt a little isolated, so Claudia tried to see them as much as she could. As long as our house was back in order before she and my father returned on Sunday night, we were free to use it however we wished.

That night, we rented *A Nightmare on Elm Street* and *Hoosiers.* The former had been selected by Pam, a junior forward, who did not consider a movie worth seeing unless about twenty-five people met their deaths in gruesome and interesting ways; and the latter by Celine, our shooting guard, who couldn't believe that people played basketball in the country, and shot at hoops that were nailed to the sides of barns. Pam insisted that we watch *Nightmare* first, and no one took issue with that. People rarely took issue with Pam. She was a big, stocky girl, a shot-putter in the track season, who I was always having to extract from altercations. She talked a lot of trash on the court, and had a huge, deep belly laugh off of it; she was also an outrageous flirt, and boys clamored for her attention.

"Man," she said as the opening credits rolled, "can you imagine if Freddy Krueger played hoops? He'd give a whole new meaning to the idea of sticking a hand in someone's face."

"I don't know why you like these gory movies," said Celine from the couch. Celine was quiet, skinny, and far too mild-mannered; we all knew she'd be hiding her face in her arms within ten or fifteen minutes. She was so shy that she covered her mouth with her hand when she laughed, and blushed when a four-letter word escaped her lips. Every once in a while during a game, though, someone would offend her so much that she'd get angry, and it was then that she proved most effective. Sometimes I'd tell her that our opponents had insulted her when they hadn't, just to get her fired up.

"They entertainment and shit," said Pam. "They make me forget my problems. Besides, they funny as hell."

Celine raised her eyebrows. "You think this stuff is funny?" she said. "Girl, you totally whack."

Telisa, who was sitting on the floor, petted the dog's head thoughtfully. "I don't know about this Freddy Krueger shit, but *Hoosiers* is a hella good movie. I wonder what would happen if *we* went to Indiana. We could play on those dirt courts, against some of those big-ass country girls."

I heard someone scoff on the couch. It was Bonita, our number-one substitute—a sophomore and a potential future star. "I don't think they'd like us out there in the country, you know what I'm sayin? It wouldn't be like *Hoosiers* for us—it'd be more like *Children of the Corn.*"

Bonita was usually sullen and she rarely talked; we were all so surprised that she'd spoken just then that we forgot to laugh at her joke.

"Hey," she said to me, after a moment of silence. "Why's your dog named after Ann Meyers and not my girl Cheryl Miller?"

"We got her like seven years ago," I said. "Before I even heard of Cheryl." I didn't add the fact that Ann, like her namesake, was a blonde.

In the middle of the first murder, I went into the kitchen on a food run. I came back with tortilla chips and Bartles & Jaymes, which was the drink of choice that year. Then I sat on the floor between Telisa and Shaundra. Shaundra, our center, was my other good friend on the team, a six-footer who looked even bigger because she was a little overweight. She had a jheri curl and big owl glasses, and her cheeks were full and round. Her father was black and her mother Vietnamese, and her middle name was Kieu, pronounced Q. We called her by both names, although we normally used Q because it was shorter and sounded cooler.

Besides being my best friends on the team, Telisa and Q were both seniors, and also the two best other players. Q, in fact, had gotten some recruiting letters in the last year. None of the places that were interested in her were particularly illustrious—they were mostly Division II and III schools, and a few lower-level schools from Division I. But still, it looked like she might end up having the chance to become the first person in her family to go to college. Her father was a postal worker who'd basically raised his kids alone; Q's mother had been killed during a robbery when Q was three. Now he was set on the idea of Q getting a scholarship, especially since his first two kids' lives hadn't turned out as he'd planned. Q's sister, Debbie, had mothered two kids by the time she was twenty, with neither of the fathers in sight. And her brother, Robert, had become a cop, which was one of the two main career opportunities—along with the military—for people without a college degree. He'd worked in Compton for three years, cracking down on the drug trade, until the big-time dealers down there convinced him that he could make more money working on their side. He'd switched over two years before and Q rarely heard from him now. Anyway, all of their father's expectations had been transferred to Q, and the problem, as Q realized, was that a scholarship was by no means assured. At barely six feet she was too short to be a college center, and those couple of inches, plus her extra twenty pounds, were going to hurt her chances. And as if that weren't enough to deal with, she hadn't passed the SAT. According to a new rule, Prop. 48, all incoming freshmen had to score at least 700 to be eligible for collegiate athletics. Q had taken the SAT twice already and had just missed getting 700; she'd try it again in December. Raina and I had both passed it the previous spring, and Telisa had gotten some disgustingly high score which was probably double what Q had received. With all of these things in question, no one could really say if Q would end up getting a scholarship. She and I tended to avoid the topic.

Needless to say, my teammates were highly amused by the new living arrangement.

"Nancy," Pam had said when I first told her about it. "Girl, you housin an *enemy."* Pam considered anyone who wasn't from our school the enemy.

Raina was still at home when we started the movies. Stacy was there, too—they were hanging out for a bit before going to meet Toni in Westwood. They emerged from Raina's room around nine, and passed through the living room on their way to the door, turning on lights and eliciting groans of protest from the rest of us. Stacy was carrying one of the Cheryl Miller dolls that had been popping up in basketball circles for the past couple of years, and she waved it at us when she walked in. She made Raina look small, although she wasn't particularly large herself—a little under 5' 9", and thin. Although her mother was an earthy brown, Stacy's skin was high yellow, and she had a shoulder-length jheri curl. Raina was two steps behind her, wearing khaki shorts and a burnt orange sweater that I knew to be Toni's. Toni was always lending Raina clothes and encouraging her to wear them, but this seemed less an act of generosity than a method of identification, as if Raina were simply a possession she could mark as a message to prospective wooers to lay off. Still, Raina didn't wear street clothes very often, and my heart jumped when I saw her. She looked beautiful. I felt self-conscious about looking at Raina in front of my team, but also, about being with my team in front of Raina.

"Hey, ladies," she said.

People tossed out hellos at her from various parts of the room, except for Telisa, who yelled out cheerfully, "Hey, girl, get outta here."

"Hey, Telisa."

"No, I'm serious. Get out. Teammates and significant others only."

I had to smile at that one.

Stacy stepped forward. She and Telisa were friends from having been out to some clubs together. "Yo, *fuck* you, bitch," she said, thrusting her chin out in mock hostility.

Q pulled herself up, which took a long time. "Don't be talkin shit now, girl," she said, towering over Stacy and Raina both, "else I'm gonna have to smack you upside the head."

"Oooooohs" came up from all over the room.

"All right, all right, we're on our way," Raina said, taking a few steps forward and pulling Stacy along.

"Yo, hold up," called out Telisa. Raina turned. "As long as you stayin in our district now, why don't you come to our school?"

Everybody laughed at her sudden change in tactics. Raina cocked her head and smiled. "You mean you actually want me to *play* with you sorry-ass losers? Who do I look like, Mother Teresa?"

"Aw, c'mon, Raina. Think about it. With you, we'd kick the shit outta *everybody.*"

Stacy crossed her arms. "No *way* would she leave us, man." She smiled. "Besides, y'all are *weak.*"

Various calls of "Aw, fuck you, man," and "Bitch, get out."

"You better watch your mouth, girl," I put in, laughing. "It's about fifteen of us here and only two of y'all."

"All right, homes. Later," said Stacy. We gave each other the basketball players' signal of greeting and farewell, that half-handshake, half-high-five meeting of the hands, where first the thumbs interlock and then, as you pull away, the fingers.

When they were gone, we rewound the movie back to where it had been when they'd come in.

"Seriously, though, can you imagine?" Telisa said as the VCR whirred. "With Raina on our team we'd kick some serious ass."

"Yeah," Q replied, nudging me with her elbow, "if we could get her and Miss Thang here to share the title of top shit."

"They'd have no problem with that," said Telisa. "If there was any problem, it'd be that they play too much alike."

"Girl, what you talkin about?" I asked, laughing. "We don't even play the same position."

"Maybe not, but y'all still play alike."

"Get outta here," I said, although I knew what she meant. Raina and I played different positions, but we were noted for a lot of the same things—defense, intensity, getting the job done against people and teams much stronger and faster than us. But still, to compare my game to Raina's seemed ridiculous. I could see what might make someone draw parallels, but it was so clear to me that Raina was simply *better*—a better person, because she truly inhabited her life and moved through the world with such purpose; a better player, because she loved the sport for itself, and wanted to honor it by devoting herself to it completely. I knew more than anyone that my efforts amounted to a poor imitation of Raina's, that for the last two years *I'd* pushed so hard because *she* did.

CHAPTER 6

By mid-November, my level of stress was at an all-time high—our season was about to begin. And if the high school season—in terms of recruiting—had always been the *least* important part of the year, now I was convinced it was the most important. After all the camps and leagues, the AAU tournaments and nationals, your senior season of high school was all you had left. And in your last season you had to confirm all the good opinions that scouts had developed of you during the summers, or, if you were coming off of a bad summer, you had to prove that that performance had been a fluke. Many of the top recruits would sign their letters of intent that month, and thus spare themselves this pressure, because no matter how their senior year turned out, they were already committed to a school, and the school to them. But some of us, including Raina and me, decided to hold off, either to await a better offer, or simply to keep from making a premature choice.

By that time the thrill of being the recipient of such relentless attention had deflated, for me, into something else, something new and not altogether pleasant. In a way, I suppose, the recognition we received—not just from colleges, but from reporters and other players, from people who stopped us on the street—was somewhat wasted on us. We had never not been wanted—at least not since we were very young; we didn't know, yet, what it meant to be an anonymous face in the crowd. I liked the newsprint and the honors that came my way, but they would have meant so much more to me just five or six years later, when I *was* a face in the crowd; when I knew too much to assume my right to anything. But by November of my senior year, I'd become tired and a bit uncomfortable with all the recruiting. I continued to file the letters that arrived, thought halfheartedly about my options, talked politely to the coaches who called on crackling long-distance lines.

The joy of it, though, was gone.

It wasn't that this long-distance courtship didn't have its funny moments. There was, for example, the time that the Ohio State coach called Natalie's house, and the phone was answered by Natalie's three-year-old sister, Kara, who'd just woken up from a nap.

"Is Natalie home?" asked the coach.

"No," answered the sleepy child.

"Is your mommy home?"

"No."

"Is your daddy home?"

"No."

"Well, where *is* everybody?"

Pause.

"I don't know," cried Kara, who then promptly dropped the phone and started to wail. The alarmed coach, imagining Natalie and her parents dead in a back room somewhere, called the Compton police department all the way from Ohio, and had them go and check the place out. Everything turned out to be fine—Natalie's mother had been in the bathroom the whole time, and hadn't heard Kara's cries. Natalie cheerfully shared this incident with everyone she knew, and then ended up signing early with Ohio State.

It also wasn't that I'd grown indifferent to the attention, or that I was tired of being hassled all the time—no, I *wanted* to get a scholarship; I wanted that final sign of affirmation. Rather, it was that the process of selection itself had become bewildering. I had the feeling that my whole future would be determined by the act of signing one piece of paper, that each decision I made would limit the number of options I had from there. If I stayed close to home, I might end up limited and stifled, but if I went someplace far away I might change so much I'd eventually lose contact with the things that had made me who I was. My whole future, it seemed to me, would be like the irrevocable falling of a fixed pattern of dominoes, all set into motion by the one domino I tipped over by choosing a college. I was completely terrified of that future.

Raina, on the other hand, was lusting for it. She kept talking about how great it would be to live someplace different; how much she was looking forward to meeting new people. She also talked about the things she wanted to do *after* college, a time I found impossible to imagine. One Saturday afternoon, while we were running some errands, she tried to get *me* to discuss this, too.

"So where you wanna be ten years from now?" she asked.

"I have no idea. I don't even know where I'm gonna be ten *minutes* from now."

"Well, *I* know that," she said. "You're gonna be at the grocery store, with me."

We'd been sent out to buy broccoli so that my father could make a stir-fry, and to pick up some Nyquil for Claudia. Raina was driving her mother's Honda, and we were headed east on Manchester, out of Inglewood and into L.A.

"Do you think you'll try to play pro?" she asked.

I shrugged. "I don't know. I ain't that crazy about the idea of livin in a foreign country. Besides, it all depends on how college turns out." We stopped at a light, and a young Mexican boy who was standing on the center island held a bag of oranges up to Raina's window. "What about you?" I asked.

"I don't know, either," said Raina. She waved the boy off and he moved further down the island, offering his product to the car behind us. "Whenever I imagine basketball stuff, though—you know, screaming fans, last-second shots, cameras going off everywhere—it's always in terms of college, not pro. Maybe it's 'cos I've never seen a pro women's game, I don't know. It's not like goin pro never crosses my mind—and it'd be cool to play in Europe; I heard you can make thirty, forty grand a year there, even more if you're a six-footer, like you. But when I picture my life after college, I tend to think about *jobs,* you know what I'm sayin? And about where I'm gonna live and all that." The light changed, and the car moved forward. "But whatever happens afterward, college is gonna be great."

I turned and looked at her. "So you still got no idea about where you gonna go?"

"Nope," she said. She stopped to let an old man, who didn't seem particularly attached to reality, stumble across the street. When we'd passed him, Raina shook her head sadly. "It sure ain't gonna be in L.A., though." She was silent for a moment; then she brightened. "Remember all those places we got to go for camps and AAU? They were *cool* places, too—New Mexico, Arizona, Washington, Virginia . . ."

". . . Connecticut," I added. "New Orleans."

She smiled broadly. "Just imagine actually *living* in one of those places, and being able to take trips to *other* places, for free, because of basketball. And if you play for a good team, you'll be on ESPN and shit, with Ann Meyers doin the color commentary."

I didn't say anything, and stared out the window. Her enthusiasm bothered me, because I wasn't enthused. None of the things she was talking about sounded good to me. I *couldn't* imagine living in the places she'd mentioned—I couldn't fathom the idea of living anywhere except L.A.—and while I'd enjoyed the trips I'd made, this was only because I'd gone with friends, and invariably, I was homesick by the end. I didn't understand how Raina could be so excited about things that caused me such discomfort and terror. And I was hurt, too, because her desire to leave L.A. and high school behind was also linked, in my mind, with a desire to leave *me.* I, of course, had no desire to part with *her.* Living with Raina, for me, had been like breaking in a new pair of jeans—they didn't fit very well at first, but got comfortable quickly, and now I wanted to wear them all the time.

I didn't talk to her much—that day, or ever—about where she wanted to go, but I watched the proceedings of her recruitment with great interest. If I couldn't be at the same school with her, I wanted at least to be in the same region. This would be difficult, because we were both getting calls from all over the country, but I would try to coordinate my interests with hers without being too obvious about it. The second signing period in mid-April loomed much larger to me than graduation in June. Graduation marked the end of one era, but signing day marked the beginning of another, and so, of *all* others. I didn't want that day to come. I wanted time to freeze *now,* with Raina living in my house, eating at the same table, sleeping on the other side of the wall. What I felt about her was like nostalgia in advance. Since nothing of significance had occurred between us yet, this sense of wistfulness should have struck me as odd. It didn't, though. I don't know why. But it was as if I knew even then that I'd recall the events of this time for the rest of my life, that this was the experience against which I'd measure all others.

Just after Thanksgiving—which my dad and I spent at home while Claudia and Raina went down to San Diego—my team had our annual alumni game. The purpose of this event was twofold—to give us a practice run, along with the earlier scrimmage, before our first official game; and to encourage alumni interest in the current team. Often teachers showed up to cheer on the old stars they'd once had in their classes, and afterwards, all of the players would go out for pizza.

Telisa, Q, and I got there early enough to survey the competition. I dropped my sports bag next to our bench and took a walking lap around the court. This was always the first thing I did upon entering the gym—it was as if the gym were my estate, and I was checking the grounds to make sure that everything was in order. It had been part of my pregame ritual since the beginning of my junior year, when I'd inherited the team from Vicki Stewart, the All-State guard, who had graduated the previous June. Today I took special note of everything, since it was our first time playing at home that year. I noticed how good the newly painted lines looked, but squatted down at one point to touch a spot that hadn't been properly waxed. I got to the wooden bleachers and shook my head in dismay—they were brittle and ancient, and looked about as stable as a house of cards. I glanced up at our scoreboard, which, since my freshman year, had been in the habit of getting stuck when there was 2:23 to go, and I hoped, as I always did, that it wouldn't break down altogether during some crucial juncture of a game. Two of the overhead lights had burned out, so it always seemed like dusk. The floor was warped in the northeast corner, where some water had leaked in during one of the heavy winter rains. Maybe the rains had also contributed to the yellow paint chipping off the walls; sometimes I'd leave the building with flakes of yellow stuck to the bottoms of my shoes. As I walked through the gym that night, I took deep breaths, inhaling the rich, pungent odor of sweat that hung heavily in the air. I'd always loved and welcomed this smell, and I think that every true athlete does. It is the smell of effort and competition; of people challenging their own limits; of bodies glistening and taut and alive.

We still had plenty of time before the game started, so I went to the bathroom, and then to my locker, where I got one of the wristbands I always wore when I played. On the inside of my locker door there was a newspaper clipping—the report of our loss in the playoffs the previous winter. We'd only made it to the second round before being upset by a lower-ranked team, and I was still haunted by that defeat, by my subpar performance. I stood there and read the article twice.

By the time I got back out to the court, about ten of the alums had arrived and were warming up at the far basket. Most of them were people I knew—girls who'd been senior or juniors when I was a freshman—and the first thing I noticed, as always, was how much weight they'd put on since their playing days.

"Yo, Nance!" yelled out one of them, a big center named Tracy. "Come over here and talk to my son."

"Wassup, Tracy?" I yelled back, and then I walked over to Chris, her three-year-old, and squatted down to talk to him. "Wassup, little man? You've grown about two feet since last year." He was wearing a Bulls cap and a black sweatshirt, and trying, without much success, to bounce a basketball. He stared up at me in a daze, and then looked back at his ball.

"What you been up to, Tracy?" I asked his mother as I stood back up. The last I'd heard, she'd dropped out of junior college.

"Not much, homegirl," she said. "Got a job now, but other than that, just kickin it, tryin to take care of him." She nodded toward her son. Chris had the round eyes and broad nose of his father, who'd been killed in a drive-by two weeks before Chris was born.

"That's cool," I said. "Gotta keep gettin paid, right?" I didn't know what else to say to her. Too many of my former teammates had similar stories—junior college, a dead-end job, more school for a while, and then nothing. Three other girls besides Tracy had their kids with them that night, and I couldn't believe these were the same girls I'd played and partied with just a couple of years before. There was another girl, Letrice, who was sinking jump shots from the corner—she'd been just this side of good enough for a scholarship. Now she was an assistant manager at Lady Foot Locker in the mall, and it was the best job held by anybody there. In the bleachers sat another ex-player—Pauline Rider, who'd been a sure shot to get a scholarship until she'd blown her knee out the summer before her senior year.

She never went anywhere, not even to a JC, and I didn't know what she did with herself now, but she often showed up at our home games and then left without saying a word. Only one of my ex-teammates had made it to a four-year college—Vicki Stewart, who had a scholarship to Oregon.

The same people were playing for the alumni team as the previous year, minus one, my friend Rhonda Craig, who was doing time for selling speed. I chatted with them all for a few minutes before heading back to our side of the court. Then I heard a voice behind me shout, "Hey, it's the Asian Invasion!"

I turned around and grinned. It was Rhonda. "Wassup, girl?" I said. "When'd you get out?"

"Couple weeks ago, and shit, am I glad."

We walked toward each other and I hugged her, the most genuine hug I'd given anyone that night. Rhonda was short, 5'4", and stocky, but muscular and deceptively fast. She'd been like a big sister during my first year of high school. She was a senior point guard when I was a freshman, and she'd named me "Maddog" for my overzealousness on the court. That year she'd driven me around to open gyms at different schools, taken me out with her drinking buddies, given me all kinds of advice on high school and how to deal with team dynamics. The speed thing hadn't started until after she'd finished school, when her mother had stopped working because of a shoulder injury and Rhonda had wanted to help her out. She'd just dabbled in sales, sold a little on the side of her regular job at Vons, and luckily, she'd never gotten into crack. Even though we were still hanging out a lot when she started with the speed, I didn't follow her down that path. I had *done* speed, and weed, and wasn't adverse to dabbling in other mischief; I'd gone along for the ride a few times when some of the friends I had then had broken into cars at the beach. But Rhonda, despite her own choices, had picked me up by the collar and set me firmly on the high road. She was the one who had made me understand the value of my talent in basketball, and once I believed it could lead me into a future, the mischief didn't seem so appealing anymore.

"So how was the pen?" I asked, clapping her on the shoulder.

"Fucked up," she said. "But check this out. I only been there a couple days, right? And guess who I ran into?" She named a player from Morningside, who'd graduated the same year as she and who was in on a robbery charge. "So we got this three-on-three tournament goin. And me and her picked up this other girl Rita from Compton, and we kicked everyone's ass and took the whole thing."

"You played with a girl from *Morningside?*" I said. "You traitor!"

"Hey," Rhonda protested. "When you in jail, you do what you got to."

We talked and laughed some more, and tried to figure out when we could get together. Then I heard the loud, Midwestern-tinged voice of our coach calling me from across the gym. I told Rhonda I'd talk to her more after the game, and went over to Coach Fontaine.

"You girls can have your little party after you play," he said. "Right now you've got a game to worry about."

"All right, Coach," I said, annoyed.

"Now get everyone doing the lay-up drill, and stop with this horsing around."

"O.K."

Telisa, who'd been standing nearby, shook her head. "Chill out, man," she said when he was out of earshot.

Coach Carl Fontaine was a former assistant football coach—my father had coached against him—who'd been "demoted" to girls' basketball eight years before because of a minor scandal involving drunk driving and an off-duty cop's new car. He was in his late fifties, and overweight, and he wore ridiculously tight green polyester shorts to practice. He had a huge purple eggplant of a nose, and sickly pale skin, and about five long gray hairs which he combed over the bald dome of his head. Although he knew a lot about basketball, he couldn't relate to any of us, and sometimes, after he'd made some incomprehensible remark about politics or the neighborhood, we'd all look at each other and roll our eyes and wonder what planet he'd come from.

I went back over to our side and started my team on the lay-up drill. We got loose, slapped hands, encouraged each other. The game began a few minutes later.

We played sloppily at first, and much to our embarrassment, the alumni were all over us. Despite being overweight, their superior size and strength translated into a lot of garbage points under the basket. By the middle of the second quarter we'd pulled ourselves together, and we made a run at them and tied the game by halftime. Coach Fontaine was not happy, though—in the locker room he chewed us out for being distracted and not playing with our usual intensity. We got the message. In the second half we stepped up our game, and soon the difference in conditioning began to show. The alums were out of gas by the end of the third quarter. We pulled away and won by twenty.

After the game, I gave my wristbands to a couple of the junior high school girls who always came to watch me play. Then all of us, current players and alumni, went off to Numero Uno. We pushed a few tables together, creating a big, sweaty mass of basketball players in the middle of the restaurant. There were enough older people—Rhonda, Tracy, and some other players from even earlier—to order a pitcher of beer, and we younger ones snuck gulps when none of the waitresses were looking. We ordered four pizzas, with various toppings—half of one of them covered with anchovies, at the insistence of Letrice.

"I hate fish," Pam informed us, putting one fist on her hip and the other squarely on the table.

"Me, too," Telisa said. Then, turning to me, "Hey, don't you and your pops eat fish raw?"

I smiled. "Only on special occasions."

"And you *like* that shit?" she asked, wrinkling her nose.

"Hell, yeah," I said, still smiling. I chose not to remind her about the one time I'd made her try a piece of raw tuna, at my sixteenth birthday dinner in Gardena—after eating it, she'd sheepishly asked for another.

"Listen, y'all," said Rhonda. "That ain't even the problem here." She turned to Letrice and shook her head. "Girl, the whole table gonna stink when that anchovy shit come. Ain't none of us gonna wanna eat."

"Well then that's *good,* homegirl," Letrice said, grinning. "It'll keep y'all from puttin on any more weight."

She was immediately showered with curses and little sugar packets.

"Look who's talkin," Tracy said. "Quiet as it's kept, Ms. Letrice, look like *you* put on a pound or two yourself."

Letrice crossed her arms and patted each of her shoulders. "I ain't gettin fat, though. I'm just fillin out."

When the pizzas arrived—despite Rhonda's concern—we all dove in as if we hadn't eaten in weeks. Telisa inhaled a piece of the pepperoni, and then, despite my threats that I would refuse to drive her home, ventured a piece that had anchovies on it.

"Y'all should try some, too," Letrice said, addressing everyone on the current team. "It has protein. Give you strength. And the way y'all played tonight, it look like you gonna need it."

We had run out of sugar packets, so we threw our napkins at her instead.

"What you talkin about?" Telisa said, gesturing with her hands. "We beat your ass by twenty. Remember?"

"Only 'cos we let you. Right, Tracy?"

"Yeah," Tracy agreed. She'd been cutting up her pizza into tiny pieces and feeding them to Chris, but now she looked up at us and grinned. "We was feelin kinda sorry for y'all."

Pam and Celine, who were sitting directly across from her, both snorted in disgust. "Yeah, right," Pam said. "You was just plain sorry."

It went back and forth for a while, like a verbal passing drill—each person trying to throw an insult at the next with more accuracy, more bite. Finally the alums from each era began to argue about which team had been the best, and they *all* contended that their teams had been superior to the present incarnation.

"The best team ever," Rhonda said, "was the year that Tracy and me were seniors. That was the only time we ever beat Morningside, and they won the whole state that year." She turned to me in triumph, as if challenging me to dispute her.

"Don't look at *me,*" I said. "I ain't arguing. I was on that team, too, remember?"

"Yeah," Rhonda said, "but you was just a Maddog freshman punk who only played fifteen, twenty minutes a game."

"That was a hella good team, though," remarked Letrice, shaking her head at the memory. She'd been a junior then, and the third-leading scorer behind Vicki Stewart, the All-State guard, and me.

"Uh-huh," Tracy agreed. "I remember that Morningside game. They led all the way into the fourth quarter, and then we caught 'em and won by like ten or twelve."

"You won by *five,*" corrected Telisa, who'd been on the JV team with Q that year, and had watched the whole game from the stands.

"They tried to press us," Rhonda said, ignoring her, "but we just passed our way through that shit. You scored like thirty, thirty-two points that game, Letrice."

Telisa shook her head. "She had nineteen," she said, "and only six in the second half."

Letrice turned to Rhonda and Tracy. "And remember how we shut down Angela Smith?" Angela Smith was their All-State forward, a crunch player who normally came up big when the game was on the line. "It was like we put handcuffs on her and shit. She didn't score a single point in the fourth quarter."

Telisa covered her eyes with her hand, groaned, looked up again. "That's 'cos she was *hurt,*" she said. "She didn't even *play* in the fourth quarter."

Letrice reached across the table now and smacked Telisa on the forehead. "Shut the fuck up, computer brain," she said.

After the older players recounted a few more of the high points from their careers, the talk turned, somehow, to everyone's present lives. We young ones heard tales, then, of child-rearing and junior colleges; of the frustrations of shitty jobs and of well-meaning but ignorant social workers; of the pecking order and inedible food in prison.

"This little rich girl tryin to tell me to go back to El Camino," Tracy said, referring to the caseworker with whom she had to meet in order to receive her welfare checks. "But what's the point? If I got a AB, then I could work for maybe five dollars an hour 'stead of four-twenty-five or four-fifty."

"And work's a pain in the ass, anyway," Letrice said. "Nine to six or seven every day, gotta smile at stupid people you'd rather smack upside the head."

"Y'all should try jail," Rhonda said. "Shitty food, gotta watch your ass every second, and you walk around all day in this tiny cell that's smaller than the bathrooms in the gym."

They were all silent for a moment.

"You know, I never would of thought I'd say this," Letrice began, "but I kinda miss bein in high school." She waved a hand toward us, the current players. "Things get harder when you done with school. Y'all still got it easy."

"What makes you think we got it easy?" asked Telisa, as she pushed her plate away. She wiped her mouth with a napkin and looked at Letrice. "It's hard for everybody these days. Shit. *We* don't got it easy."

"Yeah, you do," said Rhonda sadly. "You just don't know it yet."

I glanced over at Q, who'd been quiet all evening, and saw that she was staring down at her plate. I thought I knew what she was feeling. It was fun to hang out with our former teammates, but I was scared by what their lives had become. A few times Raina and I had run into some older girls at the park, washed-up ex-high-school stars who'd never made it anywhere, and we'd looked at each other and the same thought had been in both of our minds: *that will never happen to me.* Those girls at the park, and a couple of the girls at the table, had been the hopes of their neighborhoods once, as we were now. But by my senior year, I thought of them as sad, bitter specters—the ghosts of seasons past.

I tried to catch Q's eye, but she wouldn't look up. It occurred to me that she might have been even more frightened by our former teammates' lives than I was. The few small schools that had expressed interest in her still seemed a bit uncertain, and her father was putting a lot of pressure on her to get a scholarship—so much so that he didn't seem to be considering any of the other routes she could take to college. But then again, as Telisa said, how would *he* know about that kind of thing? No one in the family had ever gone. In fact, Raina and I had a big advantage over many of our friends and teammates simply because our parents had gone to college themselves, even if, in Claudia's case, it was only for a while. Therefore, they expected *us* to go, too, basketball scholarship or not, whether it took loans, financial aid, robbery, blackmail, or a combination of all of the above.

At any rate, the conversation was getting a little too heavy for me, so I brought up a topic which I knew everyone would have plenty to say about—Coach Fontaine.

"Y'all should be glad you was coaching yourselves tonight," I said. "Coach Fontaine really gave it to us at halftime."

All of the alumni groaned—both out of disgust at the man, and relief that they didn't have to deal with him anymore.

"*That* motherfucka," said Rhonda, "still got the worst garlic breath I ever smelled."

"Naw, it's a dog shit smell," argued Tracy, and so for the rest of our time at Numero Uno, we debated about the best ways to describe Coach Fontaine's breath, and clothes, and hair. I was feeling better, and I noticed that Q was laughing now, too. We slapped hands at one point, and I held on for an extra second, wishing I could send a message through my touch. We're gonna make it, I wanted to tell her. We're gonna be fine.

CHAPTER 7

The next night it was Claudia's turn to cook for her friends. When Raina and I got home from the park a little after seven, we were greeted by the sweet, tangy smell of teriyaki sauce. My father was nowhere in sight—he must have fled the house again. Claudia was in the kitchen, and Rochelle, Kim, and Paula were sitting in the breakfast nook. All four of them were talking easily, and laughing; it looked like the tension from the previous dinner had completely blown over. This made sense—they'd all seen each other at a couple of their group's meetings, and had probably worked things out. It no longer seemed strange to me that Claudia was having people over. My life was so full of her presence, and Raina's, that I couldn't remember, anymore, what it had been like before they came.

"Hi, girls!" Rochelle called loudly when she saw us, raising the wine glass she held in her hand. She seemed genuinely happy to see me as well as Raina, and I was glad; I liked her—but at the same time, her attention made me nervous.

"Hey," said Raina, walking ahead of me.

"Hi," I said.

Kim greeted both of us as we got the table. Paula said hello to Raina, and then nodded at me.

"The chicken's not quite done yet," called Claudia from the kitchen. "But you can have some when it's ready."

"Great," Raina said.

Since there wasn't any room for the two of us to sit, we stood behind the table and leaned against the wall. I wanted to go upstairs and change, but I knew it would seem rude if I left right away. Rochelle asked Raina, then me, where we were thinking of going to college. She was wearing a loose, flowing, blue-and-green jumpsuit, which looked great on her ample frame. As she talked, she kept glancing over her shoulder.

"Girl, get over yourself," said Kim, who had on jeans and a blue cotton short-sleeve shirt, her typical restaurant attire. "I see you checking yourself out in the window."

Everyone laughed. Rochelle put a fist on her hip. "Honey, I look *good* tonight. And what's wrong with admiring myself when I don't have anyone else to do it for me?"

Claudia came over to the pass-through and shook her head.

"You keep shaking your head at me, girl," Rochelle said to Claudia, smiling, "and we'll see what happens with the deal I've been getting you on work clothes."

"Oooh," said Raina, grinning.

"Speaking of clothes," said Kim, "what are you going to wear to the conference, Claudia? One of those boring suits the *Times* makes you wear? Or something a little more interesting?"

"I haven't thought about it yet," answered Claudia, who was clad, at the moment, in a sweatshirt, jeans, and apron. "What are *you* going to wear, Kim?"

Kim leaned back and folded her hands behind her head. Her chipmunk cheeks lifted as she smiled. "Well, I just got me this fitted green dress. Maybe that and some pantyhose and heels."

Rochelle leaned over. Her blue-and-green sleeves hung loose, like the sleeves of a kimono. "You go, girl. You've got such a nice figure, and it's always hidden in those loose-butt ugly pants you got on. I wish you'd wear dresses more often."

Kim smiled. "Well, there ain't much use for dresses in the restaurant."

Raina went to the refrigerator and pulled out two Cokes. She tossed one over the table at me, and opened the other. "Hey, what's this conference y'all keep talking about, anyway?" she asked.

Claudia opened the oven. She and Ann looked in at the chicken intently; then Claudia frowned and closed the door. "The Black Businesswomen's Alliance," she said, turning toward her daughter, "is holding a conference for black women in the workplace. We're doing a huge publicity campaign—newsletters, phone calls, flyers in stores and companies and at Department of Social Services offices. Yvette Harrington's going to be the keynote speaker. You know who she is?"

Raina and I both nodded. Yvette Harrington was somewhat of a legend. Born and raised in Compton, she'd worked as a grocery clerk for several years before starting to bottle her own salad dressing in the back of her house. The dressing had sold so well that she began to make other things, like soup and spaghetti sauce; finally she'd rented an old warehouse in Lynwood and started Harrington Foods. Although her inexpensive, home-style products still sold best in black areas, they were stocked in stores, now, all over Los Angeles. She'd eventually turned to politics, and a few years before, she'd been elected to the California State Senate.

"Anyway," Claudia continued, walking over to the table, "this conference is for all black women—professional, blue-collar, even women on welfare. We're having talks and events for the group as a whole, and then special, smaller workshops designed to address specific needs. There'll be a whole range of different things. For example, we'll have a panel for professional women about breaking through the glass ceiling; and on the other end of the spectrum, a workshop for unemployed and underemployed women about basic job-search skills—how to write a cover letter, how to act at an interview, etc. But you should ask Paula about more of the specifics—this thing is her baby. She and a few other women from the BBA came up with the idea, and she's the head of the speakers committee."

I was impressed with Claudia. She sounded so efficient and businesslike, and I'd never seen this side of her. Raina nodded and scratched her cheek. "That sounds like a really broad range of women," she said. "Do you think they'll all feel comfortable together, or have a lot to say to each other?"

Paula looked at her like a teacher whose favorite student has just come up with an intelligent question. "That's a concern of mine, too," she said. "We'll have to see. There *are* some professional women, sellout sisters, who don't want to go to the conference, for exactly the reason you're talking about. And I'm sure that some of the blue-collar women and women on welfare will be too intimidated to show up." She smiled. "But what we're hoping, of course, for the women who *do* go, is that some networking will happen—that some of the unemployed and underemployed women will meet potential employers, and vice versa. Also, on a more subtle level, I think it'll be good for everybody there just to *see* each other—good for the underemployed women to see sisters who are making it, and good for the professional women to see that we've still got a long way to go. If it all comes off, it'll be a hell of a weekend—a day and a half at the Airport Hilton, and a big party at the end of the second day."

Paula seemed, now, to be in business mode. With her level, serious voice, her self-confident manner, and the crisp, elegant suits she wore, she must have cut an impressive figure in the working world. Despite Raina's claims, though, that Paula was one of the most generous people she knew, I couldn't bring myself to like her after what she'd said about my father. I wanted to make her address me, so I asked her a question. "So what's Claudia going to do?"

Paula looked at me with an expression I couldn't read, and then turned to Claudia and smiled. "Claudia," she said, "is giving a speech to the whole group about being bigger than your position."

Raina and I looked at each other. "Huh?"

Paula laughed. "She's talking about how to have more influence on the work environment than your job description calls for—getting people to pay attention to race and gender concerns, getting things done that you want to get done."

"Basically," Rochelle said, "how to be an uppity black woman."

"I still don't get it," Raina said.

"It's like this," said Rochelle. "We've all done it at some point or another. For example, just a couple of years ago at Robinson's, the work clothes for women were all boring and prissy and small in the butt—and you *know* Liz Claiborne said she didn't make clothes for black women." She smiled while Claudia turned around and patted her butt. "Anyway, I got them to order business clothes that were better cut, better suited for sisters. I also got them to stock makeup for black women, which of course we didn't have, and now we're gradually building a larger black clientele." She took a sip of her wine and put her glass back down on the table. "Paula got 20th Century to seek out more black home buyers by placing listings in black newspapers and local offices in black communities. And your mother," she said to Raina, "has gotten one of the most historically conservative papers, the *Los Angeles* motherfuckin *Times*—"

"Rochelle!" said Claudia.

Rochelle dismissed her with a wave of the hand. "Anyway, she's gotten them to consider adding a section that addresses community interests and concerns, a kind of open section for real people, not newspaper people, to write their reports and opinions. She took an informal poll the last time they made a big round of subscription calls, came up with a proposal, and ran it past the old white men who run the paper." She leaned forward conspiratorially. "You may not know this, Raina, but your mama is *bad*."

"Oh, hush up, Rochelle," said Claudia, but I could tell she was pleased.

"And at the conference," said Rochelle, ignoring her, "on the second morning, she's going to give this talk. And believe me, she'll be something to see." Rochelle offered her palm, and Kim placed her hand on top and pulled; it was an older, gentler version of our high five.

"Yeah," said Claudia. "I can't wait. And I'm gonna tell stories about *all* of y'all."

I leaned over and petted the dog, who'd come over to say hello. "Are you nervous about it?" I asked Claudia.

She turned toward me, and I saw the same spark in her eyes that I knew must have been in my own when I was thinking of an upcoming game. "A little," she said. "But I'm really looking forward to it. I've got about half the speech written already."

"She's a real good talker, you know," said Kim.

I *didn't* know. I didn't know her much at all. And Claudia's public life was as much a mystery to me as the personal lives of the famous.

"Anyway," said Claudia. "Let's change the subject. All this buildup's making me tense." She went back over to the oven and looked in. "Besides, the chicken's ready, so why don't you all move out to the dining room?"

Rochelle, Kim, and Paula refilled their glasses, and went to sit down at the table. Claudia prepared plates for Raina and me, then shooed us away so she could talk with her friends. After saying goodbye, we left them, Raina heading upstairs to her room, me standing with my plate around the corner. I wanted to hear more about this Claudia I didn't know, this Claudia who laughed with her friends, and spoke well in public, and influenced the policies of the *Los Angeles Times.* The four of them covered movies, and local news, and gossip about people I'd never heard of. I thought they'd get through the meal safely, that things between them were back to normal, but then I heard Paula ask, "Where's Wendell?"

Claudia answered, "Oh, he wanted to get out of the house again, and not interfere with our dinner."

"Out with some of the white people he works with?" asked Paula, and I could feel the ice in her voice.

"No," said Claudia, carefully. "He went to dinner in Gardena with some friends. I thought we'd finished with this subject, Paula."

Nobody spoke for several moments. Silverware clinked brightly against a plate; somebody cleared her throat.

"I've been with Wendell for more than a year," Claudia went on, "and you never said anything before. Why are you on my back about it now?"

"You weren't *living* with him before," Paula answered, and her words were slow and deliberate.

Claudia was quiet for a moment, but I could almost feel the waves of her anger. "Oh, so if I'm just sleeping with somebody, then that's O.K. But if I want to make a life with him, well that's some kind of crime?"

"Yeah, that doesn't make any sense," agreed Rochelle.

Paula sighed. "I'm not saying it's bad to commit to somebody. Shit, I wish *I* had someone to commit to." She paused. "But we've been friends for a long time, Claudia, and I just feel like, I don't know. Like I'm losing you to the other side."

"What do you mean, the other side? It's not like Wendell's white."

Paula scoffed. "Oh, come on, Claudia. He's Asian. Same thing."

"What the hell are you talking about?" said Claudia, voice rising. "Do you have any idea what his family has been through at the hands of the white people you seem to think he's so close to?"

"All that war shit was forty years ago," said Paula. "No one even remembers it now. But that's not really even the point, though." She paused, and when she spoke again, her voice sounded sad. "Claudia, I know I'm not being completely fair to you, but this is just the way I feel. I don't like him, O.K.? And I'm uncomfortable with the idea of you bringing him to the conference party."

"You're uncomfortable with . . . wait, you can't really be saying this."

"I'm just afraid that it might send the wrong message. I don't know. It might suggest that black women have to turn their backs on the community in order to succeed."

"Wait a minute, Paula," said Kim. "You're talking about two different things here. This is Claudia you're dealing with, not some sellout sister. Shit, half the women on the board of directors are married to white men, and I'll bet you're not telling *them* to leave their husbands at home."

"Maybe not," said Paula, "but it's different. Claudia's my friend, so this is closer to home."

"If you're my friend," said Claudia, "then you should see my relationship for what it is and not turn it into something else." She took several deep breaths. "I can't believe you come into Wendell's house and tell me that you don't want him to go to your damn party."

Just then, I heard a car pull into the driveway—my father was home from dinner. I ran up the stairs as quietly as I could, still holding my now-cold plate of food. A few minutes later the front door opened. "Hello!" I heard him call. He went into the dining room, and I could only imagine what he encountered, what the mood was like in there. I was still trying to process the conversation I'd heard. My feelings were complicated and hard to separate. I was angry at Paula for what she'd said about my father, but it was a different anger than I would have felt if she were white. Underneath it was a mixture of other feelings—I felt betrayed, deserted, hurt. In some other part of my mind, I found myself wondering what Claudia *really* thought—whether she was as resolute as she sounded, or if she didn't, on some level, agree with her friend. I also wondered what my father was going through. Did he think he was selling out by being with someone who wasn't Japanese? Was he having to face, like Claudia, the disapproval of his friends? If so, I didn't hear about it—he wouldn't say anything, of course, and I couldn't tell for myself, since I never saw his friends anymore. I wondered if he and Claudia ever talked about these matters. I wondered if their relationship could accommodate such pain.

A few days later, there was a special girls' basketball preview in the South Bay section of the *L.A. Times.* It included black-and-white photos of both Raina and me, and I bought an extra copy so I could cut the picture of Raina out without my family asking what I was doing. I stuck the picture—in which Raina was diving toward the camera for a loose ball—inside my folder for Trig, and carried my backpack to school as carefully as if it held the world's most precious jewel. Once there, I taped the picture up on the inside of my locker—my regular locker, not the one in the gym—so that I'd be able to look at Raina several times a day.

In the midst of basketball and my nail-biting over Raina, I did manage to make it to school on most days. That in itself was a minor victory. When I was dating Yolanda my sophomore year, the seniors were released at lunchtime, so I'd go home with her and skip my afternoon classes, returning only for basketball practice. This had started a pattern of truancy that I was just then breaking out of. By my senior year, I was a capable but erratic student; I still didn't take my classes very seriously. Despite my spotty academic record, I liked being in school, although like most other jocks I pretended not to. Actually, though, there was nothing more reassuring to me than sitting at my desk, exchanging hastily scribbled notes with Telisa or Q while the class discussion floated past our ears unheard. School was security, school was home, and it was painful to imagine that in just a year's time, I'd no longer have those hallways to roam through, no longer have lockers to gather around with my teammates, or friends wherever I turned. I did not want to leave this familiar world. Sometimes, when I was feeling especially attached to the place, I'd want to hug everyone who passed by, people I recognized but hardly knew, but who'd existed in the periphery of my life for years, and who I'd probably never see again after June.

The axis around which the day revolved was basketball practice. Every afternoon we rushed out of our fifth-period classes and hauled our butts to the gym. Practice was from two to four, Monday through Friday, and the atmosphere of those two hours varied, depending on our coach, everyone's personal lives, good or bad test scores, and me (because I was captain and top shit, my mood affected everyone else's). Practices were sometimes loose and easy and punctuated by frequent laughter, sometimes silent and hard and endless. As the first games approached they got more intense and more directed, because then we had tangible opponents to prepare for instead of the ambiguous "other team."

School was also a welcome break from Raina, although in truth it wasn't much of a respite because I never forgot her. I could never quite expel her from my consciousness; it was like she was a weed that had grown into the cracks of my mind. I didn't really have to think about her, though, because she was already in my head, lived there with me, one step ahead of my thoughts. In practice her name was always on my lips as I conjured up the energy to run faster, jump higher, play harder. In class, when I wasn't passing notes with Telisa or Q, I was jotting poems and song lyrics into the margins of my notebooks, still hearing whatever she'd said to me that morning, until the pages marked with lyrics far outnumbered the pages which had actual notes. Once the season started, I especially thought of her on game days. As I walked through the halls, sat on the bus, eyed the opposing team, I'd wonder how Raina was faring that day, how much her skill and determination were frustrating her opponents in some other gym a few miles away.

Our season opened on the first of December. The morning of my first game, I woke up tense, full of adrenaline, ready to step out of my bed and immediately onto the court. We were playing Santa Monica at their place, and they were a team we were expected to beat. I wolfed down my breakfast, kissed the dog, received good luck wishes from the parents and Raina, who also had a game that day. Then I packed up my schoolbooks and went outside. It was cloudy that morning, but it didn't matter—the world couldn't have been any brighter.

I walked down the sidewalk, practically skipping. Down the block, I saw several adults getting into their cars and rushing away. Although I knew they were going to work, I'd always seen this mass morning exodus in another way—the morning was probably the safest time, and perhaps by leaving the 'hood then, they thought they were escaping something. Several of the adults I saw were people I knew, and now, as I walked by, a few of them spoke to me.

"Kick some ass today, girl," said Mr. Johnson as he got into his car.

"Beat up on those rich kids, Nancy," said Mrs. Rose, although the kids on Santa Monica's team weren't as rich as some of the other kids we'd play.

"Hey, Nancy, kill those motherfuckas!" offered some prepubescent schoolboys who passed by on their bikes.

"We will," I said to the various well-wishers I encountered. "You got it." I walked through the 'hood proudly, loving it, never wanting to leave. It struck me again how easily the community had adopted me; how people placed their hopes in me now and expected me to represent them well. I took this faith in me as a compliment, which it clearly was—but I also worried that it was misplaced; that I didn't deserve it.

On Crenshaw Drive, an offshoot of the larger Crenshaw Boulevard, I stopped at the liquor store I'd pointed out to Raina on the day she'd moved in. It was a small place, and run-down, with none of the slickness or cookie-cutter sameness of the 7-Eleven on Manchester. Inside, the gray paint on the walls was peeling off; yellowing posters were taped onto the sliding glass doors of the refrigerators; and one lonely, uncovered bulb provided all of the light. There were a few unstable-looking shelves, propped up by stray pieces of wood, and they held simple things, basics, like bread, soup, and spaghetti. Out in front there were always four or five men, standing around because they had no place else to go, passing their days by rehashing the old times and discussing the decline of the 'hood. The men were vocal about their views, and often drunk, but essentially harmless. In the early evenings, though, younger guys would start to mill around, spray-painting the walls, selling crack and everything else you could think of in the alley behind the store, amidst the trash and discarded furniture. Toby Wilson, the old man who owned the place, chased them away whenever he could, and the kids would laugh at him, and slink away for a while, and be back within an hour. Often the crack lady was back there with them, doing whatever it was she needed to in order to get her fix.

When I walked in, Mr. Wilson was sitting down, watching the news on the tiny black-and-white television he kept behind the counter. "Morning, Nancy," he said, standing up slowly. He was just about my height, but stooped; when I'd first met him, a decade earlier, he'd been two or three inches taller. Mr. Wilson was a dark brown, the color of the bark on an oak tree; the deep wrinkles on his face were spaced wide apart and there was smooth-looking skin between them. He was almost bald, with little scraggles of gray hair on either side of his head, and he wore wire-rimmed glasses that always slid down his nose. I'd been coming to Mr. Wilson's store since I was seven. At first I'd only come for the candy—Sweetarts and bubble gum, then chocolate-covered raisins and Tootsie Rolls, and finally, potato chips, Twix, and the occasional granola bar—but what had kept me coming for all those years were his stories. Stories were something I didn't get much of from my parents and grandparents, whose way of dealing with the past was to try and forget it. But Mr. Wilson knew more and talked more—about history, about sports, about Los Angeles—than anyone I'd ever met, and I never tired of listening to him. I think I was the only one, though, or one of very few; he was like a walking history book that nobody wanted to read.

"Good morning, Mr. Wilson," I said. "How you doin today?"

"Well as can be expected," he said, scratching his forehead slowly, "considerin Mike and Robert and all them outside tryin to eat me out my own store."

I smiled. He often gave food to the people who needed it, then complained when he did not pull a profit. "What's goin on in the world?" I asked, pointing toward his TV. I noted that my team's schedule, which many of the local stores had posted, was displayed prominently on the wall behind him.

"Ol' Reagan's up to no good again," he said, shaking his head and rubbing his fingers together, as if trying to convince them to work better. "Caught lyin 'bout sellin some weapons. Seem like the only thing that ol bag *can* do is lie. I remember when he was governor, he never did have a good thing to say. But that's government folks, I suppose. Riots happened in Watts back in '65, all they could say was that we don't know how to act right."

"That was before my time," I said. "I think my dad was there, though. He don't like that Reagan much either." I picked up a Twix bar—I always ate one on the day of a game—and set it down on the counter. When I looked up at Mr. Wilson, I found him considering me thoughtfully.

"That's right," he said. "Your daddy grew up in Watts, didn't he?" He looked down, scratched his head, looked up at me again. "You know, back in '65, there was a lot of Japanese folks livin in Watts—I remember, 'cos I lived there awhile, too. My neighbor was a man name Tanaka, worked as a gardener for some rich white folks up in Hollywood. Good man—our kids used to play together. But then, pretty soon, Mr. Tanaka and his family moved away. *All* the Japanese done moved away, from *all* the black towns, soon as the white folks let 'em live in *they* neighborhoods."

He didn't say this in an accusing way—he was just telling me what had happened—but I felt strange about it nonetheless. "Well, you don't see *me* leavin here, do you?" I said, trying to sound lighthearted.

"No, child," he said softly. "But you will."

I didn't look at him, just reached into my pocket for some money; I didn't know what to say.

"It's not just you, though," he said. "You'll all leave Inglewood, sooner or later—you and your friends Raina and Telisa, all of you who got something you believe you can do. I'm not tryin to make you feel bad; it's just the way of the world these days. Just do yourself a favor, though, and don't forget where you come from, or the people you leavin behind."

I nodded, my heart suddenly full.

Mr. Wilson finally noticed the Twix bar on the counter, and now he smiled, his teeth still white and strong. "You got a game today?" he asked.

"Yeah," I said, glad that the subject had changed. "Our season opener."

He pushed his glasses into place, turned around, and peered at the schedule. "Well, look at that," he said. Then he turned back to me and waved away the dollar I tried to give him. "You show 'em, girl!" he commanded.

I stepped outside, said goodbye to the men who were standing there, heard the crunching of broken vials beneath my feet. I shook the glass off the bottom of my sneakers and began to walk. At Manchester, I waited for the light to change, and watched a bus drive by with graffiti all over its side. "ETG" it said, for the Eight-Trey Gangster Crips, an enemy set of the Inglewood Family Bloods. I passed the cemetery to the right and the Forum to the left, saluting the latter place as both a gesture of respect and as a prayer for good luck in the day's game. Across Prairie, the downtown section of Inglewood began, although everything—the discount clothes shops, the discount furniture places, the Conroy's flower shop, the little restaurants, the free health clinics—was still closed, steel gates drawn shut across the entrances. I walked the remaining mile to school quickly, still bouncing with anticipation, bending over now and then to dribble an imaginary ball.

Despite my excitement about the game, though, I was feeling a little less happy. My mind kept returning to something Mr. Wilson had said, the thing about me leaving the 'hood. He was right, I knew—I *would* move on, even if it was not for the same reasons as Mr. Tanaka. In a way, I had left already, or perhaps I'd never really arrived. The factors that had brought me to Inglewood were different from the factors that had brought everyone else there, or that were keeping them all there now—and as much as I loved my friends and tried to fit in, I would always be an outsider among them. I loved Inglewood, though—it was by far the best place I had ever lived; it was the place I felt the least uncomfortable. But I would leave it in seven months, just as Mr. Wilson said, and find new spaces I could circle outside of.

I arrived at school twenty minutes before the bell rang. Jake, the security guard who doubled as the school's graffiti removal crew, was sitting in his chair with his walkie-talkie in hand. I said hi as I approached the gate. That gate would close at exactly eight A.M., and those who got there after the bell rang would have to produce a damn good reason for why Jake should let them in, or scale the fence when he wasn't looking. Jake was a basketball fan, though, so he always made exceptions for me when I strolled up at some odd hour of mid-morning.

"Get twenty-five points and twelve boards for me today," he said.

"I'll try," I said, slapping his hand.

All that day at school, I could barely sit still in my classes. Everywhere I turned, both teachers and students offered me high fives and wished me luck. In second period Trig, the day's announcements were read over the schoolwide intercom, and Nykesha, the student announcer, made sure that everybody knew about the game.

"And finally," came her distorted voice out of the speaker on the wall, "Nancy, Telisa, and the rest of the girls' hoops crew are gonna dismantle Santa Monica in their first official game of the season. The game is at three P.M. at SaMo. Show no mercy, y'all."

We didn't plan to. As I sat through Trig, Courts and Law, Photography, and Chemistry, I drew little diagrams of all our offensive plays. I kept looking at the clock every few seconds, and I could have sworn that the hands weren't moving; now that I actually wanted time to speed up, it seemed to have stopped completely.

When we had away games, as we did that afternoon, we were let out early to catch our bus; I was released first and went around with passes for everyone else. These were the times I loved high school the most—walking around those empty hallways with my teammates, feeling the thrill of being free while the rest of the school sat trapped in classrooms, but having that freedom for a purpose. We boarded the bus in front of the school, and the starting five sat way in the rear, each of the varsity players getting a seat to herself, and the JV's doubling up. Anita Baker's new album had just come out, and when "Sweet Love" came on over our team's portable radio we sang along and exchanged solemn high fives. For the rest of the season we knew we'd win if that song came on. It was good luck, like spotting a Laker.

Still, to make sure, we had our pregame victory-assurance rituals. Telisa wore her mismatching socks, one green, one purple. Q offered a prayer in Vietnamese. I'd eaten half my Twix bar at 10:38, in Photography, and the other half just before we got on the bus. Q passed around the pack of four gumballs she bought before every game, and, as always, I ate the red one, Telisa ate the green one, and Q ate the blue one, which matched the elastic band on her goggles. Then Q popped the yellow one in her mouth, took it out again and handed it to Celine, who bit half of it off and gave the other half to Pam. The five of us chomped silently for a while. Then we all touched Clyde, our game ball, and passed him around so that the reserves could touch him, too—even though we'd be using the other team's ball that day, this way we knew that Clyde's spirit would be with us.

When we got to Santa Monica, we walked into the gym without speaking. It was badly lit, and there was little ventilation. A strange, musty odor mingled with the normal smell of sweat, and Telisa joked that it was caused by a dead body hidden somewhere in the building. Their team was already warming up. They were small, not one of them over 5'10", and no one seemed to have much of a shot. Occasionally they'd glance over at us, and we could see the fear in their eyes. "Dogmeat," Q said as we walked to our bench, adjusting her goggles and grinning.

Unlike a week before at the alumni game, this time we'd come ready to play. Q tipped the jump ball to me, and I hit a streaking Pam, who put our first points on the scoreboard before five seconds had passed. We played with the other team at will, doing whatever we wanted on offense, shutting them down on defense. Coach Fontaine had us run all our new plays, in order to work out the kinks in them before we unleashed them against tougher competition. We did several different things on the defensive end, too—person-to-person, a 2-3 zone, and a full-court press, which he called off out of pity within a matter of minutes because the other team couldn't get the ball past their own free throw line. We were like a machine, and we did not let up—we wanted to win big in our opening game so all those other teams out there would take notice. Q was awesome, making easy work of the Santa Monica center—facing up to the hoop and shooting over her, or muscling by her when she got too close. Telisa played her usual level-headed game, directing the offense and hitting jumpers from way outside if their guards were dumb enough to leave her alone. And I was hot, too, hitting shots from the corner, driving baseline, setting up Q when her defender was out of position. Santa Monica tried to double-team me, but that only meant that another of our weapons was left unchecked. And when one of *my* duo went to cover the open player, my teammates quickly got me the ball, and then it was just me against a solitary, quaking defender who had no chance in the world of stopping me. It was beautiful. It seemed, that day, like our opponents were playing a completely different game than we, a game they were just learning, and all of their reactions were half a second too slow. I felt, also, the joy of watching my body respond perfectly to all I asked it to do. The yards of wooden floor passed beneath me in a blur; the floorboards seemed to rise up and push me along. I felt the strength and adrenaline move through my legs. Each time the ball was dead I'd run my hands along my arms, which were slippery and shiny with sweat. My lungs were burning, and it felt good: my body's endurance would increase the more I pushed it. My heart was beating quickly, but not hard, not straining; it clipped along like a healthy young horse. I felt intensely present that day, like I inhabited every part of my body—I lived in my fingertips, which touched the ball; in the soles of my feet; in my hips when I clashed with another player for a rebound; in my shoulders; in my thighs; in my kneecaps when I kneeled to tie my shoe; in my throat and mouth and lips when I spoke to my teammates, when I yelled out in exhilaration. All five of us moved as if directed by one mind. By the time Coach Fontaine finally took out the seniors a few minutes into the fourth quarter, I had twenty-three points—a good three-quarter total—and we were up by twenty-five.

"Don't mess with *us,*" Telisa chanted as we left the court, "'cos Q and Nancy gonna *bust!*"

With the three seniors on the bench, Santa Monica started to make up some of the point differential, but it was as if they were chipping pebbles off a mountain. We cheered our teammates on and splashed water on each other. At one point, Pam got fouled on her way up to shoot, and she went to the line for two free throws. She missed the first one, and as she turned away in disgust, her gum flew out of her mouth and landed on the floor just in front of the foul line. We laughed and Pam looked sheepish. I guess the referee didn't see it happen, though, because as soon as Pam turned toward the basket again, he handed her the ball. She positioned herself at the line, bounced the ball a couple of times, and looked up at the basket. Then she leaned over, picked the gum up and put it back in her mouth, and shot the ball so quickly that it all seemed like part of the same motion. The ball went in and we all laughed so hard we almost fell off the bench. Even our coach had to shake his head and smile.

After the final buzzer, Coach Fontaine herded us into the visitors' locker room.

"Good game," he said, as we threw towels around and tried to sit still. "Good way to start out the season." Then he cleared his throat and assumed the even tone of voice he always used when reciting one of his practiced talks, in this case Standard Fontaine Postgame Speech No. 12. "We went hard today, and executed well, and didn't sink down to the other team's level of play. That's what we've got to do all season long—make the opponents adjust to *our* game and not let ourselves adjust to theirs."

". . . not let ourselves adjust to theirs," Telisa mumbled along with him, under her breath. After a few more minutes of postgame dissection, we got up and put on our sweatsuits. I rubbed and stretched my cramp-prone calves. Clyde, who went home every day with someone on our team, was given to Celine for the night. We boarded the bus, and Telisa moved around and sat next to different people, joking with them or congratulating them or attempting to loosen them up.

"Get your face out your shoes, girl," she said to Bonita, the sophomore, who hadn't played much that day. "We won."

Q snorted. "If I had your face," she said, "I'd just *keep* it in my shoes."

"Yeah?" Telisa said. "Well *your* face is so ugly that when you was born, they had to put tinted windows on your incubator."

Q grinned. "Yeah? Well you so *stupid* that when you passed Taco Bell, you thought it was the Mexican phone company."

Telisa thrust her chin out. "Yeah? Well *you* so stupid that you had to call information to get the number for 911."

They high-fived each other while the rest of us laughed. Then Telisa came back and sat next to me. "We *own* motherfuckin league this year, girl," she said. "We own it."

Celine nodded. "I bet we go undefeated."

"Nancy's gonna be MVP of the league," Pam said.

Telisa nodded. "Shit. Nancy's gonna be MVP of the *universe.*"

And it went on like this, people throwing out cheerful insults and rash predictions, for the rest of our drive back to school. I did not want the ride to end. I was glad our season had finally begun—this was the happiest time of the year for me, the time I felt most like my life had a meaning—but there was some loss in the feeling, too. This had been the first game of my final year of high school, the beginning of the end.

CHAPTER 8

After the bus dropped us off at school, Telisa gave me a ride home. I walked up the driveway, still hearing my friend's car as it rattled up the street, and finally wondered how Raina's game had gone. Her team had played at home that day, so she should have been back already, which she was—I found her stretched out on the living room floor in a clean white T-shirt and the light USC sweatpants she always slept in. The television was on to some movie from the seventies; all the women wore flowery bell-bottoms and all the men had huge, triangular collars.

"Hey," Raina said, sitting up. "How'd y'all do?"

"We killed 'em," I said, grinning. "It was ugly. My coach took me out about three minutes into the fourth quarter."

"That's exactly how our game went," said Raina, pressing the mute button on the remote. "I didn't play at all in the fourth."

I set my backpack on the floor and petted the dog. Then I walked over and sat down on the love seat, my feet resting just inches from Raina's leg. "But Fairfax is supposed to be good this year, aren't they?"

"Maybe," she said, shrugging. "But not today."

"Oooh," I said, "I'm scared of *you.*"

"Naw, it ain't like that," she said. "I mean, we played well and everything, but they were really off. Terry Davis usually gets like twenty or something, but she couldn't score shit today." She scratched her leg. "So what did *you* score, Miss Thang?"

I kept my eyes on the dog and said, "Twenty-three," trying not to look too pleased about what I knew was an impressive total for a little more than three quarters of work.

"All *right,*" said Raina, smiling, and I had to hold back a grin.

"Yeah, well, you know," I said. "The other team played bad defense. It was mostly just lay-ups and shit."

"Still," Raina said, "that's great."

"Thanks," I said, and I finally looked at her now. "Well, what about you? What *you* hit for today?"

"Oh," Raina said, as if she were bored with the topic, "twenty-five."

I felt something turn over in my stomach. Raina had played fewer minutes than me, but had still managed to score more points. On top of that, she'd sounded glad about my point production, and I wondered, now, if this was because it had been less than hers.

"Great," I said, and my voice sounded like it had been forced through a meat grinder.

Raina seemed not to notice. She leaned over and hit me on the foot. "Hey, you wanna order a pizza or something? I'm hungry. The parents went to the store, but by the time they come back and cook dinner, I'm probably gonna die of starvation."

"Uh, actually, no," I said, standing. "Sorry. I ain't that hungry, so I guess I can wait." This was true, but even if it hadn't been, I would have done anything, at that moment, to get out of the room.

She stuck her bottom lip out, trying to look cute, which suddenly, violently, annoyed me. "All right," she said. "But if you find me dead down here, I'm gonna hold you responsible."

I couldn't answer her, and turned away before she saw the

look on my face. I picked up my bag, trudged up the stairs, and stripped off my dirty uniform. In the shower, my annoyance got washed away and I saw what lay beneath it—frustration. I had played a good game, done just about as well as anyone could in that space of time—but Raina, somehow, had done better. Worse, she'd seemed so casual about the whole thing—casually pleased to learn of my statistics, then nonchalant about disclosing her own. Maybe she just expected to outscore me—but if so I resented that expectation, and I resented what I thought was her pleasure at living up to it. I didn't know how I was going to make it through dinner that night. Fortunately, though, Raina really *couldn't* wait until the parents got home, and she went out, I learned later, with Stacy, to a pizza place in Torrance. By the time she got home, I was already in bed, reading; she didn't bother me, and went straight to her room.

The next morning, at breakfast, the parents asked about her game; they'd heard about mine over dinner. Raina recounted it dutifully, underplaying her own achievements. My father refilled her coffee mug as she finished talking.

"One of the refs at your game," he said, "Tom Ikeda, is a buddy of mine from high school. He called yesterday, after you won. He told me that at one point, when you were tied up, you bounced the ball *off the other ref,* and then grabbed it and went in for the basket."

"I didn't do it on purpose," said Raina, sheepishly. "I was trying to pass it to Keisha, but he got in the way."

"Yeah, right," my father said. "I heard it was like the Globetrotters. I heard you ran a perfect give-and-go off the poor guy's hip, that the defense all went in the wrong direction, and that the crowd was just rolling in the aisles." He sounded pleased beyond end, and I wanted to throttle him. It was one thing for Raina's friends to adore her, or even Claudia's, but this was too much. Everyone was so *impressed* with Raina, so amused by her, and I just didn't want to hear it anymore. Sure, she was a great player, but she was no greater than anyone else, and I was suddenly tired of people finding her so wonderful. Even the play that my father described seemed infuriatingly silly. I believed that it *was* a mistake; that she had hit the ref by accident and had set herself up by chance for an easy basket. She had been the recipient of some good luck—I saw no reason to be impressed by this, and was annoyed that my father admired her.

I was annoyed, that day, by a lot of things. Suddenly I found it unbearable that Raina stayed in the bathroom for so long, primping for school, especially since, by the time she was done, her hair was all over the sink. She played her music too loud—New Edition, for God's sake—and sang along with it, off-key. She'd left a pair of shoes in the hallway, where I tripped over them on my way downstairs, and once I got to the living room, I found a dirty plate she had left there the day before. I took this into the kitchen, fuming, and then went off to school. There, my mood lifted a bit—I was glad to see my friends, and people kept congratulating us for our win. We had a good practice that afternoon, still high from our first game, and got excited about game two, which would be the next day.

When I got home, the mail was overflowing from the mailbox. I gathered it all in, and then went into the house, where I heard Raina on the phone in the kitchen. Q was expecting me to call with our assignment for Courts and Law—she'd ditched, and spent the period listening to music in some boy's car—but it didn't sound like Raina's conversation would be ending anytime soon. Her voice was low and tender, and when I peeked in at her, I saw her head bent sideways, the phone on her shoulder, the bottom of it cradled in her raised right hand. She often talked to Toni right after she got home from school, and Toni usually called again later, in the evening. Between Toni, her friends, and all the coaches who called, it seemed like Raina was always on the phone. I continued on into the living room, getting annoyed with her all over again. Why the hell didn't she just get her own line? The big pile of mail was starting to fall out of my arms, like a cat who doesn't want to be held, and I reached the coffee table just in time to dump it. Most of it was recruiting mail for Raina and me—several 9 × 12 envelopes, three medium-sized envelopes that held media guides, and a handful's worth of letters. I divided the recruiting mail into two separate piles. Raina's pile was considerably bigger. This was not a constant thing—my pile could be bigger than hers on any given day, and in the end, our mail probably evened out—but it seemed particularly painful that day that she had more mail than me.

To my surprise, Raina got off the phone quickly, so I put in my call to Q. When I went back out to the living room, Raina was sitting on the couch where I had just been, and looking through her mail. We said hi to each other. She'd just finished a glass of milk—the glass was on the coffee table—and I wondered if I'd have to clean up after her again. I sat down on the love seat and ripped open one of the 9 × 12 envelopes, which was from UConn.

"That's a press release about their tournament," Raina informed me. "I just got the same thing yesterday."

I put the envelope back down without removing the contents, and picked up another.

"And that's the Wyoming media guide," said Raina. "Kinda weird that they send it out so late in the year, don't you think? I mean, the rest of 'em came in the fall."

I closed my eyes for a moment and didn't say anything.

"Hey, don't y'all have another game tomorrow?" she asked, as I picked up the next envelope.

"Yeah," I said. "Against Dorsey."

"We play tomorrow, too," said Raina cheerfully. Some of the opened letters she put back on the coffee table, and some she tossed to the floor, to throw away. "We're playin Compton, at their place, so we probably gonna get killed."

I nodded. "They're tough." My team had played twice at Compton, and had lost both times. The only reasons I found this bearable were that Compton was always ranked higher than us, and that I'd outscored my friend Natalie in each of the games.

"The place is probably gonna be crawlin with scouts, too," Raina said. "Shit. Natalie Green signed early with Ohio State, right? But Penny Sayers hasn't signed yet, and I don't know *where* she's gonna go."

"You're both gonna have a hard time," I said, and they would. Penny Sayers was another All-State guard, and she and Raina would almost certainly be guarding each other. This matchup could result in brilliance on both of their parts, but it could also mean they'd shut each other down.

"Yeah, I know," said Raina. "But it'll be fun." She smiled. "Last year when we played Compton, the assistant coach from Texas—you know, that real skinny guy with the silver hair?—he fell asleep in the middle of the game. He'd already come to see me play a couple times, so all my teammates knew who he was. Anyway, it's the start of the fourth quarter. We look over at the Texas guy, and he's just *out*—he's leaning sideways, and snoring real loud. So Stacy goes right up to him—he's sittin in the front row—and yells, 'Wake up, man! Is this siesta time in Texas?'" Raina chuckled to herself. "That poor coach jumped about halfway up the bleachers, and even the refs cracked up. Shit, it's a good thing I don't wanna go to Texas." She paused. "But you know, that guy *always* looks sleepy at games. Have you noticed?"

I didn't look at her, and my stomach felt funny again. "He's never come to one of my games," I said.

Raina was silent for a moment. "Oh," she said finally. "Well, um, you don't really wanna go there anyway, do you? I mean, it's *Texas,* you know? All those cowboys and Alamos and shit."

"No, you're right," I said. I *didn't* want to go to Texas, but this did nothing to make me feel better just then. "Listen, I think I'm gonna skip the park today. I wanna conserve my energy for the game tomorrow."

"Me, too," Raina said, to my disappointment. "Maybe I'll get some homework done tonight."

We both stayed in all evening, and she continued to annoy me. When Claudia came home from work, Raina gave her a hug, and I thought this slightly nauseating, an obvious attempt to be endearing. When the Clipper game came on at six, Raina talked to the players on the screen, and it took a great effort to stop myself from telling her to please shut up. At dinner that night, which was pork chops, peas, mashed potatoes, and cornbread, Raina ate each course in succession. She consumed her entire pork chop, then all of her potatoes, then all of her peas, and finally cleaned off her plate with two pieces of cornbread. Raina always ate her meals course by course, and it had never bothered me before; that night, though, I found it unbearable. She asked later if I wanted to do homework with her, and I begged off, saying I needed to be alone so I could concentrate. When I was in my room, though, I did nothing but make a paper clip chain. The phone rang a couple of times—the Oregon coach, for Raina, and the Utah coach, for me—but otherwise, nothing happened, which was fine with me. I needed a good night's sleep, so I went to bed early. I could hear Raina making noise, though—it sounded like she was throwing furniture around—so finally, at midnight, I went into her room and asked her to be quiet. "Sorry," she said lightly, holding the Nerf ball in her hand. The plastic rim was still vibrating from her latest dunk. I wanted to ask why the hell she was playing Nerf basketball so late on a weeknight—and with her door open, even—but I just turned and went back to my room.

The next day, we played Dorsey, which was a fairly good team. They had a 6'4" center, who was surprisingly agile for her height; Q kept turning into her and then bouncing back, as if off of a wall. Because Q couldn't score much—she did get a few layups, but only when the center left her to help on weak-side defense—the rest of us had to step up our game. Pam had a career-high eighteen points; I scored twenty-eight points and pulled down thirteen rebounds; Telisa passed off for nine assists. The game was close through three quarters and then we pulled away in the fourth, winning by a margin of ten points. After walking to the market down the street from our school, we all came back to watch the JV game. I joked around with my teammates, absently, wondering if Raina's team had beaten Compton that day, and wondering how Raina had done.

Telisa took me home a little after six o'clock, and we agreed to meet later to do our homework—I was even going to her house, for once, because her mother was staying over at her boyfriend's. No one else was back yet, and Ann went berserk, as if she'd been left alone for a month. I looked through the mail, and felt a little better—I'd gotten six pieces of mail from colleges that day, and Raina only four. After I read all of mine, I showered, and by the time I got dressed, both Claudia and my father had come home.

"Hello, my favorite wild child," said my father when I walked into the kitchen. Claudia, who was sitting in the breakfast nook, waved.

"Hey," I said, taking the seat next to Claudia.

"Did you win today?"

"Yup."

The dog, without warning, started sprinting toward the door, which meant that someone was on the doorstep, or was about to be. We heard the key in the lock, the sound of the door opening, then Raina coming into the house. She turned the corner and walked toward us, and I could tell by the way she moved—her feet were dragging and her shoulders slumped—that they'd lost.

"Welcome," said my father in a slow, deep voice; he sounded like a maître d' on Quaaludes.

"Hi," Claudia said. "How'd you do?"

Raina leaned over, let the sports bag slip off her shoulder and onto the floor. Then she sat down at the table. "We lost," she said, sounding dejected. "But barely. We stayed real close to 'em the whole game, the lead kept going back and forth. But then they went up by four, and we had to foul 'em, and they hit all their free throws. The game was tied with 1:27 left, but we ended up losing by nine."

Claudia nodded, looking sympathetic. "But Compton's one of the top teams in the state, aren't they? It's great that you came so close."

Raina sighed. "But that's worse than if they'd killed us, you know? We got so close, which means we could of beat 'em, and we didn't."

My father took a bottle out of the refrigerator and held it out to her with a flourish. "That's too bad," he said. "Here, have a beer."

Raina shook her head, waved off the bottle. "No, thanks. I think I just want some water. How did *you* guys do?" she asked, turning to me.

"We won," I said.

She smiled, looked briefly happy. "Good for you."

Claudia, though, wasn't finished with her yet. "Well, did *you* have a good game?" she asked.

Raina shrugged. "I guess."

"What'd you score?"

"Yeah," said my father, looking at me. "And what did *you* score?"

"Twenty-eight," I said.

Raina looked down at her hands. "Twenty-nine."

She had done it again. I tried to keep my expression neutral, but I don't know if I succeeded. I wanted to go outside and scream as loud as I could.

"Well, at least *you* played well," Claudia said to her daughter.

Raina looked at her mother wearily, as if this was the most ridiculous thing she'd ever heard.

My father swooped around the table and jostled each of us on the shoulder; this was his way of telling us that he was tired of everyone being so serious. "Nancy," he said to me, but winking at Raina. "You let yourself be outscored by a *guard.*" I didn't respond—he didn't need to remind me of this, and I wasn't able to go along with his mood. "And Raina," he continued. "Why are you scoring that much, anyway? Guards are supposed to *distribute* the ball, not shoot it."

Raina smiled now, and my dad smiled, too; his strategy was working. "I'm a shooting guard, not a point guard," she said. "I can score as much as I want. You gonna tell Michael Jordan he shouldn't shoot?"

They continued to banter affectionately, and Raina's mood began to lighten. My father started dinner, and I left them, going upstairs to gather my math book and notes. As I drove over to Telisa's, I thought about the fact that Raina had outscored me again. I was angry and confused; I didn't know what to feel. On the one hand, it made sense that Raina should score more. She didn't have another recruit on her team, the way that I had Q; and besides, I'd already conceded that she was the stronger player. Still, I hated that she'd outshone me; I wanted desperately to do better than her, or at least to do as well. I didn't know how I was going to survive the season; how I'd be able to deal with coming home after games and always being second to Raina. And I was sure she was conscious of the gap between us. She probably loved knowing that she could outdo me; that she was the real star; that I could practice every day for the rest of my life and never reach the place she already was.

The next day, after we got home from school, Raina and I went down to the park. I wanted to play against her in a pickup game. It didn't happen, though—there were a couple dozen people waiting to play; we ended up with different groups; and both our teams lost badly to the team that was reigning that day. The logjam of players was even worse than usual, because there was only one game going on—one of the hoops on the second court had somehow disappeared. So instead of waiting an hour for the chance to play again, Raina and I moved over to the partnerless hoop on the other court and played Horse, then Twenty-one. Twenty-one was somewhat tricky, since there were other people shooting around, but we ended up incorporating them into our game by using them as screens. Raina was low-key about the whole thing—she was tired, and disappointed at not being able to play full court—but I took it very seriously. Normally we split these kinds of games pretty evenly, and it didn't matter much, but that day, those games were as important to me as the CIF finals. I beat her at Horse, which, theoretically, she should have won, since she was more of an outside shooter, and then killed her in two games of Twenty-one. I'd expected to feel better, but didn't. These victories weren't particularly satisfying, because she didn't seem to care, which, in turn, made me all the more angry. I couldn't understand what was wrong with her. She'd just lost to me, badly—why wasn't she mad? Maybe it was because she hadn't tried hard, and therefore had an excuse. Or maybe she considered me so far beneath her, such a nonthreat, that it meant nothing if she occasionally let me win. After we'd finished for the night, we walked home, Raina chatting cheerfully about a party she and Toni had gone to, while I dribbled along next to her, silent.

The next day we played Redondo, which was a rival of sorts. For one thing, Redondo was the high school I would have attended if I'd stayed in Redondo Beach. For another—and I didn't know if this was related—the first game I'd played against them, my sophomore year, had erupted into a fight. Although they weren't a very good team, and should have been easy to beat, there was enough bitterness on both sides to make the games interesting. That year, we were playing at our place, and I wanted, as always, to demolish them. I also wanted to have a great game individually, of course, so I'd have impressive stats to take home to Raina.

We succeeded on both counts. We won by eighteen, although it wasn't even that close, and I got a triple-double for the first time in my career. I had twenty-one points, which was nothing spectacular, and ten blocked shots, my career high. Most impressively, I'd collected just about every possible rebound. Part of it was anticipation—I was good at judging how a missed shot would fall, and I always blocked out well. But the bigger part was that the ball seemed to chase me that day, as if I had been dipped in honey, and it were a bee. I finished with twenty-seven rebounds—which, I learned from a reporter, was a CIF record. At the post-game meeting I kissed the ball, and said, "Thank you, Clyde."

Coach Fontaine laughed. "Take him home tonight. He obviously wants to be with you. Poor thing's been following you around all day."

We stayed to watch the JV game, and then I got a ride home. I couldn't wait to tell Raina about my game, to make her as jealous as she'd made me, and when I walked into the house, I found her, still in uniform, sitting on the floor and watching *M*A*S*H.*

"Hey," she said, as I sat down on the love seat. "Did you win?"

"Yeah," I said, setting Clyde down beside me. "It was Redondo. We kicked ass."

"Yeah, so did we. It was kinda boring." She spun around to face me. "I hate blowing people out, don't you? It just ain't very fun."

"Well, yeah, that's usually true, but today was kinda cool."

"Why? What happened?"

"Well, I . . ." I lowered my eyes. This was my moment of triumph, but suddenly, for some reason, I couldn't look at her. "I kinda had a triple-double."

Raina leaned forward. "A *triple-double?* Holy shit! What—points, assists, and rebounds?"

"Not assists," I said. "Blocked shots."

"You had double figures in *blocked shots?*"

"Yeah," I said. "Ten exactly." I snuck a peek at her, expecting to see the same kind of battle in her face that must have been in mine for the last few days. I didn't find it, though. She looked animated, incredulous—and happy.

She inched forward on the carpet like a caterpillar, pulling her butt to her heels, then sticking her feet out further, moving her butt again, moving her feet. "So how many points you get?" she asked excitedly. "And how many rebounds?"

I didn't feel triumphant now; I felt like she was trying to get me to admit something against my will. "Well, not that many points," I said. "Twenty-one." I put my hand on top of Clyde. "But I had twenty-seven rebounds."

Raina's eyes and mouth flew open wide. "Twen—*No.* Get the fuck outta here. You're kiddin me, right?"

"No," I said.

She just stared at me for a moment. She put her hands on top of her head, and shook it. Then she rocked backwards, stuck her arms out and appealed to the sky, and let out a huge, joyous laugh. "Twenty-seven fuckin rebounds!" she yelled. "Nancy, *you* are the *shit!*"

"Thanks," I said, half-smiling. This was not what I wanted. Where was Raina's jealousy, her resentment?

"Wait," she said, leaning forward again. "That's gotta be some kind of record."

"It is," I said. "It's a CIF record. The old one was twenty-five."

She jumped to her feet—by magic, it seemed. One second she was sitting on the carpet, and the next she was standing up.

"Damn! You broke a CIF *record!*" she yelled. "Well, shit, get up, girl, so I can hug you!"

I stood, obediently, and she gave me a long, rough, body-shaking hug. This might have meant something to me normally, but I was so unhappy at that moment that I received it like a child in the clutches of an aunt who reeked of cheap perfume. "Goddamn!" she said. "A triple-double, and a CIF record! I thought *I* had a good game, 'cos I had twenty points and eight assists, but shit, I ain't got *nothin* on you!"

She looked at me, beaming, and shook her head. Then she went off into the kitchen. I heard her pick up the phone, punch some buttons in. After a short pause she started to talk. "Yo, Stacy, wassup? You ain't gonna believe this shit. Nancy got a fuckin triple-double today, and it was *blocks,* can you believe that?—instead of assists . . . What? . . . I know, I know, but it gets better, girl. 'Cos guess how many boards she got. No . . . Twenty-seven. I'm *serious,* twenty-seven! Yeah, girl, you heard right! It's a CIF *record* and shit!"

I listened for a moment, feeling more and more miserable,

and finally, I went upstairs to take a shower. When I came back down, Raina was still on the phone—with someone else this time, telling the same story. Claudia got home a few minutes later, and Raina met her at the door with the news. She did the same thing with my father when he got home. They were both excited—Claudia hugged me, and my father opened a bottle of wine—but I just wanted to go to my room and hide. I couldn't deal with Raina being so happy for me. She clearly didn't care that I'd outshone her that day. And I knew now that she'd taken no pleasure in outscoring me before; she probably had not even noticed. I could have hated her for this, but I was too ashamed—or maybe, not nearly ashamed enough. My father made steaks and rice, and as dinner progressed, I felt my anger begin to subside. Raina ignored my strange mood and talked to me, teased me, made it clear how proud she was. I couldn't believe she could be so nice to me after how cold I'd been the last few days. Her generosity was stunning, and I would have to try, now, to be worthy of it, and also—if I could—to return it.

The day after my triple-double game, my father pulled me aside as I was heading toward the kitchen for breakfast. "Listen," he said, voice lowered. We were standing in the living room and Raina and Claudia were already in the kitchen. "Um, Claudia's parents have invited us all down to San Diego for Christmas. And I know it's a break from our, um, holiday tradition, but I think it might be fun to go. And hey—it'd mean that you wouldn't have to eat my dry turkey." He cleared his throat and seemed so worried about my response that I had to smile. My father was an inch taller than me, but probably eighty pounds heavier, and he looked, just then, like a teddy bear. "Oh, and also, Claudia and I, and her parents, are going down to Baja that night with two of my friends from school. So you and Raina can hang out in San Diego for a couple of days. Their house is only about a mile from the beach—it'll be fun, I think. Would you mind spending Christmas with a group of people for a change?"

I thought about this for a moment. Although I didn't say so, I think my father overestimated my attachment to our traditional way of celebrating Christmas—eggnog, a sad little tree, college football games on television. The holidays always depressed me. For one thing, they were the only time I ever heard from my mother. She had moved to Rolling Hills with her white lawyer husband, his bully son, and their two new half-white kids; according to my mother's parents, who still wrote to me on occasion, even my half-siblings—much to their parents' dismay— got beaten up by white kids. My mother now sent me a Christmas card and a hundred-dollar check every year, and that was the extent of my dealings with her. I didn't know what my father thought of all this. He never mentioned my mother, holiday season or not, and he wouldn't show me any pictures; he'd removed all traces of her from his life. I wasn't unlike him, I understand now—I preferred to act like she didn't exist.

The other reason the holidays depressed me was that they reminded me of my father's parents, who'd died five years before in a car accident. From the time of my parents' divorce, we'd always gone to their house for Christmas, and being alone with my father just didn't compare. It would be nice to get out of the house during the holidays for once, but it was strange to think about spending that time with someone else's family. "I guess it's O.K.," I said now.

My father looked at me. "You sound a little skeptical."

"I'm not skeptical, it's just that . . . well, what if they don't like me?"

He cocked his head, then laughed. "Why wouldn't they like you? What—because you're Japanese?"

I hadn't consciously realized the nature of my fear, but now that he had said this, I knew he was right. "I don't know. Maybe."

He smiled at me, the reassuring father again. "Sure, Nancy. They're fine with the idea of Claudia living with a Japanese man. But he has a *daughter* who's Japanese, also? Now, *that's* too much."

I grinned. "Well, how do *I* know what they think of you guys? And what *do* they think of you guys?"

He sighed. "Well, when we first started dating, I don't think they were exactly thrilled, and I still think they'd prefer for Claudia to be with a black man. But they've warmed up to me a lot in the last few months. Like any parent, they believe that their daughter should be worshipped, and they know I do a good job of that."

I nodded. "What do you think Grandpa and Grandma would do if they knew you were with a black woman?"

He raised his eyebrows. "Oh, they know."

"And what do they think of it?"

He smiled. "They're twirling in their graves."

"But, Dad," I said, "they were cremated."

He smacked his forehead. "Oh, you're right. Well, then each individual ash is twirling in its canister. They're upstairs in the attic. You can check for yourself."

I thought for a moment, uncertain. "They are not," I finally said.

My dad grinned. "Right again. I scattered the ashes, up where they honeymooned at Big Bear. How'd I get such a brilliant daughter?"

We were a patchwork family, and the edges were starting to fit. I'd finally gotten used to Claudia's presence, and to the laughter which woke me up on Sunday mornings. I'd also gotten used to seeing Raina every day, although this meant only that it no longer surprised me and not that I felt any calmer about it. After my triple-double game, and Raina's response, I wasn't annoyed, anymore, by the little things she did, and our relationship went back to normal again. I stopped counting the letters that came, and tried to stop caring about games at the park. We took to doing our homework together, splayed out on the carpet in my room, and I was more diligent about getting it done then, as an excuse to be with her, than I had ever been before she moved in.

Later in those evenings the phone calls would come, sometimes from college coaches but more often from friends—Telisa and Q for me, Toni for her, and Stacy for both of us. Stacy was always up to some kind of mischief or another, and Raina and I both lived vicariously through her decidedly more interesting social life. She went out to clubs almost every weekend night, usually with some girl she'd met at a game. Raina and I both had phone extensions in our rooms, so we were able to have three-way conversations.

"So how was your date?" I asked one evening when I knew she'd been out the night before.

She chuckled wickedly. "I saw, I conquered, I came."

Raina and I both laughed. "You ho," Raina said.

"Hey, don't be callin me a ho," Stacy said. "Besides, I'm givin up girls when I turn eighteen."

"Well, who you gonna move onto next?" I asked.

Stacy sighed dreamily. "Women."

From there our conversation turned to specific details of the previous night's encounter, to general gossip, to what we had done with our weekends, and finally, of course, to basketball. Sometimes, when Raina was talking, I'd lie on the floor and close my eyes and just listen to the sound of her voice.

Our parents did all they could to promote the myth of familial normality. Maybe for them, though, it really had become normal. Their own relationship, at least, seemed unquestionable now; despite his problems at school, my father was happier than I'd ever seen him, and Raina said the same about her mother. By now, too, Claudia's presence in our house was old news to our neighbors. She and my father still got occasional glares when they walked around the 'hood, but these were getting more and more rare. There were other signs of trouble, though. At one point, I asked my father what had happened to Tim Nakanishi, a friend from college he used to play paddleball with on weekends. "Tim," my father had answered, keeping his eyes on his paper, "is not a fan of Claudia's." My mother, for her part, would write in that year's Christmas card, "I'm concerned about you. I hear your father's taken up with a black woman." And Claudia, of course, had Paula. Judging from a phone conversation I overheard around this time, Paula had not shown up for their last group dinner at Kim's place, and Claudia was sure it had to do with their argument. "She won't return my calls," Claudia said over the phone to Rochelle. "And did you see how she completely avoided me at the last meeting?" She paused and nodded at whatever her friend was saying. "I know. But I don't know what to do anymore, Rochelle. Shit, I wish she'd just get over it."

For the most part, though, people were fairly accepting of my father and Claudia—especially those who had liked my father before, and even more so, especially those who were basketball fans. I was glad about this, because people's discomfort with our parents tended to make *me* uncomfortable; I didn't like to think much, then, about how different the patches in our patchwork actually were.

On the first Sunday morning of that month, just as on every other Sunday morning since the beginning of September, our parents emerged from their room about eleven. They were sleepy-eyed, yawning, and pajamaed, and they immediately slipped into the gentle teasing that seemed to characterize all their dealings with each other.

"How about some sausage this morning, love?" my father said as they entered the kitchen. Sunday was Claudia's day to cook—only one cook at a time was allowed in our small kitchen—and he liked to milk his advantage as much as possible.

"We only have bacon," she said. "Will that do?"

"Bacon! The last time you made bacon the fire alarm screamed for two hours!"

"Why are you always so hard on me, you lazy bum?"

He squeezed his bicep. "Hey. Don't complain. A hard man is good to find."

They grinned at each other. Raina and I rolled our eyes.

Claudia brought in the morning paper, and then, while she cooked, Raina, my father, and I all fought over the sports section. This was immediately dissected at the kitchen table and never made it out to the post-meal newspaper perusal session we conducted later on in the living room. That morning, my father got it. I had to settle for Metro and Raina for Travel, which was her second-favorite section. She spread the paper out on the table and folded her hands together on top of it. I noticed the flesh beneath her nails, which was the color of toffee; her fingers were a darker brown at the knuckles. Raina's long, squarish hands were covered with nicks and tiny wrinkles; they had the beauty and strength of old women. Two veins pushed up the skin just inside each of her wristbones, like legs beneath a blanket.

"Hey, Mom," Raina said, pointing to a picture of the Grand Canyon on the front page of the Travel section. "If you dropped a men's basketball and a women's basketball from the top of the Grand Canyon, which one would hit the bottom first?"

"Neither." Claudia answered. "They'd fall at the same rate."

"O.K., but if you put a men's ball and a women's ball in the Colorado River, which one would reach Mexico first?"

"I don't know."

"Well, let's find out. Can we go to the Grand Canyon sometime?"

"Maybe," Claudia said, over the sound of sizzling bacon. "But we've got to see what your grades are like first. You get anything below a B this semester, and you're not going *anywhere,* not even the bathroom."

Raina looked at her mother seriously. "I don't think you'd like that," she said.

"Listen, Miss Thang," said Claudia, putting her fist on her hip and smiling. "Just 'cos you're bigger than me doesn't mean I can't still whup your butt."

"Ooh, mom," said Raina, smiling, "I love it when you're tough."

They went on like this for a few more minutes, Claudia threatening to remove all sleeping, eating, and breathing privileges if Raina didn't do well in school, Raina threatening to go live at the beach. I liked watching the two of them interact. They were much closer than my father and me; they'd check in with each other every night after dinner, talk for ten or fifteen minutes about their day. Claudia and Raina were both serious people, but that was not, as I'd believed at first, the state they were always in. And the things that tempered their basic seriousness were different. Claudia could be mischievous, joyfully wicked, as if a very small devil was perched on her shoulder. But Raina was just plain weird. When they'd first moved in with us, I'd thought the quirky things she said were simply distracting, amusing—garnish for her obvious perfection. It had taken me a while to realize that this oddness wasn't an *addition* to who she was; it *was* who she was. I liked her oddness, though. It made her seem more accessible, more real. And Raina seemed comfortable with the things that made her different, made her strange, in a way I could never be.

"Yo, Mom, look at that," she said now, pointing over my father's shoulder at the sports page as Claudia sat down to eat. "Rockets 117, Rockets 112. Guess you haven't been paying much attention at work lately, huh?" Raina always held her mother responsible for any mistake involving the *Times,* whether there was a typo, or an incorrect caption, or the delivery boy had thrown the paper on the roof.

Claudia spread a napkin on her lap and smiled. "It's been really busy lately," she said. "I guess that one slipped past me."

"Well, maybe we should subscribe to a better paper," Raina teased.

"Maybe you should shut your mouth."

I looked at the sports page in order to find the mistake, but found something else that distracted me—a picture of Cheryl Miller, holding a Cheryl Miller doll in her hands. She looked as radiant, proud, and self-contained as ever, a lioness who was ruler of all she saw. "Raina, look!" I said, jumping up so fast I hit the bottom of the table and caused the parents' coffee to spill. "Give me the paper, Dad. You gotta let me cut that out."

"No, no, no, no," he said, pulling the paper back and shaking his head. "No one's touching this until I go through the scores."

Every morning my father or Claudia demanded the public reading of the high school scores, which, including pauses for discussion or disbelief, usually took about twenty minutes. On Saturdays, they read the football scores, too, but the rest of the time it was just hoops. True basketball parents, they were. Both of them knew who the best high school teams and players were, could name the top twenty men's and women's teams in college ball, made it to as many of their daughters' games as possible. Before we'd gotten our licenses, our parents had driven us the thirty-odd miles to Cerritos every Saturday and Sunday, where we both had spring league games in the morning and AAU practice in the afternoon. My father's dedication had upset a couple of the women he'd dated before Claudia. They'd been of the opinion that he was wasting a great deal of time chauffeuring me around Southern California and a great deal of money sending me to Nationals—time and money which they maintained would have been better spent on them. But he saw all of this expenditure as an investment—fork over a couple of hundred bucks every summer for camps and Nationals now, and get your daughter's education paid for later. Claudia saw things the same way.

After we'd finished eating, we moved out to the living room, where we drank coffee and read the rest of the Sunday *Times*. The paper got so strewn about that you could barely see the carpet beneath it. It always took us at least an hour to work through the thing, an hour in which the only sound made by any of us was the occasional rustling of paper. That morning the dog came in, nuzzled Raina on the shoulder, turned around three times and sat down. She usually joined these family gatherings, taking advantage of the late morning sunlight. For some reason she always lay on the Calendar section, as if she could read the title; we joked that she must have been an entertainer of some sort in a past life. From the stereo came the voice of Billie Holiday singing "Embraceable You." I read sporadically and contemplated the dying carnations on the coffee table, which had been a good-luck present from Toni for Raina's first game.

Raina read the paper while lying on her stomach, feet sticking into the air. Her feet were surprisingly large, as if all the extra inches and bulges that had been spared from the rest of her had sunk down and reconvened below her ankles. She put one fist on top of the other and rested her chin on it, which made her look very thoughtful and very young at the same time. I glanced at her around the edge of my paper as often as I could. I was trying to memorize her face. Every morning when I left her I forgot what she looked like, and every day when I returned I was surprised again at her beauty. It was as if consciously trying to recall her image was exactly what chased it away.

I doubt her reunions with me were quite so dramatic. We measured the progress of our relationship, I imagine, quite differently. For her, I suppose, our relationship just existed, a uniform whole that was not particularly altered by new incidents or occurrences. But for me each new development was something to take apart and analyze endlessly, both for its own meaning and for the light it cast on our relationship as a whole. I took her words and actions away with me and sifted through them like a stack of papers. Did she hold that smile a little too long at dinner last night because I told a particularly funny joke, or was she pleased with me for some other reason? Did she sigh like that in the living room because she was bored with the TV program, or because she was bored with me? And what about that frown while we were doing our homework last night? And that strange nod of approval when I scored on her at the park? And her refusal to speak at breakfast the other day?

She must have known how huge a part she played in my life, but if so, she never mentioned it. It was as if we had an unspoken agreement not to deal with the issue of my feelings. For my part, I never brought it up—I just didn't have that kind of courage, nor did I have the strength to withstand an outright rejection. And if I didn't want to talk about it, then she'd keep quiet, too; she'd never do anything to embarrass me or make me uncomfortable. I realize this pact of silence did not indicate a great deal of courage, in either of us. I also realize that being unable to express my feelings may have actually served to make them all the stronger. But those feelings were complicated, and I'm not sure that I could have explained them, even if I had wanted to. As much as I loved Raina, I always limited what I imagined could happen between us, and I wouldn't allow myself to hope she'd want me back. My goal was not to win her; I wasn't trying to achieve her. What I wanted, more than anything, was to *deserve* her.

CHAPTER 9

Normally, the end of the football season brought rest and relief for my father. He would be sad about it—especially if he was particularly attached to that year's group of seniors—but after a week or two, I could see the pressure lift off him, and he would ease into a slower pace of life. My senior year, though, his level of stress only seemed to increase once the season was over. His team's banquet was held the week of my opening game, and the players had chosen Eddie Nuñez as the Most Improved Player and a linebacker as the MVP. Eric Henderson went home empty-handed, and Larry Henderson had been so upset that he wouldn't even speak to my father—believing, apparently, that he had influenced the vote. Once the banquet was over and the team had officially disbanded until spring practice, the drama moved off the football field and permeated the rest of my father's life.

One night a few days after the banquet, Raina and I were upstairs doing homework in her room. In addition to the pen she held in her hand, there was one behind her ear and another sticking out of her mouth; she insisted that the extra pens helped her concentrate. I was just about to ask if I could borrow an eraser when I heard my father come in from school. He went directly to the kitchen, where Claudia was sitting, and I decided to take a break and say hello. I walked down the stairs in my stocking feet, but as I was about to turn the corner, I heard my father's voice. And there was something about it, a strange nakedness, which prevented me from taking another step.

". . . his progress report," I heard him say to Claudia. "So Larry called me in this morning and asked what was the meaning of this, and I told him that it was exactly like I wrote: Eric's work had not been satisfactory for the first half of the semester, and if I gave him a grade now it would be a D, and if he didn't improve in the remaining few weeks he was in danger of failing the class."

"How much weight does a progress report have?" I heard Claudia ask.

"None. It's just a thing we give all the parents halfway through each semester in order to tell them how their kids are doing. But that was just the first of many things that happened today."

At this point, Ann came around the corner. Delighted to find me, she grabbed a toy and crouched down into a play bow. When I didn't respond, she gave me a hurt look and went back toward the kitchen, and I had the sudden irrational fear that she'd tell the parents I was eavesdropping.

"So, what else happened?" Claudia asked.

I heard my father sigh. "Well, last week, this kid came to see me—not a football player, just a kid who's in one of my classes. And he told me he'd been in a history class with Eric Henderson last year, and that Eric somehow managed to get a C in the class even though he failed all the tests. And their teacher was Jennifer Corbitt, who is not an easy grader."

Claudia was silent for a moment. "You think maybe something strange went on?"

"I didn't know," my father said. "I didn't know what could

have happened. So I went and talked to Jennifer this afternoon." He paused, and I imagined he took a sip of whatever drink was sitting in front of him. "Jennifer's a good woman, and we're pretty much friends—we grab a beer together now and then after a staff meeting—so I figured she'd be straight with me. I asked if it was true that Eric Henderson had failed all his tests last year but still passed the class, and she said yes, it was true, and I asked her how. And she looked at me kind of funny and said, 'I thought you were in on this,' and I said no, I wasn't in on anything. And she told me that actually, originally, she'd given Eric an F. But then last June, the day after she'd turned in her final grades, Larry Henderson came in to see her while she was cleaning up her room. And Jennifer said that Larry told her she should reconsider Eric's grade. Jennifer refused at first, but then Larry got threatening and said that he could arrange for her to lose her job. And what could she do, you know? She has three kids. She couldn't afford to risk getting fired."

"Jesus," Claudia said. "Why didn't she go to the principal?"

"That's what I said, too. I said, 'Jennifer, why'd you let him get away with that? Why didn't you go talk to Dr. Shelton?'"

"And what did she say?"

"And she looked at me and kind of laughed and said, 'Wendell, Dr. Shelton was *with* him.'"

There was a moment of loud silence. Then I heard Claudia say, "Oh, my God." She was quiet for another moment and then asked, "What are you going to do?"

My father sighed. "I don't know. I mean, Eric's not failing my class at the moment, but I'm sure as hell not going to pass the kid if he doesn't deserve to be passed. And frankly, I'd be *happy* if he flunked. That would make him ineligible to play next year, and then the quarterback question would be settled."

"Well, what about Eddie?" Claudia asked. "What kind of student is he?"

"He's decent. B student. Nothing spectacular, but nowhere near failing."

"What does he think of all the stuff that's going on?"

"He doesn't know about the grade thing, of course. And as for the playing situation, I don't know. I talked to him after our end-of-the-season team meeting, and he seems to think that if he just keeps improving and outplays Eric in spring practice, Larry'll have to see the light and let him play." My dad sighed. "He's a good kid, and I don't think he wants to believe that someone would hurt him intentionally. It's the other kids who are more cynical. And pissed."

Just then we heard the sharp cracks of gunfire. It sounded like it was several blocks away, not immediately threatening, but I still jumped about a foot off the ground. The parents stood up and started to walk toward the living room, so I scrambled up the stairs and into my room. I heard them check to make sure that the front door was locked, and then my father called up to Raina and me. We left our rooms and went downstairs to join them, Raina still with one pen behind her ear. There was no more gunfire, but we all stayed sitting around the table for a while, drinking coffee and talking in quiet voices. I wondered if my father would tell me about the events of his day. He didn't. His mood for the rest of the night was sober and quiet, and Claudia kept looking at him, and touching his arm, and kissing the top of his head. I tried not to bother him, and surprised myself—and everyone else—by giving him a hug before I went up to bed. A few minutes later, as I stood in the bathroom brushing my teeth, I wondered why I'd done that. It was because he'd looked so sad, I guessed, because he seemed to need it. But it was more than that, I realized. It was because I was proud of him.

Claudia had her own bad news just two days later. Raina and I got home from the park that night around seven, as we always did; my father was in a meeting at school. When we walked into the living room, we found Claudia yelling into the phone, and she was so worked up she didn't bother to switch phones or to lower her voice.

"Yes, exactly, Rochelle," she was saying. "She called and left a message at five, when she knew no one would be here. And she said she wasn't sure that I was suitable to give a talk at the conference. I mean, what the hell does that mean, 'suitable'?"

She was pacing back and forth, and didn't acknowledge us. Her face looked grim, her shoulders were tight, and her hair stuck out in tufts, as if she'd been pulling it.

"Well, that's what I'm saying," she continued. "She didn't even have the guts to tell me to my face. She doesn't like the man I live with, so she doesn't want me to speak at her event. I mean, what are we in, here? Second grade?"

Claudia finally looked up and saw us and made a wild gesture with her arm; I wasn't sure if she was waving hello to us, or telling us to leave. We started to walk away, toward the kitchen, and I could hear the buzz of Rochelle's voice through the phone. "Well, it isn't that simple, you know?" said Claudia. "She told the speakers' committee that I was being uncooperative and confrontational, so what am I supposed to do? Meet with each person on the committee and say that the chairperson's got a problem with my boyfriend? That'd make *me* look spiteful. And besides, I don't want to go behind her back like that."

I looked behind me, and saw Claudia nodding. "I know, I know, this is really unfair. But just because someone's doing me wrong doesn't mean I should act the same way."

Raina and I were in the kitchen by now, and Claudia's voice was slightly muted. "What the hell was *that* all about?" asked Raina, and I looked at her, surprised. Then I realized that she didn't know how Paula felt about my father; she hadn't had the luxury of eavesdropping.

"I don't know," I answered. "Ask your mom."

We poured glasses of Coke, and turned on *M*A*S*H,* to drown out Claudia's voice. As I stared at the screen, not really following the story, I wondered what *Raina* thought about her mother being with my father—and what she thought of my father in general, and of me.

The next Friday, a big group of us decided to see a movie. Telisa and Shavon said they'd pick up Q and then meet us at the theater in Manhattan Beach. Raina and I had an early dinner at home, eating the food that my father had made for us before he and Claudia left for the weekend—chicken-fried rice, and inari-zushi, rice packed into two-inch bean curd pockets that looked like little footballs. Then I fed the dog, who started tapping me with her paw at exactly 6:30, as she did every night to demand her dinner.

"She's like an alarm clock," Raina commented, "only cuter, and she don't need batteries, and you gotta walk her twice a day."

"And more importantly," I added, "she don't believe in getting up early."

We piled all our dishes in the sink, and decided to do them in the morning. Then the phone rang. I thought it was Stacy—we were supposed to give her a ride—but when I picked up the phone and said, "Hey," the voice on the other end said, "Lemme talk to Raina." I stood there for a moment, weighing the benefits of telling Toni that I didn't appreciate her rudeness, but in the end I just held out the receiver.

Raina took it, put it up to her ear, turned toward the sliding glass door. "Hey," she said, and the tone of her voice—happy, loving, intimate—made me turn and leave the room. I didn't know what to do with myself, so I took the dog on a quick walk. When we got back, Raina was still on the phone, but now I could hear her all the way from the door.

"Well, why *not?*" she said, and her voice sounded distressed. "It's not like you got anything *else* to do in the afternoons! Or maybe you *do,* and I just don't know about it!" She stopped talking, but I could hear her pacing back and forth, and I wondered what had happened while I was gone. "Well, *fine* then!" she yelled. "*Maybe* I'll see you later!" She slammed the phone down, and stormed into the living room, almost running me over. "Uh, hey," she said, composing herself. I'd seen her face, though. In the moment before she'd realized I was there, it had been furious, churning, naked.

"Are you O.K.?" I asked, stepping forward.

"I'm fine," she said. "Let's go."

I stepped closer. "Are you sure? I mean, like, do you wanna talk or anything?"

She glanced at me, startled, offended. "No . . . just leave me . . . I mean . . . no."

I pulled back, afraid that I'd overstepped my bounds, not entirely sure that she wasn't going to hit me. She put her jacket on, and yanked the zipper up like she wanted to hurt it. Then she walked out of the house and down to my father's car.

I followed her, got into the driver's seat, reached over and unlocked the passenger door. Raina got in and sat there with her arms crossed. As I backed out of the driveway I narrowly missed hitting the crack lady, who just kept walking without turning to look at us even though I'd come within an inch of her legs. In the rearview mirror I saw the indifferent swing of her bandanna, the way her hands seemed too large for her skinny arms. Raina wasn't saying anything. I took a few deep breaths to collect myself, and then drove over to the Lennox area to collect Stacy.

Stacy lived in a loud neighborhood—her place sat in the shadow of the 405 freeway, and was right beneath the constant stream of planes descending toward the airport. Her house was a one-story place with three bedrooms; there were seven kids in the family, and a grandchild on the way. Stacy's dad was in jail, but I didn't know why, and nobody dared to ask. Her mother worked at Hughes Aircraft, and I think she expected Stacy, as the oldest, to act as the surrogate adult when she wasn't around. Stacy only sporadically stepped into this role—yelling at the little ones every so often for making too much noise, halfheartedly asserting that maybe the older ones should do some homework—but since these commands were so irregular, and came without enforcement, the kids tended not to pay much attention. This frustrated their oldest sister, which, in turn, angered their harried mother. The household was in constant chaos, and so Stacy stayed out of it as much as she could.

We drove through Stacy's 'hood slowly, noting how different it felt from ours. The houses were smaller and more dilapidated, there were huge craters in the streets, and every block had at least one empty lot filled with trash and old furniture. Skinny dogs ran through the streets, their coats covered with dirt, and sniffed at piles of garbage which sat uncollected on the curbs. Small buildings that had once housed liquor shops or corner markets had been converted into storefront churches. "Jesus Saves," said the hand-painted sign on one of them. "Sinners, Pray For Your Forgiveness," said another. There were other signs, too, but they were in Spanish and I couldn't read them; gradually, the blacks were trickling out of the area, and being replaced by people from Mexico and Central America. Although the entire 'hood was unsafe at night, Stacy's block was especially hazardous—there was a shut-down school across from her house, whose open-air halls, which you couldn't see from the street, were used for drug transactions and gang meetings. Several shootings had occurred there in the last few years. And once, when a group of Latino gangbangers was scattered by the sudden appearance of the police, three young guys had forced their way into Stacy's house. They sat Stacy and two of her sisters down on the couches, pressed guns to their sides, and told the girls that if the cops came banging on the door, the girls had better swear the guys had been there all day. The cops never came, though, and the gangbangers left without further incident, one of them feeling so bad about scaring the girls that he promised to watch out for their house. He kept his word. Within the next six months he chased a burglar away, and then returned the radio that an acquaintance of his had stolen from Mrs. Gatling's car.

Nicki, Stacy's sister, pulled open their front door, then unlocked the thick metal screen door and backed up to let us in. Nicki had played basketball the year before, but she'd quit the team over the summer because she was pregnant. That night she looked tremendous, inflated, like the baby was going to pop out at any second, even though she wasn't due for another three months.

"Hey, ladies, wassup?" she said when she saw us. "Y'all gonna sign with a college, or what?"

"We plan to," Raina answered, sounding serious.

"That's great, homegirls," Nicki said, touching her stomach. "You better not fuck up, now. We all countin on you to make it."

"Girl, give it up," came Stacy's voice from behind her. Then Stacy herself appeared. "Who're *you* to be givin people advice?"

"I can say what I want, Ms. Thang," Nicki replied, punching Stacy on the shoulder. "And *you* better not fuck up, either."

"Hey. Who the older sister here?"

"Yeah, yeah," Nicki said, pushing Stacy toward the door. "Get the fuck outta here and go see your movie."

We said goodbye and walked down to the car. Although it was warm that night, we rolled up all the windows. This was a precaution against carjackers, who were more likely to approach cars with open windows so they could stick the gun directly in your face. I was more afraid of getting carjacked than I was of anything else; in the last six months alone, both Q's sister and Pam's mother had relinquished their cars to armed young thieves at quiet intersections, and I couldn't get into a car anymore without thinking about what had happened to them. There were many little rules, besides the window rule, for driving in our parts of L.A.—like leaving space between yourself and the car stopped in front of you in order to have room for a quick getaway; and not pulling all the way up at an intersection, so you had a clear view of all the people on the corners. I don't know if my friends were as scared of carjackers as I was, but Raina and Stacy didn't seem too worried that night. During the twenty-minute drive to Manhattan Beach, Raina sat in the front seat quietly, while Stacy chattered on and on. I glanced at her in the rearview mirror. Stacy was O.K.-looking, but she had a sweet, unassuming smile which increased her attractiveness and undercut all her efforts at coolness. Although she was taller than Raina, she'd always seemed shorter to me—less at home in her body, and in the world. The expression on her face that night was open and happy; her wet, heavy curls were like living things on either side of her face. She was telling us about a new job she had lined up, in the accounting office of a friend of her mother's.

"I'm gonna work there during Christmas vacation," she said, "and maybe some weekends. Then starting in January, I'll be workin every day after school."

"What about practice?" Raina asked.

"I'll just go after practice," Stacy said. She slid down and put her foot over the top of Raina's seat. "But I'm hella excited about this. Now that I'm eighteen, I think it's time I started makin some real money—especially with Nicki's baby on the way. My mama's always talkin 'bout I don't do nothin for the family—'cept steal a package of diapers now and then." She laughed. "But I'll be able to help her out now, I'll be gettin a paycheck. And this is an *office* job, you know what I'm sayin? No more flippin hamburgers and shit!"

"That's great, Stace," I said. Then I started to ponder the fact that she'd turned eighteen. She was the first of us to cross that invisible threshold into adulthood; she could vote now, and join the army, and legally drink in certain states. In the course of one day, she'd taken on a burden of expectation and responsibility that was too overwhelming for me to think about, and that I certainly did not want to feel.

Raina had no further comment, and I wondered where her mind was; she must still have been thinking about Toni. I looked at Stacy in the mirror again and she was staring out the window, keeping time with the music on the radio. I hoped her job would work out, and that she'd go to a junior college. I hoped she would be all right.

When we got to the theater in Manhattan Beach, it took ten minutes before I could find a parking space among all the Porsches and BMWs. Compared to these cars, my father's creaky old Mustang looked like a bum who'd crashed a cocktail party. I noticed that the trees and grass here were a lush green, and not the yellowish tan which was the prevailing color of vegetation in the less affluent areas of L.A. The cement was smooth, uncracked, and free of trash. Manhattan Beach was an upper-middle-class white community, and going there was like stepping onto the set of one of those snobby, glamorous TV shows I alternately laughed at and resented. We sometimes went to movies there because the theaters were nice, and because it felt like a field trip for us. It all looked vaguely unreal to me that night. People were not particularly dressed up—they wore polo shirts, blouses, khakis—but you could tell they'd spent a lot of money on looking casual. They talked and laughed and flipped their hair as if they were on camera. Adults were trying hard to act sprightly and young, parents were attempting to be cooler than their kids. I saw women in their forties wearing the tight, tapered jeans that were favored by their teenage daughters. I heard fifty-year-old men refer to each other as "dude."

We walked toward the crowd lined up in front of the theater, and I found my friends right away; they were easy to spot among the swarms of white people.

"Yo, wassup?" Telisa called out when she saw us. "What y'all doin here?"

"We just thought we'd catch a movie tonight," I said.

"What you come to see?"

"Jumpin' Jack Flash."

"Well, that's convenient," Shavon said, "'cos we just happened to buy three extra tickets."

"Cool," I said. "It can be like the family night out at the movies."

"Hey," Q protested, smiling. "Speak for yourself. Ain't all of us here in the family."

We made introductions—Shavon hadn't met Raina or Stacy—and then stood in line to get into the theater. I could tell right away that Stacy liked Shavon—she was grinning, and looking at her kind of slyly, and there was a teasing lilt in her voice when she spoke. There was a lot for her to like. Shavon was one of the stars of the track team, and her body, a sprinter's body, was muscular and tight. She had a smooth, open, caramel-colored face, with wide cheekbones and bright hazel eyes. Like Telisa, she was a good student, only without the smart mouth my teammate had. Shavon was mature and stable, too, and sometimes, when I was feeling especially playful or envious of their personal attributes, I'd suggest that she and Telisa were hoarding all the good qualities that one could want in a girlfriend, and that they should split up and distribute the wealth. I didn't really mean this, though. Anyone could see that they were great together. Sometimes I'd catch them looking at each other, and it was such a loving, private look that I always felt like I was spying, and turned away.

"We should all go out sometime," Stacy said as we were waiting. "Get a big group of people and hit a club."

"That'd be fun," Shavon said, smiling at Telisa.

"Yeah," I agreed.

Telisa looked at me, surprised. "But Nancy, you don't *like* clubs."

"Well, maybe I just ain't been to the right ones," I said. Telisa was right—I *didn't* like clubs, but I wish she hadn't told everyone. What I was hoping was that we could set up a night to go out, and that Raina would agree to come, too. Raina, however, was unresponsive.

"Well, *I'll* take you out," Stacy said to me. "No one ever sees you. You gotta stop it with this incognito shit."

I muttered something noncommittal and looked past her, straight into some familiar faces. Four girls were staring at us from beneath yellow hair and furrowed pale foreheads; their expressions varied from curious to hostile.

"Yo, T," I said, tapping Telisa's shoulder with the back of my hand. "Who those girls over there?"

Telisa took her eyes off of Shavon long enough to look at them. "I'm sure we've played against 'em," she said, scratching her neck. "Ain't they from Mira Costa?"

"Yeah, I think you're right," I said. I remembered them more clearly now; they were on the team we had scrimmaged against. The tallest one, who was about my height, was their center—the girl with the deadly ponytail—and the shortest one, who was about 5'5", was their point guard and leading scorer, the girl who'd asked Telisa how much money her father made. The two others were also starters, but they weren't very good; they basically supported the other two, acted as filler. All of them were wearing Guess? jeans, and high-top Reebok aerobic shoes. The three smaller ones wore light sweaters in pastel colors. The center had on a crimson Harvard sweatshirt.

They were staring at us so openly that finally Stacy raised a hand and yelled, "Wassup?"

Their faces registered surprise momentarily; then the little point guard whispered something and they all began to laugh. I was suddenly aware of the holes in my no-name jeans, of my cheap sweater and scuffed-up shoes.

"Fuckin prissy white girls," said Telisa.

Then two boys walked up and joined the girls. One of the boys, a tall, streaked-blond surfer type in a green-and-red striped polo shirt, put his arm around the center. The other, a shorter, bulkier guy with dark hair and thick eyebrows, hugged one of the ineffective starters, a girl with the broad pink face and upturned nose of a pig. The girls began to chatter to the guys, and pointed in our direction. The boys turned and looked over at us, and there was disdain in the blond boy's eyes, and also annoyance, as if we were a pile of garbage that had been left on his lawn. Then all six of them closed in and formed a little circle, drawing their wagons together.

"Well excuse the fuck out of us for livin," said Shavon, shaking her head in disbelief.

Stacy tried to talk more about going out to a club sometime, but she didn't get much of a response. We were all feeling a little deflated. Because we'd just faced some overt hostility, we'd suddenly become more conscious of us as a little island of color in a huge sea of white—even more so than we'd been when we'd first arrived. And my personal discomfort had another dimension. I was also more aware than I normally was of the difference between me and my friends. It's not that I ever forgot who

I was, or that I wanted to. But I had no history yet—or rather, no sense of the history that I had. I was trying hard to be accepted, which meant trying to be black; I didn't know, yet, what it meant to be Japanese.

Because the people in my own 'hood were so used to me by then, it was only when we ventured out into other areas—whatever the racial makeup—that I became uncomfortably aware of how out of place I must have seemed. I wondered, that night, how we looked in those white people's eyes—like a unified group of kids of color, or like five black girls and one random Asian kid. Q was half-Vietnamese, but her Asian features—her roundish face, flat nose, and slightly narrow eyes—were only apparent if you really looked, and she was darker than many people with two black parents. These subtleties were lost on most white people, anyway—I'd heard them call her a nigger but I'd never heard anyone call her a gook.

When we were finally let in, we went to the left side of the theater and the Mira Costa kids, thankfully, to the right. I tried to maneuver myself so I could sit next to Raina, but my attempts to get close to her failed. Stacy sat between us, and I paid more attention, at times, to her and Raina than I did to what Whoopi Goldberg was doing on the screen. I situated myself so that my shoulder was leaning in Raina's direction. Some part of me—an ear, a leg, a shoulder, a hip—was always leaning towards her, as if pulled by some magnetic force; I couldn't manage to hold myself completely upright when Raina was anywhere close. Stacy and Raina whispered to each other every few minutes, and although I strained to hear, nothing reached me but an occasional chuckle. I wanted to be in on the conversation, too, and found myself annoyed at Stacy for not including me, for sitting between us, for talking to Raina at all.

After the movie was over, we all stumbled out into the lobby. I felt groggy, uncertain, like I'd just woken up from a dream. We stood in front of the snack counter for a while, discussing the scene where Whoopi's sparkling blue dress got eaten by the paper shredder. Finally, Stacy looked at her watch.

"It's still early," she said. "Y'all wanna go out?"

"Naw," Telisa said, putting her arm around Shavon and grinning. "Shavon's dad's out of town this weekend and she's supposed to dog-sit, so we're gonna go chill at his place."

Shavon raised her eyebrows at Telisa and smiled. "What makes you think I'm gonna take *you?*"

We laughed.

"I don't wanna go out, either," said Raina. "I gotta go meet up with Toni." I just looked at her; I couldn't believe that she was seeing Toni that night after the fight I'd overheard.

Telisa turned to her. "Hey, Toni's place ain't that far from where we're goin. You want us to give you a ride?"

"Sure."

I was disappointed that Raina was leaving, but Telisa couldn't have known not to offer. Then I thought that maybe it was better the way that things had turned out—*I* certainly didn't want to deliver Raina to her girlfriend.

After the rest of us had also declined the offer to go out, Stacy, Telisa, and I went into the bathroom. Stacy and Telisa grabbed the two empty stalls, and I waited for a moment until one of the others freed up. A few seconds later, just as I had gotten into a stall, I heard the voices of the Mira Costa girls. I peered out through the crack in the door and saw all four of them enter the bathroom. The point guard went up to the sink and looked at herself in the mirror; the center stood to the right of her and the two others to the left. They'd been talking about the movie, but then the center shook her head as she pulled a compact out of her purse.

"I can't believe those Inglewood players are here," she said.

The pig-faced girl leaned toward the mirror, mascara in hand. "Yeah, it *is* a coincidence, huh?"

"No, I mean I can't believe they're in Manhattan *Beach,*" the center said. "If you ask me, they shouldn't even be allowed to *come* here."

The pig-faced girl turned to her. "Who cares, Kristi? Relax."

"Yeah, really," said the fourth girl, who was Stacy's height, and skinny. "What's your problem? This is a movie theater, not a private club or something."

"I'm with Kristi," said the point guard, who'd just applied some rose-colored blush. "You don't see us going to Inglewood, do you? So why should people from Inglewood come here?"

The pig-faced girl shook her head. "That's stupid, Dana."

"No, it's not," said the point guard. "If those girls want to see a movie, they should see it in their own damn neighborhood." She smirked. "Except they probably don't even *have* theaters in Ingle-watts."

With that, I burst out of my stall. Telisa came out of her stall, too. The four Mira Costa girls spun around and looked at us, wide-eyed. There were a couple of older women in the bathroom, standing at other sinks, and when they saw us they scooted out quickly.

Telisa went right up to Dana, the point guard. "You know," she said calmly, "maybe if you didn't spend so much time in front of the mirror, you'd be a better basketball player."

Dana stood her ground and considered Telisa distastefully. "Well, maybe if you didn't spend so much time playing basketball, you'd be a better student."

I laughed out loud. "She couldn't *be* a better student," I said. "She's probably gonna be first in our class this year."

The center, Kristi, snorted. "*That's* not saying much."

Stacy threw open the door to her stall and charged over to the sinks. She pulled Kristi away from the mirror, and pointed her finger like a sword in the girl's face. "You wanna take this outside?" she asked.

Kristi backed off, looking scared. The three others just stood there. Telisa and I each grabbed one of Stacy's arms and pulled her out of the bathroom. "Forget it, Stace," I said. "She ain't even worth it."

Raina, Shavon, and Q were all standing by the popcorn machine, and they looked at us quizzically as we approached. "What happened?" Raina asked.

"We kinda got into it with those Mira Costa girls," I said.

"Did you kick their asses?"

"Yeah," Telisa said. "We flushed their heads down the toilet."

"Good for you," said Shavon, as we all moved toward the door.

My car and Telisa's car were in the same section of the parking lot, so we all walked out together. There were even more cars now, driving back and forth, people trying to find spaces for the ten o'clock shows. It was cloudy that night, but the breeze was warm and pleasant, and we walked along slowly, talking about some of the other movies we'd like to see. Telisa had her arm around Shavon, and I was keeping pace with Raina, thinking I'd give anything to walk along with her like that.

Just as we turned the corner to the row where our cars were parked, we heard a loud male voice yell, "Hey!" We all turned, and saw the two boys who were with the Mira Costa girls. The blond one was walking towards us purposefully, one step ahead of the dark-haired boy, who looked more reluctant. The girls themselves were a few feet behind.

The guys stopped just short of us, and the blond one glared at each of us, one by one. "I heard you punks were threatening the girls here."

Telisa put her hands on her hips and thrust her chin out. "We weren't threatening 'em. Shit. We were just havin a conversation. If we'd of threatened 'em, they'd be *runnin* by now."

"I don't care what you call it," the boy said, narrowing his eyes. "You just don't *talk* to them like that."

The other boy, who was standing a couple of feet behind him, reached out and tugged his arm. "Brent, come on," he said. "Forget it."

"Yeah, c'mon y'all," said Raina, to us. "Let's leave these fools alone."

The blond boy, Brent, shook his friend's hand off. "I don't *want* to forget it, Rick," he said. Then he turned to us. "Now why don't you just get the fuck out of here and go back to where you came from?"

Telisa crossed her arms and looked back at him. "Free country," she said.

Brent looked her up and down, and then crossed his own arms. "Yeah, well some people were never meant to be free."

Shock and anger bubbled up in my throat.

"Jesus, Brent," said Rick.

We all took a step toward Brent, as if by agreement; our shoulders tightened and we clenched our fists. "You say something like that again," Telisa hissed, eyes narrowed, "and I'm gonna have to fuck you up."

Brent laughed. "You can't scare me, you bitch. Don't you know where you are?" He gestured to his friends and then pointed at me, smiling. "Look, it's a Japanese nigger."

My breath caught, and I wasn't sure which aspect of his epithet most enraged me, but I knew that I wanted to kill him. I tried to yell or swear, but my mouth would not work.

Telisa spat out, "*Fuck* you, motherfucka."

Behind the boys, the pig-faced girl looked angry. "Come *on,* Brent," she said. "Stop being such an asshole. Let's just get out of here and leave them alone."

Brent turned and looked at her. "Just stay out of this, O.K.?" Then he turned back to us. "Ooohh," he said, grinning and pretending to shake. "I'm scared."

"You should be," Telisa said. "You really think you got a chance against the six of us?"

"No problem," he said. "Maybe if you were a *real* man, we'd think twice before we messed with you, but you're not, you're just a weak imitation." I wondered if he meant what I thought he did, and if so, why he had singled out Telisa. Then I realized that she and Shavon, the affectionate couple, were the only ones who were obviously gay. He turned to Shavon. "Hey, baby, you're pretty cute," he said, in an oily voice that made my skin crawl. "You need to get fucked by a *real* man instead of some imitation man like her."

Shavon crossed her arms and glared at him. "She's imitation

nothin," she said. "And she knows how to please a woman better than a fake-macho, perfume-sweatin, surfboard-ridin, trust-fund-livin, limp-dicked glass of lukewarm milk like you *ever* will."

Brent looked like he'd been slapped. "*What* did you say?"

Telisa smiled, but there was no humor in her face. "You heard her, motherfucka," she said.

He took a step forward, and so did she, and we all moved in closer, getting ready to fight. Then we heard a car pull up behind us. We turned to look at it, and stepped away from each other: it was the Manhattan Beach police.

"Problem, kids?" asked the cop on the passenger side, a beefy blond guy in his thirties.

"Yeah, there is," Brent answered, looking annoyed. "These bitches have been harassing our girlfriends." The four girls, who'd been standing well behind the two boys, slowly drew up closer to them now; Rick and all of the girls looked relieved.

"Aw, man, give it up," Telisa said, and I grabbed her arm, telling her with my touch to keep quiet.

The two cops got out of the car, and the driver, who was older and graying, came around to the passenger side. "Do you want to tell me how this started?" he asked.

He'd been addressing Telisa, but it was Brent who answered. "They were all in the bathroom together, and *these* people," he said, gesturing at us, "these goddamn *hoodlums* started threatening the girls here."

"That's bullshit!" Telisa insisted, half to him, and half to the cops. "We were just in there usin the bathroom, and they started sayin a bunch of fucked-up shit about us!"

The younger cop, the beefy one, turned toward her slowly, and it was like watching a mountain move. "You need to clean up your language, missy."

Telisa's mouth dropped. "What you talkin about? *That* asshole just swore," she said, pointing at Brent, who was sneering.

The young cop moved his arm slightly, rested his hand on his billy club. "I don't like your attitude," he said. "Maybe you could use a night in jail to cool down." He looked at us, smiled slightly, and I caught a glimpse of his white teeth. "We've got lots of room in the slammer," he said. "Maybe you could *all* spend the night."

Brent began to snicker, as did Kristi and Dana. Dana stuck her tongue out at us, and it took a great effort not to go over and punch her. We all stood there silently for a moment, until finally the older cop, who'd been looking at me the whole time, stepped forward and addressed me.

"Hey, aren't you Nancy Takahiro?" he asked.

Everyone, including his partner, stopped and stared at him.

I looked at him uncertainly. "Yes."

The older cop smiled, and took a few more steps in my direction. He had a stern face with blunt features, but his eyes were warm and friendly. "My daughter plays for South Torrance," he said. "I saw you play in their tournament last year. You had thirty-four points against Long Beach Poly in the final. It was a beautiful thing to see."

I smiled a little, and felt relief wash through my chest like spring rain. "Thanks," I said. "Yeah, I really like that tournament."

The older cop threw his head back and laughed. "I'll bet you do," he said. "You guys win it every year. Pretty soon they're going to have to stop inviting you back. I'm Michael Donaghy by the way," he said.

The younger cop, his partner, just glared at him and didn't say anything. Brent, Dana, and Kristi all looked furious.

"Nice to meet you," I said, shaking Donaghy's hand. Then I pointed toward my teammates. "That's Telisa Coles, our point guard, and Q . . . I mean . . . Shaundra Murray, our center."

"Oh, right," Donaghy said, nodding. "I recognize you now. Nice to meet you."

They looked at him a little suspiciously, mumbled, "Nice to meet you, too."

I gave Donaghy a big smile. I wasn't sure whether he was reacting simply to my basketball status, or to the fact that I was Asian and not black—after all, almost everyone else in our group, including Raina, another star, had also played in that particular tournament. This was not the time to ponder these issues, though. My more immediate concern was getting us out of there as fast as possible, so I decided to press whatever advantage I had. I smiled even more widely now, and pointed toward the others. "And that's Shavon Stevens, our buddy, and Raina Webber and Stacy Gatling, who play for Leuzinger."

He greeted them, too, and they nodded. "Listen," he said, "I'm sorry about this misunderstanding here tonight." He made a sweeping gesture that included the Mira Costa kids. "I know you young people have got a lot of steam to blow off. But have some *fun,* for God's sake. Don't waste your energy on being mad at each other. Go on home, now, all of you, and don't let me catch you causing a big ruckus like this again." He'd addressed this last part to Brent, sternly, and now he turned to me. "It was a pleasure to meet you, Nancy," he said. "Good luck in college next year."

CHAPTER 10

At nine o'clock the following Monday, Raina and I threw on our workout clothes and headed out into the night. We ran hundred-yard sprints up and down the street, gasping painfully at times but never stopping. We did defensive slides and jump shot drills, shot hundreds of lay-ups and free throws. The air was cool, and fresh because it was winter; if you breathed in deeply and closed your eyes, you could almost smell the ocean. There were a few stars in the grayish black night, but they seemed blurred or diluted, as if we were looking at them through wax. I loved playing at night. The darkness made it seem as if the rest of the world had fallen away; as if we were taking part in some private ritual. The gusts of wind felt cool and refreshing, like wet towels running over my body. We stayed close to the house, in case something happened and we needed to rush inside, but we didn't really think about the possible danger because our attention was focused on the workout. We were dead serious about our task. And I worked harder than usual because I was out there with Raina, who never gave less than a total effort. She needed to achieve and to shine and to have her accomplishments acknowledged; it was as if she feared that if she stopped playing well and receiving recognition, she would somehow cease to exist. This kind of need made her hard to live up to, but it was pushing me to improve. On the previous nights, despite our parents' concern for our safety, we'd gone on like this until 10:30 or 11:00, not speaking except to say "nice shot," or "come on, now," between sprints, drills, baskets.

I often wondered if anyone else—Stacy, Toni—was aware that Raina spent so much time working on her game. How well did her teammates know her? To them, Raina was the usually low-key star who occasionally lapsed into total silliness. After that first time I'd seen her play at my high school, she'd trudged up into the stands with her teammates to watch the next game, the look of intense concentration that had so struck me before completely absent now from her face. She was wearing a red cycling cap, and I saw it bob up and down every few minutes as she threw her head back in laughter. She was the center of attention that afternoon, as she often was when she chose to be, telling stories and cracking everyone up. I liked watching her with her friends, and saw no contradiction between her game-time single-mindedness and her postgame clowning. And that day, she was acting for her teammates, entertaining them, as if it were part of her role, inherent in being team captain. I understood what she was doing, because I did it sometimes myself. But the difference was that her confident comedic act, just like her game-time determination, convinced me, while my own did not.

I'd been surprised, when she moved in, to discover that she spent so much time alone. Also surprised by how absolutely she was committed to basketball. This, they never see, I thought as she sprinted up the block in the soft yellow glow of the streetlight. This they know nothing about. They might have an idea it exists, from repeatedly witnessing the will that carried Raina, and sometimes even them, through the toughest moments of a game or practice. But the preparation, the endless, tireless repetition of even the most monotonous or exhausting drills, the shooting free throws so late into the night that the neighbors leaned out their windows and complained—this they have never laid eyes on.

Basketball—the crisp sound of the ball swishing through the net, the rough feel of leather against my hands. That night, after five straight days of sprints, taking a breath of air was like drinking something luxurious, sweet, and filling. I felt light on my feet; I could tell that I'd dropped three pounds in the last couple of weeks, and that my heart rate was gradually slowing. Our bodies were in the best condition that they would ever be in. But as these after-dinner sessions became a nightly event, I began to wonder if there wasn't more to Raina's obsessiveness than just the need to stay in shape. It seemed to me that Raina saw her body as a tool, as an instrument she could use to get what she really wanted, which, I think now, was validation. I was happy to be pulled along. That winter I could have run or shot or played twenty-four hours a day. There was no better task, no more delicious exhaustion, and Raina was right there beside me.

I suppose we also threw so much of ourselves into these night sessions because we were afraid we'd never play each other in a real game. The competition between us could not be measured or decided on a scoreboard. It was much less direct than that now, or maybe *more* direct, because we didn't have scores or time limits or the presence of other people to interfere with the testing of our wills. It was not a matter of who scored more, or who won; it was a matter of who tried harder, who gave. The former could be affected by a million different variables; the latter was fundamental, unchanging.

It was a competition, though, that Raina won hands down, and I knew this before we even started. There are two main ingredients in the composition of an athlete—ability and degree of commitment. Enough of one can sometimes make up for the lack of the other, as in the case of Larry Bird, who did not possess unusual speed or jumping ability but was still one of the greatest players ever to play the game. I had one of these ingredients—degree of commitment. But Raina had both. And what's more, she even outdid me in the one ingredient I'd always taken pride in—or had used to, until I'd come across her. Raina's drive and discipline made my stomach turn with shame. Sure, I was out there running sprints under the streetlights, too, but the difference was that I would never have been doing this if she weren't there, whereas she would certainly have been doing it if I weren't. I loved basketball, but I could have given less to it, while Raina's love for the game was pure and complete and she did not see anything else. She had the kind of hunger that is necessary for any venture into greatness. But the only thing that I had was her.

That night, after a particularly draining effort, we dragged ourselves into the house around eleven. Raina went upstairs to take a shower, and I headed toward the living room, dribbling the worn-out ball on the linoleum. I was concentrating on the details of our workout—the way Raina had tugged at the bottoms of her shorts between sprints, the way she'd closed her eyes and lifted her face to meet the wind. I thought I should preserve these images, and so I hoarded them away in my memory banks like a squirrel storing nuts for the winter. I don't know how I knew I'd need them later in my life. It was instinct, and I didn't question it.

"Don't bounce that ball in here," Claudia called out from the kitchen. She came into the living room wearing a big blue nightshirt and furry yellow slippers, and joined my father, who was watching the news.

"Sorry," I said, picking up the ball.

My father looked at me, gave a weary sigh. "Don't you two ever get tired?"

I sat down on the carpet and rubbed my calves, which were

starting to cramp. Ann came up and licked the sweat off my chin. "Wassup, homedog?" I said.

"Why can't you just take it easy at night?" my dad continued. "Or do some more homework? I mean you already practiced all afternoon at school."

"And at the park," added Claudia.

"Tournament coming up," I said vaguely.

"You know," my father said, sounding serious, "there are other things in the world besides basketball."

"Like what?" I asked.

"Lots of things."

Claudia sat up straight and looked at me. "It's good to see you and Raina working so hard at something, but sometimes I think you take it too far. It's like you're both afraid that if you let up for even a second, your whole life is going to fall apart."

I stayed silent and kept petting the dog.

Finally Claudia just shook her head. "You two are crazy."

My father reached over and took her fingers into one of his mammoth hands. "Blame it on your daughter," he said. "Nancy doesn't usually take this quite so seriously."

Claudia laughed. "Neither does Raina. She didn't *used* to be this way. I mean, she always took basketball seriously, but not like this. Not to the point where she was doing sprints at eleven o'clock at night."

My father looked at me. "It's just a game, Nancy," he said.

But I didn't react to him right away. I was thinking about what Claudia had said—that Raina didn't used to be this way. She didn't used to go running in the middle of the night. Was her sudden desire to do so completely related to the importance of her senior year and her need to impress the scouts? Or could it possibly have something to do with me? I never knew. Of course I never asked. But I was smiling when I looked back up at my father. "You're right, Dad," I said, "It's just a game."

• • •

I should say that around this time Claudia noticed something. Not anything dramatic, since there was really nothing dramatic to notice—just some tiny clue, or accumulation of clues, which must have let her know that what existed between Raina and me was not your average pseudo step-sibling relationship. I realized this one Saturday morning, after I emerged from my room and joined her at the kitchen table. My father was still in bed.

"Morning," she said. "Raina up yet?"

"Up and gone already."

"Really? Where'd she go?"

"With Toni, I guess. I think they went biking or something."

She lowered her eyes and sighed. Her hair was held back by two silver clips, and her face, free of makeup, seemed lighter. With her head bent like that and the sadness in her face, she suddenly looked her age. I was surprised by this transformation—Claudia usually looked so well-put-together—and sitting there, I realized how little I actually knew her. I had always thought of her primarily as Raina's mother, and then as my father's girlfriend—a girlfriend who was, at that moment, losing a friend because of him. But I didn't even know, really, what she thought about *that.* The woman before me had her own life, her own pains and hopes and fears, and as I watched her looking down at the table that morning, it occurred to me that I had little idea of what they were.

"Everything all right?" I finally asked.

Claudia sighed again, looked at me, looked away. She rubbed her hands together as if they were cold. "I'm not sure Toni is worth all of this . . . effort Raina makes."

We'd never spoken of Toni, or for that matter of anything related to her daughter's personal life, and I was startled that she'd brought her up now. I tried not to show it. "Toni's all right," I lied.

"Maybe," said Claudia. "I worry about Raina, though. She's so intense about things. You both are." She glanced at me. Those intelligent eyes showed both curiosity and concern. She really was a beautiful woman.

I took a sip of my coffee and hid my face behind the mug. "Yeah, well, what do you expect? We're both only children."

"I suppose. I guess I'm just being an oversensitive mother. Maybe it *is* a cliché, Nancy, but I do really only want what's best for her." She paused. "I know that you do, too."

She smiled at me, warmly, and right then I knew that she knew. I have no idea how she figured it out—maybe she was simply more observant than other people. Maybe it was the super-sensors a mother extends toward her only child. Or maybe she just knew a lot about love. At any rate, I was not about to ask her how she'd come to possess this knowledge. I felt a burst of panic that she'd tell my father, but then immediately knew that she wouldn't—both for my sake, but also for his, because Claudia, like Raina, would never make people deal with things they were not yet ready to face. More strangely, as my cheeks flamed, I understood that she preferred me to Toni; I realized she actually approved. Still, the kindness of her smile terrified me. "Of course," I said finally. "Raina's my buddy."

Toni must have noticed something, too. I can think of no other reason for the strange talk she corralled me into about this time. Toni had been coming around to our house semiregularly all that fall, about two or three times a week. I didn't see much of her because she usually just picked Raina up and didn't stay, and on the rare occasions when she was in the house for more than a few minutes, I retreated into my room. I don't think Toni came by as often as Raina might have liked—not because she wasn't particularly welcomed by the rest of us—although she wasn't—so much as because she seemed to have a full social schedule quite outside of her relationship with Raina.

Anyway, I knew that something was up when suddenly Toni started paying attention to me. She had always ignored me before, or said hello distractedly. But then one afternoon in mid-December I came home from practice and found her sitting in the living room with Raina. I was carrying Clyde, but as soon as

I saw that Toni was there, I opened the connecting door to the garage and set him down inside, as if exposure to her would cause contamination. On the coffee table there was a bag of homemade peanut butter cups from a nearby bakery, which Raina loved and which Toni always brought for her when she came.

"Wassup, kiddo?" Toni said when I walked in. This was her usual manner of addressing me, which would have been enough to make me dislike her if I hadn't disliked her already.

"Hey," I said, glancing from her to Raina, who looked sullen, and wondering if I'd interrupted an argument.

"How's the hoops?"

"Good. We're 3 and 0."

"Cool," Toni said, in the tone of voice that people use when they couldn't care less about what you've told them. She sat with her knees spread and her arms extended in either direction on the back of the couch; Toni always took up a lot of space. As we looked at each other, I had the fleeting hope that an earthquake would hit just then, destroying only the wall behind the sofa and burying Toni in the rubble. But earthquakes never happen when you're thinking about them. I often worried that one would hit at a particularly embarrassing time, like when I was taking a shower or sitting on the toilet. I was only slightly more scared of earthquakes than I was of Toni.

"Why don't you go change your clothes, honey?" she said now to Raina, who got up and left the room without acknowledging me.

Toni grinned. "She's pissed at me. People sayin I been runnin around on her."

"Oh, yeah?" I said, looking at a spot on the wall behind her.

"Women," Toni started. Then she cocked her head and looked at me, as if noticing me for the first time. "You got yourself a woman, Nancy?"

"Nope," I said. She knew damned well I didn't.

"Well they keep you busy. They cool, though. Only thing

is, when you got a woman and everybody knows about it, it's like the relationship becomes public property or somethin. People start, like, watchin it, you know? Pickin it apart. Pretty soon you hear it got dragged out at some party, and then the next thing you know people start givin you advice and shit, like Dear fuckin Abby. I don't *like* that mess. You know what I'm sayin?"

"Yeah, I guess so."

"And see, the thing is, Nancy, no matter what people think, no one knows nothin about other people's business. No one knows *shit.* You understand?"

"Yeah," I said. "I understand."

She leaned forward and looked me straight in the eyes, and pressed her fists together, knuckle to knuckle. "No woman could ever mean as much to me as Raina. Ever. You got it?"

I thought, Then why do you shit on her?, but nodded yes.

She kept looking at me, even when Raina returned in street clothes and announced that she was ready. Raina's shoulders were hunched and her face appeared drawn. She wouldn't meet my eyes, but she looked at Toni, despairingly; some pained communication passed between them. The dog trotted in and laid her head on Toni's leg. I felt betrayed. But like I said, Toni had a way with women.

After they left, I wondered about Toni's little tirade. Why had she directed it at me? Did she think that I was one of the people responsible for the blemishing of her image? Well, I wasn't. I never said anything to anyone about Toni—not for her sake, of course, but for Raina's, and also, because I never wanted to be associated with any of the slander that got back to Raina, I suppose for my own as well. I wondered if Toni had just been posturing in her little pledge about Raina, but there was something about the frankness of her stare. Was she telling me the truth? Maybe. And yet she constantly stood Raina up, lied to her, made little effort to hide her interest in other women. I could not explain this behavior, nor could I explain Raina's reasons for putting up with it, beyond the fact that Raina seemed to love people the same way she loved basketball—for themselves, for what they were, and not for what they gave her; not because she expected anything in return. It wasn't even Toni's "running around," though, that made me think she wasn't good enough for Raina; it was that it was clear to me that she didn't understand her.

This was how I saw it, anyway. I could have been wrong. It's a common tactic of spurned lovers to assert that their beloveds' chosen partners aren't capable of understanding them, with the assumption being that *they,* however, are.

On the last Wednesday night before Christmas vacation, I was in my room doing some much-needed studying when I heard Raina come into the house and slam the door. I looked up for a moment from my Courts and Law notes. There was some muffled talking in the dining room; then Raina started trudging up the stairs. I knew she was angry by the sound of her ascent, each step sharp and final as an exclamation point. I thought she'd go straight to her room, as she usually did when she came home upset, but to my surprise I heard a knock on my door.

"Come in," I said, trying to sound like I was deep in thought.

She opened the door and leaned against the frame, her hand still curled around the knob. "Hey. What you doin?"

I looked at her. Her whole body was stiff, and she stood there twisting the doorknob so hard I was afraid it might come off in her hand. It must have been a bad one, I thought, for her to come to the first available person, me, for some company.

"Nothin much," I said.

"You busy?"

"No, not really."

"You wanna go for a drive?"

I had two tests the next day and a math assignment due. To go with her would show a blatant disregard for my studies, and also mean breaking a promise I'd made to my father to be more serious about school. It could result in my failing the tests, and therefore possibly my classes, which in turn would mean I couldn't graduate in June. "O.K.," I said.

We told the parents we were leaving and went outside. I wondered why Raina hadn't just gone by herself in Claudia's car, and was momentarily thrilled at the notion that she wanted to talk to me. Then, seeing the empty driveway, I remembered that Claudia's car was in the shop. So much for that theory. Still, you don't question good fortune when it drops in your lap, and so as we walked down the driveway and into the street, I had to hold back a smile.

We took my car, or rather my dad's car, the old blue Mustang, keeping all our windows rolled up until we were out of the 'hood. Raina didn't seem to care where we went, so I got on the 405 north and headed for Hollywood. Neither of us spoke. Twenty minutes later I took the Sunset Boulevard exit and drove east, pushing eighty around those wide, hilly curves. There was no reason to take such a risk beyond the fact that this was Sunset, and that it gave me a terrific sense of pleasure to feel the way the car hugged that dangerous road. Raina didn't seem to mind. When we got to Hollywood Boulevard, all big-haired prostitutes and neon, we looked out the windows and let the sound of the radio fill up the inside of the car. I turned left and climbed up the dark Hollywood Hills, revving through those silent residential streets with their houses looming and still as sleeping giants. I parked in a clearing near the top, and the two of us stared down at the lights of the city. They lit up the ground to the south and the east; to the west they just stopped, met by the blackness of the ocean. Finally I looked at her.

"Beach?" I asked.

"Beach," she answered, and with that I started the engine, zoomed down the hill, and drove like a maniac toward Santa Monica. We stopped at a liquor store for a six-pack—all thoughts of my tests were out the window—and then parked in one of the big lots just north of the pier. I smiled at the irony of being there with Raina; this was the very same spot I'd gone to think about her so many times before.

"Wanna stay in the car?" I asked.

"No, let's get out."

The parking lot was usually filled with couples steaming up back seat windows, but the cold weather must have driven them elsewhere that night because the lot was almost empty. It was not too chilly, though, to kick off our shoes and socks and walk barefoot in the sand. The moon was almost full, and as we walked toward the ocean, we could see the moonlight painted on the surface of the water. Tiny figures of people crawled on the pier a few hundred feet away, and every now and then a particularly loud laugh would reach us over the sound of the surf. We walked toward the water in silence.

I'd been to the beach at night many times. It was a popular spot for drinking, for long talks, or for just hanging out, the cheapest entertainment in Los Angeles. It was also a prime spot for serious window steaming, especially for a lot of the gay girls we knew, who couldn't bring their lovers into their homes. The beach was a place we'd come to think of as our own. With a high school social scene that didn't acknowledge our existence and a basketball scene dominated by gossiping straight girls, a space to claim for ourselves was both valuable and necessary. As Raina and I trudged along in the cold sand, I thought of how amazing it was that we'd all managed to find each other. My entry into the gay basketball community had begun with my coming out to an AAU teammate during my sophomore year; she'd then informed me, to my surprise, that some other people I knew were also in the family. I contacted them, or they me, and so on, until I'd become a regular part of that undercover network which had finally led me to Raina.

Raina reached the end of the soft sand and stepped onto the wet sand packed hard by the surf. She picked up a small rock and threw it sidearm into the ocean. "God, I can't wait to get outta here," she said.

I hugged myself and said nothing. I wondered what other people heard in her voice. It was medium-pitched and clear, but also, I thought, a bit hesitant, as if she didn't quite trust it to convey the subtleties of her thoughts.

She continued. "I can't wait to get my scholarship, my diploma, my plane ticket, and just get the hell *outta* here. I feel like one of those horses at the starting gate, you know? All itching to go, but held back by some stupid gate I got no control over." Another rock flew out over the ocean. Raina stared straight ahead. I remember wanting, then, to stand apart so I could watch her, but also to enter her mind, her consciousness, to see what she was seeing.

"I just wanna get . . . *started,*" she said.

"Started on what?"

"I don't know. Life."

"This ain't life?"

She glanced at me, annoyed. "You know what I mean."

I looked down at my feet, wondering at this outburst. The way Raina was talking, you'd have thought we lived in some small town in the country and not in the huge metropolis which was our home. But I knew what she meant. She was choking in L.A., the walls were closing in, and the first impulse you have when you're feeling claustrophobic is simply to get yourself *out.* Maybe later, when she had breathed awhile, she'd come back into the city, as both of our parents had done, but for now she just wanted to taste the air on the outside. I'd be leaving in a few months, too, and I did want to go to college, but I felt less eager to get out of Los Angeles than Raina did. Not just because I loved it—we *all* loved it, really—but because I was afraid of what came next.

"You just don't know how bad I wanna leave," she continued. "I mean, if I knew I had to be here forever, seeing the same people, staying in the same situations, I think I'd go totally crazy. I'm just too *affected* by everything, you know what I'm sayin? I'm too fuckin *sensitive.* All the pain I see around me, I take it on as my own." She paused and I held my breath. "You know, sometimes I'm driving along in the car, and suddenly I get this urge to swerve off the road. Or I see an accident on the freeway and I wish that someone would hit *me* sometime, you know? Hit me and get it over with."

She covered her face with her hands and bent her head for a moment, then slowly drew her hands back as if smoothing out her skin. I was startled by what she'd said, but didn't respond. I didn't think it was my place to. It seemed that my function was not to comment but simply to hear, to bear witness to the fact that she was speaking. She might have said the same things to the ocean, alone, and my presence there had less to do with me than it did with the dragging muffler on Claudia's car. It occurred to me that while Toni had been the catalyst of this outburst, Raina wasn't going to talk to me about her. What she *would* talk to me about, or at least talk about in my presence, were the kinds of things she couldn't share with Toni. Whether it was because she didn't trust Toni, or because Toni wouldn't listen, I didn't know. But there were some things she didn't tell her. This I was sure of. Not that it meant, of course, that she could bear to be without her.

Now Raina locked her fingers behind her neck and took a step into the surf. "You just can't count on people," she said.

I stepped forward, too. "You can't judge the whole human race by the fuckups of one person."

She turned and looked at me, surprised, perhaps, by my presence. One good thing about talking at the beach is that you don't have to face the person you're talking to, and until that moment our eyes hadn't met all night. She turned back toward the water and laughed softly. "I don't just mean Toni. But it would be nice if she'd start proving people wrong."

I glanced at her. "So you know that people think she might not be the best . . . match . . . for you."

"Of course I know. How couldn't I? It's not what you think, though. It's just that I guess we got different ideas of the way things should be. I mean, I know what y'all say about her, and maybe you're right. She's a badass, she don't give a fuck, but that's kind of why I *liked* her, you know? I'm always playing by the rules, but Toni don't do that, she just does whatever the hell she wants. But she can be so good to me sometimes, Nancy. You wouldn't believe it. You just don't know Toni. You wouldn't believe it." She paused. The receding waves left white foam on her ankles. "I just wish she'd . . . I don't know."

We were silent for a moment.

"You think you guys'll stay together after you leave?" I asked now.

"I don't know. No. No way. She's been trippin about it, though."

I pushed some wet sand around with my foot. It occurred to me that Raina might be depending on college to provide a breaking point, since neither of them seemed likely to end the relationship herself. Much later I'd have a different view of the abandon with which Raina threw herself into this relationship. I'd still see that there was a purity in the all-accepting way she loved Toni, but I'd also see the self-denial, the self-destruction.

"But really," she continued. "There's no one you can count on, even outside of girlfriends. The last person I really counted on was my dad, and look what happened with him."

I glanced at her. I didn't know anything about her father, except that Claudia had divorced him when Raina was ten. "What about your mom?" I asked. "Don't you count on her?"

Raina sighed. "Yeah, I guess so, but not the way I used to count on my dad. We don't really talk about stuff—not important stuff, anyway. I mean, she knows about Toni, but I don't think she likes her, so I can't really talk to her about our problems. Besides, I'm older now, and I just don't trust people as much." She paused. "After my dad took off," she continued, "I kept waiting and waiting for him to call or something, but he never did. I don't know how my mom got through it, except that she's the strongest fuckin person I know. Five years he went without getting in touch with me, and then one afternoon he just strolls up to our front door like it was something he did every day. Suddenly he wants to be my best friend. He keeps quiet all that time, and then he wonders why I don't wanna hang out with him."

"Do you still talk to him?"

"Hell, no. I wouldn't take his calls. That day he came back was the last time I ever saw him."

A wave broke thirty feet offshore, curled into itself and rushed forth again, sent fingers of water shooting up the sand. A muscle in her cheek twitched and her eyes shone, either because they were reflecting the light of the moon, or because they were filled with tears. There'd been one other time I'd stood with Raina at water's edge, by the duck pond at Blue Star a year and a half before. I had thought I loved her then, although I couldn't have; I didn't know her. But something of significance did happen that day. Maybe I understood that I *would* know her eventually. Or maybe once you decide to love someone, you'll love her, no matter who she turns out to be.

"But the point is," she began again, "you're the only person you got. You're the only one you can depend on, you know what I'm sayin? I mean, maybe this doesn't happen with other people, but I've always thought I was gonna end up being alone. I've always known that. I got someone now, and maybe I'll have someone else after her, but sooner or later it's just gonna be me. That's O.K., though. As long as I know better than to depend on other people. You gotta learn to count on yourself, you know? Because who the hell else you gonna count on? Who the hell else is gonna be there for you?"

She stared out over the water and pressed her fists against her thighs. There was such an intense look on her face that I thought she saw something, but if she did, it was nothing that was there in front of her. The third-quarter moon lit her eyes, and made them look soft despite the expression she wore, which was hard, hurt, frustrated. For the first time, it occurred to me that Raina had been wounded, irrevocably damaged, and that this damage had something to do with why she pushed herself so hard. I didn't know what might have caused such damage—her father was surely a part of it, but only a part. And I didn't know what kind of achievement could make her feel complete, or if she'd ever let anyone help. Her last question, asked of no one, still echoed in my mind. I'd be there for you, I thought to myself. I'd always be there for you.

CHAPTER 11

Sometimes it doesn't take much to make you think your life has totally changed. It took just five minutes into the first Laker game I saw at age nine for me to feel an exhilaration so intense I knew I'd seek it forever. It took one miserable tenth-grade geometry test to make me realize that whatever I did in my grown-up years would not involve graphs or numbers. It took my father one sight of Claudia's proud, perfect back to impress upon him that his life, as he said later, had "found a junction to a whole 'nother freeway.'" And it took that talk at the beach with Raina to make me think our relationship had turned some kind of corner.

Although I wasn't particularly superstitious as far as athletes go, I did believe in fate. What else could explain why Claudia's car had been unavailable on Wednesday night, thereby making it necessary for Raina to come to me for a ride? What else could explain why Raina, the picture of self-sufficiency, had decided to open up? She had finally allowed me a look at what stirred beneath that implacable front, and somewhere, in the back of my mind, tiny voices of hope began to clamor. For the first time since I'd known her, the thought of Raina brought me a joy that was based on something tangible, something real.

The other way in which fate had intervened was by arranging for this to happen just before Christmas vacation, when, out of both design and necessity, Raina and I were certain to spend a lot of time together. We'd both be off from school, we'd planned to go shopping together, and then, on Christmas Eve, we were driving with our parents down to her grandparents' place in San Diego. Late on Christmas Day, the four adults would drive to Baja with some friends of my father's, and so for the twenty-four hours after that we kids would have the grandparents' place to ourselves. Although my father had said the house was only a mile from the beach, this wasn't its primary attraction. The main appeal was simply that it wasn't home. It was not our house, it was not our city, no one could reach us and we'd be alone. A full day of sun, water, basketball, drinking, and lots and lots of talking. Needless to say, I couldn't wait.

The morning after our talk at the beach, I flew out of bed an hour before my alarm went off. I hadn't slept for a second. All night I'd replayed our conversation in my head, fast-forwarding over the relatively unimportant parts, slowing down and repeating the parts where Raina had revealed something new. I reconstructed the entire night, all the way up to the moment at the end just before I unlocked the front door, when Raina had actually hugged me and whispered "thanks." The memory of that whisper fueled my day. It took me first to Raina's door, where I pressed my ear against the wood so I could hear her breathing on the other side. It took me to Mr. Wilson's liquor store, where I bought my usual Twix. It took me through my tests; I breezed through them both, hardly noticing them. I fell asleep for a few minutes on the bus ride down to Torrance for our game, and then, running solely on fumes, I proceeded to have one of my best games ever, with four scouts conveniently watching from the stands. On the way home I sat alone in the back of the bus with my Walkman cranked up to full volume and a big grin on my face. I thought of Raina the whole way back. It felt like I hadn't seen her in days.

When I finally got home she wasn't back yet. My disappointment was tempered by the parents' enthusiasm about planning Christmas dinner.

"Do you want turkey or ham?" Claudia asked when I went into the dining room after my shower. "My mother's trying to decide what to cook."

"Turkey. Can we get some extra legs?"

My father waved a head of broccoli at me. "She didn't say we'd *buy* it for you, she just asked what you'd *prefer.*" He looked especially large that night because he was wearing a small white apron that belonged to Claudia; it said "World's Greatest Mother" across the front.

I gave him a fake snarl while Claudia put a bowl of salad on the table. "So what do you two plan to do in San Diego after we leave?" she asked.

I shrugged. "I don't know. Just chill. We both need a break."

"Just don't tear the house apart," my father said.

We sat down to dinner, my father's chicken-and-vegetable stir-fry. Somehow I managed to function on two levels at once. Half of me participated in the family discussion, while the other half conjectured wildly about the events of my impending time alone with Raina. When Claudia and my father debated about the best way to cook a turkey, I pictured Raina and me, on the twenty-sixth, making cold turkey sandwiches and eating them on her grandparents' porch. When Claudia mentioned how nice the beach was by her parents' place in San Diego, I pictured Raina and me watching a sunset there with cold beer bottles sweating in our hands. Each of these thoughts brought a huge grin to my face, which my father took to be the result of my having had a great game with several scouts in attendance. I gathered, too, that I was acting quite giddy, since my disproportionate burst of laughter at a relatively stupid joke prompted my father to cock his head and ask, "Are you drunk?"

After dinner I bounded around the house in, of all things, a cleaning frenzy, which really must have made my father think something was wrong since normally not even the threat of torture could induce me to vacuum. But now the house seemed an unacceptable mess, an eyesore; I wanted to clean it to make it worthy of Raina. After an hour of dusting, vacuuming, and scrubbing, I took the dog outside and ran sprints up the street. I imagined that Raina was sprinting beside me; the three of us did six 40's and four 100's before I crawled back inside and went upstairs to take a shower. The real Raina was not yet home. What was taking her so long? We had some talking to do, or at least some hanging out, in the afterglow of the night before. What would things be like between us now? It seemed to me that our time alone in San Diego would be a litmus test for the future of our relationship. If we took what we'd found and ran with it, our post-Christmas chill-out time would at the very least cement our friendship. It could possibly do a lot more than that. But if we didn't build on what had happened, or if we ignored it, our friendship might stagnate, or worse. That wasn't going to happen if I could help it. It had to work out. It just had to. This thought occurred to me with such intensity that I punched the door of the shower, which brought Claudia running to the bathroom door to ask if everything was all right. I said that it was. Then I got out of the shower, went into my room, and fell asleep still wrapped in my towel.

The ringing of the phone woke me up. I fumbled around, disoriented, saw that the clock face read 9:30. I picked up the receiver, said hello. Raina, on the other end, said, "Hi."

I woke up immediately. "Hey. Where are you? Did you win today?" Just a little extra intimacy crept into my voice.

"Yeah," Raina said. Nothing else.

I paused for a moment. "When you comin home?"

"I'm not. I'm stayin at Stacy's. Tell the parents for me, all right?"

Now I was puzzled. She rarely spent the night at someone

else's place, and this was a weeknight. "Well, what's up?" I asked. "Is something goin on over there?"

"I'll tell you later. I really gotta go now. Bye." I heard the receiver click, and she was gone.

For a few seconds after I hung up the phone, I wondered if something was wrong. Had I pissed her off in some way without knowing it? That was impossible—I hadn't even seen her since the night before. I decided that Stacy was having some sort of problem, and that Raina was staying over to help. That must have been it. Probably her curtness on the phone was related to whatever was happening. I put on some shorts and a T-shirt and went to bed.

On Friday morning, the last day before vacation, I was totally exhausted. I dozed off in two of my classes, but when I was awake, I managed to move around in a happy daze. I had another good game, but for once it wasn't basketball which dominated my thoughts—the whole Christmas plan could now claim that distinction. At dinner, which Raina once again decided not to show up for, the parents and I finalized our arrangements for the drive down. We discussed the menu for dinner, and also the complicated transfer of keys from children to grandparents once we finally left the house on the twenty-sixth. Meanwhile, I worked on my personal agenda. I'd bring along some romantic but not mushy music. I'd bring a football to toss around at the beach. I'd buy a bottle of wine, perhaps, and also, instead of eating leftovers for all of our meals, maybe I could take us out to dinner one night. The part of me that was paying attention to the mealtime conversation continued to laugh loudly at all that was said. Claudia and my father looked at me strangely; I knew they were wondering what was up. What they couldn't see was that while my butt was planted firmly in the chair, my head was roughly five miles above it.

Raina had a tournament game that night, but none of us knew where it was. The parents waited an hour for her to call and tell them, but she didn't, so they finally gave up and went to a movie. I sat in my room eating ice cream and flipping through a two-year-old issue of *Sports Illustrated.*

One of my biggest strengths, and biggest weaknesses, was my unshakable belief that things would work out for the best in the face of all evidence to the contrary. This was why I could walk out of a test with half the questions left unanswered and still imagine I'd get an A or a B. This was why we could be down ten points with two minutes left in a game and I would simply assume—often correctly—that we'd come back and win. This was why it didn't bother me much when Raina failed to come home the night after we'd talked, and also why it didn't alarm me when she was late on Friday. I myself referred to this outlook as healthy optimism. But it could also be called self-delusion.

When the phone finally rang at nine, I picked it up on the first ring.

"Are the parents home?" Raina asked without saying hello. I could hear balls bouncing and people talking in the background. She sounded far away, and it wasn't just because of all the noise.

"No, they took off already. Where are you?"

"In Lakewood. Where'd they go?"

"To a movie. They waited awhile for you to call, but then they figured you must be playing already."

"No. The game got moved back. They're running late here. I don't even think we'll start playin till after nine."

"Oh, really? Cool. I'll pick up Q and Telisa and come watch."

"Don't bother."

I spread my fingers across the open pages of the magazine. For a moment I thought she meant, we're playing an easy team, the game will be boring, so don't waste your time. But it began to occur to me that maybe that wasn't what she meant at all.

"All right," I said, deciding not to push the subject. I stood up, walked to the window, put the phone down on the dresser. Something was obviously wrong, but I'd figure it out later. "Listen," I said now, "are you gonna be home later? 'Cos me and the parents have been talkin about this Christmas thing, and you and I gotta work out the logistics of stayin at your grandparents' house after everybody else goes to Baja."

When Raina answered, her voice was artificially casual and high. "Oh, yeah. I meant to talk to you about that."

"What do you mean?"

"I don't think it's such a good idea for me to stay down there."

I made myself take a deep breath. "What?"

"Well, we got a game on the twenty-eighth, and even though we don't practice till the twenty-seventh, I don't think I should take days off right now, especially with league coming up. I haven't played so hot the last couple of games, and there's been scouts here, so I need to be doin a lot better."

I paused. "You could work out in San Diego."

"It wouldn't be the same. I wanna use our gym and our weight room and shit."

As she talked her voice sounded more and more like that of a stranger. I couldn't believe that Raina would do this. My vision of our time together grew momentarily bright and clear before it evaporated completely. I didn't want to whine, to complain about the plans I'd made, and so I said softly, through clenched teeth, "Goddamn you."

I'd meant it to sound lighthearted, but it must have come out sounding bitter, because right away Raina said, "I gotta go."

I didn't reply. A buzzer went off in the background. Raina sighed. "Nancy, it was only gonna be for an extra day."

"An extra day is a long time."

"Come on. It wasn't like this was a huge big deal or anything."

"Maybe not, but I was still looking forward to it."

"Well, guess what? You got a long life ahead of you. Look forward to something else."

My mouth dropped open. "*Excuse* me?"

"You put too much stock in things that don't mean as much to other people. You gotta learn to just, like, chill out a bit."

I stood there gripping the phone. "Thank you, Raina, for that incredibly valuable piece of advice."

"Don't be so oversensitive. I'm just trying to help."

"Well, keep your fuckin help to yourself."

There was a long silence. Several times I started to speak, but I couldn't get a handle on the jumble of thoughts that were whirling around in my head. All I could finally come up with was a terse, "You know, you got some nerve tryin to tell me what to do."

"Oh, shit," Raina said. "Listen, I just can't deal with this right now. I got a game to play."

"You were the one who brought it up."

"Well, I'm ending it now. Goodbye."

"Great. Goodbye. Have a wonderful game."

And with that, instead of hanging the phone up, I lifted the offending bearer of bad news and hurled it at the wall. It made a thick crashing sound and landed upside down on my bed; I picked it up again and smashed it to the floor. The dog, her interest piqued by the explosion of noise, came to the doorway and gave an inquisitive bark.

"Shut up!" I yelled, and pushed past her on my way out to the hall. I went straight to the closet, opened it, and grabbed an armful of basketball shoes. These I threw one by one at Raina's door, enjoying the dull thud they made when they hit the wood, stopping only to dig deeper in the closet to root out hidden pairs.

After that, I grabbed my running shoes and took off on a long run, even though it was 9:30 and there'd been two shootings in the last few weeks. It's possible that, in my state of mind, the danger was part of the attraction. I headed first toward the park, and saw the crack lady there; she was swaying back and forth and laughing out loud, and I was sure she was laughing at me. Then I left her behind and ran on toward the ocean. I ran through run-down residential streets, past schoolgrounds and empty, dark industrial buildings. It had rained earlier in the evening, and the sidewalks were soaked; the fog had settled down from the sky. I ran straight into it, barely able to see, and the world around me was an eerie white, absent of other people and noise. I could discern the vague shapes of houses through the billowy layers of fog, and the acrid smell of wet concrete filled my lungs. I had no idea where I was going and I didn't care. It seemed to me that I was one giant bleeding wound, and I could not outdistance my pain and disappointment. What made things even worse, though, was the knowledge that I'd contributed to this disaster myself. How could I have thought that Raina's openness at the beach was more than just a momentary lapse? I should have known she'd pull away. She didn't want to be alone with me in San Diego or anywhere else, and she had made that very clear by staying away from the house for two days. Not that it was all my fault—I was furious with her, too, for the way she'd spoken to me, how nasty and cold she'd been. Still, as I hurtled down the sidewalk, I knew the pain I felt was as much my own doing as it was hers. I had willfully chosen to ignore the signs of her withdrawal. I hadn't held in the reins on my hope, and it had stampeded out of control.

It took an hour to wear the edge off that first burst of emotion. After that I turned around and ran home. I went into the house and headed straight for the bathroom, where I knelt in front of the toilet and retched. Nothing came up, but it felt like my stomach was turning inside out, so I stayed there on my knees for ten minutes. When the nausea passed, I leaned against the wall and shut my eyes. I was exhausted. I didn't even shower. Slowly, painfully, I dragged myself into my room, where the unrelenting glare of the overhead light seemed like a blatant affront to my misery. I began to strip off my soaking clothes, but then, like a protruding nail snagging a passing sweater, something on the other side of the room caught my attention. It was the mark the phone had made in the wall. There was a triangular dent in the plaster where the corner must have hit, which opened into a flat indentation that looked like the mark the spine of a book might leave if pressed into rolled-out dough. There were green marks in and around the triangular section, and in a couple of places inside the flat part. I stared at this complicated scar. Whenever I saw marks like this in other people's houses, I always wondered how they had gotten there, and if there was a story behind them; whether a hole in the wall was the legacy of a mischievous, bat-bearing child, or perhaps instead the testimony of an adult's surrender to fury or passion. But now, as I stood there breathing hard in the middle of my room, the mark I suddenly thought about was the one I'd made myself. Would some future resident of this house conjecture, as I did in other places, about the story behind this scar in the wall? Would I, if the house remained in the family, ever look at it with wonder or regret? Or would it come to mean nothing to me, be just another mark in the wall, devoid of all history and significance?

By the time I saw Raina the next morning I'd regained my composure. The emotional storm of the previous night had passed, leaving a dangerous calm in its wake. This calm, though, made it possible for me to function. So when Raina emerged from her room, waded through the sea of sneakers that still littered the carpet outside her door and said, "Try on some shoes last night?" I was able to meet her eyes for a long, hard moment and turn away without saying a word. At breakfast the parents chatted cheerfully about the movie they'd seen the night before. They asked Raina about her game, which she dutifully described, and then they asked me if I had ended up going to see it.

"Nope," I said. "Pass the butter."

And maybe I said it a little too coldly, because as Raina handed the butter over without turning to face me, the parents exchanged a glance. They knew that something was wrong between us. I didn't have it in me to care.

The next few days were like a nightmare I couldn't wake myself up from. Although I managed to eat, and play, and do my Christmas shopping, it was as if I was moving in a dream. Raina was out most of the weekend, although she did call a couple of times to see if anyone had called for her. I felt like her message service. I also felt like asking her for an address so I could send along the rest of her possessions. There was this distinct sensation that I can only liken to a magic carpet being pulled out from under me, and because I'd been flying along so high, the fall, when it came, was much worse than it might have been if I had stayed more restrained in my imaginings. I was like the penny a baby-sitter had once told me about, the one dropped from the top of the Empire State Building—I'd fallen so far, so fast, that I didn't just *hit* the ground, I sank *into* it.

What I remember most about that time is that I felt disconnected from everything, even my own body, which seemed more like a machine then, a collection of so many movable parts. The blood vessels were no more than wires, the nerves just message centers which transmitted commands to muscles to move or stay still, expand or contract, with no impulse or life behind the movements. This new soulless me did not function well, of course, on the basketball court. I had a game on Saturday and was so down and listless that my coach and teammates thought I was sick. We lost and were eliminated from the tournament. I hardly noticed. All the basketballs in the world could have shriveled up like raisins and I wouldn't have cared in the least. In my deadened state it did occur to me that I was being unprofessional, that Raina, for one, would never have let her emotions interfere with her play. But that was because she was so *used* to having drama in her life. Suddenly I felt no compassion. So what if Toni was hurting her? If she was going to keep allowing herself to get screwed over, then she deserved whatever she got. Let her suffer. By herself. I didn't care.

On Wednesday afternoon, after an hour of rearranging groceries, duffel bags, and Christmas presents in the backs of the parents' cars, we started our drive to San Diego. My father seemed to be the most excited of all of us; he was glad to be out of school, and eager to get away from his problems with the Hendersons. Claudia and my father went in my father's Mustang, and Raina and I in her mother's Honda. We hadn't explicitly planned it this way, but it was an unspoken rule that whenever we took two cars, parent always rode with parent, and kid with kid. Raina drove. And while she spoke every once in a while to comment on a license plate or a song, I held my tongue and sat as far away from her as possible. When she solicited my opinion about which of two dresses she should wear for Christmas dinner, I glared at her, annoyed. Finally she turned on the radio and stopped trying to talk. This made me feel better. I still couldn't stand to be in the car with her, though, so when my father waved us off the freeway so that Claudia could use a gas station bathroom, I was out the door as soon as we'd come to a stop. I paced back and forth for a couple of minutes, then walked over to the side of the Mustang.

"I wanna ride with you," I said to my father, who'd just opened his door, swiveled, and stuck his feet out onto the pavement.

He shaded his eyes with his hand and looked up at me. "There isn't any room in back, Nancy. We've got all the bags."

"Then let Claudia ride with Raina in the other car."

He looked puzzled. "Well, O.K., sure. What's the problem?"

"There *is* no problem! I'm just fuckin sick of being cooped up in that goddamned car!"

I knew I was causing a scene. People at the gas pumps looked over, nozzles in hand. Claudia, who was walking toward us from the back of the station, slowed to a near-crawl. Raina, in her mother's car, looked down as if in shame. As I stood there, out of breath from yelling, I again had the sensation that I was falling, and falling, and falling through space, powerless to stop and not knowing what I'd hit at the bottom. I expected my dad to yell at me for swearing, but instead he gave me a long look, pulled his legs back in the car, and reached over to open the door on the passenger side. Claudia went to the other car; I slid in next to my father and slammed the door. We got back on the freeway. He was mercifully silent and let me be silent for the rest of the trip down. We drove behind Claudia's car, and so for an hour I stared silently at the back of Raina's head. I missed her. She looked so small to me then, and I pondered the fact that she was moving just ahead of us in a bubble of impenetrable steel. It seemed fitting, somehow. She was precisely that shut away from me, impossible to reach.

When we got to Claudia's parents' place, her father, James, a skinny man bent three inches by age, grabbed our duffel bags and shuffled back into the house. Her mother, Gail, was tiny and covered with an intricate web of wrinkles, but when she flashed her disarming grin it took twenty years off her age and you could see the family resemblance. I watched them for signs of discomfort as they talked with my father, but there were none, they were fine; they acted like he was an old and dear friend. We all sat in the living room and talked; then Raina took off for the beach while I stayed and watched the adults get drunk on eggnog. Claudia treated her parents lovingly, as Raina treated her, although I didn't want to remember any of Raina's good points just then. At bedtime she wasn't back yet. Her grandparents put our parents in one of their extra bedrooms and set the other up for Raina and me. I lay motionless and awake until one A.M., when Raina crept in and crawled into the other bed. I considered the irony of our finally sleeping in the same room together at a time when we weren't even speaking. It seemed that she was doing some thinking, too. She tossed and sighed and shifted for at least an hour. At one point she turned and I could feel her looking at me, and she took several short, sharp breaths, as if she were getting ready to say something. I willed her not to speak. She didn't. Finally she got settled and her breathing assumed the slow, regular pattern of sleep. I lay there rigid, staring up at the ceiling, until the soft, gray light of morning began to creep in through the shades.

The next day, Christmas Day, was like one of those comic tragedy versions of a holiday turned on its head, except that only I was able to recognize the disaster. No one thought it strange that while Raina and I had presents for everyone else, we didn't have any for each other. (I'd chosen not to buy one out of spite, and felt justified when I realized that she hadn't gotten me one, either. "It hasn't come yet," she explained. "I had to order it.") No one thought it strange that when I did manage to smile, it was the kind of ghastly grimace that sick people use to assure their visitors they're not in any pain. And no one remarked upon the fact that I hardly touched my Christmas dinner. For an hour I sat rearranging the piles of food on my plate while everyone else ate heartily. As I played with my turkey and stuffing and yams, the four adults and Raina engaged in a fast-paced, lighthearted discussion about who had messed up at what critical juncture of the preparation of the meal. Raina, by the way, looked beautiful. She was wearing a dark purple dress that made her look regal, and her hair, free of its usual braid, was glorious and wild as she shook it out before sitting down to eat. Everyone joked and laughed all through dinner and dessert. I'd never felt more alone in my life.

Late that afternoon my father's friends came by to take the adults to Baja, and Raina drove back up to L.A. I finally had the place to myself. Claudia's parents had been kind enough to let me stay there even though Raina had left, and I was determined to have a good time without her. That night I watched football and an old rerun of *The White Shadow.* Then I walked around the neighborhood—it was safer down here—and looked at people's Christmas decorations. I had a fleeting urge to call Lisa, the girl I'd had the summer fling with, who was now a freshman at San Diego State, but, knowing that this urge came purely from spite, I managed to fight it off. Finally I took a six-pack out of the fridge and headed down to the beach. And as I sat there on the cool sand, thirty feet up from the water, the numbness of the last few days wore off and I realized how upset I still was. The last time I'd been to the beach at night was, of course, the time I'd gone with Raina. That night had been like a teaspoon of water to a woman who was dying of thirst—it hadn't provided any relief; it had only made me want even more. Foolishly, though, I had thought it was some kind of breakthrough—Raina had actually talked to me about herself, and hugged and thanked me afterward. Very sincere, I thought now. Yes. Thank you, Nancy, for being there this one time, but please understand that I must now shut you out. Thank you for listening while I talk about a life you can hear about but never take part in. Well, fuck her if she couldn't deal with me now. As I sat there thinking, all the anger came back in a rush. I was so furious with her for opening up to me and then punishing me for it that I wanted to rage and cry until she understood how much she'd hurt me. But she wasn't there to hear me then and never would be, so I screamed instead at the ocean, which seemed, that night, as angry as I, and which answered with a deafening roar.

The next morning, without consciously realizing I'd decided to do so, I packed up my things and drove home. I was supposed to stay in San Diego for the rest of the day, but for once I couldn't stand to be alone with my thoughts. It wasn't that San Diego was the problem, or that Inglewood, when I returned there, would be any better. I didn't really know where I wanted to be; for the last few days I'd just wanted to be anywhere except the place I actually was.

Raina was home when I got back. I went straight upstairs to my room, ignoring the "hi" she offered from the kitchen. I shut my door, dropped my bag, and flung myself down on the bed. Within moments I was drifting off—the drama of the last few days had left me so exhausted that I fell asleep whenever there was a lull in the action. So when Raina's knock came at the door a few minutes later, I thought I'd manufactured it in a dream and didn't answer. But when it came again, louder, I sat up. "Come in," I said.

"Hey," she said as she opened the door. She stuck her head in and looked around, as if she thought I might have rigged something heavy to fall on her when she stepped into the room. Finding nothing out of the ordinary, she came in. "Your present got here today," she said.

I looked at her skeptically and was about to turn away, but then I caught sight of what she held in her hand. It was a soft, floppy, chestnut-colored figure with curly brown hair and maroon clothing. "A Cheryl Miller doll," I said before I could stop myself. It was. Someone, I never found out who, had been making these handmade Cheryl Miller dolls for the past three years. People brought them sometimes to USC games, showed them off to their friends, had them signed by Cheryl Miller herself. I had mentioned a few weeks earlier that I'd love to get my hands on one but didn't know how I could. And now Raina had found one for me. She'd gone through all that trouble. Even though we had barely spoken.

Since neither of us was making a move toward the other, Raina lay the doll down carefully on my desk. "I hope you like it," she said. "Made in America. Although the Nikes might of been made in China, you know, with child labor or some shit like that." She glanced at me uncertainly. "But probably not," she continued, "since they're made out of cloth. Do they make cloth in China? I don't know."

She stood there and looked at me. I realized that this was her peace offering, her apology, but I couldn't bring myself to say anything just then, and so, after a few moments of awkward silence, she turned and left the room. I walked over to the desk and picked up the doll. It was a raggedy doll, about two feet long, made of soft brown cloth and stuffed with cotton. The detail was wonderful—there were red Nike swoops on the little white shoes; the sides of the hair were cut short, just like Cheryl's; the number thirty-two and the name Miller were embroidered onto its maroon-and-gold Trojan uniform. Suddenly, as I stood there looking at it, my eyes went hot with tears. I'd been bitterly angry at Raina for acting the way she had, and now I was angry at her for making it impossible to *stay* angry. Damn it. Just as I was getting used to hating her, she had to go and do something nice. I was totally unprepared for such kindness. And I had no idea until then that love tinged with pain could be just as formidable, if not more so, than love untouched by cruelty or betrayal. Holding the doll tightly against my chest, I sat down on the carpet and rocked. Underneath all the layers of anger, disappointment, and resentment, I discovered a capacity for sorrow I hadn't known I possessed. Slowly but steadily, the tears rolled down my cheeks—at first the tears of that sorrow, but gradually, the tears of relief. I felt like a person who'd just survived a horrible accident—I didn't know yet how injured or maimed I might be, but I knew, at least, that I was alive.

After I'd finished crying, I sat and pondered what my next move should be. I went into the bathroom and looked in the mirror. My eyes were puffy and my hair a ball of frizz, but after a few yanks of the brush and splashes of water on my face, I was somewhat more presentable. I made my way downstairs and into the living room, where Raina lay on the couch reading Kareem Abdul Jabbar's *Giant Steps.* She looked up at me as I came in. She had offered me an apology, and I had to let her know that I accepted the offer. "Wanna shoot some hoops?" I asked.

She closed the book and smiled. Our eyes met for a moment, and in that look was an understanding of how close we'd come to real disaster, how fragile the peace was now. It didn't matter. She was in sight again. We'd narrowed the gap between us. She said, "Sure."

CHAPTER 12

The future that Raina so desired was rapidly closing in. We'd both played several games by then, and I no longer noticed anything that wasn't directly related to basketball. Once the season began every year, it was like I entered a time warp until it ended four or five months later. During that period the world rolled along without my knowledge of it, and I was always amazed at how quickly the time had passed when I emerged to discover that seasons had changed, books had been written, revolutions had occurred in my absence. My senior season was speeding by even faster than usual because I didn't want it to end. Once it was over, I'd only have a few more weeks to make the decision about college. I did what I could to put the brakes on the passage of time. I tried to hold on to the individual moments but they slipped through my hands like water.

After Christmas, as she'd promised, Raina began preparing for her tournament. She claimed to have gained four pounds on Christmas Day—which, of course, no one else could detect—and she did a combination of sprints and longer runs in order to burn them off. Both of our teams were practicing, and afterwards, Raina would hang out with her teammates, so I didn't see her much the next couple of days. My father's friends brought our parents home the night of the twenty-seventh; they both looked rested, tan, and happy. We sat on the floor of their room while they unpacked.

"We didn't miss you in the least," my father said. "Did you miss us?"

Raina and I both said, "No."

He grinned. "They why are you in here watching us put our clothes away?"

I rolled my eyes. "Because we're *bored.*"

Claudia picked up a handful of clothes, threatened to throw them at us, but then dropped them in the laundry basket. "Well, what have you been doing?" she asked.

"Nothing," I said.

"Playing basketball," Raina said. "And hanging out a lot." She fiddled with her shoelace, looked up at her mother. "I saw Paula today," she said.

Claudia looked at her, quickly, and so did I—she hadn't told me this.

"Really?" said Claudia. "Where?"

Raina clasped her hands over her knees. "At Barry's Chicken & Waffles," she said. "I went there with Stacy after practice, right? 'Cos Kim'll feed us sometimes for free. And Paula was there, too, eating lunch."

Claudia pretended to be very interested by something in her bag, and when she spoke, her voice was noticeably subdued. "How is she?" she asked.

"Good," Raina answered. "It was great to see her. She sat with us while we ate, and then Stacy and I went over to her place and just chilled on her balcony. It was a perfect day to do it, too—the sky was real clear. I'd forgotten how nice the view is in Baldwin Hills."

Claudia didn't say anything; she just looked down at her clothes.

"She's all excited about the conference," Raina continued, and I thought her mother flinched a little. "You know Paula—she's the happiest when she's got a big project to work on. Anyway, she gave me a couple of books for Christmas, and she even gave Stacy one, isn't that cool?"

Raina sounded so normal, so cheerful, and I wondered why she was doing this. It was possible that she didn't know what was happening between her mother and Paula. But then she looked at Claudia searchingly and said, "I *miss* Paula, Mom." And I knew she understood that *something* was wrong, even if she didn't know exactly what it was.

Claudia unfolded a pair of pants, and then folded them again. "Yes, she's been—we've *both* been—very busy these last few weeks." She didn't lift her head, and Raina just looked at her. My father, who'd been quietly unpacking through this, touched her very lightly on the shoulder. "Anyway," Claudia said now, glancing over at us for a moment. "Wendell and I are very tired. Maybe you should leave us alone now."

Raina nodded silently, then stood up and walked out of the room. I followed a few seconds later, after saying good night to our parents. The dog, who was lying at the foot of the bed, looked from me to my father, and decided to stay where she was. Down the hallway I heard Raina's door close. I wondered if she and Paula had talked about Claudia, but somehow I didn't think that they had. Maybe Raina was trying to force her mother to deal with her friend, or maybe she was just sticking up for her. At any rate, I knew she wouldn't discuss it with me. I stopped for a moment, wondering what was happening in the parents' room. But all I heard through the open door was silence.

In the week between Christmas and New Year's, my team had a tournament at Artesia High School. Artesia was a basketball powerhouse—both its boys' and girls' teams were always strong, and it hosted a girls' winter tournament and spring league every year. The boys had a star freshman named Ed O'Bannon, and eight years later, he and his younger brother Charles would lead my father's beloved UCLA to its first NCAA championship in twenty years. At any rate, the Artesia tournament was one of the biggest and most talked-about tournaments of the season—there were thirty-two teams, including enough state- and CIF-ranked teams to make the level of competition unusually high. A lot of my AAU buddies were playing, and because of the high concentration of potential college material, the top of the bleachers would be packed all week with vultures. I was anxious about how we'd do—there were the scouts, of course, and although I'd played in front of them enough by then not to let their presence affect me, I still didn't want to fall on my face. But what concerned me even more was how my team would perform. We weren't seeded, because of the abundance of ranked, big-name teams. My team was considered a squad with one star and four no-names by the people who made these rankings, who must not have been noticing the ascendance of Q. This tournament was a good chance for us to show everyone that they'd been taking us far too lightly.

Our first game was like a warm-up—we played hard, but there was no question of the outcome, which had been determined, in my view, as soon as the pairings were announced. We were matched up against a weak team from Orange County, and we led by fifteen at the end of the first quarter. I worked hard to keep everyone's concentration level up—it was important to continue to execute well, because sloppy play in an easy, meaningless game might result in sloppy play in a later important one. Since there was no pressure on me to carry the team that day, I set up Q as much as I could. She played well, making easy work of the other team's center. Q would do a reverse pivot as soon as she got the ball and then shoot from way over her head, which effectively nullified the height advantage that the other center usually had. When the player moved closer to try and guard Q more tightly, Q put the ball on the floor and plowed right past her. Q's extra weight helped in that kind of situation—she was so strong that I'd once seen her hit a power lay-up with three people hanging off of her shoulders. Sometimes the player guarding me would drop back to cover Q, which left me wide open on the wing or in the corner. Then Q would dump it back out to me, and boom, I'd have an easy open jumper. We played with them like this all day.

Despite the easy flow of the game, there was another factor which was making me nervous—the presence of Raina. Her team was playing early those days at another tournament nearby, so Raina, who was being very considerate in the spirit of our delicate truce, had promised to come to all of my games. I forced myself not to glance into the bleachers where she was sitting, but each good play I made was like a tribute to her, an offering. Somebody up there was watching out for me. My passes were all sharp and reached their targets. My shots flew off my fingers with perfect backspin and arch, and most of them hit their mark; although I only shot twelve times that day, I hit nine of them, plus several free throws, to finish with twenty-three points. I was actually kind of glad that Raina was there—her presence kept me on my toes, and prevented the blowout from getting boring. Q scored twenty-six points and grabbed twelve rebounds, and I hoped that the scouts had taken notice. Her father certainly had. He came down and hugged her after the game, and was even friendly with me, for once.

After I'd stretched my calves, which had been threatening to cramp the entire second half, I went up into the stands to join Raina. She was sitting with a big group of our AAU friends, next to a bunch of neighborhood girls who kept pointing at them and giggling excitedly. Two more games were on tap for that evening, so we had at least three hours of hang-out time. That made me happy. I was glad to see these folks; it was like a mini-reunion of the basketball elite. There were about twelve of us that night, a collection of the reasons that the scouts were in attendance, and I could see them looking over at us and scribbling on their clipboards, although we all pretended not to notice. These were the players I'd spent my springs and summers with; I'd hung out with them at camps and tournaments all over the country. About half of them had already signed, and as I approached, I heard them telling Raina how glad they were to be done with recruiting. She listened to their stories, but I knew she didn't regret holding off. Most of them had signed early for reasons of status or security, and without much concern for the differences between the actual schools, but Raina was so deliberate that she needed to weigh all the factors before she could make a choice.

We didn't just talk about serious things, though. We also exchanged stories about our teams, ragged on each other, recalled strange or funny episodes from the summer—like the time when a group of us stole our coaches' beds at Blue Star, and then returned to our rooms the next afternoon to find they'd stolen ours right back. I loved hanging out with this group of people, even if I wasn't particularly fond of every individual in it. My high school teammates were great, and I spent a lot of time with them, but there were parts of my basketball life that they could never understand, experiences we didn't have in common. But *these* girls had gone to the same places, played in the same tournaments, been through the same wringer and expected the same reward. Despite differences in neighborhood, and race, and class, we had this one defining experience in common.

There were two other gay girls in this particular gathering of people—Rebecca Hill, a white girl from Ventura who had signed with Washington, and Theresa Golding, a black girl from Lynwood who hadn't signed yet, but who was rumored to be leaning towards Vanderbilt. Rebecca was funny, irreverent, and completely down-to-earth; she was one of the few white kids from the suburbs who mixed well with us. Theresa was on the quiet side. She was an avid churchgoer who never swore, but who could make "shoot" or "darn" slide off her tongue in a way that sounded utterly obscene. I liked them both, and felt the kind of sisterhood with them that I always felt with other family members in a big group of straight girls.

There was one point at which the bond felt particularly

strong. It was at halftime of the first of the two games we were watching, and we had all just returned from a food run laden with hot dogs and popcorn and nachos. Theresa had been talking about a player we all knew, a girl from North Carolina who'd called her the night before because she too was thinking of signing with Vanderbilt. Then Lydia Slater, a prissy but deadly blond center from the San Fernando Valley, piped up:

"Yeah, she's a really great player. But you know what?" She leaned in close and looked around conspiratorially. "I think she might be gay!"

Theresa shrank back a bit, and Rebecca looked down at the court.

Raina, though, pressed both hands to her cheeks and gasped. "No! Really?"

Lydia nodded, looking serious and concerned. "Yeah," she said. "I was using the phone next to her at Blue Star last summer, and she was being all mushy to someone named Chris, and then later I saw her showing a picture of Chris to her roommate, and you know what?"

"What?" Raina asked, leaning closer, eyes wide and palm cupping her chin.

"It wasn't a boy!"

Raina drew back and put a hand across her heart. "Oh, my God!"

Rebecca and Theresa and I fell out laughing. Natalie, who'd just joined us, rolled her eyes and shook her head.

Lydia looked at us. "What are you guys laughing at?" she asked, which only made us laugh harder.

"Nothing," I said. "Just forget it." A couple of years before, I might have withered in this situation, felt very acutely the other girl's privilege and my own status as outcast and weirdo. By now, however, my views had changed—in my eyes, it was she who had the problem.

The next day, we had what was probably the most unpleasant game of my high school career. The trouble started right before the opening tip-off, when one of the other team's players, a light-skinned girl on an all-black squad, lined up next to me at the circle and said, "Yo, ain't you playin on the wrong team?"

I looked at her quizzically and asked what she was talking about.

"North Torrance already played a couple hours ago," she replied, and then I understood what she was saying. North Torrance, which was Stephanie Uchida's old team, had an all Japanese-American roster.

I shook my head in disgust and didn't say anything. Telisa, however, had heard the whole exchange, and glared across the circle at the offending player. "Do you know who you talkin to?" she asked angrily. Telisa didn't sound like this very often, and the rest of our team, including Q, who was waiting in the middle for the jump, turned around and looked at her in surprise.

The other player, who was slightly shorter than me but a good thirty pounds heavier, laughed dismissively. "Naw, why? Who the fuck is she?"

Telisa shook her head. "Well, I feel sorry for you, man, 'cos you about to find out."

Then the ref came into the circle. He asked if we were ready, decided that we were, tossed the ball up and started the game. Q lost the tip, and the other team set up their half-court offense and scored on their first possession. It was my fault—one of their guards slipped right past me—and I was pissed at myself for being distracted by the conversation at the circle.

When we got the ball, Telisa dribbled up the court deliberately, waiting to see what kind of defense they'd spring on us. It was a zone. We moved the ball around to see how well the defense adjusted (fair, not great), and then Telisa hit me on the right wing. I made a head fake and moved past the first defender, and then got hit hard enough by the center on my way up to the basket that my shot wasn't even close. No matter, though—I had two free throws coming. We got into position, and I made the first shot. Then, just after the ref handed me the ball again, my friend on the other team piped up.

"Yo, how come you ain't little like the rest of your people?" she asked.

Again, I just looked at her, but I saw Q bristle. Telisa, who was standing next to the player, said, "Girl, you diggin your own grave."

I sank the second shot and we ran back to set up our defense.

The first quarter was close, and our two teams were trading baskets. My tormentor, Number Five, was a decent player—she kept muscling past Pam for easy baskets, and then laughing whenever she scored. When I moved over to the left side of our zone and sent Pam to where I had been, Number Five just followed Pam and wouldn't let me have a crack at defending her. This was the type of situation where I would have loved to have gone player-to-player—that way I could have stayed on her case all day—but their center was 6'4" and awesome, and there was no way Q could have handled her alone. Fortunately, though, they couldn't handle us, either. All of their size and bulk meant that they were also very slow, so Telisa was doing damage at the guard position, and there was no one who could stop my drives. I had ten points in the first quarter, six of them coming from lay-ups I made after burning someone out at the wing.

After one of these lay-ups, a play on which I'd also been fouled and so had a free throw coming, Number Five nodded in appreciation. "You pretty good, Viet Cong," she said. "You know how to talk in English?"

Q spun around and glared at her, but the girl didn't notice. I bounced the ball at the free throw line and tried to control my own anger. It didn't work—I bricked the shot, which only angered me more.

The second quarter was more of the same. The game was close, and we were mad, and Number Five kept up with her comments. Q stayed quiet—it wasn't in her nature to talk shit—but Telisa had a running conversation with the girl, letting her know that every time she messed with us, she was going to pay for it with points on our side of the scoreboard. Things reached a boiling point just before halftime, when the other team's center was shooting a free throw. Number Five screwed her face up and started speaking gibberish, and I could tell that this was her approximation of an Asian language. One of her teammates, who was clearly tired of this performance, asked, "What the fuck you doin?"

"I'm talkin like a Viet Cong," she said, gesturing in my direction, "so that girl over there can understand me."

Q was on her in an instant. She flew across the key and shoved Number Five so hard that her big, heavy body reeled back ten feet. Telisa and I grabbed Q before she could go after her again; her goggles were askew and she was baring her teeth. The ref, who either hadn't been hearing Number Five's pronouncements or didn't care about them, hit Q with a technical foul. We all had to stand behind the half-court line while their point guard sank the two penalty shots.

I took the opportunity to try and calm Q down. "Don't let her get to you like that, girl," I counseled. "Just put it into your game. She *wants* you to react, and we can't afford to lose you if the refs decide to throw your ass out."

She nodded, but still looked furious. I didn't blame her—I was mad, too. Somehow, though, we made it through the rest of the half without further incident. Number Five shut up for a while, and we poured on the scoring, taking it to her side of the court as often as we could. I burned her badly a couple of times, but refrained, with some effort, from rubbing it in. It wasn't that I was morally opposed to trash-talking—in truth, it was sometimes very satisfying. I was not above telling someone after I'd scored on her that she'd deserved it for fouling me all game, or telling a big talker after we'd won that if she planned to talk shit in the future, she had better be able to back it up. But those were rare occasions. Most of the time, I let my playing speak for me. Number Five, though, was making things personal in a way I didn't like, and that was exactly why I'd stayed silent for the first half of the game—if I even started to express what I felt about her, I wasn't sure I'd be able to stop.

Coach Fontaine didn't know what was happening, but he knew we were upset, so at halftime he gave us Standard Fontaine Halftime Speech No. 8, the one about keeping our emotions under control. None of us really listened—this had nothing to do with him. As we warmed up for the start of the second half, we looked at each other solemnly, knowing we had some serious work to do.

The other team was ready to play, too. We led by four at the start of the third quarter, but they quickly tied the game on a couple of jump shots. Number Five laughed right in my face when their point guard made the second one, and I had to just stand there for a moment and clench my fists so I wouldn't go over and punch her. On the next play, Telisa took the ball down and passed it to me on the left wing, and I immediately lobbed it in to Q. Number Five collapsed on her, so Q kicked it back out, and I sank the shot from the wing. On their next possession Pam made a steal, and we set up our offense again. I lined up on the right side this time, got the pass from Telisa, and pump-faked to lose my player. Then I took two dribbles around her and went up for the shot from the right corner of the key. Swish. I looked at Number Five, who was standing under the basket, to let her know that her lesson had just begun.

In the third quarter, the game became mine. I had entered The Zone. When you're in The Zone, you feel invincible; and ridiculous, impossible things become as easy as breathing. The basket suddenly seems as big as a swimming pool; rebounds fall at perfect angles and present themselves to your hands; you know how all the players are going to move, as if you'd programmed them, or told them where to go. Everything seems clearer than usual; it's like putting on a new pair of glasses, or suddenly understanding a language that you've been struggling to master. A player in this condition is also said to be unconscious, and this is a good way to describe it. There's a certain feeling of unreality when you're playing like that, and the best way to take yourself out of The Zone is to acknowledge the fact that you're there.

The crowd, sensing what was happening, began to titter. People came in from the snack stand, returned from the bathroom or the parking lot to watch the show. I ripped down rebound after rebound, made diving steals, drew the other team's defenders to me and then left them in the dust. We were up by eight or ten through most of the fourth quarter, and we knew we had the game in the bag. Number Five had been relatively quiet, and I thought she was finished talking, but then finally, as I was shooting a free throw with a couple of minutes left, she said, "Hey, is it true y'all eat dogs?"

That did it for me. On our next possession, after they'd scored, I had Telisa give me the ball right under our basket. I dribbled toward Number Five, who was retreating down the center of the court. When I got close to her she tried to guard me, sliding sideways to my left and just in front of me. Then, at midcourt, I spun hard backwards and to the left, pulling the ball around with my right hand and barreling into her with my shoulder. It was a body-block my father would have been proud of. She went down with me on top of her, and as we fell, I gave her an extra elbow in the gut. I heard the breath come out of her when we hit the floor.

"You keep your goddamn mouth *shut* from now on," I growled, "or else this basketball's gonna go *in* it."

She looked up at me, eyes wide and voice silenced at last, and then the ref rushed over blowing his whistle. He added insult to injury—she hadn't established position, so the call he made was blocking, on her.

After I stood up and brushed myself off, Q and Telisa came over to make sure I was all right. They'd seen the whole thing and Q was grinning. "I thought you said to put it all in the game," she said.

We would win by ten, and after the free throws I was about to make, I'd finish the day with forty-one points. I put my hands on her shoulders and shook her a bit. "Q," I replied, smiling, "I just did."

That game was our last win of the tournament. The next day we lost to Compton, which was Natalie's team. There was no shame in such a defeat—they were the fourth-ranked team in the state, and we only lost by five—but still, each loss felt like a failure to me, and now I was banished to the stands for the rest of the week. My team had made a good showing for itself, though, and both Q and I got messages from scouts—through two or three different intermediaries, since direct communication was not allowed—that they'd been impressed by our performances. Q was thrilled about this, and I was happy for her. She'd played three good games and her timing could not have been better. As for me, I was feeling pleased, too. My display in the second game had been one of the highlights of the tournament, and I knew that my vengeful little trick at the end, rather than putting people off, had only served to increase my toughness quotient. Better yet, though, my performance had impressed a more important critic—my housemate. Raina had cheered loudly and enthusiastically through all of our games, and always clapped me on the back when I went to join her in the stands.

"Girl, you kicked *ass* these last few days," she said after our loss, which had been another good game for me, although not transcendent like the last one—and not enough to give us the win. "Shit, it's fun to watch you play."

And that compliment from her—and the smile of appreciation that came with it—meant more to me than any of the comments or praise that were floating down the stands from the vultures.

Raina and I came to the games together for the last two days, to watch the semifinals and the final. We cheered for Natalie's team in their semifinal victory against Lydia Slater's team, and then cheered for them again as they fought it out with a San

Diego team in the final. I was disappointed, of course, that my team was out of the tournament, but on the other hand, it was a nice change of pace to hang out at the gym without having to worry about staying focused for a game. Our AAU crowd sat together on both of those nights, and when I looked around at our little group I noticed how relaxed people seemed—how sure of themselves, and of their right to the space they took up. We were admired and envied by all of our peers, and coveted by dozens of respected institutions. We were all proud and brash and convinced of our worth, and I found myself wondering if, twenty years from then, any of us would still be feeling that way.

Other things, silly things, went on in those couple of days. A bunch of the neighborhood girls came up and asked me to sign their shoes. Raina had several guys following her around, and whenever she left the stands to go to the bathroom or get something to drink, they'd all descend upon her and try to impress her with their wit and charm. She'd listen to them, amused, and wait politely through their obvious efforts. She was actually very kind—she never told anyone off, or cut them short, or made them feel bad in any manner. But when they asked for her number, she'd decline their requests, smiling, and say it had been nice to talk to them.

She was markedly less polite to the couple of guys who approached me. At one point during the semifinal game we were standing in line for a drink, and a guy who'd been trying to impress me all tournament came up and stood beside us.

"Come on, Nance," he said, trying to strike the proper balance between solicitous and cool. "Just let me take you out one night. I've been waiting for someone like you—I mean, where you been all my life?"

Raina laughed out loud. She said, "Hiding from clowns like *you.*"

He looked flustered, and went away. I actually felt a little sorry for him, especially since he reminded me of the one guy I'd dated, when I was a freshman, a poor soul I'd fooled around with for two dull months before I finally admitted that I wasn't interested in boys. I laughed, too, though, and looked at Raina. "Thanks for defending my honor."

"Anytime," she said, grinning, and I wondered why she'd bothered.

Certain girls tried to talk to us, too, and in this case, I got more attention than Raina did, because most of the girls in the family were aware that she was taken. Needless to say, I wasn't interested. All I wanted to do was hang out with my AAU friends, and as the final game wound down—with the San Diego team beating Natalie's pretty handily—I found that I was conscious of the minutes ticking away. I didn't want to leave this haven of friends. But more than that, I was afraid I'd never spend time with them again—not like this, not all of us at once. We were seniors, and the next summer, for the first time since seventh grade, there'd be no camps, no tournaments, no Junior Olympics. There'd be no more of the traveling party that the summer basketball circuit had become. Sure I'd see these friends, maybe all of them, but it would only be one or two at a time. Never would we function as a group again, and I was afraid, as I sat there, that this was the last time we'd all be together, that we'd all leave in a few months and disappear into our separate and uncertain futures.

After the awards ceremony, which I had to stay for in order to pick up an All-Tournament trophy, Raina drove off with a couple of her friends, and Natalie and I went to grab a bite at Wendy's. Natalie was 6' 3", and squarely built; she was one of the few people who could make me feel small. She was extremely dark, the daughter of a Kenyan father and a black American mother, and so stately and impressive that I was sure she was descended from royalty. Over hamburgers, fries, and Frosties, she talked about her disappointment at having lost that day; her excitement about leaving California; and her relief at having signed early with Ohio State. She talked a bit about Charles, her boyfriend, and about how sad she'd be to leave him. He was only a junior, so they'd be separated for a year, but then he was planning to move out to Ohio after he graduated. Natalie told me he couldn't wait to be through with school.

"And there's some strange shit goin down with that team, girl," she said, and the bite of burger in my mouth turned to stone.

"What do you mean?" I asked.

"I think the head coach is trippin 'cos he knows all the players are behind Eddie Nuñez."

I managed to swallow, and took a sip of my Frosty. "Oh yeah?"

"Then a couple weeks ago, he called in some of next year's seniors, and gave 'em this speech about leadership and team unity. He said he heard certain players been questioning some of his decisions, and that talkin behind his back like that was just gonna end up dividing the team."

I dragged a couple of French fries through a puddle of ketchup. "And Charles was there?"

"Yeah," Natalie said, "and so was Eddie." She took a bite of her burger, swallowed, looked at me. "And then one of the guys mentioned something about your dad, and Coach Henderson said he wasn't sure if your dad would even be *back* next season. He said they been 'having their differences.'"

This was all news to me. I said, "Really?"

"Yeah. And the guys ain't happy. I mean, your pops is their *friend,* you know what I'm sayin? And *he's* the one they listen to, not Henderson." She stuck a fry in her mouth and chewed. "And have you heard what's goin on with your dad and that fool *Eric* Henderson?"

I kept my eyes on my food and tried not to look too concerned. "What do you mean?"

"Well, there's this rumor goin around that one of Eric Henderson's teachers passed him last year in a class he should of failed, and now your *dad's* got Eric in a class. I guess he been messin up again, not doin his homework and shit. And in the last few weeks before Christmas vacation, Eric wasn't showin up at all, almost like he was daring your dad to do something about it."

I couldn't think of anything to say.

"I don't know, girl," Natalie continued. "Charles and the guys is pretty upset about the whole thing. They say that if Eric Henderson's the starting quarterback again next year, they just gonna keep lettin him get hit till someone fucks him up good."

"Jesus," I said. "I can't believe this shit."

"I know," she said, shaking her head. "I think Eddie's finally startin to get pissed, too. And he should be. He's the *shit.* Charles say that if Eddie would of played this year, he could of been the best quarterback in the league. And he's a cool guy, too. Real laid-back. Charles and them been hangin out with him more since this whole big mess got started." She shook her head again and looked at me sadly. "I don't get it, you know? I don't know why people in power gotta fuck with other people like they do."

"I don't know either," I said.

By the time we left Wendy's, it was already dark. As we walked out to the parking lot, I heard a sharp crack, which sent me scurrying behind a car. Natalie laughed.

"That's a firecracker, fool," she said, and then I remembered it was New Year's Eve. This realization only comforted me for a second—people *would* be shooting guns that night, firing rounds into the air at midnight and probably several hours before. That was why I, and most of the people I knew, intended to stay inside.

Natalie and I talked about our plans for the night—she was hanging out with Charles and his friends, and I was going over to Q's to watch Dick Clark—and then we said goodbye and took off in our separate cars. I got on the 91 freeway, and as I headed west I could see the last traces of daylight, a strip of gray against the bottom of the sky. I let my eyes blur a little, and the red from all the taillights bled together in my vision. The radio offered me songs that I would normally have been glad to hear, but that night, as I drove home, I hardly noticed them. My head was swirling with the things that Natalie had said about my father, and with the questions that arose if those things were true. Was Larry Henderson arranging to have him fired? Would Eric Henderson really challenge him so openly? What would my father's course of action be if Eric continued to cut his class? The trip back to Inglewood, which usually took about forty minutes, seemed to pass in half a second. I took the 91 to the 110 to the 405 north, got off at the Manchester exit. Only another ten minutes, from there, to home.

Maybe because I was so preoccupied with thoughts about my father, I forgot to take the usual precautions. My window, which I'd opened at Wendy's, was still rolled halfway down. At each stoplight I came to, I pulled all the way up behind the car in front of me, and didn't look to either side. The light turned yellow as I approached La Brea. The car in front of me made it through the intersection, but I slowed down to a stop as the light turned red, and the nose of my father's Mustang just broke the plane of the crosswalk.

It was only by luck that I saw him. I was half-leaning against the door, waiting for the light to change, when I looked into the side-view mirror to see if there was any gray still left in the sky. There wasn't, but what I did see was a young guy, maybe fifteen or sixteen, stepping off the curb and heading quickly toward my car. He was on the small side, with thin delicate features, and he wore a big, bulky Lakers jacket which seemed to engulf him. He walked toward me with such purpose that I just watched him approach, wondering if he was someone I knew. Then, when he was still about ten feet away, he reached into his jacket and pulled out a gun.

I didn't understand, at first, or *believe,* what was happening; it was like the interval between when you hit your hand against something and when the pain of it finally comes. I still didn't move as he got closer, as he reached the side of the car, as he raised the gun and tried to put the muzzle in the open window. It was like a slow-motion fantasy—not possible, not existing in real time—but somehow, finally, I snapped out of my daze.

Then I did exactly what you are not supposed to do in that situation—instead of getting out and handing over the car, I pressed the gas pedal down to the floor. The light was still red, but I drove through the intersection anyway, ducking down to avoid seeing the cars that I knew were about to hit me, and also to keep from getting shot. Miraculously, though, I wasn't hit by another car, and I was just registering my thankfulness for the lull in the traffic when the back window, and then the front one, was pierced by a bullet, and cracks like spiderwebs blossomed out around each of the holes. Only then did I hear the gun's report. I kept driving, my head up just high enough to see over the dash, as my heart beat so violently that it seemed to take up the entire inside of my chest. I waited for another bullet, but it didn't come. At all the intersections I stopped at after that, I looked around frantically, as if expecting the same kid to step off of each corner. In another few minutes I made it home.

I rushed inside, almost forgetting to shut the car door, and called out for my father. He, Claudia, and Raina were all sitting at the kitchen table, and when they heard my voice and saw my face, they just looked up at me for a moment, their eyes filled with concern.

"What happened?" my father asked, standing up quickly. "Are you all right?"

I couldn't explain to him, couldn't say anything, so I just grabbed his arm and pulled him outside. Raina, Claudia, and Ann all followed behind. When we got out to the driveway and my father saw the car, he pressed his lips together, and his nostrils flared, and he just stared at it for a moment. Then he walked up in front of the car and put his index finger into the hole left by the bullet, went around to the back and did the same thing. Behind us, I could hear Raina and Claudia saying, "Holy shit," and "Oh, my God." My father flattened both of his hands against the back windshield, and I saw a shiver go all the way through him.

"Are you all right?" he asked again, looking at me.

"I'm fine," I said. "Just freaked."

"How did this happen?"

"This kid tried to jack me at Manchester and La Brea. I was just sittin there waiting for the light to change, and he started walkin toward me, and he had a Lakers jacket on and I thought maybe it belonged to his brother or something, 'cos it didn't fit him, it was way too big. But then he opened it and there was a gun underneath and maybe that's why he was wearing that jacket. And I don't know what kind of gun it was but it looked fuckin huge, and he came up around the side of the car so I drove away, I drove through the intersection, and then, and then—"

The words just stopped coming. Everyone was looking at me. I stared at the shattered windshield and noted, absently, that the reflected images of Raina and Claudia were oddly disjointed, as if Raina and Claudia themselves had been broken and then hurriedly put back together.

"You could of been killed," Raina whispered. And somehow hearing this made me feel even more frightened, made the danger I'd faced more real. Although it wasn't cold that night, I started to shake badly. My father must have seen this, because he came over to me then. He stood in such a way that my left shoulder bisected his chest, and he enveloped me with his arms.

"It's O.K.," he said. "You're home. And I won't let anything hurt you."

I wanted to relax in his arms. I wanted to let go of my fear and lean into his chest and think everything would be all right. It didn't work, though, because I couldn't believe him—this was a man who was having trouble protecting even himself. I knew he meant what he said, that he would do everything he possibly could to keep me from being hurt. But I also knew that it wasn't enough.

After the police came out to the house and told us there was almost no chance of catching the kid who'd shot at me, we all decompressed in the living room. My father brought me a cold beer and asked about every five minutes if I wanted something to eat. Raina had planned to go over to Stacy's, but instead she stayed home, sitting next to me on the couch the entire evening and making jokes about Dick Clark's hair until I laughed. I tried not to jump when firecrackers went off. At midnight, as the apple fell in Times Square on the television, we heard several reports of gunfire. I cringed, more than usual, and Raina shook her head.

"That's a stupid fuckin tradition," she said.

We stayed up for another two hours, still hearing firecrackers and the occasional gunshot. I drank another cold beer, and then another, until my body relaxed enough for me to go to bed. I let Ann sleep in my room just to have some company, and put the pillows over my ears to shut out the noise from outside. It took me another several hours to get to sleep.

When I woke up in the morning, I was still a bit dazed from the alcohol, and surprised to find the dog in my bed. Then I remembered the events of the previous night. They seemed incomprehensible though, like the strange, distorted incidents of a nightmare, and I wasn't completely sure, for a moment, whether or not they'd really happened. I went outside to look at the car, and discovered that it was gone. The paper had been picked up already, so I went back inside, and found Claudia and Raina at the kitchen table. Claudia looked up when she saw me.

"Happy 1987," she said.

"Yeah, wonderful," I said. "Hey, where'd the car go?"

Claudia got up and poured me a cup of coffee. "Your father took it down to the garage," she said.

"They're not open today, are they?"

"No," she said, as she poured some milk into the cup, "but I think he just wanted to get it out of our sight."

I nodded, and then sat down in the chair beside Raina.

She turned and looked at me. "How's it goin?"

"All right, I guess,"

"Did you sleep O.K.?"

"Yeah, I did. I think the alcohol helped."

She nodded seriously. "Beer's a good thing."

I thanked Claudia for the coffee, took a sip of it, shook my head. "That was a crazy thing to happen, though," I said. "Especially on a holiday."

Raina grinned. "Well, at least you started the new year off with a bang."

Claudia rolled her eyes, and I just looked at Raina, and then finally, we all started to laugh.

My dad got home about twenty minutes later, and then cooked a huge breakfast of French toast, home fries, and sausage. After we ate, I called Telisa, Q, Stacy, and Natalie to tell them what had happened. They all expressed horror and concern, but I realized, in the middle of the first conversation with Telisa, that this wasn't really what I was after. I discovered that as I spoke to people, and described the scenario over and over, it seemed to diffuse its power somehow. It made the shooting less a real, threatening event, and reduced it, at least for a while, to just an interesting story, a topic to mull over with friends.

I spent the rest of the day watching the bowl games on TV, and by evening I was feeling close to normal. It seemed like several weeks had passed since I'd driven away from that kid at the intersection. When we got the car back from the garage three days later, the first thing I did was press my hands against the new windshields. It was hard to believe that they'd so recently been shattered. I drove the car immediately, just cruised around for a while, to get over my fear of being in it. With Raina in the passenger seat, I went back to the corner of Manchester and La Brea—it looked harmless and uneventful in the daylight, and the lunchtime traffic passed through as if nothing had happened. My strategy worked—after seeing the intersection, and driving around for half an hour, I was fine. And while I didn't forget what had happened, of course, I put it away somewhere, in a compartment in the back of my mind. This was how I'd always dealt with the violence around us; this was how most of us dealt with it. You had to keep a certain distance, a certain mental control; if you thought about it too much, you'd go crazy.

CHAPTER 13

On the day after New Year's, my team resumed practice. We still had a few days of vacation left, and by throwing myself back into basketball, and back into my life with Raina, I was able to distract myself from what had happened with the car. My team practiced at eight A.M., on mornings so cold we could see white tufts of breath in the air. Every morning after practice I'd have a long breakfast at McDonald's with Telisa and Q, and then get home just in time to see Raina off to her practice, which started at the much more reasonable time of noon. I watched *All My Children, One Life to Live,* and the first part of *General Hospital* while she was gone. Then she came back and we fixed ourselves some lunch; together we watched the rest of *General Hospital,* and then *Oprah Winfrey.* One day I arrived at home wearing one of my team's new practice jerseys, which had been designed by Coach Fontaine. "There Is No 'I' In 'We'" it said in bold blue letters.

"Yeah, right," Raina said. "I'd like to see how your 'we' would be doing if a certain 'I' wasn't throwin in twenty-four points a game." I laughed. It did not escape my attention that she knew exactly what I was averaging. She *had* been keeping track. I was happy.

Every day at four o'clock we left for the park—stopping at the liquor store for a minute or two in order to chat with Mr. Wilson—and after dinner we headed down there again. I always kept my eye out for the kid with the big Lakers jacket, but he never appeared; after the games started up, I forgot him. Normally we played with the regular pickup crowd—all guys—but a couple of times Letrice, Tracy, and Telisa showed up, too. Telisa didn't play at the park much anymore—schoolwork and Shavon had become her priorities—and I was happy to have her there. Usually a few of the Inglewood Families would be hanging out by the picnic tables, and occasionally one or two of them would join us. We'd play full court if we could, three-on-three if we had to, Tracy leaving the court every once in a while to chase after Chris, who tended to wander. If there was a storm, though, the park would be empty. Raina and I would go down to the courts anyway, and I loved it when we played in the rain. We'd be the only people out there, and we'd laugh and act silly, bouncing the ball in big puddles in order to splash each other. Raina's clothes would get wet and cling to her body, thin cloth outlining the curves of her hips and breasts. I'd see the rain that collected in the hollow at the base of her neck. I'd see it stream down her arms and legs, so smooth it seemed to be caressing her; she'd turn her face up toward the sky, and I'd want to trace with my fingers the paths the water followed down her cheeks and forehead. Her whole body was slick and wet and I wanted to move against her, feel her skin sliding over my own.

We finally dragged ourselves home from the park around ten, showered, and went straight to bed—both of us sleeping long hours, I suppose, because we'd worked so hard during the day. Our days were filled with basketball, and there was no homework or school to distract us. For a change of pace we'd watch the sport instead of playing it, either on TV or in person, at the USC, UCLA, or Long Beach State women's games. USC was not the same team that year without Cheryl Miller; it was like a basketball game without the ball, a beach without the ocean. There was nothing to distinguish them now from any other college team, and I was going to their games more from habit than out of a real desire to see them play. A few times, at the games, we spotted old college stars who were playing pro ball in Europe or Japan; they had come home to California for the holidays. Even the youngest of them was five or six years older than us, though, so we didn't have much to say to them. We tended to stick with our AAU friends, although only a few of them would show up on a given day. The group of us would sit halfway up in the stands, and I'd see Raina eyeing the high school seniors who were in the reserved seats behind the home team's bench. These were the players who'd signed early letters of intent with those schools, and they were proud and self-aware as peacocks. I noticed that Raina looked down at them almost hungrily. I imagine she wished her future was as determined as theirs.

We spent a lot of time together during the latter half of vacation. Normally we both retreated to our rooms for a couple of hours in the afternoon or evening, but that week we were always in each other's company. Every morning Raina would ask if I'd slept O.K., and it was a good question, because often I hadn't. I'd wake up every other night or so, the gunshot still echoing in my mind, the image of the shattered windshield appearing for just a moment on the darkness of my ceiling. I was glad that she was making such an effort—it seemed to say that she considered our relationship important. The time between us, though, had taken on a different quality. On the one hand we were always together, but on the other we didn't talk much unless there was something meaningful to say. This made sense, I suppose. After what we'd been through in the last couple of weeks, it was impossible to go back to being casual.

On the first Friday after we returned to school, Claudia and Raina went out to dinner by themselves. I was sure they were going to talk about Raina's future. She'd been even more obsessed with the subject lately than usual, despite, or maybe because of, the temporary reprieve we were having from games. Because neither of us was playing for a week, there were no scouts watching over us and making note of our every move—although we still couldn't get through the evening without some fast-talking coach tying up our phone line. I liked that they couldn't come to watch us for a while; not seeing all the college people made it easier for me to ignore their existence. While Raina made lists and charts about the pros and cons of the schools she was considering, I just skimmed over each new letter I received and stuffed it away in my files. My father, meanwhile, always wanted to talk about the choices I had, and Claudia brought the subject up, too. Not to mention that Raina had started asking my opinion of this or that coach, this or that program, this or that city or state. It seemed like the person who was least interested in my future was me.

Because one half of the household was having a special night together, my dad figured that the other half should, too. I was not in any mood to be chummy, though. Earlier that day I'd learned from Letrice that Rhonda was back in jail, and not because she'd done anything. She'd simply been in the car when her boyfriend was pulled over and then arrested for possession, which was enough to violate the terms of her parole. No one knew yet how long she'd be in this time.

My dad, however, had no idea about this. He made, not one, but two of my favorite dishes—beef curry and yakisoba—and I wondered what favor he was planning to ask. What my dad had in mind, though, was worse than any favor—he was giving me this royal treatment because he wanted to talk.

I had just taken my first bite of curry when he cleared his throat and put his fork down. "So Nancy," he said. "What's your thinking on the school situation?"

I finished chewing, swallowed, took a sip of my drink. "I don't know."

"Have you at least narrowed it down a bit since we met with all the coaches?"

I shrugged. "Yeah, sure, I guess. I mean, I know I don't want to go to UCLA."

"Listen," he said, trying to catch my eye, "I don't want to rush you, but you've got to start thinking about this a little more seriously. You're going to be going on your campus visits pretty soon, so you've got to figure out which five places you want to see."

"I know," I said, looking down at my food. "You're right."

My father took a sip of his water, and then looked at me closely. "Nancy, why have you been having such a hard time with this? I mean, I know it's a tough decision to make, but it's almost like you'd rather not even deal with it at all."

I didn't look at him, but nodded. "Yeah, I guess that's kind of true."

"But why?"

I could tell that he was looking at me searchingly, but I kept my eyes on Clyde, who I had for the night, and who was sitting in Raina's chair. It always made me feel uncomfortable when my father tried to have a serious talk with me, especially when it related to my future. I cast around for something to say which would give him an idea of how I felt. What I came up with was, "I really like being in high school."

He laughed a little. "Well, *I* like being in high school, too. Obviously, I guess, since I work in one. But the future is out there *waiting,* Nancy. All you've got to do is go and meet it. And kids like you and Raina, you're in a wonderful position. I would love to have had the opportunities that you have."

I shook my head. "It's not that simple, Dad."

"Listen," he said, "I know that this time seems really confusing, with all of these people coming at you from all different directions. But once you make your choice, everything else is going to look a lot simpler. And all of this stuff you're going through now, you're not even going to *remember* it. Once you get to college and then out in the real world, you're going to be so glad to have your own life that you'll probably never want to come back to this place. And frankly, I'll feel a hell of a lot better when you're out of here, especially after what happened on New Year's." He paused. "I know you're really attached to your friends and everything, but you're going to make *new* friends soon, and those will be the ones that'll last. Your real life hasn't even begun yet, Nancy. Up to now, it's just been practice."

I finally glanced up at him, and he looked so earnest. My father was a wonderful man. He'd made sacrifices for me, he'd accommodated all my needs, and one of the appeals of getting a scholarship to college was that I'd spare him from having to pay. He was a popular teacher at his school, and related well with kids. But as I sat there at the dinner table, I was struck by two things—how much he loved me, and how little he knew me. I couldn't have said who was responsible for this. It was true I didn't tell him much, but more and more, as I got older, I wondered if he was making a conscious effort not to ask me anything for fear of learning things he didn't want to know. It wouldn't occur to me until years later how well my father *did* actually know me—or, at least, how familiar he was with my strategies for protection. We were so similar in the ways we dealt with the world. We each kept it at arm's length—he with humor, me with the illusion that it didn't really trouble me—each of us affecting a detachment we did not really feel; each afraid to go out and enter the world because every part of it we touched made us bleed.

I wasn't sure what to say to him now. How could I explain to my father that in high school, despite the dangers, I was *safe?* I'd made a place for myself there over the last four years; I knew where I stood, and what my status was. I could walk through my school, or through the 'hood, with confidence and pride, knowing that people knew and respected me. But all that was going to change by the end of the school year. In a few months, I would have nowhere to belong.

It was even larger than that, though. I knew that Raina, for one, felt a sense of responsibility, felt the weight of other people's expectations. And I felt it, too—every high five I got from a local store clerk, every word of encouragement from neighbors or folks at the park, every starry-eyed gaze from some young kid in the 'hood, made me realize how much people were counting on me. I loved my community, and I wanted to do well by it, make it proud—but I wasn't completely comfortable with the burden of its hopes. For one thing, I wasn't sure I had a right to them. But also, more simply, so many other young stars had reached the point where Raina and I were now, only to be shot down by injuries or SAT scores or some problem at college; the proof of their failures was all around us. And it was terrible, in those instances, to see the collective disappointment in the 'hood, to see that the redemption which people had hoped for had not been achieved. I did not want to contribute to that pain. And at that point, halfway through my senior year, all my possibilities were still ahead of me. As long as I didn't act, I couldn't make a wrong move. The future was still wide open, full of promise and potential, and trying anything, *anything,* could mean disaster. It seemed better, therefore, to do nothing. If I stayed still, and made no choices, and committed myself to no course of action, at least I was staving off any chance that I could fail. At least I wasn't letting anybody down.

The next night I had a stressful conversation of a completely different nature. This one was with Stacy, in our living room. The parents had gone down to San Diego for the weekend, so I'd invited several people over, but Q and Telisa had other plans already, and Raina had gone to spend the night with Toni. Stacy came over in time to watch the Laker game at 7:30, bringing two forty-ounce bottles of Miller that she'd stolen from 7-Eleven for her mother. Mrs. Gatling didn't want them—she preferred Colt 45—but Miller was my favorite beer at the time, and I was happy to have it. The Lakers looked unstoppable that night, and killed the other team. In June, they'd beat the Celtics to win their fourth championship of the eighties, the perfect gift for our graduation.

After the game was over, Stacy filled me in on her social life. She was recently single again, after having spent a month with a girl named Cynthia, a pretty but duplicitous girls' basketball groupie from Lakewood. Typically, Stacy had been very caught up in her—writing her sweet letters all the time, giving her flowers and little presents I knew she couldn't afford. Finally, though, she'd gotten sick of being lied to, and had managed to break it off. She said it was strange to be unattached again, although she knew that Cynthia had been all wrong for her. Then she turned, gave me a serious look, and started in on one of her favorite topics.

"You gotta get out there, girl," she said. "You gotta get out there and . . . circulate."

"Circulate?" I repeated, amused.

"Yeah, girl," she said. "No one knows about you. I mean, people *know* about you, but they don't know nothin *about* you, you know what I'm sayin?"

I smiled. "Why would I want them to know anything about me?"

Stacy looked exasperated. "So you can get a girlfriend, stupid! Shit!"

"I've *had* a girlfriend," I said. "I've had a couple of 'em. And I ain't exactly desperate for another."

Stacy shook her head. "That's ancient history, girl. You need somethin *now.* I mean, when's the last time you got some play?"

I counted backwards. "A little over two years."

Stacy pressed all her fingers to her head, as if she were adjusting the way it fit onto her neck. *"Two years?* Holy shit! *Why?"*

I shrugged my shoulders.

Stacy wiped her hands on her shorts and shook her head again. "You missin *out,* girl. Sex is *good.*"

I laughed. "I wouldn't remember."

"Well, don't you miss it?"

"Yeah, sure. But there are other ways to keep yourself . . . satisfied."

"That's right," she said. "You have a dog."

I threw a pillow at her. "Fuck you!"

She deflected the pillow away and laughed. "O.K., O.K., I'm sorry. But shit, two years." She thought about this. "Well, you got strong, pretty hands, girl. I hope you been usin 'em."

I smiled and wiggled my fingers. "You know how good I am with my hands."

She rolled her eyes. "But still, that shit's so lonely. It's a lot more fun when you with someone else. You know, like they say in the Bible—'Do unto others as you would like to be done.'"

"That sounds great," I said. "But it just ain't happenin right now."

"But it *could* be happenin, Nance. You just gotta get a girlfriend."

I decided to humor her. "And how would I go about doin that?"

"It's easy. Gettin a woman, it ain't that complicated. You spot some fine woman at a club, right? Or at a game. And you come on real strong at first—maybe ask her to dance, get her number, just hang out and talk to her a bit. You do this a few times, whenever you see her around. You give her all this attention, till she gets used to it, and then suddenly, you just lay off and ignore her. And then, bam! She'll come *runnin.* I promise."

"It's that simple, huh?"

"It's just that simple. And for you it'd be even easier. You look *good,* girl. You got that curl goin on, and those sweet brown eyes, and that smile that light up your face. You got that pretty tan skin, and you a kick-ass motherfuckin basketball player. If you just put yourself out there, Nancy, women would be linin *up!*"

I laughed. "If it's so easy, how come *you* ain't got a new girlfriend yet?"

"Me? I don't want one, girl. They hurt you."

This was true. Stacy had ended up with a series of bad people—people who'd cheated on her, left her, and generally treated her like shit—of which Cynthia was just the latest incarnation. I knew a lot of Stacy's tough-girl act was meant to cover all the sore spots underneath. She didn't like people to know how softhearted she was, but her softness was part of why I liked her so much. It was unexpected; it made her vulnerable and complex.

"So girlfriends hurt," I commented now, "but you still think I should try to get one?"

She shrugged her shoulders. "Maybe it'd be different for you, girl. Things always seem to work out good for you. It's just that I hate to see you sittin around and wasting your youth like this, waiting for something that ain't never gonna happen."

I glanced at her. We hadn't talked about Raina this way in a long time. "What makes you think I'm waiting? Or wasting?" I asked.

She took a gulp of her beer and set the bottle down, hard. "Nancy, I know you still like Raina. It's like all your energy, or something, is pointed toward her. I mean, you can almost *see* it. And listen—I know Raina's great and shit. She's a great fuckin person, and I love her to death. But she don't *like* you, girl. You gotta let it go. You gotta put it in the past and move on."

I finished off my own beer and set it down on the coffee table. "Does she ever talk to you about me?" I asked.

Stacy shook her head. "Naw. You know Raina, she don't talk about shit. Only time she ever talked about you was a couple years ago, when you was following her around all the time. We was drivin home from the UCLA-USC game, you know, that time the Bruins won? She asked if I thought you liked her, and I said yes. And she said she couldn't believe it, she didn't know why, she didn't understand what you saw in her."

I looked down, amazed at the possibility that Raina did not see, in herself, what I saw.

"But that was the only time," she said. "I guess she just ain't thinkin about it now, and neither should you. You gotta find somebody else, Nance."

"But I just ain't interested in nobody else."

Stacy leaned toward me. "Of course you ain't interested in nobody else. You don't *see* nobody else. You ain't givin no one else a chance." She retreated a bit. "Listen, there's other possibilities out there. There's other people that like you. But you? Shit. You wouldn't know that someone liked you if she came and waved a fuckin banner in your face."

She sounded disgusted, and I wondered why she cared so much about the state of my love life. I didn't want to talk about it anymore. I got us another round of beers and a bag of pretzels and suggested that we turn on the television. Stacy seemed to have finished her diatribe. She didn't bring up Raina again, and became rather quiet, only speaking occasionally to comment on something funny Arsenio said. Finally, around one, I announced that I was tired. I fixed Stacy up on the couch with a blanket and pillow, and then went on up to my bedroom with Ann. Raina did not come home that night. I lay awake for a long time—angry at Toni, and at Raina for not wanting me, and at our parents for being gone so that she could stay with her lover. At the same time, though, I knew that the situation was not as bad as it could have been—I don't know what I would have done if Toni had spent the night at our place. I thought, for a long time, about what Stacy had said. She was right, I knew—I should have been getting out there. And at certain times, like that night, when my feelings for Raina seemed unbearable, I actually half-wished that I were drawn to other people. But I wasn't, and it was hopeless; I was trapped by my own doing. And I couldn't see how it was ever going to change.

CHAPTER 14

The next Tuesday, after we'd been back at school for a week, our team played—and won—its first league game. I got a ride home from Telisa because it was raining, the water coming down on our roof so hard that I found Ann hiding under my bed. Raina came home right after me—her team had won its game, too—and the parents got in a little later. Because the parents were feeling too tired to cook, we ordered a couple of pizzas. After dinner, Claudia stayed at the kitchen table to work on her speech, and my father went upstairs to grade some homework. Toni called, and so Raina disappeared into her room; I flopped on the couch downstairs and read *Sports Illustrated.* It had been a long day and a tiring game. I was just starting to nod off when the doorbell rang.

Ann rushed toward the door and made a huge racket, and because she didn't let up after a few obligatory barks, I knew that whoever was out on the stoop was not someone familiar. I dragged myself up off the couch and made my way to the door. Through the peephole I saw two middle-aged white men. One

I recognized as Larry Henderson. He had the same tall, squarish body and sandy crew cut as his son, and he wore what seemed like the standard outfit for a football coach—casual gray slacks, white sneakers, yellow windbreaker over a white polo shirt. The man standing next to him was smaller, balding, and dressed in a gray suit; his pale forehead was shiny and he appeared to be sweating, despite the chilly air. Although I'd never seen this man before, I realized immediately that he was Dr. Shelton, the principal of my father's school.

I held Ann back by her collar and opened the door. The rain was coming down in torrents now; it sounded like the pavement was sizzling.

"Is your father home?" Larry Henderson asked without saying hello. "We'd like to have a word with him."

He didn't really seem to see me, but I felt Dr. Shelton's cold, scrutinizing glare, and it made me shiver with discomfort. "Yeah, just a minute," I said. "Let me go get him."

I went upstairs and into the parents' room, found my father leaning over his desk. "Dad," I said. "Larry Henderson's here. And I think Dr. Shelton's with him."

He'd been writing a comment on one of the homework papers, and his pen stopped moving in mid-sentence. He stared down at his desk for what seemed like a long time. "Thank you," he finally said.

My father stood up then, not looking at me, and walked quickly out of the room. I followed a few steps behind, and stayed halfway up the stairs while he opened the door. "Hello, Larry," I heard my father say. "Hello, Bob."

"We need to speak with you, Wendell," I heard Larry Henderson say.

"Well, come on in."

"No, I think you should come outside."

My father didn't answer for a moment, and I could hear the rain through the open doorway. "Since you drove all the way over here," he finally said, "you might as well come in."

"No, we really need to speak to you privately."

When my father answered this time, his voice sounded like frozen steel. "If you have something to tell me," he said to the men, "then you can do it in my house, in front of my family."

Dr. Shelton spoke now, his voice higher and more disdainful than Larry Henderson's. "This is business, Wendell," he said. "This is between you and us. Now you just step out here on the driveway so we can talk."

"No," my father said. "If you want to talk to me, then you can do it inside. And I'd recommend that you come in here, anyway. If some bored gangbanger rolls by here and sees you on the stoop, he might think you're a couple of cops and *shoot* your ass."

There was silence for a moment, and then the sound of the two men, my father's superiors, stepping up into the house. I retreated up the staircase to get out of their sight, and perched in the same spot I'd staked out four months before in order to listen to the coaches talk to Raina. All three of them sat down in the living room. Claudia didn't appear and I wondered if she was still in the kitchen, being quiet, and listening, like me.

"So what is it you want to discuss?" my father asked.

Larry Henderson took a deep breath and then exhaled sharply. "Well," he said, "something is going on here we don't like. We think you're trying to undercut the team."

"What are you talking about?"

"We think you have some kind of vendetta against my son, and that you're giving him unreasonably low grades in your class."

My father laughed, sounding almost—but not quite—amused. "That's ridiculous," he said. "Eric hardly ever comes to class, and he doesn't really do his homework, and the homework he *does* bother to do is crappy. I'm just giving him what he deserves, and actually, I'm giving him *better.* A harsher grader would flunk him without a second thought."

"I disagree," Larry said. "I think you're letting your feelings cloud your judgment." He paused. "It's pretty obvious that you're determined to make Eddie Nuñez the quarterback next year."

My father was silent for a moment. "That has nothing to do with it," he said. "That has no relation whatsoever to Eric's grades."

"I think it does," Larry countered. "I think it has everything to do with them. It's no secret that you and some of the more . . . misguided . . . of the players believe that Eddie is better than Eric. But team decisions are not made by committee. You're all wrong, and Eric's the starter, and Eddie will stay on the second string. And you, Wendell, need to get with the program."

"If Eric keeps doing what he's been doing, he is going to fail my class. And then it won't matter who you think is better, because he won't be able to play."

"Listen, Wendell, you—"

"Hold it, Larry," said Dr. Shelton, who'd been silent so far. Then his voice changed a little, and I knew he was speaking to my father. "Star athletes do not flunk classes at my school."

My father half-laughed, and then stopped. "Well, Eric Henderson just might be the first."

"He will not fail," Dr. Shelton said, "as long as I am the principal." He paused. "I know the players love you and look up to you, Wendell. It would be a shame if you weren't with us next year."

My father took a moment to answer. "What are you trying to say?"

"We're not trying to say anything," Larry said. "We just want you to think about what you're doing. Think hard. Because there's a lot more at stake for you here than what grade you give my son." He paused. "You know, I could swear—and Dr. Shelton agrees with me—that the boys on the line pulled their blocks a few times this year and let Eric get hit pretty bad. Knowing how you feel about the quarterback situation, some people might wonder if you had anything to do with it."

There was a long, loaded silence. Then my father said, "Oh, give me a fucking break, Larry. You know that's bullshit. If the kids pulled a block or two, then it was their own damn idea. And if the two of you are going to threaten me, then at least have the balls to really *threaten* me instead of hiding behind these stupid insinuations."

"We're not trying to threaten you," said Larry. "We just want you to think a little before you do anything."

"Oh, you want me to think, huh? Well, think about this: get the fuck out of my house."

I heard the rustle of clothes as the two men stood up. "You show that kind of disrespect again," said Dr. Shelton, "and you won't have a place to go to work tomorrow."

"Right, and I have witnesses that you came over here and wanted to talk to me. Now get out of here."

The two men rose and left the house, and my dad slammed the door behind them. He stormed off toward the kitchen, and I ran down the stairs after him, the dog following right at my heels. I got there just as he was pulling a bottle of beer from the refrigerator; Claudia was leaning against the sink. His lips were pressed tightly together, and I noticed that his hand, the empty one, was clenched into a fist. Claudia and I both stood there looking at him, not saying anything. He finally saw us, looked annoyed. He said, "What?"

"Are you all right?" Claudia asked.

He fumbled in a drawer for the bottle opener, found it, popped the cap off of his beer. "I'm fine," he said. "I'm wonderful. I've never been better." Then he pushed by us, sat down at the table, and used the remote to change the channel on the television. He ignored us and stared at the screen.

Because neither of the parents would talk about what was happening with my father, I tried to ignore it and distract myself with league. This wasn't especially hard, because I liked to play in league. There were certain teams that were always particularly fun to victimize, like Beverly Hills, whom we hated on principle, and whom we never beat by less than thirty points. Their school had a two-story *indoor* parking lot, a huge, perfectly clipped front lawn straight out of a brochure for some Ivy League college, and a retractable basketball court that closed over a pool. We played them at their place in mid-January. As we stood by the edge of the hybrid thing waiting for the two halves of the court to come together, we tossed peanut M&M's into the water. All of their players wore diamond earrings, which they took off at their bench before the game. It was very important to us to kick the shit out of them.

During the junior varsity games, which were held immediately after ours, my teammates and I would wander around the neighborhood of the school where we'd just played. Wealthy neighborhoods were the best. The whole group of us strolling through Beverly Hills or El Segundo turned more than a few peroxided heads. We were like kids let loose in a store full of expensive china—everyone watched us uneasily, expecting disaster, and that made it all the more fun for us to be there.

If we'd played at home, we'd make a quick trip to the corner store, and then, home or away, we'd come back and make a nuisance of ourselves in the bleachers. The JV game would be about half over by then, so for the last two quarters we would comment on the other team.

"They fadin fast like Michael Jackson's skin," said Q.

"They weak like solar-powered vibrators," said Telisa.

"They nonexistent like Reagan's brain," said I. Then: "Number Twenty-one look pretty good, T. Why don't you go try to talk to her after the game?"

"Not my type, homegirl. Besides, I got a woman already. Why don't *you* go try sweatin her, Q?"

Q put her hand on her hip in mock offense. "Girl, you barkin up the wrong tree. Why don't *you* go, Nance? You the one that's been single 'bout fifty years."

I pretended to be insulted. "Aw, girl, why you dis me?"

"'Cos you deserve it," Telisa answered. "Foolish Asian girl."

"Foolish black girl."

We both turned to Q. "Foolish Asian and black girl."

It was our senior year, and we were determined to have as much fun as possible. On the bus rides home Telisa and I would make up raps; after a particularly exhilarating win we'd all dance or roughhouse in the aisles until the bus driver pulled over and threatened to make us walk. We didn't care. These girls were my friends, my family, and I only had a few more months to hang out with them. Our time was passing—I could almost *hear* it, as if the last few seconds of my most important game were ticking away on an invisible scoreboard. We taped our newspaper clippings up in the locker room and drew word bubbles on the pictures of our opponents. We wore our green-and-white letter jackets everywhere—even, in Telisa's case, to church.

For some reason, around this time, I kept remembering an old man we'd encountered when we were sophomores. We were at Denny's one day after a game, and Q took the cherry off her chocolate sundae and tied the stem into a knot with her tongue. Telisa and I thought this was brilliant. We kept asking the waitress to bring us more cherries, and then lost ourselves in laughter while Q repeated her trick. There was a man sipping milk in the booth across from us; he was the oldest man I'd ever seen. "Check out the mummy," Telisa said when she noticed him watching us, but we soon forgot him and turned our attention back to Q. When we started to leave, though, the man sat up straight, and grabbed my arm as I tried to walk past. His gnarled hand felt like something dead against my skin. His eyes, though, were bright and lucid, and the tiny purple veins that laced his eyeballs seemed to grow darker as he stared at me like a messenger from some unimaginable country. "Savor it, all of it, even the pain," he said in a surprisingly steady voice. Then he let go, and we walked out of the restaurant, Q and Telisa making jokes about crazy old men. I laughed along with them, but my arm still tingled where the old man had touched it, and I never quite forgot what he'd said.

During the league season I wasn't home as much, or at least it felt that way, because even when I was present in body, my mind was always on our next or our previous game. The house seemed more like a pit stop—just a place to roll into, fuel up, and get the damaged parts fixed before I sped off again into the never-ending race of the season. My father I didn't notice that much. I think that most kids relegate their parents to scenery at times, taking it for granted that they'll always be there to cook dinner, do laundry, and nag about homework, but allowing them no significance apart from their function in our lives. When I did bother to pay attention, he seemed burdened; I'd find him staring out the window sometimes and looking very sad, or sitting slumped at the kitchen table with his head against his fist. The humor which had always been his way of deflecting painful matters seemed now to have vanished completely. He'd relax more when Claudia was home, though, and it was getting harder and harder to remember a time when he had ever been without her. During his better periods, he continued to be shamelessly romantic, and had a penchant for demonstrating his love in ways that were quite embarrassing—to me—like when he hired the singing telegram people to come sing "Wonderful World" for Claudia's birthday. The only time he really seemed to focus on me was when he tried to talk about my picking a school, which was, of course, talk I quickly deflected. Otherwise, while Claudia occasionally gave me a searching look after Raina left the room, my father remained oblivious. I avoided being alone with Claudia for fear she'd bring something up, and saved my love-related complaints for Ann, whom I'd taken to walking every night. She was, of course, extremely sympathetic.

And what was Raina up to all this time? I don't know. We saw less of each other once the league season began, and I was almost too busy to miss her. I didn't care as much, now, about how her season was going—partly because I no longer asked about her point totals; partly because, when I did happen to hear them, they seemed to be about the same as mine. If only one of us had been a recruit—or if there'd been a big disparity in the number or quality of the schools recruiting us—our relationship, I'm sure, would have been more tense. Fortunately, though, things seemed fairly even between us. For every coach that stopped calling me, one also stopped calling her; for every school that stepped up its efforts for her, one also stepped up its efforts for me. We were two of the most sought-after players in the state, and we were getting equal amounts of attention. I doubt that Raina would have particularly minded if I had gotten more. But if *she* had gotten more—despite my attempts to be mature—I think I would have minded a lot.

Raina's love life was a mystery to me, as always. She appeared to have forgiven Toni again—a fact that I found frustrating but not surprising. I think her resolve was broken when Toni presented her with her belated Christmas gift. But even I could understand this, when I found out what it was: floor seats to the Lakers-Celtics game. For the several weeks that followed, Toni called Raina at least three or four times a day. This was unlike her, and I wondered if it had to do with the fact that Raina would be graduating soon, and leaving at the end of the summer. Sometimes she left mushy messages on the answering machine when Raina wasn't home, which annoyed me. Didn't she know that I usually got home before Raina and was the first one to check the machine? Maybe she did know. Maybe that was the point. Finally, I just started to turn the machine off in the morning before I left for school.

Neither Raina nor I was home much during those weeks, but when we did spend time together—in her room, watching *Moonlighting,* shooting baskets in the driveway—it was apparent that some tiny new bridge of understanding had been forged between us. It was the paradoxical sense of familiarity and discomfort which comes from heightened knowledge. At any rate, we did not pretend to be so unaware of each other. One day when Raina came home from being out somewhere with Toni, upset once again at something she'd done, I said, fed up, "You know, you deserve better than to hang out with people who are always bringing you down."

I expected her to get mad, but instead she smiled and replied, "And *you* should give yourself more credit than to think that people wouldn't like you if they knew how much went on in your head."

Our eyes met. I smiled back at her. A month before, neither of us would have spoken like this, and we certainly wouldn't have been able to look at each other if we had. But things were different now. Maybe it helped that we had each seen firsthand a bit of the other's weakness. And while her reaction to our talk at the beach had angered and disappointed me, my general discovery that she feared being open to people seemed to round her out somehow. It did occur to me, though, that despite what she'd said about the things that went on in my head, our friendship was still dependent upon my never voicing what I felt. And there were certain topics we never touched upon—our missing parents, what my father might know about me, my utter lack of love life—because we couldn't have talked about anything real without talking about what existed, and didn't exist, between us. But the irony of our holiday crisis, the unforeseen result, was that our friendship, having survived it, was actually stronger. Because of the pain we'd experienced and the knowledge we'd gained, there was a fullness to our relationship that hadn't existed before. We appreciated it now, we meant more to each other. I don't mind admitting this scared the hell out of me.

During this period, both Raina and I went on our recruiting trips. I spent two days each at Iowa, Washington, Virginia, UNLV, and Arizona. Raina went to Michigan State, Michigan, Stanford, Virginia, and Washington. The trips were fun, I suppose, especially since I got to miss school, but the novelty of being flown somewhere, then dined—if not wined—and taken around a school for two days, wore off almost immediately during my first trip, which was to Iowa. I met coaches, players, professors, alumni, and athletic directors, a revolving-doorful of people whose names escaped me as soon as I was out of their presence. I watched practices and games, and got shuffled around between the coaches and players, who took me to their classes, their dorm rooms, their apartments. I saw the schedules which outlined who was responsible for me at what time, and I felt, more than anything, like a child whose babysitting arrangements were being made. Most of the players I met were cool, and some were honest enough to tell me the drawbacks of their programs and the idiosyncrasies of their coaches. I tended to gravitate, though, towards the players who were from L.A. The coaches, not ignorant of the ties of geography, had set things up so that I stayed overnight with a player from California on every single one of my trips. In two of the cases, the player's roommate was Asian, and that was probably intentional, too. The coaches couldn't have planned, though, the conversation I had with the sophomore point guard during the first night of my visit to Iowa.

From the moment I met her, I was sure I'd seen her before, even though she was from Washington, D.C. And where I'd seen her, I thought, was at a gay club at home. When some of the Iowa girls took me out to a local house party, I maneuvered the player, Jamie, away from the others, under the pretense of wanting to ask about the program. She was good-looking, with skin the woody color of maple syrup, and bright, liquid eyes. We talked for a few minutes about how Iowa was doing that season, and then I asked her if she ever went out to L.A.

"Yeah," she said, pulling at the hair which hung just to her shoulder. "My dad lives there. I go out and stay with him for two or three weeks every summer."

"Oh, really?" I said. "I thought you looked kinda familiar. What do you do when you're in L.A.?"

She suddenly looked at me with greater interest. "Oh, I go . . . out."

"Oh, yeah?" I said, smiling. "What kind of places you go?"

She smiled back at me now. She knew. "Oh, just places. You know. Long Beach, Pico-Union, West Hollywood."

Some of the most popular women's clubs were in Long Beach, Pico-Union, West Hollywood.

Just then, two other players joined us and we cut our conversation short. We already knew what we needed to, though. I hung out with Jamie for the rest of the weekend, and learned about her life there. She told me that no one in the athletic department knew she was gay, and that if there were any other gay players on the team, they kept it to themselves. She'd had a hard time meeting people in Iowa and was looking forward to moving back to D.C. My visit there was like a vacation for her; we stayed up until three A.M. both nights, and had a snowball fight once while the campus slept, me soaking my borrowed jacket. There were a couple of times when I got vibes from her, and I was sure she would have been up for something if I had been interested. I wasn't, of course. Still, I liked hanging out with her, and knew we could have become good friends, although the school didn't win me over. Too cold, too flat, too country for me. Even Jamie's presence there wasn't enough to make me go.

The other eventful visit I had was to Washington, because Raina was there at the same time. We actually didn't see that much of each other—we were whisked off to separate classes, met with the coaches at different times, and were only together at their game and at a practice. But it was still intriguing and fun to know that she was around somewhere, going through the same routine. And when our paths did cross, we compared notes, and gave each other our real impressions. During the game, which Raina and I watched from right behind the home bench, I commented that all of the Washington players, even the guards, were big and stocky.

Raina nodded in agreement, and grinned at me. "They ain't called the Huskies for nothing."

When my campus visits were completed, I had an overwhelming amount of new information to process. Like Raina, I decided to make a chart listing all the good and bad things about each of the schools. Some of these distinctions were easy—Virginia, which was close to D.C., was a plus for location, and Washington a minus for weather. Las Vegas was ugly but had great support for its women's basketball team, and Arizona was exactly the opposite. Seattle had large numbers of Asians and gays, whereas Iowa was the whitest, straightest place I'd ever seen. It seemed like every place was a trade-off in some way or another—a few good qualities for an equal number of bad ones. The one thing the schools had in common, I noticed, was that they were all in states I'd been to with my AAU team. I worked on my chart for days, until my head began to hurt from looking at it. I consulted my Cheryl Miller doll for advice, but she didn't have much to say. And I still wasn't any closer to making a choice.

CHAPTER 15

On the last Wednesday night in January, Claudia got home a little earlier than usual in order to cook dinner for her friends. Although it was 5:30—prime time for pickup ball—I was home studying for my upcoming finals. Raina, who had her schoolwork more under control, had gone to the park by herself. My textbooks and notes were spread out on top of the coffee table in the living room; I sat on the floor and leaned over them while Claudia shuffled around in the kitchen. She was making some kind of pasta dish with lots of basil and oregano, and as I stared, unseeing, at the chemistry book in front of me, I wondered if Paula would come. She had boycotted their last two dinners. And while Rochelle and Kim, apparently, had spoken to her on the phone, Claudia hadn't talked to her yet. Meanwhile, as far as I could tell, Kim and Rochelle had been lobbying on Claudia's behalf; Kim had left a message about a conversation they'd had with some other person on the speakers' committee.

A little before six, the doorbell rang. It couldn't have been

Kim or Rochelle, since they weren't due until 7:30, and I was trying to figure out who would show up unannounced when Claudia came into the living room.

"Glued to the floor?" she asked, smiling, when she saw I hadn't moved.

"I was about to get up."

"Uh-huh," she said, continuing on toward the door. "Right. And it's probably one of your friends, anyway."

I got to my feet, slowly, to see who it was, but when Claudia opened the door, she just stared for a moment. "Hello, Paula," she finally said.

I didn't know what to do, and sat down again. From where I was, I couldn't see Paula, and I wondered how she looked. It took a few seconds before she replied. "Hello, Claudia. It's been a long time."

Claudia stood very straight, her hand pressed tight against the edge of the door. "Are you here for dinner? I told Kim and Rochelle not to come until seven-thirty."

"Yes, I know," said Paula. "I mean, no I'm not. Staying for dinner. I came by early because I knew they wouldn't be here." She paused. "I'd like to talk to you, Claudia."

Claudia looked at me, caught me staring, turned back to Paula. "All right, let's talk out here," she said. She stepped outside and shut the door.

I scrambled around the love seat, went up to the door, and pressed my ear against the wood. They must have been standing just a few feet out in the driveway—although their voices were muffled, I could hear every word.

"I've missed you, Paula," I heard Claudia say, and I was so surprised by this that I pulled back for a moment.

"I've missed you, too," said Paula.

There was caution in their voices, but also pain, also caring; it made me wonder what their friendship had been like before.

"Listen," Paula said. "I'm sorry I tried to keep you from giving your talk. You should do it. The committee still liked the outline of your speech, and oh, I don't know. I just came to my senses. It was immature of me to use the BBA to try and work out my issues with you."

Claudia was silent for a moment. "So you're apologizing?"

"About the speaking thing, yes. But I'm still upset about everything else." She paused. "I feel like you've deserted me, Claudia."

Claudia gave a joyless laugh. "I feel like you've deserted *me,* Paula."

They were both quiet for a few seconds. Then Claudia said, "What do you want me to do, Paula? I mean, what do I have to do to show you that I haven't changed?"

"But you *have* changed, Claudia. Ever since you moved in with Wendell. Ever since you've *been* with him, really. You're not around as much, and you don't call us as much, and you just seem, I don't know. More *distant.*"

"I'm just *busier,* Paula. It's not that I care any less. What—you think this is Wendell's fault?"

It took Paula a moment to answer. "Well, you weren't like this when you were still married to Carl. Or when you were with Mark or Darryl."

Claudia laughed. "Carl, if you remember, spent more time with his other women than he did with me. And Mark and Darryl were never serious." She paused. "I guess you're right, though. I probably *have* been less available, and that's *my* fault. I promise to make an effort to spend more time with you all. Meanwhile, can't you just try to be happy that I've found somebody? I mean, I know you'll probably never like Wendell, but can't you be happy for *me?*"

"I don't know, Claudia," Paula answered. "I just don't know."

"I'd be happy for *you* if you found somebody."

"I know you would. But that'd be different. I'd never put you in this position."

"*What* position?" said Claudia, and it sounded like her patience was running thin. "Paula," she said, trying to be calm again. "I haven't *done* anything to you."

"Well, it's nice that you think so," said Paula. She paused. "I just can't believe you've let that man be more important than our friendship."

"I *haven't,*" said Claudia. "*You* have."

Just then, the phone rang, and I jumped as if someone had caught me. I ran into the living room and picked it up on the third ring. "Hello?" I said.

"Hi, is this Nancy?" asked the voice on the other end.

"Uh, yes."

"This is Rochelle. How you doing? Honey, could you tell Claudia that I'm going to be a little late? I've got a few more calls to make here at the office, and then I have to go home and feed my cat."

"No problem," I said, and then hung up as quickly as possible so I could go back to the door. When I got there, though, it seemed that Claudia and Paula had moved further down the driveway, and while I could hear the murmur of their voices, I couldn't make out what they said. Finally I gave up and returned to my books. A few minutes later, Claudia came back inside and headed straight for the kitchen, where she banged pots around until her friends arrived. I said hello to them, and went up to my room. For once I wasn't interested in eavesdropping; I didn't want to hear any more.

The semester ended the following week. On the night before our finals began, my father and Claudia cooked a big dinner for Raina and me. They made barbecue ribs, black-eyed peas, potato salad, and cornbread. We ate at six, the two of us kids not talking to the parents much because we were studying at the table—Raina had Government and English Lit. the next day, and I had Trig and Chemistry. I kept licking my fingers before I handled my flash cards for Chemistry, but the cards still got covered with red-orange smudges from my father's special barbecue sauce.

"Dad, why couldn't you have made something less messy?" I asked.

He'd been buttering a piece of cornbread, and he looked up at me now. Creases formed at the corners of his eyes, and he almost smiled. "I try to do you a favor and cook a good meal before you descend into finals hell, and you complain that the food is *messy?"* He looked at Claudia and shook his head. "What are we going to do with this child?"

"I don't know," she answered. She smiled, but looked subdued. "We could concoct some horrible punishment. Make her wash all the dishes with a toothbrush."

"Good idea," he said. "And maybe we can get the other child there to help her."

Raina, who'd been staring at her notebook, looked up at my father. "'By thy long grey beard and glittering eye/Now wherefore stopp'st thou me?'"

My father really smiled now. "No reason," he said. "Just checking to see if you were with us."

Raina put a hand on his arm and gave him a mock serious look. "I'm with you, brother," she said.

He shook his head, looked greatly pleased. "Are you engrossed in English Literature?"

She nodded. "Deeply."

I looked at her notebook and laughed. "Raina, there's nothing but basketball stats on that page."

Claudia looked up sharply. I could tell she wasn't amused by Raina's lack of concentration. She'd been in a horrible mood since her confrontation with Paula, and also busy, obsessed with her speech. I remember thinking that her concern was unnecessary—Raina always did fine on tests—and that she was being a bit uptight. It would take years before I'd understand why she watched Raina's life so closely, or how desperately, because of her own thwarted hopes, she wanted for her daughter to succeed. "Can I ask what you're thinking about?" she said now, her voice heavy with disapproval.

Raina's smile, when she answered, was a little strained. "I was thinking about dead British poets."

Claudia raised her eyebrows. "Dead British poets who played basketball?"

Raina leaned back in her chair and sighed. "O.K., you're right, I wasn't thinking about dead British poets. Actually, I was sitting here wondering where I'll be in a year."

My father nodded and stroked his chin. "I've been wondering that myself," he said.

At first I thought he meant this in relation to Raina, that he wondered where she'd be in a year, and I found it a little strange that he was so concerned about her future. Then I thought he meant it in relation to me, and felt a flicker of annoyance at his meddling in my business. But finally I realized that I'd been wrong in both assumptions; that he had meant it, in fact, about himself. Claudia must have come to the same conclusion, because she gave him a searching look.

"Why?" she said. "Where do you *think* you're going to be in a year?"

My father sighed. "Well, that's just it, isn't it? I really don't know."

The light mood of a few minutes earlier had suddenly vanished. Claudia sat straight up in her chair and put her fork down. "Do you really think that the school would fire you?"

My father stared down at his plate. "Yes, I do."

She was silent for a moment. "Well, I guess that's just a risk you'll have to take, then," she said. She picked up her fork again, stirred some peas around on her plate. "I don't know, maybe I'm just being an optimist, but I think that if you do what's right, do what you have to, it'll all work out somehow in the end."

My father didn't answer for a long time. I tried to make myself smaller, and Raina stared at her notebook; we both pretended not to listen. When my father spoke again, his words were careful, his voice intense and low. "I *love* those kids," he said slowly. "It would be *terrible* if I couldn't coach them anymore."

Claudia nodded. "I know. I know how much you love being a mentor. But if worse came to worse, you could always go coach at another school, couldn't you? And I'm sure you'd love the new kids, too."

I glanced up at my father to see how he'd react to this. He shot Claudia a look which seemed composed mainly of annoyance, but which also contained a bit of anger. "That's not the point," he said. "And besides, it's not as easy to get a new coaching job as you think." He took a gulp of his beer, and stared at a spot on the table. "A couple of weeks ago, I tracked down Cameron Smith, who was the assistant coach at Hawthorne before I came. He had to resign ten years ago because there was this rumor going around that he was providing drugs to some of the players. It never became public, and none of the boys who supposedly got drugs from him ever materialized, but the whole thing was enough of a scandal to force Smith to lose his job." He paused. "I always believed what Larry told me about him, but then when all of this stuff started happening with me, I wondered if there was more to that story. So I found Smith through some other teachers who were still in touch with him. He's down in Long Beach now, working in a real estate office, not coaching or teaching at all. And the story he told me was pretty damn different from the tale that Larry's been spinning all these years."

Claudia was watching his face closely. "Well, what was *his* version?"

My father sighed. "Smith's version, yes. What a version. According to Smith, Larry's wife, Cathy, had her eye on him—on Smith, I mean. He was single at the time, and Cathy was unhappy, which is one thing that hasn't changed much since then. Anyway, she launched into a full-scale pursuit of him—calling him at home, hanging all over him after games, writing letters that Larry would intercept from their pile of outgoing mail. She didn't try very hard to hide her intentions, and maybe she actually wanted Larry to know. At any rate, Larry was pissed as hell. Nothing ever came of Cathy's efforts because Smith wasn't interested, but I guess just what she had done was enough for Larry. Suddenly the rumors about drugs were floating around. And Smith had to resign. And no other school would touch him—even though he was a first-rate coach, even though they knew the drug thing was a lie. So now he's out of teaching altogether. And Larry Henderson is still the head football coach, and Cathy is still his wife."

Claudia was silent for a moment. "So Larry's powerful," she said. "And vengeful. But that doesn't change the fact that you have to do what's right."

"I'm in a position where I can help these kids, and guide them. It's a privilege and a responsibility to be where I am, and I don't take those notions lightly."

"I know you're really invested in your players—"

"Those kids count on me. They talk to me. They do not want me to leave."

"Yes, they love you, Wendell, but you've still got to do what's right."

"I know," my father said. "I know I have to do what's right. But the hard part is figuring out just exactly what that is."

The next day I descended into the land that my father had aptly described as finals hell. It was the land of coffee and scantron sheets; of potato chips and cookies; of watching the first blush of sunrise color our windows pink and gray. It was the land of grueling two-hour exams, after which we somehow had to pull ourselves together enough to make it to a practice or a game. Raina and I didn't talk to each other much during the three days of our finals, and neither of us talked to the parents. My last final was on Thursday, and after our game, I walked home and went straight to bed without eating my dinner.

On Friday, we had no school, and I slept all morning before getting up to go to practice at two. When I got home, I took a shower, and then sat with Raina in front of the TV in the kitchen. She was in a shitty mood, despite her finals being over, because Toni had left a message saying she had to cancel their plans for that night. I was glad that Raina was staying home, shitty mood or not. Claudia came in at seven, and when she called out for my father, no one went to the door to greet her except for Ann. She set her briefcase down in the living room and came into the kitchen. She was wearing a long blue dress with yellow flowers on it, and blue heels which brought her almost to Raina's height.

"Where's your father?" she asked me.

I shrugged my shoulders. "I don't know."

She went upstairs and changed out of her work clothes, reappearing a few minutes later in jeans and a sweatshirt. "Has he called?" she asked, as she poured herself a glass of Coke.

"Nope," I said, not looking at her. Raina and I were drained and barely functioning. We were also caught up in a rerun of *The Cosby Show* and didn't ponder my father's absence.

"Well, maybe we should call him," she said. She pressed the mute button on the remote control, which brought grunts of protest from Raina and me, and then dialed the number of my father's school. She stood there in the corner of the kitchen, brow furrowed and phone pressed to her ear, for a good minute and a half or two minutes. Finally she sighed and hung up. "No answer," she said.

Raina turned the volume back on, and Claudia continued to look concerned; I knew she was thinking about what had happened to me on New Year's. "Well," she said finally, "I wish he'd at least call and say whether he plans to be home for dinner."

He was not home for dinner, nor for coffee afterwards, nor for *Miami Vice* at nine. He was not home at 10:30, at which point Claudia stopped working on her speech and began to call some of his colleagues, and even I was beginning to get concerned. Then finally, just after Claudia had completed one of her calls, we heard his car pull into the driveway. Raina and I were in the living room, where we'd moved for the larger TV. Claudia came in from the kitchen and looked at the door.

"He'd better have a good explanation for this," she said.

The door opened, and my father came in, and the dog ran up to greet him. We heard a helicopter pass overhead. My father crouched down to pet Ann, and when he stood up and looked at us, we all saw that he swayed a little.

"Where have you *been?*" Claudia demanded, sounding equally worried and mad.

"Out," my father said. He took a few steps forward, and when he came into the light, we could see that his face was almost as red as the Clippers shirt Raina was wearing. He tried to unzip his jacket, but his fingers seemed to pull in all the wrong directions.

"You drove like *that?*" Claudia said, hands on her hips. "What were you *thinking?* At least you could have called so I could come pick you up."

"Leave me alone," my father said, holding his hands up in defense.

"No, I won't leave you alone. What do you mean, leave you alone? You had me worried half to death. I was just about getting ready to call the police."

"I turned in the kids' grades today," he said.

Claudia went silent. Raina and I were sitting on the couch, and it felt like something cold crawled up the back of my neck. I didn't know what Raina was doing, because I couldn't bring myself to look at her.

My father managed to get himself around the love seat and sit down. Then he stared straight ahead, not really looking at anything. "I turned in the kids' grades today," he said again, his voice completely flat. "I finished grading all the finals and figured out the kids' grades, Eric Henderson's last of all."

Claudia stood right where she was, but her shoulders slumped a little, and when she spoke again, her voice was much softer. "And what did you give him?"

My father broke out with a short, bitter laugh, and began to rock back and forth. "I gave him a B," he said. "B for 'bastard.' I could've given him an A for 'asshole,' or even a C. Oh, except I forgot. The C is my grade. C for 'coward.'" He closed his eyes and kept rocking, fingers entwined over one of his knees. Claudia went over and stood next to him. She touched the space between his shoulder and neck, then pulled his head to her stomach and stroked his hair.

"It's all right, Wendell," she said softly, as my father squeezed his eyes tighter and grimaced.

All of this enraged me—my father's admission, Claudia's response—and I jumped up off the couch and glared at him. "How *could* you?" I yelled, and I saw him flinch a little. "I can't *believe* you! How could you *do* that?"

"Nancy," Claudia said, but I was already gone. I ran up the stairs, went into my room, and slammed the door. I didn't know what to do; it was as if my father had changed right in front of my eyes, transformed into someone I did not want to know. The feeling was deeper, somehow, than disappointment; it felt like an utter betrayal. Years later, I'd have a better understanding of what my father must have been going through. I'd know that sometimes, standing up for your principles costs more than you think you can afford. My father would have lost his job if he hadn't passed Eric, and new jobs were not easy to come by; on top of that, he really believed that he'd be helping his kids by staying. But that night, and for several months afterwards, I would listen to no excuses. I was ashamed of my father, and angry at what he'd done, and also, I know now, afraid that I might be like him. I did not want to have anything to do with him, or with the part of myself that might be capable of the same kind of weakness and compromise. I was ashamed that Raina had seen this, too—in him, and perhaps in me—and the way I dealt with that shame was by blaming him, running away. From then on his pronouncements held no weight anymore, and his advice was insubstantial, something to walk through, unobstructed, like idle conversation, like fog.

One Saturday night in mid-February, Raina's team had a nonleague game. Coaches arranged these sometimes if they were old rivals who would not otherwise have the chance to let their teams loose on each other, or if they just needed some competition in the middle of an undemanding league schedule. This particular game had some additional intrigue, because a few of Raina's teammates, including Stacy, had gotten into a minor scuffle with some girls from this team after a USC game in December. Now both sides were out for blood, and the bleachers of Raina's high school were as packed as I'd ever seen them, despite the big storm we were having. I sat with a few of my teammates behind the home team's bench. Most of us were in standard jock gear—ratty shorts, sweatshirt, hip-pack. We almost always dressed this way, with the allowable substitution of jeans for shorts, partially because it was comfortable, but also because we looked upon the street clothes of nonathletes with the same disdain I imagine military people have for civilian attire. Anyway, Claudia sat with my father about five rows behind us; I didn't even turn to look at them, because I did not want to see my father's face. Behind them, in the last row, were three college scouts, there for Raina no doubt, set apart from the rest of the crowd by their silence, their dress (no-nonsense polo shirts with the names of their colleges embroidered on the pockets), and the clipboards they held in their laps. No one seemed to notice them, though, but me. People had come to see some intense basketball action and maybe even a little blood; already they were scrutinizing the players for signs of overt hostility. Members of the two teams glared at each other as they warmed up on opposite ends of the court. Toni was conspicuously absent.

I sat in the stands and looked at Raina, who was stretching alone in a corner and calmly eyeing the other team. Right then I decided that wherever I lived for the rest of my life, I'd have to go to the local basketball games. Gyms were my natural habitat—like this one, with its shiny blond wood, its stale air, its wooden bleachers so old and creaky they seemed ready to collapse. There were long red pads behind the baskets, placed there to cushion the impact of those who'd run downcourt too fast to stop for something so insignificant as a wall. Two bulbs on the scoreboard were burned out, so that the 8 became a 3. There was the sound of twenty-odd basketballs hitting the floor at short, irregular intervals, and the loud squeak of shoes on polished wood, which was like the call of some high-pitched bird. I was a creature of this place and all others like it. Everything about it—

the sound of the ball swishing through the net or clanging off of the rim, the black and white lines on the court, the smell of age-old sweat—was as natural and desirable to me as the earth, trees, and fresh air might be to a creature of the woods.

Raina, however, was oblivious to her surroundings. She was bent over a ball now, eyes shut, psyching herself up. The game that night was important, but to Raina every game was important; every game required the same level of commitment. I'd always thought that what made Raina such a wonderful player was her tremendous strength of character, but by now I knew it also was her pain. I wondered what Raina felt when she was out there on the court. I wondered what wound she had suffered, to make her need to prove so much.

A few minutes later, the game began, and as Raina grabbed the ball after her team's center won the tip-off, my face broke into a smile. I had fallen in love with Raina on the basketball court, and every time I saw her play again I remembered why. She was so unbelievably focused—even during warm-ups she seemed to have forgotten that any world outside of the game at hand existed. Usually reserved off the court, she became the leader on it, yelling out directions with an urgency and authority she completely masked when she wasn't playing basketball. Raina played the game as I could only dream of playing it, with an intensity I could equal only when I was playing against her. I loved watching her during games because I could stare at her openly. I took in everything about her—the grimace she wore as she sprinted downcourt; the hair slicked back and twisted into one perfect braid; the muscles of her legs, which were long and subtle, like swells formed by something moving underwater. She missed an easy lay-up and then berated herself for it, using a tone of voice she'd never use with someone else. The perspiration on her body made her skin glow.

There was something wrong that day. Her whole team was too tight, overanxious. The problem with playing on emotion is that while it can motivate you, it can also get you so wound up that it's impossible to function normally. That was what was happening to Raina's team now. They were missing easy shots, throwing passes to empty spaces, cracking under the pressure of the other team's full-court press. And they were yelling at each other, shifting blame, which only made them more angry, and so more tight. Raina was the only one who seemed unaffected. It was not that she wasn't as intense as her teammates; in truth, she was more intense, because her ability to focus had nothing to do with the anger that was defining the game for all the others. She not only managed to block out everything off the court, she also blocked out the distracting emotion on it. Firmly but calmly, she directed her teammates. She played her usual in-your-face, don't-give-up-an-inch brand of defense, made most of the shots she managed to get off, and set up a few shots for her teammates. Despite her efforts, though, she could not make up for collective mistakes, and when the buzzer sounded to mark the end of the half, her team was down by twelve. Raina and her teammates dragged themselves to their locker room, looking tired and frustrated.

At halftime I went to chat with the parents, snuck a few looks at the scouts, and bought some horrible concession-stand nachos. These I ate with Telisa while we discussed the prospects of Raina's team making a comeback (slim). We talked about our own three remaining league games, which we were sure to win, and about the girl that Telisa was checking out on the other side of the stands. Soon both teams came back onto the floor, shot around a bit to warm up, and the second half began.

The first three minutes of the third quarter went much like the previous half. Raina's team committed four turnovers, which led to three baskets for the other team, while scoring only once themselves. It looked like the game was over. But then, with 4:52 left in the quarter, something happened. Stacy made a steal, passed the ball to Raina, then got it back under the basket to cap off a three-on-one fast break. Score. Then Raina stole the in-bounds pass and took the jump shot right there from the baseline. Score. Then their center, of all people, a lanky 6'2" girl who just a few minutes earlier had tripped over her own feet and fallen in slow motion like a giant redwood, picked off a pass at midcourt. Two passes later, Raina had the ball. She pump-faked, got her defender in the air, drove around her, stopped under the basket. Pumped again, sent another girl flying, and went up with the ball just as the girl was coming down.

Basket and foul. The gym exploded.

Raina sank the free throw and they were down by nine. Telisa and I stood up and high-fived each other so hard that my hand still hurt two minutes later. This thing wasn't over yet.

To put it simply, she took over the game. After her team's initial comeback surge, things evened out again, and the teams traded baskets for a while. But suddenly Raina was at the center of everything. She controlled what was happening. She gathered the game into herself and parceled it out again as she saw fit. She didn't try to be flashy, but that only made her incredible plays—her drives between three defenders, her last-second thread-the-needle passes—seem all the more spectacular. It occurred to me for the first time that this sport was like music—that Raina was singing with her body the way that other people sang with their lungs.

How would Raina's voice sound if she sang like she played? It would be deep, not in its tone but in its layers, with each layer suggesting another beneath it until you were aware of a profound complexity granted only to geniuses or prophets. It would be the kind of voice that didn't immediately strike you, but then, when you listened more closely, startled you with its undisguised intensity. Her singularity would be manifest not in the words that she sang, or in the style with which she delivered them, but in the timbre and intonation of her voice. Singularity is rare. Some people try to disguise their lack of it, their lack of a new story to tell or a new way to tell an old one, with their false and blown-up notion of passion. They always fail. You are as naked behind a microphone as you are on a basketball court; in both cases all the masks you've so carefully constructed are totally stripped away, and no amount of flashiness or rehearsal or even perfect execution can hide the absence of that Great Intangible which makes an unforgettable singer, or athlete, unforgettable. Raina had that Great Intangible. Listening was revelation. I heard the music that she not only sang but seemed to be writing as she went along. I heard the ebb and flow of exquisite verses, the sudden rushes up and down the scales, the glorious resolution of a chorus. I saw the way she took the other players on the court and arranged them, like notes, so that they somehow came out in perfect order. Most of all, though, I heard the longing, the need, the struggle to prove her worth, that poured endlessly out of her, that *was* her.

I knew her team would win. I knew it the way you know upon waking up on certain mornings that it's going to be a wonderful day; the way you sense a letter from a long-lost friend the week before it finally arrives. It was inevitable. Halfway through the fourth quarter they were still down by five, and the other team wasn't giving an inch. But this was Raina's song now, so when she grabbed an offensive rebound, put it in, then stole the ball and scored again to cut the lead to one, nobody was less surprised than me. When she drove left off the wing to score the winning basket a few moments later, and then quickly nodded, as if to say she'd known they'd pull it off all along, I wanted to lift the ceiling with my shouts.

I was seventeen years old, and always hearing from my father that everything that seemed so important to me then would someday come to mean very little. He did not mean Raina, of course—he meant basketball, and impossible math tests, and the friends I had made at school. But the basic premise applied to everything—that the things I was experiencing then were not quite real, and would only factor into my impending personhood in the form of pleasant but insignificant memories. Even Claudia, in all her wisdom, said that Raina and I were too intense, too devoted to things we'd dismiss as mere episodes of youth once we reached that distant shore of adulthood. It didn't seem to me that this was right. It didn't seem that I could ever separate my love for Raina from myself and still keep that self intact. It was too deeply intertwined, *she* was too deeply intertwined, with all that I was. They were wrong, our parents, and not only because they underestimated the power of my emotions—and so Raina's as well—but also because they completely misunderstood the nature of them. It wasn't simply that I loved Raina; it was that she filled my life, she flowed through my veins, she splashed out into every corner of my body. And it wasn't simply that I admired her, envied her; it was that I sometimes wanted to *be* her.

CHAPTER 16

In the week after Raina's game, two major things happened which shook several of my friends' lives to the foundation. The first was that Telisa got kicked out of her house. I, along with the rest of my household, was among the first to know—she came banging on our door at two in the morning on a weeknight. The parents must have assumed, correctly, that it was someone for one of us kids, because neither of them came down right away—and when I opened the door and saw Telisa, I was glad that they hadn't. She was carrying a big duffel bag, and she wore a grim, frightened expression I'd never seen on her before. Her eyes were dry now, but I could tell she'd been crying, and her hair, which was normally brushed and perfect, was sticking out in all directions.

"My mom just threw me out, girl," she said, and her voice sounded raw and strained.

"Jesus," I said, not quite knowing what to do. "What happened?"

Telisa shook her head. "I don't wanna talk about it just yet. Can I come in and sit down for a second first?"

"Yeah, of course," I said. "Come on in."

We went into the kitchen and sat at the table. I got a beer for my friend, and a Milk-Bone for my dog, who'd been trailing along after me with her ears perked. Just then my father trudged in, wearing his pajamas. He was clearly annoyed at having been stirred from his sleep, and, since his mood had been so bad in recent weeks, not as accommodating as usual. He must have seen Telisa's face, though, because when he spoke, he sounded much calmer than he looked.

"We've all got to get up early in the morning," he said to my friend. "You can't just come knocking on people's doors in the middle of the night."

Telisa nodded seriously. "I know, Mr. T. I'm really sorry. But some crazy shit just went down at my house, and I had to get outta there right away."

He sighed heavily, and I knew he wasn't mad. "I suppose you'll be wanting to spend the night."

"Yeah, I would, if that's O.K. with you."

He sighed again and scratched his chin. "Yes, it's O.K. We'll talk about this in the morning. Nancy will get you some blankets." Then he turned to me. "Now don't you stay up half the night."

"We won't," I promised, not looking at him.

With that, my father dragged himself out again, the dog following on his heels. Telisa turned to me. "I'm sorry I woke y'all up," she said. "Your pops is really pissed at me, huh?"

"Whatever," I said. I didn't want to talk about him; I didn't care what he thought about anything. He'd been spending time outside of school with Larry Henderson lately, going to bars once or twice a week, and I couldn't understand this sudden turnaround, this strange defection; it made me even angrier than I'd been about the grade. A few days earlier, right after Raina's game, I'd found a note from Larry that my father had left on his nightstand. The note, written on official Hawthorne High School stationery, had said, "We're glad to have you back on our team." It had taken a great effort not to rip it into shreds. I threw this out of my mind now and turned back to my friend. "What happened?" I asked.

Telisa took a big gulp from her beer, set it down again, turned the bottle around in her hands. "I got home around midnight," she said, "and like a fool, I brought Shavon in so I could give her this tape she wanted to borrow." She sighed. "My mom usually goes to bed early, right? So I thought it'd be O.K. Me and Shavon went into the living room and got the tape, and then we just chilled there for a while. We weren't really doin nothin—just sittin there with our arms around each other—but then my mom walks into the living room and finds us." She stopped and shook her head, tapping the bottom of the bottle lightly against the table. Tears welled up in her eyes. "Man, she *lost* it. She went after Shavon and started punchin on her, and I just told Shavon to get outta there. Then she started yellin and cursin at *me,* tryin to punch on me, sayin she didn't raise me to be like this, and she wasn't gonna have no sick crazy people livin in her house. It was bad, girl. Then Earl woke up and got into it, said to leave me alone and that *she* was the one who was whack, and then *he* left, and I don't know where he went. Then she started screamin at me and sayin that I'd come between her and Earl, and that if I didn't pack up my stuff and leave she was gonna put it out in the street."

"Shit," was all I could think of to say.

"Yeah," Telisa said. "So I packed up as many of my clothes as I could, but I gotta go back over there and get the rest of my shit later."

"But I thought she knew about you and Shavon," I said.

"She did. But she didn't have to *deal* with it, you know what I'm sayin? Kind of like your dad is, now, with you. He probably knows, but he don't *wanna* know, and as long as you're single, he doesn't really have to face it."

I felt a wave of nausea pass through me. Once, when I was

with Yolanda, my father had come home unexpectedly while we were napping together on the couch. We'd jumped away from each other, just in time, and I think he'd willfully ignored our guilty looks. There'd come a day, though, when he wouldn't be able to ignore things anymore. But in order to talk about my being gay, we'd have to smash so many barriers that I wasn't sure we'd be able to face each other again.

"And even though I've got a girlfriend," Telisa continued, "I guess my mom just pretended it wasn't happening. But when she came out into the living room and saw us like that . . ." She shook her head. "I guess she couldn't pretend anymore."

We sat and talked for another half an hour. Then I set Telisa up with some blankets and pillows on the living room couch, and that became her bed for the next week. Although I was still too mad to convey my thanks or approval, my father was great through this time—he never asked what the fight had been about, but he knew Mrs. Coles was crazy, and so he told Telisa she was welcome to stay with us as long as she did her share of the chores. I saw him look at me every once in a while, trying to gauge my feelings; I knew that part of the reason he was being so nice to my friend was that he was trying to win me over. It wasn't going to work, though—what he'd done was not something he could just sweep under the carpet. I only talked to my father when there was no way to avoid it; it was hard for me even to look at him.

Word quickly got around our team that Telisa could be found at my place. We'd just finished the league season and were beginning to prepare for the playoffs, but one of our starters had been put out of her house, and this was not exactly good for team morale. Meanwhile, Q was in horrible spirits—she still wasn't getting seriously recruited, and like most people who were hoping to receive an athletic scholarship, she hadn't applied to any schools. No one asked about her situation or even acknowledged it, especially me—I was probably the last person she wanted to talk to—and when she was feeling particularly crabby, which was most of the time, she tended to avoid me altogether. The playoffs would be the last chance she had to prove herself, and her future would be determined by her performance. All of these factors made us very uptight, and at one practice Q and Pam started snapping at each other so viciously that Telisa and I had to get between them and calm them down. Everyone was on edge. We needed to pull ourselves back together, or the playoffs would be a disaster. Unfortunately, though, the other calming influence on the team besides me—Telisa—was wrapped up in her own set of problems.

Although it meant that I got even less homework done, I was actually glad to have Telisa in the house. We spent a lot of time together, joking around during the day and having deep philosophical discussions late at night, and I could feel that we were getting closer. The only aspect of her presence I didn't like was that it meant I saw a lot less of Raina. She was around as much as usual, but she tended to go off by herself if Telisa and I were together; she never really wanted to join us. I only got to spend time with her when Telisa was out, which wasn't very often. It was hard for Telisa to see Shavon—her mother had called Shavon's mother, and Shavon's mother had hit the ceiling, too. She was using the opposite tactic from Telisa's mother, though—instead of kicking her daughter out, Shavon's mother kept her in. Shavon had to go right home after school, and then her mother would subject her to rages and tears. She was not allowed to go out at night and her mother screened her phone calls. Finally, at the end of the week, Shavon left to go and stay with her father.

Telisa was quieter than usual, and sad, but she managed to get her schoolwork done and to be sociable with the parents. She did go get the rest of her things eventually, sneaking in one day while her mother was at work to pack boxes of clothes, and books, and records. She left all of her furniture there, but lugged the boxes to our garage, where I peeked in on her at one point and found her sitting with her face in her hands. I didn't say anything, and backed out before she noticed me. Although I was worried about her, I didn't want to intrude, and she, for her part, didn't seem to want to talk very much. I knew she must have been hurting beneath all those layers of composure, but she wouldn't let anyone see it. At school she acted normal, telling no one besides the team what had happened, and even then she gave an edited version. At practice she was more intense than ever.

But this would turn out to be one of those instances when fate tempers a terrible blow by then reaching into its hat and producing something wonderful. For it was also during Telisa's stay with us that she got a piece of incredible news. It happened four days after she'd been kicked out. Her brother called that night just after Claudia got home from work, and told Telisa she'd better come meet him at McDonald's right away. She left, and when she came back about an hour later, she was so excited that she started jumping up and down and thumping on the walls. There was a look of happiness and vindication on her face.

"What happened?" I asked.

She clenched her fist in triumph and then slammed it down on the couch. "I just got into Berkeley," she said.

I said, "Huh?"

She turned and beamed at me, her eyes lit with joy. "I just got into motherfuckin *Berkeley!*"

I cocked my head at her, confused. "Wait a minute. What you talkin about? I didn't know you applied to Berkeley."

My friend did a little jig and then looked at me again. "That's 'cos I didn't *tell* anyone, homegirl! You think I'm gonna *tell* people 'bout something like that? Shit. What if I didn't get in?"

Her news, finally, began to sink in. "Holy shit!" I said. "You just got into Berkeley!" I stood there and thought about this for a moment. No one, I mean *no one,* ever got into Berkeley. No one I knew had ever even applied. Only the very smartest kids in the state could go there on the strength of their academics alone—and now, my friend was one of them. "You're a fuckin *genius,* T!" I yelled, and then we high-fived each other, and that wasn't enough, so we high-fived each other again. We hugged and whooped and danced around, and then Telisa almost split my eardrums with her yell.

"Whheeoooeew!"

The dog got into the act, jumping on us and barking. All the commotion brought Claudia out from the kitchen, and just as she came into the living room, my father walked in the front door. He put his book bag down, smiled at us, and asked, "What the hell is going on?"

"Telisa got into Berkeley," I announced. But I bristled a bit, not entirely happy that he should share this.

My father's mouth opened, then closed again, and he smiled even wider. He nodded at Telisa, looking impressed. "That's wonderful," he said. "Congratulations."

"Telisa, that's great," added Claudia, going over and giving her a hug. Then she turned toward my father, not looking happy. "Where have you been, Wendell?" she asked. "It's almost nine o'clock."

My father bent down, suddenly engrossed in the zipper of his book bag. "I was out having a drink with Larry," he said.

"You could have called," she said gently. "I didn't know whether you wanted dinner or not."

I was not feeling so gentle, and, because I was excited about Telisa, less likely to keep a lid on my thoughts. "Why you hangin out so much with that asshole, anyway?" I said, and I knew my voice was dripping with disgust.

My father stood and raised his head, but didn't look at me; his eyes settled on a space beyond my shoulder. He cocked his head a little, and held his mouth in such a way that it looked like he was in pain. "I have my reasons," he said.

"Right," I said. "Like if you can't beat 'em, join 'em?"

He said nothing, but seemed tired and grim, and I felt a thrill of anger, a bitter pleasure at my cruelty.

"And what about Eddie?" I asked, almost gleefully. "Did you invite *him* to have a drink with you, too?"

Claudia stepped forward, put her hand on my arm, and gestured toward Telisa. "Nancy, let's talk about this later."

I glared at her. I was mad at Claudia, too, or maybe ashamed that she was defending my father to her friends when he had failed us all so miserably. But then I remembered Telisa, who was standing there, looking confused. "O.K.," I said. "You're right. We'll talk later."

My father and Claudia went into the kitchen. I felt bad that we'd made Telisa see this; that we'd interfered with her moment of triumph, so I turned back to her now and jabbed her on the shoulder.

"Sorry about that. Hey, how'd you find out you got in?"

It took Telisa a moment to switch back into gear, but when she did, anger flickered across her face. "My brother. Girl, he dug the letter out of the *trash!* My mom just threw it away without opening it, but he took it out and read it, and then he went straight to McDonald's and called me." She grabbed me by the shoulders and smiled again. "But it don't matter how I found out," she said, shaking me. "I got *in,* Nance! I got my ass into fuckin Berkeley! I'm gettin *outta* this place. You hear me? And this messed-up crazy city can kiss my skinny black ass goodbye!"

There was a new bitterness in her voice as she said this, and I wondered at the similarity between her sentiment and Raina's. I didn't have time to think about it, though. Telisa hugged me again, and then my father suggested we order some pizza. We all ate a lot that night, and my dad let us drink beer with our food, and Telisa laughed and glowed and told us that she'd been worrying for weeks about the status of her application. Raina came home in the middle of this, and when she heard the news, typically, she was more impressed by Telisa's new security than by the brains it had taken to get in.

"You're so lucky," she said. "You know where you gonna be next year."

And this, I suppose, was an element of my own reaction, too—Telisa was the first of my immediate circle of friends to have a definite plan for the fall. But more than that, I was conscious of the shift this would cause in our relationship, and in the way that other people perceived her. I was so proud of Telisa. Of the two of us, it had always been me whose achievements garnered praise, me who people talked about with envy and wonder. I'd often felt vaguely guilty about all the recognition I received for my athletic skills while Telisa, who was so much smarter than me, got none. In any situation other than basketball, it would have been she who was the star. But things had changed just in the course of that night, because now, at least in my eyes, she finally was.

Telisa's family situation had just begun to lose its drama when, a few days later, Stacy got arrested. I was among the first to know about this development, too. The phone rang around seven one night, when the parents were out to dinner.

"Nancy?" said the voice on the other end. And it was so guttural and quavering I couldn't tell who it was.

"Yeah," I said, "who's this?"

"It's Stacy," the voice answered.

"*Stacy?* What's wrong?"

"I'm in jail, girl," she said. "I got my ass thrown in jail."

And even though she sounded upset, this news would not register, I simply could not take it in. I smiled and shook my head. "Shut up, girl. Stop playin."

"I ain't playin," she said. And there was such insistence in her voice, and agony, that I knew she was telling the truth.

I stood there uselessly, not knowing what to do. "Jesus," I said finally. "What happened?"

"I did somethin stupid, girl," she said. "I just did somethin stupid."

"Shit," I said. "What are they doin to you? Do they have you in a cell?"

"Not yet," she said. "They let me come into this little room and make a phone call first. Is Raina home now? Can I talk to her?"

"Yeah, sure, hold on," I said. I stayed on the line for a second, trying to think of something comforting to say, but nothing came to mind. Finally I put the receiver down and called out for Raina. She appeared in the kitchen a moment later, and when she got close, I whispered, "It's Stacy. She's in jail."

Her mouth opened in surprise, and then she suddenly looked very serious. She picked the receiver up off of the table. "Hey," she said. "It's Raina."

They talked for a few minutes, and I couldn't make out what was happening from Raina's end of the conversation; she mostly said, "Mm-hmm," and nodded her head. I petted the dog absently and tried to figure out what Stacy could have done. Drugs were the most logical answer. Stacy smoked weed sometimes—most people did, although I tended to stick with beer—and maybe she got caught with a joint or a dime bag. She could also have been making a drop for someone, although I hoped she wouldn't be that stupid. As far as I knew, she didn't carry a gun, but if she *was* strapped, that was grounds for arrest, too. I was still thinking about this last possibility when Raina got off the phone. She turned to me, looking exasperated.

"She wants me to go tell her mom," she said.

"Well, why didn't she call her herself?"

"Because she was afraid that her mom would trip."

"Oh, that's nice," I said. "So she's gonna trip less when *you* tell her?"

"No, but I guess at least this way Stacy doesn't have to deal with it."

"Great," I said. Then, after a pause, "What'd she do?"

Raina sighed. "She took a two-thousand-dollar check that was addressed to her employer and signed it over to herself. I guess the bank or her boss or someone got suspicious, so they investigated, and the cops came and arrested her at work."

"Holy shit," I said, and we just stood there for a moment. Then we went upstairs and got ready to leave.

The parents had taken the Honda out to dinner, so we took the Mustang. I handed the keys over to Raina, because I was still nervous about driving at night. At Stacy's, I waited outside in the car while Raina went in and talked to Stacy's mom. She came out looking grim. After she'd shut the door and belted herself in, she took a deep breath and closed her eyes.

"Girl, she is *pissed,*" she said. "You know, she *got* Stacy that job, and she's real upset that Stacy dogged out her friend. And then, you know, Stacy's dad's in jail, too."

I shook my head. "I know." Out the window, I saw a few dark shapes moving in the schoolyard across the street. "What's she gonna do?"

Raina shrugged. "Wait and see what they set the bail at, I guess, and then try to scramble it up. She said she had some folks she could call. And J.R. offered to kick in some cash."

I smiled wryly. Stacy's younger brother, J.R., was a small-time dealer, a smart, sly kid whose elusiveness had served him well on the street. He was the most likely member of the household to have cash on hand, and the least likely to have legally earned it.

There was nothing more for Raina and me to do now, so we headed back home in silence. We were both too distracted to concentrate on our homework, so we sat in front of the television and didn't talk much, except to tell Telisa, when she came in, what had happened. The parents came home eventually, too, but we didn't fill them in on the events of the evening. I finally went to bed around midnight and it took me a long time to get to sleep.

Two days later, Raina and I dropped Telisa off at school, and then we borrowed her car and came straight back to the house. Raina called Stacy's and learned from Nicki that their mother had just gone to bail Stacy out. We kept calling every fifteen minutes or so to see if they were back yet, until Nicki finally got sick of us and said she'd call us herself when there was something to report. So we waited all morning—pacing, worrying, painting possible scenarios, and I remember thinking to myself, oddly, that we were acting like two people who were waiting for the birth of a baby. Finally, around noon, the phone rang. We both jumped to answer it, and I got there first.

"They're back," Nicki said. "And if you wait about twenty

minutes, our mama's goin to work, so you can have my sister all to yourselves."

We went straight out to the car, both of us figuring it was better to go somewhere than to keep pacing back and forth inside. When we got to Stacy's, though, her mother's car was still there, so we circled around the block a couple of times until it was finally gone. We parked, went up the walkway, and Raina knocked on the door. I felt nervous. It was as if I were about to encounter someone I had never met before, or that I knew but hadn't seen in several years. Then Stacy answered the door.

She looked awful. Her eyes were puffy from crying, and there were dark blotches in her yellowish face. I wondered if she'd had any sleep in the last few nights, and if there'd been anyone in the cell that she could talk to. Seeing her like this did something strange to me. It made me feel closer to her, but also, somehow, more distant—because I knew, now, how different our lives had become, and felt, as I often did regarding my friends, that I had no right to care about her as much as I did.

"Wassup, ladies?" she said, moving aside to let us pass.

"Wassup?" I replied. "Welcome home." We squeezed past her, and once inside, I looked around me as if I were in a strange, unfamiliar place. There were several football-sized holes in the walls, where you could see through to some of the wooden beams, the old house's bones. A stack of telephone books supported one corner of the worn green couch, where the leg had broken off. The coffee table was littered with half-smoked cigarettes, bags of Fritos, and an empty baby bottle. The recliner by the television had permanently reclined.

"Thanks," Stacy said. "Don't know how long I'm gonna be here, though. The trial's on April 23rd. I gotta go meet with the lawyer again this afternoon, and everyone knows I did what they say I did, so . . ." Her eyes filled with tears, and she turned away.

I stood there looking at her, and felt completely unable to help. "It'll work out," I said. "Your lawyer's gonna figure something out."

Stacy shook her head doubtfully. "I don't know, girl."

Then suddenly, Raina, who'd been looking away, whirled around and glared at Stacy. "What the fuck were you *thinking?*" she demanded. I turned and looked at her, surprised. She was standing there with her fists clenched, and what struck me most was not the anger in her voice, but the pain. It was as if Stacy had done something against her personally. And Stacy must have taken it that way, too, because she stood there with her eyes on the floor like a large, repentant child.

"I'm sorry," she said. "It's just that we needed the money, with Nicki havin the baby and all, and it just seemed so easy, and I was sure I could get away with it."

Raina shook her head violently. "It ain't a matter of *getting away* with it! Jesus! You just don't fuckin *do* shit like that!"

Finally Stacy raised her eyes and met Raina's glare. She looked a little angry now. "Well, that's easy for *you* to say. You got your ticket outta here. Your future's wide open, and when you leave this place, you can do whatever the fuck you want. Well, that's all real nice, Raina, but for the rest of us, it just ain't that fuckin easy."

There was a complicated expression on Raina's face. She looked furious, but also sad, and something else I couldn't interpret. At any rate, she didn't say a word. She turned and walked out the door, and a few seconds later I heard the car start.

Nicki, who'd been listening from the kitchen, came in now and shook her head at Stacy. "You steal and you lie and you hurt the people who love you," she said, almost gleefully. "You just like your no-good father."

Stacy closed her eyes and sighed. "Shut up, Nicki," she said.

Since Raina had stranded me, I suggested to Stacy that we go for a walk. We went to the liquor store to buy some sodas, and then jumped the sagging fence to get into the schoolyard. Some high-school-age guys were playing hoops on the run-down courts, and the usual shady, secretive traffic was taking place in the doorways of the boarded-up old classrooms. Once, Stacy had told me, while the school was still open, some gangbangers had driven past it and fired shots over the yard while the kids were out for recess. The kids, accustomed to the sound of gunfire, had apparently dropped to the ground and crawled calmly inside, while their teachers ran around in a panic. That afternoon, the grass was overgrown and lush, thanks to the rain of the last few weeks. We could hear the traffic and smell the car exhaust from the freeway behind us. We sat in some old swings, hands curled around the cold metal links, and Stacy tried to explain what had happened.

"I feel like I let everyone down," she said, "but I was really just tryin to help out. My mama's always complainin 'bout how we can't afford to do this, we ain't got money for that, and that's the reason I even *got* this job, right? Only I wasn't workin that much, just evenings and weekends, and after the tax season's over, I was supposed to get a lot less hours." She paused and looked thoughtful. "So one night, I find this check that no one logged in, and I figure I can just take it and that no one'll miss it 'cos they never even knew it was there. And it's real easy signin it over and everything; they didn't hassle me at the bank. That week I gave my mama four hundred dollars and she was happy to have it, so the next week I gave her four hundred more. She knew I wasn't makin that much, so she had to know I was gettin it from somewhere. But she never asked where it come from, you know what I'm sayin? It's like with J.R. He give her money, and everybody *knows* he make it over there . . ." She gestured toward the people in the doorways. ". . . but she never says nothin about it, she just thank him for the help. It's like she don't care where the money come from as long as she don't have to know about it. I can't even tell if she's pissed that I stole something, or just pissed that I got myself caught."

At that moment, we heard the roar of a particularly loud plane, and looked up to see a 747 passing over us. It was approaching the airport, which was a couple of miles away, and it was so low we could see the lines in its belly. Stacy watched it go over, then shook her head and looked back down at the ground. "I don't know why anyone would wanna come *into* this city," she said.

When we got back to Stacy's house, I called home but received no answer. I needed to get to practice, though, and my clothes were at my place, so I decided to take the bus home. Stacy wasn't going to her team's practice—she'd arranged to talk with their coach at school the next day. And she was seeing her lawyer again that afternoon, so she was nervous by the time I left. I caught my bus and sat near the front, closing my eyes and letting the events of the last few hours wash over me. The thought of Stacy going to jail seemed too outrageous to believe, but I knew that it was real. And she was right—things *would* be easier for Raina—and also, by the same token, for me. They had already been easier, really, for the last several years. We were stars, recruited athletes, who'd been showered with praise and attention; who'd always been treated like we were valuable, like we were chosen. And just as importantly, we'd been given a taste of life outside of L.A., and this had immediately changed our relationship to the city—because no matter how bad things got for us, we knew that we could leave. I felt, on the bus that day, a tremendous sadness for the people who didn't have the same kinds of options, like Stacy, and for the people who didn't know what their options *were,* like Q. And it occurred to me, then, that the reason my friends were so much more bitter than I, the reason they were so anxious to leave, was that the city meant something different to them than it had ever meant to me. No one on the outside cared too deeply about whether I stayed there or not. But they wanted very much for my friends to stay, and not only for them to *stay,* but to *suffer.* For the first time I realized that my friends and I had been traveling on separate but parallel tracks. We were moving in the same direction, negotiating the same landscape, and carrying weighty and similar baggage—but the tracks did not meet, and *their* path was completely different from mine. It was bumpier, had more obstacles, and there were a host of bandits at every turn. I never lost sight of my friends; we rode side by side, and looked back and forth at each other, and talked across the space between the tracks. But it was as if I had always been watching their faces through a window. I loved my friends, and I could see that their journey was dangerous and painful. But the only ones who could really understand the dangers of that journey were those who traveled on the same hard track.

CHAPTER 17

The Black Businesswomen's Alliance held its conference during the third weekend in February. Claudia was gone all day on Saturday, and by the time I got home from the movies that night, she and my father were already asleep. On Sunday, Raina went to the conference, too, in order to see her mother speak; that evening, my father drove over to join them for the party. Although I was tired, I made myself stay up. I wanted to find out what had happened.

At 11:30, I heard the cars pull into the driveway. Ann stretched, yawned, shook her leg out, and then walked over to the door. Claudia came in first, looking weary. The dog sniffed her hand, and licked it, before running outside to greet my father.

"Hello," I called out from the couch.

Claudia jumped a little. "Hi, Nancy," she said. Then she came over to where I was sitting. She looked at me closely, in a way she hadn't before; I saw the affection in her eyes, and the sadness. Something about this look made it impossible for me to ask her anything. She smiled now, a tired smile. "Shouldn't you be in bed?"

"I was just about to go brush my teeth," I lied.

"Well, that's what I'm going to do, too," she said. "I'm exhausted. I'll see you in the morning."

I watched her go up the stairs, and then my father came in. He turned and waited for Raina, who appeared just as the door to the parents' room clicked shut.

"Hey, how'd it go?" I asked.

"Good," said my father as he fiddled with the lock. He sighed, took his jacket off, hung it up in the hall closet. "Anything exciting happen around here?"

"No, not really. I watched the Lakers game. They won."

"Mmm," said my father, looking distracted. Then he, too, went up the stairs and into their room.

Raina walked over and sat down on the love seat.

"I guess they're tired," I said.

She sighed. "Yeah, it's been a really long day."

I tried to read her expression. She seemed fine, although a little subdued. "So how'd your mom's speech go?"

Raina brightened up a bit now. "Oh, it was great," she said, smiling. "She had everybody nodding and like, agreeing with her and shit, and everyone was laughing at her jokes. I didn't know she could *be* like that, you know? People were talkin about it afterwards, they were all pumped up. It was kind of like she was a coach or something, giving a really good pep talk."

I smiled, liking Raina for liking her mother so much. "You're proud of her, huh?"

Raina nodded. "Hell, yeah."

"So how was the rest of the stuff today?"

Raina shrugged. "I don't know. The conference stuff was kind of boring. They were talking about all this work shit that I'm just not down with yet, you know? Employee relations, management, tax information, that kind of thing. And then the party." She stopped and looked down at her hands. "The party was kind of a trip."

I took a sip of the juice I'd been drinking, and tried not to look too interested. "Really? What happened? Did you have a good time?"

Raina put one hand on top of Ann's head, using her thumb to stroke the dog from nose to brow. "Well, I guess. It was just kinda weird. I hung out a lot with my mom's friends, right? 'Cos I didn't want to hang out with the parents."

I nodded. Hanging out with one's parents was almost always a social error—especially at one of *their* events, where they forgot they were parents, and tended to act embarrassing.

"And Rochelle and Kim, you know, talked with the parents a lot. But Paula completely avoided them."

I stared at my juice and didn't look at her. "I don't think she likes my dad much," I said.

Out of the corner of my eye, I saw Raina nod. "Yeah, I think you're right."

I wasn't sure if Raina knew the reason for Paula's disapproval, but I suspected that she did; at any rate, I was tired of the whole situation. "Paula's a bitch," I said.

Raina looked at me thoughtfully, and sighed. "She *isn't,* though. She's great. I wish you could of known her before . . . all of this." She looked down at her hands, and then back up at me again. "She's been like an aunt to me, or something. I mean, Kim and Rochelle have, too, but Paula . . . Paula would cook me dinner when my mom worked late. Paula bought me clothes when my mom couldn't afford them. Paula took me to AAU practice when my mom's car was broken down. She let us stay with her for a week after my father left, when my mom was too upset to be alone. The first year or so after the divorce, when my mom was sad all the time, Paula would call her almost every day and talk to her, get her laughing. I mean, she's always been there, she's always been great, and I just don't know what the problem is. I don't know if they're ever going to get through this thing, and it just seems so fuckin stupid and sad."

I listened, getting more and more depressed, and feeling terrible, now, for Claudia. For the first time, I wondered if any of *my* friends had faced hostility because of me. My father and I occasionally saw signs of disapproval—from my mother, from some of his friends, from Asian strangers when the four of us went out somewhere together—but it didn't affect us much, because other than Q, who was different, we didn't see other Asians very often. We didn't have to deal with their sense that we'd betrayed them. Telisa, Stacy, and Raina, however, had welcomed the stranger in their midst, and I wondered now, finally, what it had cost them. I also wondered what it had cost my father and me to *be* those strangers, and what it was costing my father and Claudia to be together. I went to bed that night, sad for all of us, lamenting the price we had to pay for the choices we made, lamenting that prices ever had to be paid at all.

The CIF playoffs began the next week. Not surprisingly, both Raina's team and mine had won our leagues, and when the thirty-two-team field for the playoffs was announced, we were on the same side of the bracket. It was highly unlikely, though, that both of our teams would make it to the round where we were slated to meet, even though her team was ranked tenth in CIF now, and we were ranked ninth. The competition in the playoffs—at least after the first round—was always intense, and every progressively higher-round game was played as if the championship of the entire world was at stake. Raina's team would have a tougher time of it than we. Their second-round game—assuming they got that far—would be against the sixth-ranked team in CIF, and because the third-place team they were playing in round one came from a very tough league (first-place teams played third-place teams in round one, and second-place teams played each other), they, too, would be a formidable opponent. To make matters worse, Raina's coach had suspended Stacy. This probably wouldn't hurt them too terribly—Stacy was not one of their top scorers—but still, she was a starter, and it would throw the other starters off a bit to have a different cog in their usual machine. Luckily for her, the local press hadn't learned of her arrest (she wasn't prominent enough to keep track of—if it had been Raina or me, the story would have been all over), and their coach's official statement on her suspension was that it was for "disciplinary reasons." He wasn't completely coldhearted, though—he was going to let Stacy sit on the bench with the team during games.

Our playoff picture—or at least our first game—would be easier, because we were not playing a very good team. Also, the tensions about Q, and about Telisa's home situation, had calmed, and everyone was cheerful and ready to play. Part of this feeling was the usual hope and anticipation that surrounded the postseason tournament. The three weeks of the playoffs were a time during which basketball seemed like the most wonderful invention ever; a time of collective excitement so great that even members of teams who didn't qualify were infected enough to go watch the games. Those collapsing high school gyms were suddenly packed with fans, and everything—from the lines on the courts to the leaves on the trees—seemed brighter, more defined, more itself. Part of the feeling, also, was that the clouds and rain of the last two months had finally lifted. The air was crisp and clean; the gold light of the sun seemed like a rare and thoughtful gift; the mountains stood huge and majestic to the east, their top halves covered with snow. It was as if the city had been unveiled, and its beauty was breathtaking. And all of this—the feeling of the playoffs, the look of the world around me—was especially vivid, because that year I was taking note of it and wishing it did not have to pass.

The first round of games took place on a Saturday. Raina's team had a two-hour trip to make, so she left early in the afternoon and we wished each other luck. Our game was at home, which I was glad about. The whole school seemed caught up in our endeavor, and we had its undivided attention, because the boys' team had not been strong that year and had missed out on the playoffs entirely. There'd been a pep rally the day before, and all of our teachers and acquaintances—all the jocks, and student council people, and gangbangers, and nerds—had told us they planned to come. I got to the gym at six—an hour and a half before game time—and found my teammates hyped, practically bouncing off the walls of the locker room. Pam was running around and showering everyone with punches, which hurt, because she was strong. Q was slamming lockers shut loudly and letting out an occasional yell. Telisa, who'd gotten a ride from Shavon, was pacing up and down pumping her fists in the air, and when she saw me, she came right over.

"Did you see them come in, homegirl?" she asked. "They're big and slow, and they look scared already. Dogmeat."

"Dogmeat!" Pam agreed.

"Woof!" Q said.

I smiled, glad my teammates were so excited. Telisa was probably right—our opponents were from the Valley; they were the kind of people who would never come into a neighborhood like ours by choice. But I said, "C'mon y'all, chill out. Don't matter who they are. We got ourselves some work to do."

When we lined up an hour later and ran onto the court to begin our warm-ups, I felt a chill go through my body. The stands were already full, the crowd was buzzing, and we were a few minutes away from the start of a game we had to win to extend our season. My body was loose and relaxed, the ball felt right in my hands. The buzzer went off so we headed over to our bench, and I spotted my dad in the bleachers. Claudia was at Raina's game, of course, and he looked lonely up there. He pumped his fist at me and nodded. I raised my own fist, more for the crowd than for him, and all the kids in the stands—my schoolmates, my friends, our little junior high fans—stood up and started to cheer. This, I thought, as I looked up at them, is what it's all about.

After both teams had gathered at their benches, the starting lineups were announced. I was the last player to go, and the crowd went crazy as I ran onto the court. I had to smile. The rest of our starters met me at the free throw line, and we exchanged high fives and pounded each other on the back, yelled that victory was ours. I felt a sense of pride and importance, then, as we walked back to our bench, that I wished I could hold on to forever.

When the game began, though, it was clear that my concern had been justified. The other team was nothing special, but we were tight as a wire. We forced shots, threw passes away, tried to make plays that weren't there. We played the other team even for the first three minutes, committing four careless turnovers in the process. Once I went down hard on my back, and the whole crowd gasped. I was all right, but even after I got up, brushed myself off, and waved to acknowledge the applause of the crowd, we still couldn't get it together. It was terrible. Finally, Coach Fontaine called a time-out, and yelled that if we starters didn't care about the game, he'd be happy to put in the second string. We got the message. As we walked back onto the court, I gathered the five of us together and told everyone to calm down, take it easy, and remember to have some fun.

One or both of these speeches had the intended effect, because from there, the game was ours. The other team had decent inside players—a 6'3" center and a couple of six-foot forwards—but they were slow, and overweight, and became as helpless as beached whales against our fast breaks and swarming defense. The game was over by halftime. We led by twenty going into the locker room, and Coach Fontaine's speech this time—Standard Fontaine Halftime Speech No. 3—concerned keeping our intensity up in the second half and not lapsing into sloppiness.

The second half it just got uglier. Every door we tried simply opened without resistance, and the other team, obviously, just wanted the game to be over with so they could go home. I didn't enjoy blowouts—there was no challenge in them, and they didn't push us to get any better—but if they had to happen, I preferred that they happened to a team like this, which was wealthy, coddled, white. When Coach Fontaine took out the starters halfway through the fourth quarter, I sat on the bench and thought about the fact that we were ending our opponent's season, and I wondered what their seniors would be doing the next year. None of them, I was sure, would have anything to worry about. College awaited them, or maybe jobs, and no matter what the situation was, those kids would always have their parents to fall back on. That's why I couldn't feel too awful about what was happening to them on the court. When, late in the game, the junior high school girls in the stands adapted the words from a song by Tears for Fears and sang, "Shout, shout, look at the score! You are losing by thirty-four!"—I didn't feel sorry for the other team. They were having a bad night, but their lives, it seemed to me, were uncomplicated, and their futures were bright and assured. I knew we were all glad that we were beating them so badly—this was the one place where we had the goods and kids like them didn't; this was the one area in which we knew we could win.

That night I had a party at my house. My father, very considerately, went out to a bar in Marina Del Rey, where he planned to meet up later with Claudia. Everyone on my team came over, plus various boyfriends and girlfriends and people from school. Telisa showed up late, with Shavon, and they were both grinning like they'd won the lottery.

"Y'all have sex in the car or something?" I asked.

Telisa laughed. "Well, yeah, but that ain't why we're happy."

"Why you happy?"

Telisa gave her girlfriend a squeeze. "Her dad's gonna let me stay with them for a while."

"What?" I almost shouted. "He knows what's up with you guys, doesn't he?"

"Yeah," Shavon said, smiling. "But you gotta understand. My dad's been through some shit with relationships, too." I knew this was true—Shavon's mother was white, and her parents' marriage had been a big scandal in both of their families. "So he just took us out to get something to eat, right? And he told Telisa she could stay. He said, 'I'm mad at you both for not telling me the truth for so long, and I can't say that I approve. But I know what it's like to be in love and to have the world against you, and I don't wanna take part in all that hatred.'"

"Holy shit," I said, and I was grinning, too. This was incredible, unbelievable—it was giving me some faith in the world.

We had a loud, happy night. We talked about good plays we had made, ragged on our coach, predicted victory in our second-round game. Eventually someone threw on some music and people started dancing in the living room, but I stayed in the kitchen with Q and Pam, talking to a couple of people from our photography class. At one point, while I was opening a new bag of pretzels, I heard a guy ask Q how many she'd had that night.

"Twenty," she replied.

"Twenty?" the guy repeated, sounding incredulous. "Stop playin, girl. For real?"

"Well, Nancy had twenty-six."

"Twenty-six! Naw, girl, that ain't possible!"

We were both confused by his surprise at our not-unusual numbers, until it came out that he hadn't been asking about the number of points we'd had that night, but instead about the number of wine coolers.

"Oh, well, in *that* department," Q said, laughing, "I can top Nancy's numbers anytime."

Telisa and Shavon came into the kitchen, still grinning. With some prodding from Pam, Telisa told her story about finding out that she'd gotten into Berkeley, and everyone was duly impressed. A bit later, after the beer was gone, someone broke out the weed. I chased him into the small backyard so the house wouldn't smell, and a bunch of people followed him out to partake.

"Don't you want some?" the guy from Photography asked when he noticed me standing in the doorway.

"Naw," I said. "It don't do much for me."

"Yeah, Nancy's the straight and narrow one of the bunch," said Pam.

Q laughed. "Well, the narrow one, anyway."

Raina didn't get home until almost two—her team had won easily, and they'd gone to Denny's after their long ride back. Our parents came in soon afterward, and then things wound down pretty fast. Most people left, but some of my teammates stayed, and I rustled up some sleeping bags and blankets. Raina and I each discovered one of my teammates crashed out in our beds, so we found a few more blankets and joined the multitudes downstairs in the living room. Everyone talked and giggled for another couple of hours. We finally went to sleep around dawn.

A few hours later, I was awakened by a strange snuffling sound and a horrible smell. When I opened my eyes, I found Ann standing over me, holding the socks I'd worn the night before and pushing them into my face. She grunted and wagged her tail when she saw I was awake. I got up and fed her a bone. We let everyone else sleep a while longer, and then went around the living room, Ann sniffing at other people's faces—without the socks—in order to wake them up. When I got to Raina's spot I saw that she was completely covered, not an inch of her showing, the blanket drawn up over her head. I grabbed the top of it and pulled it back. She was awake already; I found her lying there grinning up at me with her teddy bear wrapped in her arms. I smiled, and in the instant before she said, "Good morning," I felt the delight of seeing her for the first time that day; I knew she was the most adorable thing on the planet; and I fought the overwhelming urge I had to kneel down and hug her. We had won our first playoff game, my teammates had spent the night, and Raina was there smiling up at me. It didn't seem possible that life could be any better.

Claudia, Pam, and Q, who barely fit into the kitchen together, made a big cholesterol breakfast of pancakes, eggs, and bacon. We decided to eat in the living room so we could watch the Knicks game. Q and I stood there ragging on each other while we put food on our plates, and Claudia shook her head at us and laughed.

"You two go back a long way, don't you?" she said.

Q stood up straight, looked serious, and touched a spot maybe an inch down on her forehead. "We been friends since we was this tall," she said.

In the living room, Telisa sat staring at the television. She was a huge Patrick Ewing fan—she loved to imitate his scowl, and wore blue-and-gray Nike Georgetown shoes to practice. We ate and laughed and cheered for the Knicks, and everyone seemed reluctant to leave. They did, though, around three, and the house seemed empty when they were gone. We had finally finished celebrating our first playoff win. And that night, after dinner, I helped Telisa move in with her girlfriend.

Our next playoff game was on Wednesday. School hardly seemed to exist that entire week; it was a waste of time, irrelevant. The only thing that was real for me was basketball. Our practices were long and intense, but I don't think anybody wanted them to end. There was a feeling of huge significance in the air, and on Tuesday, the unspoken thought on everyone's mind was that that afternoon's practice might be our last. I remember feeling a love and appreciation for my teammates which was greater than I'd ever felt before. There were people I planned to keep in touch with—Telisa for sure, and maybe Q—and of course I'd known all year that these would be our last few months together. But I was thinking more now about my other teammates. Although I wasn't as close to them, theirs were the faces which had populated my life, and I knew that I would miss them when I left.

I wondered if Raina was feeling the same way. She was spending a lot of time with her teammates, hanging out with them in the evenings, not getting any homework done. She'd made up with Stacy, too, which I was happy to hear.

"I still think what she did was pretty stupid," she said on Tuesday night. "But being pissed at her don't help anything."

On Wednesday morning, we were having a family breakfast when my father suddenly leaned in close to the sports section and then looked up at Raina and me. "Wait a minute," he said. "Do you two know who you play if you both win tonight?"

Of course we knew, but we hadn't said anything, and we didn't say anything now.

"Who?" Claudia asked, as she buttered a piece of toast.

My father pushed the paper towards her. “Each other.”

Claudia raised her eyebrows as she looked at the pairings. “You’re right,” she said. Then she looked at each of us. “Did you know that?”

I said, “Yup.”

Raina said, “Uh-huh.”

Neither of us looked at the other.

Raina’s team was playing at home that night against a higher-ranked opponent, and I’m sure that part of the reason we hadn’t discussed the possibility of our teams colliding—although certainly not all of it—was that no one expected her team to get past this round. Our fate was in question, too. We were playing Lynwood, my friend Theresa Golding’s team. And while we were ranked slightly higher, we were playing at their place, which would definitely be a factor. Lynwood was in an even rougher area than our school, and they had loud, devoted fans; it was difficult for anyone to come out of there with a victory. On the bus that evening, we didn’t horse around as much as usual. We just did our bubble gum ritual, and passed Clyde around, and stayed quiet while we psyched ourselves up.

The game was just as tough as I’d expected it to be. Lynwood ran a box-and-one defense, which meant that four people played a zone while one player followed me wherever I went. I had a hard time shaking her off; she was like a big and persistent mosquito. Telisa couldn’t get a pass to me because my defender was denying me the ball, and when I did manage to break free long enough for my teammates to find me, my defender was on me again before I even had a chance to square up to the basket. Meanwhile, everything was going right for Theresa. She was hitting outside jumpers, leading the break, somehow squeezing between Q and me to grab rebounds. The crowd loved it. At the end of the first quarter, our opponents were up by five, and I felt winded already from contending with my shadow.

At the break, we heard the wrath of Coach Fontaine. “Stop trying to force it to Nancy,” he yelled, his face red and all five hairs falling onto his forehead. “Q, pop up into that big gap in the key. Telisa, look for her, she's wide open, and so's Pam on the other wing. And if they keep collapsing on Nancy and Q, then just take the open shot. They're going to be giving it to you all night long."

He was right. Their guards were leaving Telisa alone, so she woke them up by hitting a couple of jumpers. When they finally came out to guard her, she dumped it off to Pam or Q, and Q made use of the gap in the middle, hitting several easy shots. Even with me out of the picture, we pulled even by halftime. My teammates were picking up the slack.

In the second half, it was more of the same. Tough defense from them, lots of points from Theresa, every possession extremely hard-fought. They made the mistake of trying a full-court press, which gave me some more room to operate, and then called it off quickly after I had three quick scores on fast breaks. Q, Pam, and Telisa were still doing the bulk of the scoring, though, and my teammates managed to keep us even through three quarters. Then, with just a few minutes left in the game, the girl who'd been guarding me all night finally began to tire. I still felt good—all my late-night sprints with Raina were paying off—and as my defender lost a step or two, I intensified my attack. I managed to shake her off now, and Telisa, who actually grinned the first time I broke free, hit me with a crisp, perfect pass. I scored then, and again on the next possession, and again on the one after that. Meanwhile, the other team failed to score on three straight trips down the floor. The crowd grew restless and impatient. Finally they put someone else on me, a substitute with fresher legs, but she wasn't half the defender the first player had been, and I hardly noticed her presence. In the last two minutes we were flawless. Telisa stole a pass at half-court and hit Q for the score, and that turned out to be the final basket. A minute later, when the buzzer sounded, the scoreboard showed that we had won by six.

The bus ride home was surprisingly quiet. We all felt good about the win, and went around giving each other high fives, but there was something less euphoric about our mood after this victory; we all seemed more serious and thoughtful. It was as if the initial excitement of our adventure had worn off, and suddenly the danger of the situation had become more real. We were far enough into it by then to realize that we were on new and unsafe ground, and that a wrong step in any direction could mean disaster. The person who seemed least affected by this mood was Q. She'd played a great game—she'd had twenty-five points to my sixteen, and had pulled down thirteen rebounds—and a little clump of college scouts had been sitting in the stands. She'd furthered her cause tremendously that night, and I was glad for her, although I also wished I'd been a little more impressive. I didn't let myself dwell on it, though—the most important thing was that we had won.

The bus dropped us off in front of our school, and my father, who'd been driving behind us, picked me up and took me home. Claudia's car was parked in front, and I wondered if Raina was back yet. She was. She came rushing into the living room, still wearing her uniform, looking wired and very alert.

"What happened?" she asked breathlessly, leaning forward.

"We won by six," I said.

"We won by three."

She stood there looking at me, and I looked back at her, and something of huge dimensions happened, as if the whole world tipped off its axis and then righted itself again. I found I was short of breath and that my heart was beating fast. "I'll see you on Saturday," I said.

CHAPTER 18

For the next three days, we avoided each other. We went straight to our rooms when we got home from school, and when we emerged for our meals, we hardly spoke. Our parents were amused by the situation, but also, it seemed, a bit self-conscious and careful—I realized that each of them, too, had a stake in the game. It had been easy for them to remain impartial, uninvolved, as long as their daughters' careers had been separate; but now we were actually competing, directly, and neither of them was comfortable. It probably didn't help matters that Claudia's friendship with Paula appeared to be over, especially in light of my father's failure to stand up to his bosses. I watched our parents circle each other, and wondered if Claudia thought she might have made a mistake.

Meanwhile, Raina and I were not amused by the game at all. It wasn't that we were angry, or trying to psyche each other out; no, I don't think that ever occurred to us. Rather, it was that the present situation fell outside the bounds of what we'd established as our friendship. This game, which was a CIF quarterfinal, had a great deal of meaning for both of us, and would have been important no matter who we were facing. But it was all the more important because we were facing each other. Raina's reticence, and avoidance of me, made it clear that she, too, had a lot riding on the outcome. But our friendship, with its definable boundaries and allowable topics, could not accommodate an event of such clear significance. It was too dangerous for either of us to admit how much we wanted to win.

At school, I was useless as always. I sat in my classes, preoccupied, and wrote notes to Telisa and Q about how our lives depended on beating Leuzinger. We were all solemn; we'd raise our fists as we passed each other in the hallway, and talk each other through the long practices. It was as if everything we cared about was wrapped up in the game, and all that mattered was what would happen when we played it.

The only nonbasketball thing that occurred during this period was that Stacy's boss dropped the charges against her. She called us on Thursday night to give us the news.

"He said to just forget the whole thing," Stacy said gleefully, and sounding like she'd already raised a glass or two in celebration. "He fired me, of course, and I gotta put in some volunteer work, but shit—at least I ain't goin to jail."

"What changed his mind?" I asked.

"My mom," Stacy answered. "I mean, she didn't try to talk him out of pressin charges or nothin, but they go back a long way, you know, and I guess he just didn't want to send her kid to the pen."

"I'm real happy for you, girl," said Raina on the extension in her room. "But don't *ever* pull that kind of shit again."

"I won't," Stacy promised. "You don't get but one mistake."

"And some people don't even get that."

This development broke the tension between Raina and me, at least for half an hour—it gave us something to focus on besides the game. She came into my room for a while, and we talked about our teammates' plans for the next year, never touching on what we ourselves might be thinking of doing. It would turn out that Stacy *would* pull that kind of shit again. She'd get arrested several times over the years for various petty thefts, and occasionally for drug possession. In these later theft cases, the wronged parties wouldn't be as generous as her mother's friend, and so Stacy would spend a couple of years in jail. On that night, though, our senior year, Raina and I didn't know this yet. We were just sitting there talking about our friends, about school, about everything except ourselves and the bond and competition that existed between us. It didn't matter. I was happy, and I remember thinking that I could spend every evening for the rest of my life the way I was spending that one—talking to Raina, looking at her, feeling the warmth of her presence spread through my body like wine.

On Saturday morning, my eyes flew open at 7:30 and I jumped out of bed. I hadn't slept well but when I awoke, I felt rested, full of nervous energy. I went downstairs to the kitchen and found that Raina was already up.

"Hey," she said when she saw me.

"Hey," I replied.

I got two bran muffins out of the cupboard, and we sat reading the paper at the kitchen table. We didn't speak, and were both so tense that we jumped whenever the dog made a noise. I glanced at Raina a few times. Her shoulders were high and tight, she was leaning forward a little, and both fists were clenched on top of the table; she looked, more than anything, like she was about to take off on a sprint. Finally she said she was going out to meet her teammates for breakfast, and I was relieved when she was gone—if *she* hadn't left the house, *I* certainly would have had to. My father came downstairs in his bathrobe a little after nine, and he was wide awake, hungry, and cheerful. This was my father's nature, and I understood it well. No matter what else was going on his life, he was always happy about the promise of a good battle.

"So who's going to win?" he asked, smiling and petting the dog.

"I don't know," I said.

He went over to the coffee pot and poured himself a cup. "Well, you better know, because Claudia and I have a wager going. Whichever one of us loses has to take the whole family out to dinner."

He was clearly excited, and I felt my hard, cold anger toward him soften and warm just a little. "Well, don't count on me," I said. "It's gonna be a tough game."

"Hey," my father said, grinning at me. "What makes you think I bet on *you?*"

I had half a muffin left on my plate, and I threw it across the kitchen at him, smiling. It bounced off his shoulder and was recovered by Ann, who took it off into the dining room grunting happily.

"O.K., O.K.," he said, laughing. "I *did* bet on you. So you'd better not cost me dinner. Although if we went to *your* favorite place and got a few Big Macs, it would only run me five or six bucks."

I smiled and rolled my eyes. "Yes, Daddy."

After watching a couple of college games on ESPN, I went over to Q's place at three for our pregame pasta load-up. She and her family lived in a two-bedroom apartment which was three blocks west of the Forum. Q's father slept in one of the bedrooms, and Q, her sister, Debbie, and Debbie's two young children in the other. Debbie and Mr. Murray had made us three huge pots of spaghetti and sauce, and we all ate sitting on the living room floor, beneath the framed poster of Malcolm X. We discussed, sans coach, the things we needed to remember for the game—how their center, Diane, was a killer right beneath the basket but hopeless even five or six feet away from it; how Keisha, their best forward, always drove left and was easy to shut down by overplaying that side; how Raina, who had no visible weaknesses, preferred to see what the flow of the game was like before stepping in and taking over. Also, she was the kind of player whose first few attempts to establish herself often affected the way she performed for the rest of the game; she tended not to play as well if she was thwarted in the first eight minutes. Our game plan was to take away the strengths of Diane and Keisha; to try and establish the tempo right away; to realize that Raina wouldn't dominate in the first couple of minutes and to not be reassured by her initial silence. Also, once she did finally step up and make her presence felt, we had to prevent her from wreaking havoc. I found that the more we kept talking about Raina, the more I was getting scared. She was the player I'd measured myself against and tried to live up to for the last three years. And even though I knew I had her respect, I was afraid that I didn't deserve it—that I was a fake, an impostor, nowhere near the real thing. I drove home as soon as we'd finished our meal and prayed that I wouldn't embarrass myself.

There are certain rare, astounding moments when you feel especially alive. Everything comes into sharp focus, and it is as if the vast, gray, unused portion of your mind has suddenly begun to function. You can feel each cell in your body; you can feel your muscles wrapped round your bones; you hear the messages jump from synapse to synapse. The rest of the time you wade blindly through life, simply trying to get through the day with a few small pleasures and a minimum of pain, and nothing distinguishes one day from the next; nothing has any particular meaning; everything is variable and haphazard. But in those one or two moments when you are truly *alive,* everything takes on the importance of life and death. And you begin to think of the rest of your life in terms of before and after, as leading up to those times or away from them. Because you are functioning in those moments on such a heightened level, the world stuns you with its magnitude and complexity, and you are able to take it in, to understand. And later, when you refer to your knowledge of life, it is those moments that you mean; it is those moments which stand out like blood-red flowers in the desert and they will never be lost from your heart.

Our game with Raina's team was one of those moments for me. I understood, all throughout it, that what was happening was *real,* and it made me think that nothing before then ever had been. It seemed like everyone felt that way, or at least understood that something unusual was happening—Raina, our teammates, all the people in the stands. There were times when the crowd made more noise than it ever had before, but also times, more significantly, when a huge, loud silence fell over the place, as if the people had seen some feat of miraculous strength, or had witnessed, all together, religion. Late in the contest, they'd start to whisper that this was the greatest game they'd ever seen, and it was, without question, the greatest one I ever played in. The papers would describe it in terms normally reserved for epic battles. The most hardened, disinterested observers—the scouts—would leave the gym that night with tears in their eyes.

The game was at our place, and I walked into the locker room a little before six o'clock. I put my uniform on slowly, handling my jersey, shorts, and shoes with great care, knowing that this could be the last time I ever wore them. My teammates began to trickle in, and all of them looked the way I felt—determined, and also, terrified. I didn't want the personal quality of my emotion to spread, because I didn't know, yet, whether it would inspire me or cripple me, so I tried to bring the game back down to normal terms, and talk about it in the context of the playoffs.

"Y'all see this?" I said, pointing to the year-old article taped to the inside of my locker door. "Y'all see what it says? It says we can't stand up to the pressure of the playoffs, we can't win when the stakes are too high."

My teammates looked at me grimly. Telisa was sitting down, and she nodded, fists clenched tightly on her bouncing knees. "Well, the same reporter is gonna be out there again tonight, and when this game is over . . ." I ripped the article down and held it out for all to see. ". . . I wanna crumple this thing up and throw it in his face and tell him that he better think again."

"Yeah!" yelled Pam.

"We gonna *show* those motherfuckas!" yelled Telisa.

We strutted around the locker room and gave each other stinging high fives. It was only 6:20—still an hour and ten minutes before game time—so we went out on the court to do our shoot-around. People broke off at various points—Q to get her ankle taped, Telisa to go into a corner and pray—but everyone was back and shooting by the time that Raina's team emerged from their locker room. I felt my blood beating in my ears. I took several deep breaths and turned toward the wall, so I could close my eyes and try to calm down. I was so nervous that my arms were shaking, and the first shot I took after Raina's team appeared caromed badly off the side of the backboard. This was not good. The best thing to do, I thought, would be to burn off some of my nervous energy and then face the situation head-on. I jumped up and down in place a few times, and then jogged back and forth across the width of the court. Then I made myself look at Raina.

She was sitting on their bench, staring at the ball in her hands so intently that she might have been trying to hypnotize it. After a few minutes, she stood up and adjusted her uniform, then bounced the ball and walked onto the court. She shot, got the ball back, went to another spot, shot again. Stacy was standing under the basket in street clothes, rebounding missed shots and tossing the balls back out to her teammates. When she saw me she waved and yelled, "Wassup!" But while Raina glanced at me a few times when I pretended not to be looking, neither of us acknowledged the other.

A little before seven, we went back into the locker room, and Coach Fontaine gave some speech I didn't hear a single word of. What could he possibly say that would be of any use? The outcome of this game was not going to be decided by a coach's strategies and ideas, nor by any diagrammed plays. The real story of this game existed on a plane different from the one our coach had access to.

At 7:15, we lined up and ran onto the court in our official warm-up formation, and a few minutes later our opponents came out again, too. The stands had filled up by then, and there was a steady buzz of excitement in the air. Neither of our teams had made it to the third round before, and most people who were familiar with us also knew that Raina and I were housemates. Several of our AAU friends were there, too, including Theresa, who'd warned me that in light of her team's loss to us, she was going to root for Raina. Letrice was there, and Tracy, with Chris on her lap, and I wished that Rhonda could have come with them. A little pack of college coaches sat at the top of the bleachers, and I was sure that they, too, were intrigued by the drama being played out that night, or at least by what they knew of it. In the exact middle of the stands sat our parents, my father dressed in our team's green and white and Claudia in Leuzinger's blue and yellow. Rochelle and Kim were with them, and further to the left, in the visitors' section, was Paula. I didn't look up at any of them, and I didn't want them there—what was happening seemed too intimate for them to witness.

My teammates and I shot lay-ups and free throws, did a three-on-two drill and defensive slides. Then the referees called for captains, and I went to midcourt, where Raina was already waiting. The head ref instructed us to introduce ourselves to each other, but Raina just held out her hand. I stepped forward and took it. And I thought, as we stood there, that I had never really shaken anyone's hand before. I felt all the contours of her bones and the soft, warm skin and the way her thumb and fingers encircled my hand. We gripped each other firmly, and her handshake said the same thing that her eyes were saying—I respect you, you are my friend, but I will do everything I can to defeat you. The referee gave his normal spiel about playing clean and calling time-outs and keeping the rest of our teammates under control. We never took our eyes off each other. When he was done, Raina nodded to indicate that she'd heard. Then, to me, she said, "Good luck."

We went back to our teams, and the teams headed over to their benches. By then I just wanted the game to begin—I'd be much less nervous once we actually started playing. We went through the introductions, and it was unreal to me; it was incredible that Raina and I were being introduced for the same game. My teammates and I surrounded our coach while he gave us some last-minute general instructions; finally, just after 7:30, we lined up around the circle for the jump. We all got into our spots, and after what seemed like an interminably long time, the referee threw the ball up and the game had begun.

Their center, who was a couple of inches taller than Q, managed to tip the ball to Jamelle, the forward who was filling in for Stacy. The crowd gave a large, collective cheer—not because Diane had won the tip, but because the fans, too, were nervous, and glad the game was finally under way. Jamelle passed the ball to their point guard, Robin, who saw that they had no advantage and waited for her teammates to run down and set up their offense. We had fallen back into a two-three zone, because Raina's team was so much faster than ours that it would have been dangerous to guard them player-to-player. They worked the ball around a bit now, seeing how we responded to their movements, until Raina shook free using a screen from Diane and took a wide-open shot off the wing. Swish. So much for her sitting back and letting others determine the flow of the game.

They had drawn first blood, they had exhibited no early jitters, and now we had to come up with an answer. We did. They came after us player-to-player, and I blew by Keisha, my designated victim, and encountered Diane, who'd come over to block my path. But that left Q alone under the basket, so I dumped it off to her. She made the lay-up and the game was tied.

We hustled back on defense but they got another quick score. Diane had been offended, I think, at how badly we'd burned her, and she muscled in a power lay-up off of a beautiful pass from Jamelle. I cursed and reminded Pam and Q that we couldn't let her get the ball so close to the basket. This was one of the things we'd talked about for the past several days—but there was a tremendous difference between knowing what had to be done and actually being able to do it.

On our next trip down, we were more deliberate, running a series of picks for each other and working the ball around the perimeter. Then finally, I got the ball in the left corner, and saw that Keisha was leaving me a foot between herself and the baseline. Big mistake. I was not a fast player, but I had an extremely quick first step, and that is all you need, really, to get by your defender. Now I swung my right leg over to the open space that Keisha was leaving by the baseline, turning my whole body to the left to shield the ball. In one motion I hurled myself past her and dribbled, and by the time she reacted, I was already gone. Jamelle and Diane ran toward me, waving their arms. I head-faked, crouched, and they both flew by me; it was like ducking under a wave. I shot the ball, and let out a yell as it dropped through the hoop.

That was the way it went for the first five minutes. They scored, then we scored, and both teams were so effective on offense that it seemed like the first team to miss would lose the game. We finally did both miss, of course—them before us—but neither team led by more than two throughout the entire first quarter. We were playing with the intensity of the last two minutes of a game, and all the people in the stands—except for the scouts—kept jumping up out of their seats.

No matter where I was, whether I could see her or not, I was always conscious of Raina. When they were on offense, I kept an eye on her, trying to deny her the ball when I could, and making sure that she didn't get past me. When they were on defense, I could just *feel* her. She'd yell at her teammates to make sure they knew where I was, and collapse back on me when she could afford to leave Telisa for a second, so I knew that she was conscious of me, too. I kept track of what she scored, and held off from immediately going down after each of her baskets and trying to retaliate with a score of my own. She made some beautiful plays—a reverse lay-up through the branches formed by Pam's and Q's arms, a falling jumper from the top of the key with Telisa's hands right in her face, a no-look pass to Keisha which made Q jump in the wrong direction. I swore under my breath each time she did something like this, but I also admired the plays, and wished that I could ooh and ah along with the crowd, and that they were happening to anyone but us. She seemed to like what I was doing, too. "Nice pass," she said after

I'd hit a cutting Telisa for an easy bucket. "Good shot," she said, as she helped me to my feet after I'd been hammered going in for a lay-up.

I was not as encouraging of her. While I did help her up once after Q knocked her down, I couldn't say anything appreciative; there was too much at stake. We slammed into each other a couple of times when we were both going after loose balls, and I'd whirl around with my fists clenched and see that it was Raina. Then I'd grit my teeth to quell the hostility I'd normally unleash in that situation, and want to let it out at her anyway. My need to outdo her was as passionate as hate. On the strength of pure fury, I pushed my team to play even more aggressively while Raina's team let up for a short stretch in the second quarter. We took advantage of their lapse and scored on four straight possessions, giving us a six-point lead at halftime. I ran into the locker room, still bouncing with nervous energy. Raina and I both had fifteen points.

At halftime Coach Fontaine talked about blocking out better on rebounds and keeping up our intensity—as if that would be a problem. I drank several cups of water to stave off dehydration and then called Q and Telisa over for a private huddle.

"We gotta win this, y'all," I said.

"We will," said Q. We had our arms draped around each other and our heads bent together; sweat dripped off our foreheads and onto the floor.

"T," I said, "save yourself on offense if you start to get tired, 'cos you ain't gonna wear Raina out. She's in great shape, and if you runnin low on energy, just pace yourself and keep it for the end. Q, Diane *will* get tired, so just keep pushin her around when we're on D, and then make her move as much as you can when we're on offense."

"All right," said Telisa.

"Got it, homegirl," said Q.

I had my right arm around Q, and my left arm around Telisa, and now I shook my friends and raised my head to look at them. "Let's make sure this ain't our last game," I said.

Telisa looked back at me, and I saw several different emotions play across her face. "I don't want there ever to *be* a last game," she said.

We shot around for a few minutes to warm back up, and then the second half began. I don't know what Raina had told *her* teammates at halftime, but they came out playing as if possessed. They poured on their offensive power. Diane made use of her size and set up camp beneath the basket, and the forwards found her three times for easy scores. Keisha took advantage of our preoccupation with Diane and Raina, and got open a couple of times for easy jumpers. When we sank back on Diane or sent somebody out at Keisha, Raina stepped into the open spot and her teammates delivered her the ball. Then she'd either shoot right there or make a quick move to shake off her defender and take it all the way in to the basket. Twice she beat Telisa and came straight at me. One time I reacted quickly enough to cut off her drive and force her to pass, but once she got to me and made a quick spin move, which left me guarding a patch of empty air while she continued on by for a lay-up. "Fuck," I said aloud, and the ref warned me to watch my language. I glared at him and ran up the court.

We were playing hard, and not doing badly, but Raina's team was brilliant. They completely overwhelmed us. It was as if we were running along as fast as we could, and their team zoomed by in a Ferrari. All we could do was hang on and not panic and wait for their outburst to end. This was not easy, of course—my teammates looked shaken, and our coach screamed incessantly during the time-out he called for damage control, and even I was beginning to get nervous. Basketball is a game of runs, and often one team plays as if superhuman for a while, and then comes back down to earth while the other team gets its turn to shine. But that's hard to remember when you're flailing in the face of someone else's perfection. We just kept playing as hard as we could, and at one point, I caused us all a minor scare by landing awkwardly on my arm when I dove into the stands for a loose ball. I shook it out, but it still hurt, and it didn't seem to be lined up correctly. I didn't care, though—it was my left arm, it was expendable. At the end of the third quarter, we crawled back to our bench. There'd been a fourteen-point turnaround since halftime, and now we were down by eight.

"Goddamnit!" Coach Fontaine yelled, and he was so mad he seemed to be foaming at the mouth. "What're you trying to do, *give* them the game? My *grandmother* could put up a better fight than you guys, and she's been dead for twenty years!" We all hung our heads. "Don't hang your heads!" he yelled. Then he put his hands to his own head, and I was afraid he was going to sacrifice his few remaining hairs. He didn't, though; he brought his hands back down empty and looked at us. "All right. What we're gonna do is switch to player-to-player. We need to put more pressure on their offense. Q, you take their center, and make sure you deny her the ball. Telisa, you get their point guard. Celine, you get Jamelle. Pam, you take that Keisha girl, and Nancy, you take Raina."

I looked at him, surprised.

"I know she's a guard," he said, "but I figure you know her game as well as she does."

This was probably true, and defense is three-quarters anticipation anyway, so I nodded and said, "All right."

We huddled, gave a cheer for both our school and our city—"'Wood!"—and walked back onto the court for the start of the final quarter. The crowd noise increased as we prepared to resume play. All the spectators leaned forward in their seats, and that's how I felt, too—on edge, excited, sensing that the rout of the third quarter was not the end of the story and that there was more to be written that day.

We played them even for the first two minutes. They weren't giving at all—it was like trying to move the Great Wall of China with our bare hands—but at least they weren't increasing their lead. They'd also switched to a zone defense, which meant they were probably getting tired. Meanwhile, our player-to-player seemed to be having an effect—they hadn't expected us to spring it on them, and it forced them to reset their offense, and to work harder for everything they got. I did not let Raina out of my sight. Coach Fontaine was right—I *did* know her game; I knew where she liked to cut, and the difference between a head fake and the beginning of a real shot, and the way she slipped down under the big girls to position herself for rebounds. She didn't score in those first couple of minutes, and slowly, so slowly that maybe no one even noticed, the tide began to turn. We chipped away at their lead, scoring a three-point play for one of their baskets and then a basket after they missed, making up the difference one or two points at a time. At four minutes, Raina beat me to the baseline to score her first bucket of the quarter, and then I posted up on the other end and answered her. After the ball came through the net, we stopped and stared at each other, and all of our teammates looked from her to me and back again. A strange hush came over the crowd, and somehow everyone in the building—players, fans, coaches—seemed to understand that from then on, the game belonged to Raina and me.

The next time her team came down on offense, they made no pretense that anyone else would shoot. They set a double pick for Raina, and I got caught up for a moment, and she had a split-second chance to hit the jumper, which she did. On our end, the same idea. Telisa passed straight in to Q, but Q found me at the baseline and I sank the open shot. Then Raina displayed a move I hadn't seen before and drove past me to get to the basket. Then Telisa fed me the ball on the right wing and I beat Raina for a short jumper in the key. The crowd cheered and leaned forward even further.

There are certain times when a basketball game becomes a contest between two people. Wilt Chamberlain vs. Bill Russell in the NBA finals. Magic Johnson vs. Larry Bird anytime. That was what was happening between Raina and me now. Our teammates, sensing this, stepped aside and let us go at each other, helping us when they could or when we'd let them. I still played Raina tightly on defense, jockeying for position, getting her elbows in my chest or shoulders before she cut out to meet a pass, bending my knees and keeping my feet ready to move when she got the ball and squared up to the basket. I couldn't seem to stop her, though—she scored on nearly every possession—and she wasn't doing any better with me. Raina wasn't actually guarding me—they were still in a zone—but I tried to challenge her directly as much as I could. She made sure that I knew she was there. She bumped into me whenever I passed, blocked me out whenever a shot went up, and I'd feel her hips and shoulders press into my side; feel the rough material of her uniform against my hands.

My team had whittled the lead down to three. There was a minute and a half left, and everyone was tired—we took longer to get to our spots when the ball was dead, and all of us, in the universal sign of basketball exhaustion, were leaning over and grabbing the bottoms of our shorts. Raina and I were both gasping for breath, and we knew it was now that we'd each see what the other was made of. A player's character is most evident in two situations: when the game is on the line, and when she's exhausted. It's easy to play well when you're feeling rested and there's nothing at stake, but the truly great players step up and take the game into their hands; the truly great players reach down and draw things out of themselves when they think they have nothing left. Raina and I had both been in—and shone in—the first situation many times, but I don't think either of us had ever been as tired as we were in the fourth quarter of that game. We had used all our strength; we were barely able to stand, and when I lifted my feet to move, it felt like there were fifty-pound weights in each of my shoes. Worse, I was dehydrated, and I began to feel the twitches in my calves that were always the precursor of cramps. There was only a minute and a half left in the game, though. I prayed that I would make it.

Raina's team got the ball out of bounds after their last timeout, and they came down and set up their offense. Raina got free of me—my mind moved with her but my body refused to follow—and Jamelle hit her with a pass on the right wing. By the time I got to her, I was a sitting duck, and she went past me and headed on toward the basket. Then Q, who'd been guarding Diane on the weak side, somehow managed to swoop across the key and leap into the air just as Raina was going up for the layup. Raina was past her, but Q reached over Raina's body with her left hand and swatted the ball, from behind, clear out to the sideline. It was a spectacular block, but we didn't have time to celebrate. I saved the ball from going out of bounds, and passed it to Telisa, who took off downcourt on a fast break. I filled the lane, barreling down the left side of the court, and she hit me with a bounce pass ten feet from the hoop. Jamelle was there, but I blew by her, and then encountered Keisha in the middle of the key. I started toward the left side of the basket but then spun backwards toward the middle; then Keisha's hand came down hard on my left arm as I put an underhand scoop shot in with my right.

The noise from the crowd almost blew the roof off. My teammates clapped me on the shoulders and whooped and yelled. Both refs called the basket good, and Keisha was hit with the foul. I walked to the free throw line and then bent over to grab my calves; they were twitching even more now and I knew the cramps were likely to hit at any moment. I tried to put that possibility out of my mind. The ref handed me the ball, and I bounced it three times, then took a slow, deep breath and shot. It went in. The game was tied. There were fifty-eight seconds left.

We sprinted back on defense, and picked up our players, but they weren't in any hurry to shoot. They set screens and passed the ball around—over to Raina, in to Diane, over to Keisha, back to Raina. Then, with eight seconds left on the shot clock, Raina rubbed me off on a pick from Jamelle. She got the ball about three feet above the top of the key—a good twenty-three feet out and probably well beyond her range—and everyone in the building knew that it was time for her to shoot. And in that moment when I was fighting through the pick, a strange series of thoughts went through my head. First, I thought about how desperately I wanted her to miss, so that we could go down and make the basket and win the game. But then I realized that I fully *expected* her to score, and that this was the way it should be. Raina *was* basketball to me, with all the hope and pain and passion that the sport had come to entail. She was the person I loved best and the only thing I believed in, and I did not want her to falter.

She hesitated for a moment, and I was sure she was waiting for me to rush out at her so she could leave me in the dust. I pulled up two feet short, so she couldn't drive around me, and just as I stopped I realized my mistake. She actually was within her range—I remembered seeing her shoot from the same spot in the park in September—and now, as if to remind me, she let fly. The ball hit nothing but net. There was no three-point line yet in high school play, so the basket only counted for two. But that still put us down by two points now and there were thirty-four seconds left.

Coach Fontaine called our last time-out, and I sat down and massaged my calves while he talked.

"O.K. What we're gonna do is this," he said, drawing a diagram on his clipboard. "Telisa, you take the ball down and pass it off to Celine on the right wing. Q, you're gonna be over on that side, too, and Pam you'll be down on the baseline. Nancy'll be alone on the left wing. Then Celine will reverse the ball to Telisa, and you, Telisa, will kick it over to Nancy, and at the same time, Q, you'll cut across on the low post. Their guard and forward are gonna jump out to cover Nancy, and Nancy, Q's gonna be wide open so you can dump it in to her. And then you just *score* it, Q. Everyone's gonna be expecting Nancy to shoot, and they're gonna leave you all alone. You've got the last shot, and you *sink* it, Q, and that'll send this game into overtime."

Everyone was silent. Q, who normally would have been thrilled to get the call, just raised her eyebrows at him.

Coach Fontaine looked around at all of us, and sighed, and then he did something he'd never done before—he capitulated. "O.K., fuck it," he said, laying his clipboard down. "Just get the ball to Nancy."

We went back out on the floor, and Celine threw the inbounds pass to Telisa, who brought the ball up uncontested. When she crossed half-court, there were twenty-seven seconds left on the shot clock, and thirty-one seconds left in the game. I was lined up on the right baseline, Celine was at that wing, Pam was on the left wing, and Q was in the low post on the left side. Raina was even with the free throw line and next to Pam. Telisa passed it to Pam, and she held the ball for a moment, and then passed it back to Telisa. Twenty-three seconds left on the shot clock. Telisa swung it over to Celine, who passed it down to me, and I faked over to Q, and then gave it back to Celine. Seventeen seconds left on the shot clock. Then Celine made a near-fatal mistake—she threw it over the top of the key, but telegraphed the pass so badly that Raina got a hand on it and would have stolen it if Pam hadn't stepped up to meet the ball. Pam quickly kicked it out to Telisa, to get it away from Raina's grasp. Thirteen seconds left on the shot clock. Telisa dribbled the ball once, and then passed it back to Celine, and just as Celine caught it, I cut hard across the baseline, using a double screen from Pam and Q to break open on the left wing. Celine reversed the ball to Telisa, who threw it over to me. The pass was a bit late, though, and Raina arrived at the same moment. I pivoted a couple of times, but Raina was a flurry of arms and legs—there wasn't an inch on either side of her and it was impossible to shoot. Pam had cut across to the other side, so I dumped it in to Q; there were seven seconds left on the shot clock and eleven seconds left in the game. We both knew that she was not going to shoot. Keisha collapsed back on Q, though, leaving an open space in the corner, so I jabbed straight at Raina and then cut hard toward the baseline. Q held the ball up, held the ball up, and then hit my outstretched hands, and I got off a fadeaway jumper just as Raina came and waved her arms in my face. She was too late—the shot was launched, and it was good. There were six seconds left in the game when the ball went through the hoop, and they couldn't stop the clock now because they'd used their last time-out. There were four seconds left by the time Raina picked the ball up and stepped out for the in-bounds pass.

She didn't have to put the ball in play. You're allowed five seconds to make the in-bounds pass, and she could have just waited for the clock to run out and let the game go into overtime. That would have been the wise thing to do; that would have been the choice she made ninety-nine times out of a hundred.

But for some reason, just then, she wasn't thinking. She tried to pass the ball in to Keisha, not seeing that I was still lurking nearby and hadn't run back with my teammates on defense. I was a good five feet behind Keisha, but she was standing near the top of the key, and the soft, floating pass that Raina threw hung in the air just long enough for me to run over and slap it away. Keisha didn't see me coming, so she didn't step up to meet the ball, nor could she react quickly enough to grab it once I'd knocked it out of her hands. I picked it up just inside the free throw line, and took two dribbles toward the hoop. There I met Raina, and when I went up for the shot, she hammered me to prevent the sure basket. And as I left the ground, my calves finally locked up with cramps, and I hit the floor yelling in pain.

I don't think my teammates understood what was happening; my yell had been obscured by the sound of the buzzer. They all swarmed around me as I lay on the floor, and Telisa thumped me hard on the shoulder.

"You are *it,* girl!" she yelled. "You are *it!* Hit one of these free throws and this game is *over!*"

Out of the corner of my eye, I saw Raina walking around, fingers locked behind her head and face twisted into a pained grimace. She squatted for a moment and rocked back and forth, and when she stood again, and turned away from Keisha's offer of a hug, I saw that there were tears in her eyes.

When my teammates had calmed down enough to notice my expression, they finally realized that something was wrong. By this time, I'd rolled over onto my back, grabbed a calf in each hand, and stuck my feet up into the air. Telisa called for our coach. He ran onto the court, yelling at everyone to give me some room. Then he extracted my legs from my hands, sat me up, and massaged my calves vigorously, one after the other. I felt various pats on my back and shoulders. I heard the voices of the refs, and was vaguely aware that they sent all the players back to their benches. Coach Fontaine rubbed and rubbed, and I squeezed my eyes shut and swore and howled, until finally, after several minutes, the cramps began to loosen. We stayed there for a few minutes, he pulling my toes up toward my knees to stretch the muscles. Every time I brought my toes back down, though, so that my feet were at even slightly more than a right angle with my legs, my calves twitched and the cramps threatened to return.

"It's gonna be a bitch to shoot," I commented solemnly. "I can't extend my feet at all."

"It'll be O.K.," he comforted. "Even if you miss them both, we'll just go into overtime."

He didn't say what we both knew—that if the game did go into overtime, my team would play without me; I'd be doing no more running that night.

After another few minutes, I was able to stand. The crowd clapped happily when they saw I was all right, and then yelled out in earnest when I walked to the free throw line. All the players milled around at their benches; since time had expired, they didn't take their normal spots at the key. I glanced over at Raina before I lined up to shoot. She wouldn't meet anyone's eyes, and she looked like she wanted to jump off the nearest pier. I wanted to tell her it was all right, but it might not be. I had two free throws coming, and there was no time left on the clock, and the score was tied at seventy-three. Two misses would send the game into overtime. One make would end their season, and Raina's high school career.

The ref handed me the ball and backed away. I bounced it three times, spun it backwards in my hands. But then, because I was afraid that the cramps would return, I tried to shoot without going up on my toes, which is nearly impossible. There was no strength behind my shot, and the ball just skimmed the bottom of the net. I turned away in disgust. The crowd groaned, and a few people in the visitors' section heckled and laughed. I walked around a bit to try and get a grip on my nerves, and when I got close to our bench, Telisa stepped out and slapped me on the butt. "Come on, girl," she said. She looked pissed, although I knew she was just trying to encourage me, and I nodded in reply. I went back to the free throw line, and the ref handed me the ball. And as I stood there and bounced it my usual three times, I felt the strange convergence of feelings again. Raina waited there, behind me, and if I made this shot, the game would be ours. And I wanted to win—I wanted to win very badly—but in my heart I did not want to beat her.

In the end, though, this was just a game, a playoff game in the closing stretch of the season of our final year. And I was not going to blow a chance at victory because I was afraid of a little pain—or, for that matter, because of Raina. I emptied my mind of all thought. I took a deep breath, and bent my knees, and prepared for my calves to lock. Then I went up with the shot, and yelled in pain as it left my hands, and hit the floor clutching both of my calves again so I did not see the ball go through the hoop.

The crowd exploded. I was mobbed by my teammates. They came and smothered me, jumped all over each other, shouted and laughed as tears streamed down their faces. The cramps were not so bad this time, and I was yelling for joy now as much as from pain. Telisa got down and rubbed my calf muscles, and in a minute I stood up and joined the celebration. What I saw around me was madness—there were people swarming onto the court, whooping, people jumping up and down in the bleachers. I raised my face to the ceiling and let out a roar. My teammates were pumping their fists in the air, and when I looked at Q and Telisa, I saw in their faces the same thing that I felt—we did it, we meant something, we won. A reporter pushed her way through the crowd and tried to get my attention.

"Nancy, how do you feel about this victory?"

"Holy shit!" was all I could think of to say.

Telisa, who had her arm around me by then, threw her head

back and laughed. "Girl, your shit *is* holy now, far as I'm concerned."

It was the happiest moment of my life—the happiest, and also, the most heartbreaking. For I had outdone Raina—I'd finished the game with thirty-seven points and she with thirty-three, and more importantly, my team had won. But I wanted more than anything for her to be able to share my joy. I wanted to bring her into the winners' circle with me; it was her example that had enabled me to get there. But she'd disappeared from view, and she wouldn't have been able to join me anyway. And I felt an odd pain as I stood there, because I realized, suddenly, that things were more complicated than just my having beaten Raina. It was as if, in defeating her, I'd also defeated a part of myself. And so later, when things had calmed down a bit—after we'd accepted congratulations from fans and talked to our parents and gotten a wrap-up speech from our coach; after we'd shaken hands with our opponents and I'd met the full force of Raina's eyes with their pain and loss and pride—I left my teammates whooping in the locker room and went into a bathroom on the other side of the gym. And I locked the door and covered my face and cried.

CHAPTER 19

That game against Raina's team turned out to be the last victory of my high school career. The next Wednesday we played Buena, which was the number-one ranked team in CIF and the eventual state champion. We didn't have a chance—they had a relentless full-court press, and twelve robotlike players whose programming did not allow for errors. And in contrast to their perfection, we seemed to have expended all of our energy and emotion during our game against Raina's team. My team was as flat as stale champagne. We didn't embarrass ourselves—the final margin was eight points, and Q and I both scored over twenty—but we had nothing special left to show anyone. It had taken a tremendous conflagration of hunger and will to reach the heights we'd achieved the previous game, and there was no way that we—or I—could have duplicated that effort. Despite our respectable statistics in the loss, the difference was apparent to everyone.

"I wish you'd played like that against *us,*" Raina joked after the game.

I smiled. "It's because we played like we did against you guys that we played like that against them."

Raina had been quiet for the first two days after we'd played each other. That night, she'd gone out with her teammates, and then they'd all stayed over at Keisha's. On Sunday she'd come home and dragged around the house, staying in her room most of the time and occasionally appearing at the table to be fed, or in front of the television to be distracted. She kept to herself, which was understandable, and I tried to stay out of her way. There was a sadness about her I thought I recognized—the sadness of having lost, of course, but also, the sadness of knowing you were responsible for the situation which was making you sad.

Claudia was quiet, too, although there was, about her quietness, a certain peace. And while no one talked about this, I thought it might have had something to do with what had happened after our game against Raina's team.

By the time I'd come out of the locker room that night, the gym was almost empty. The custodians were pushing the bleachers back against the walls and sweeping up the trash that had fallen beneath them. There were two clumps of parents—one from Raina's team, one from mine—standing close to the door; Diane and Q were talking to reporters. I looked around for Raina, but couldn't find her. Claudia was leaning against the wall on the far side of the gym, and, a few feet away from her, my father was talking to Pam's dad.

"Hey, big shot," my father said as I approached. "You coming home with me, or are you and your teammates going to go out and cause some trouble?"

I smiled, wearily. "We're gonna cause trouble," I said. "But I gotta shower first, so I guess I'm coming home."

Just then, Raina and Stacy emerged from the visitors' locker room. Even from where I stood, I could tell that Raina's eyes were red; it looked like she, too, had found a quiet place to cry. I didn't know what to say to her, and I hoped Claudia had brought her own car so that we wouldn't have to ride home together. Raina made her way towards us, slowly, and people turned as she passed; they watched her go, but seemed afraid to talk to her. When she'd almost reached her mother, though, someone finally stepped in front of her. I saw, to my surprise, that it was Paula. Raina stopped, and her face changed, and Paula took her into her arms. They hugged for what seemed like a long time. Raina's body relaxed slowly, giving itself up to this comfort. Then Paula let go, mumbled something to Raina, and began to walk over to me.

I stood there, watching her approach. I didn't know what she could possibly want, and half-expected her to curse me, or slap me across the face. When she reached me, though, she stopped and held out her hand.

"I just wanted to tell you," she said, "that you played a great game."

She looked me straight in the eyes. Her hair was a bit disheveled, her face was moist with sweat, and her voice was hoarse from yelling. I was so stunned that it took me a moment to remember to shake her hand.

"Thank you," I finally said.

"Your team has a lot of guts," she said. "Good luck in the next round."

I couldn't say anything, but Paula didn't seem to notice. She let go of my hand, and turned to my father, who looked as surprised as me. She nodded to him, slowly, and with great significance, as if she were conceding something, or handing me back over. Then she turned away from us, toward Claudia. Claudia looked oddly shaken; I realized that she'd seen the whole thing, and I wondered if Paula would talk to her now. Paula just stood there, though. But then she smiled. It was a tired smile, a complicated smile, containing sadness and anger and pain. But there was love in it, too, and this love rippled out and softened the rest of her face. Claudia smiled back, and her eyes welled up. They looked at each other like quarreling sisters, like hurt but hopeful lovers. Finally, Paula nodded again, and Claudia nodded back. Then she turned and walked out of the gym.

Raina and I didn't talk about this, although I was sure that she had seen it. We didn't talk much at all over the next few days, and we weren't going to touch the subject of Claudia and Paula if we couldn't even speak about our game. On Tuesday morning, at the breakfast table, I tried to get her to discuss it.

"You played great, Raina," I said as we both bent over our bowls of cereal. Our parents were still in the bedroom getting dressed. "You played great, and we couldn't stop you, and you got nothing to be ashamed of."

She didn't look up from her cereal. "I fucked up in the last five seconds," she said. "So whatever I did before that don't mean shit."

I straightened up and looked at her. "But if it hadn't been for you, there wouldn't of *been* a last five seconds. The last five seconds wouldn't even of *mattered*."

Her shoulders were slumped and she kept her eyes lowered; she looked tired, sad, defeated. "Listen, Nancy," she said. "I know you're trying to make me feel better, and I appreciate it, but it ain't gonna work. So let's just drop it, O.K.?"

I considered this for a moment, and then spoke cautiously. "O.K.," I said. "I just want you to know that I think you're the shit."

"I'm a big fuckin loser is what I am."

"Raina, that's so wrong. You know that's—"

She slammed her spoon down and glared at me. "Listen, you won, O.K.? What more do you want?"

I didn't know what to say; it was like she'd reached across the table and slapped me. I must have looked stricken, because Raina's face softened a little. She brought her braid around over her shoulder and started pulling on it, her hands moving one on top of the other, as if she were climbing a rope.

"I'm sorry," she said. "I didn't mean to snap at you. But can we please not talk about the game no more?"

And we didn't, not for weeks. Soon after we abandoned the subject that morning, our parents came in, and maneuvered around each other in the kitchen to make eggs and toast. They may have sensed the tension between Raina and me, but they didn't acknowledge it; I think they still had their own tension. I didn't wonder about them much, though, because I was still trying to make sense of what had happened with Raina. For some reason, until that morning, I had believed that her view of our meeting had been different from mine. I had known that she'd wanted to beat me, but I'd thought that the stakes had been different for her, that it had somehow been less personal. But now, seeing how upset she was—not just because she'd made an error, but because she had lost—I realized that she'd been competing against me as much as I had been competing against her. And I had won. It still didn't seem quite real to me; I still didn't know what to make of it. I'd been so used to thinking of her as better than me that I'd never considered the possibility of outdoing her. Now that I had, I saw that she wasn't invincible, and I wondered if I'd thought too much of her all along. Although I didn't want to, I admired her less, and it was obvious that she thought less of herself as well. The balance between us, clearly, had shifted. She seemed, now, to think that I *had* something, something she didn't, and I was afraid that it was true, but also afraid it *wasn't* true; that someday, I'd fail to live up to her expectations, just as she had failed to live up to mine.

Then another thought occurred to me, as obvious but startling as when you unexpectedly meet your own reflection. *I* was driven by hunger, too—perhaps a different kind from Raina's, but it was hunger just the same. I, too, wanted to show people what I was capable of, and to prove myself—to the teachers who thought I was undisciplined and lazy; to the white kids who'd beat me up when I was little; to the black kids who'd laughed at the idea of a Japanese kid playing basketball; to Raina, who I admired but also envied; to my father; to my mother; to anyone who had ever believed that I couldn't succeed. This realization brought up other questions, though, because I didn't understand how the need to prove myself could coexist with my fear of acting. But it did occur to me that as much as I loved L.A., my hunger was exactly why I'd leave it. It was the reason I was as fated to go as those, like Telisa and Raina, who couldn't seem to get out fast enough.

The tension remained between Raina and me, but we submerged it, and it finally got hidden, or almost hidden, by our reactions to other events. The biggest one, for me, was my team's elimination from the playoffs. The night of our loss to Buena, I stared grimly out the window on our bus ride back to school. I felt hollow. Losing was always devastating to me, but that night I felt like someone had died. I went out for a last sad meal with my teammates, and sat with Telisa and Q. We had just played our last game together. I knew, vaguely, that I'd never again put on our uniform; never again ride in a creaky yellow school bus with torn seat covers and stale air—but that wasn't what was hurting me just then. What hurt was that we had lost. We had gone all the way to the CIF semifinals, and lost to the eventual state champion, but it simply was not enough. It didn't matter how well we'd done, or who had finally beaten us. We had lost. I hadn't been good enough. I had failed.

Around eleven, I finally went home, keeping my windows rolled up and my eyes wide open, as I always did, now, when I drove. The house was dark and silent—everyone must have gone right to sleep when they got back from the game. I played with the dog for a while, then went upstairs, sprawled spread-eagle on my bed, and tried to contemplate the fact that my high school basketball career was over. It didn't register. I said it aloud but still didn't believe it. Maybe it would hit me once the whole season, and not just ours, was over—another two weeks down the line. As I lay there an unfamiliar question worked its way into my mind. I wondered if basketball would continue to mean so much to me, apart from the histories and ties of high school, maybe even apart from Raina. For three years she'd been the reason I had pushed myself so hard. Could anything ever matter like that without her?

After a few more minutes of staring at the ceiling, I got up and took a shower. Just as I finished putting on shorts and a T-shirt, I heard Raina come out of her room, then the sound of the floor creaking as she tiptoed down the hallway. She knocked on my door and opened it when I told her to come in.

"Hey," she said.

"Hey," I replied. "How come you're still up?"

"Couldn't sleep," she said. "You have a good time?"

I picked my dirty uniform up off the floor and threw it in my laundry basket. "Yeah, right. We ate stale French fries and cried in our Cokes."

Raina nodded. "If you'd of cried on your fries instead of your Coke, it would of made them saltier and they would of tasted less stale."

I looked at her wearily, too immersed in my sadness to untangle what she had said.

She smiled warmly. "I know how you feel."

I walked around my room, picking things up absentmindedly and putting them down again. "Well, it feels pretty bad," I said. "Any suggestions about how to relieve it?"

"Sure," she said, smiling. "Let's get drunk."

I knew I wouldn't be able to sleep that night anyway, so together we crashed in the living room and lamented the end of an era. We drank everything in the house—the six-pack in the fridge, a quarter bottle of rum, even a few shots of our parents' whiskey, straight, which was awful but highly effective. For the last three years, after the season had ended, there had always been the next year to anticipate, dream of, prepare for. There had also been countless leagues and AAU tournaments to keep us on our toes and to showcase us. Now, however, there was only some as-yet-to-be-named college team in the unimaginable void of next autumn. It was unthinkable that we'd be going to places where we didn't know the routine, where nothing was familiar or certain, where we were no longer coveted, but captured, and where we'd have to struggle along again at the bottom of the ladder—so at first we didn't think of it. Instead, we talked about the past. We conjured up old games, remembered in remarkable detail; we laughed about stupid mistakes we'd made, complained about the losses we'd never have the chance to avenge. Neither of us said what I think we both feared—that perhaps we'd done our best already. There was no guarantee that we'd be stars in college, and it was possible that we'd already reached, and passed, the summit of our careers.

"This is crazy," I slurred finally. "We're too young to be feelin nostalgic."

Raina seemed to find this highly amusing, and laughed so hard she nearly slid off the couch. "Let's talk about next year, then," she said. "Where you gonna go?"

"I've got it down to four. But you first."

"Down to three."

"Tell me."

She threw a glazed look somewhere in my general direction. "Washington, Michigan, and Virginia. What about you?"

"Washington, Virginia, UNLV, and Arizona. When you gonna decide?"

"I don't know. Soon. Depends on them, though, too."

This was true. The way that most schools let you know you were no longer being recruited was by suddenly halting all contact, like some cowardly lover who stops calling instead of simply telling you she's no longer interested. We had both received such messages from a couple of schools that had been top choices, and now it remained to be seen if those schools still recruiting us would continue to do so. I noted that two of our choices—Washington and Virginia—overlapped, and if Raina chose either of those places, I swore I would follow.

"Tell me when you make up your mind," I said.

"You'll be the first to know."

She spread her fingers wide on the carpet, looked down at them, back up at me. "Nancy," she said, "why don't you have a girlfriend?"

I thought, Here we go. But I said, "I don't know. I just don't."

"Don't you want one?"

"I don't really think about it. And besides, it ain't exactly like women are throwin themselves at my feet."

"You just don't know where to look. Maybe you gotta look *up* from your feet, although it's hard, 'cos they're so damn big."

I smiled. "Fuck you."

"Fuck *you,*" she said. "But listen—I know plenty of people who wanna talk to you."

"Yeah, right. Name one."

"Stacy. That girl's been sweatin you for ages."

"Yeah, but she's sweatin everybody. I don't think there's anyone else who likes me."

"That's 'cos you can't see the things that are right there in front of you."

She cupped her hands over her knees and looked at me. I wanted to hear more about my mysterious and probably fictional admirers, but just as I opened my mouth to speak she pitched forward and gagged. I jumped to my feet and half-led her, half-carried her to the bathroom, just in time for her to throw up in the toilet. Her whole body shook as the liquor poured out of her. We knelt on that cold linoleum floor, in our T-shirts and shorts, for twenty minutes. I had my arm around her tighter than I would ever have dared if we'd been sober.

Somehow we managed to drag ourselves to a standing position, and I held her up while she rinsed her mouth out and washed her face. Then I fumbled for the doorknob, opened the door, and started to lead her to her room. We got as far as the hallway. There we crumpled in a tangled heap of arms and legs, laughing, and once we were on the floor neither of us had the energy to get back up. The carpet seemed incredibly comfortable. Raina yawned and curled up against me, and I consciously made myself think, This is probably the closest you'll ever get to her. Her head was resting between my chin and my shoulder; I touched the smooth, warm skin of her arms.

So how does it feel to hold the woman you love for the first and only time? Mostly it feels like the world has fallen away, and that time has stopped, or at least slowed down to a crawl, because you are aware of each passing second. It's not a feeling of joy, really, so much as one of pure astonishment. There is no "I" in "we"; I couldn't believe that down in the vicinity of our feet there was a dark shape impossible to identify as part of her body or my own. And although I held her, although she lay encircled in my arms, I felt like *she* surrounded *me,* as if I'd been trying to embrace a thunderstorm, or the ocean. Trembling, I touched her cheek, my fingertips starting just below her left eye and going down to the back of her jaw, then tracing the line of that perfect jaw around to her chin. My hand stopped there for a moment, and then I curved it over her shoulder, moving all the way down the length of her arm until I reached her wrist. I encircled her wrist with my middle finger and thumb; the feel of her pulse made my own heart jump. I brushed my lips against her forehead for just a moment, and wished that she'd awaken and turn her face up to mine. I imagined running my tongue softly along the length of her lips, feeling the gentle curve of them, the tiny wrinkles beneath my tongue; it would be like licking a wedge of an orange. I imagined her lips parting and her tongue meeting mine; I imagined holding it gently in my mouth, and licking around it, the way I'd lick the tapered, tart end of a strawberry. I wanted our lips to intertwine like fingers; to feel the soft, incredible smoothness of the inside of her mouth; to feed her, and be fed by her, this wet, delicious fruit; to drink in all the flavors of her mouth and try to taste her soul. But she was asleep now, and would not have wanted these things with me anyway, so I just held on to her more tightly and tried to remember the way she felt in my arms. She slept easily, her breath warm against my neck. I tried to match my breathing to hers. I tried to relax so I'd be more comfortable to sleep against, but my muscles were unyielding as stone. How could she possibly sleep? I would have liked to also, of course—I was thoroughly exhausted. And sleep, it seemed to me, was the nearest we could get to entering the void, the place where we all came from and would return to someday, and if I slept, too, we could be there together. But my eyes stayed open by some will of their own. Raina threw an arm and a leg across me, and I pressed my face into her hair. I couldn't get her close enough.

Those few weeks just after our season ended were a time of general chaos. It felt like every day was devoted to dealing with one in a seemingly endless string of postseason banquets, all-star games, and other miscellaneous honors. Q was named first-team All-League, but this did nothing to lighten her mood—the four-year colleges seemed to have cooled on her, and it looked more and more like she'd be attending a JC.

In addition to being All-League ourselves, Raina and I were both named All-South Bay, All-CIF, and All-State, and these awards were especially meaningful that year because it would be the last time we received them. We were also, to my amusement and pleasure, named Most Valuable Players of our respective leagues. Instead of Claudia paying up on the wager she'd made with my father, our parents took us out for a joint celebration dinner, and hung our plaques side by side in the dining room.

Throughout those weeks, my inner life was a mess. Normally, the only thing I thought about at that time of year was the NCAA basketball tournament. That year, however, the term "March Madness" could have referred to my mental state. My emotions seemed magnified and incompatible. About "the future" I felt an intense fear, composed equally of dread of the signing period, which was closing in ever more quickly, and of my terror at the thought of Raina choosing a school that was a universe away from me. I'd basically decided by then that I wanted to go to Washington—it seemed nice up there, and the school was in a city, and there was water everywhere you looked. Also, I knew there'd be at least one other gay girl—my AAU friend Rebecca Hill, who had signed there in November. I called the coach and said that I was probably coming, but didn't give him a firm commitment. This was all a secret, though, even to the rest of my household. I wanted to keep my options open. If Raina chose Washington, then I could sign with them as planned. But if she decided to go to Virginia, I could switch over to Virginia, too, without anyone besides the Huskies coach ever knowing my original choice. Although I was scared by the implications of the half-commitment I'd made, I found—much to my own surprise—that I was actually starting to look forward to getting out of L.A. Part of it, maybe, was that I now had a set place in which to picture myself; I knew I wouldn't be stepping into a void. And part of it was that the carjacking attempt—although I still couldn't face it head-on—had shaken me enough to make me think that it might be a good time to leave.

Off the court, at home, I was happy to be with Raina, but also suspicious. Although things between us seemed to have stabilized, gotten good again, I knew better than to have too much faith in this—there were still reverberations of her team's defeat, and what had happened over Christmas was more than enough reminder of how quickly the bottom could drop out of our friendship. I felt frustration, too, at not being able to do or even say anything about my hunger for her, and of course a terrible jealousy whenever I was reminded of the existence of Toni. Strangely, though, I also felt a cautious joy, like that of a scared kid peeking out from under the covers after a thunderstorm, at the simple fact that Raina lived with me. That I could see her and talk to her every day. Somehow these emotions seemed to exist in equal parts, and all of them grew proportionately. I didn't know how they fit; in the past, one of them would form in me and then expand and expand, and the others would subside until the first one had run its course. But now all of them were there, all the time, not only not competing for space but somehow working together, making everything seem more alive and more crucial, so that the sight of a sunset could bring a lump to my throat and set me marveling at the wonders of the universe. Throughout those weeks of intense awareness I often tried to imagine a time when my senses wouldn't be as sharp as they were then. I knew such a time would come. No one could live her whole life in such a constant state of heightened emotion; it would be unbearable. As it was, I felt like one of those overloaded computers you see in old science fiction movies—pretty soon smoke would come out of my ears and I'd explode.

I think my father's life was in chaos, too, although he didn't talk to me about it. Sometimes I'd catch him deep in thought, or walk into a room where he and Claudia were sitting and feel the presence, like another person, of the conversation they'd just been having. He made a lot of phone calls from his room, and received calls from several people whose voices were unfamiliar to me. I didn't ask him what was happening. I didn't talk to him much at all.

Then one night, as I headed out to meet Telisa and Q, I ran into a strange kid on the sidewalk.

"Hi," he said, gesturing towards the house. "Is this Coach Takahiro's place?"

"Yeah," I replied. "He's my dad."

The kid held his hand out and smiled at me. "I'm Eddie Nuñez," he said.

I took his hand and looked at him closely—this was the kid over whom battles were being fought and my father's career decided. He was two inches shorter than me, and almost exactly as broad; his skin was light brown, his eyes were bright, his hair was shaggy and black. He had jeans on, and unlaced sneakers, and a black Raiders jacket that was coming apart at the sleeves, but he stood with the grace and self-possession of a man who was wearing an expensive tailored suit. "I'm Nancy," I remembered to say.

He smiled again, in recognition, and pushed his long bangs out of his eyes. "Oh, yeah," he said, nodding. "I know who you are. Your dad's real proud of you. Talks about you all the time." He seemed sincerely pleased to meet me, and I could see why people liked him—he was genuine, and open, unassuming.

"Oh, really?" I said. Then, because I didn't want to talk about my father, I said, "I hear you a kick-ass quarterback."

Eddie laughed, and I couldn't tell if there was some bitterness in his voice. "Yeah, well some people don't seem to think so."

I pointed him toward the door, and then drove off in my father's car, wondering why Eddie Nuñez had come to our house. Over at Q's, we watched the Laker game on cable, and I stayed there a while after the game was over to trade homework answers with Telisa. When I got home at 10:30, Eddie was gone, and the parents were sitting at the kitchen table, looking like they were in the middle of a serious talk. I glanced in at them and started to walk away, but my father saw me and waved me over.

"No, wait," he said. "Come here. This involves you, too, so you should hear it."

I walked over and stopped a few feet short of the table. "What?"

My father looked me straight in the eye, which he hadn't done since before my finals in January. "Larry Henderson and Dr. Shelton are being fired," he said.

My mouth dropped open. "What?"

"They're being fired," he said again, not taking his eyes off of my face. "I took the matter to the superintendent, George Bishop, who is not a football fan."

I just stood there, not knowing what to do. "What? What are you talking about? How'd you get him to believe you?"

My father smiled now, looking pleased with himself. "Well, you know, Bishop kind of likes me. Ever since I got District Teacher of the Year that time when you were in junior high, we've gone out for a beer now and then. So I just went to his office a couple of weeks ago and told him what had happened. And the day before yesterday, he came into the sports bar on Rosecrans where I've been going with Larry and Dr. Shelton, supposedly to watch the Lakers game. He came up and joined us, talking about how excited he was about next year's football season. Then he joked about how he'd heard that the two of them really had to twist my arm to get me to give Eric a passing grade. Larry and Shelton looked kind of scared for a second, but Bishop and I started to laugh, so pretty soon *they* started laughing, too. And then they told Bishop—*still* laughing—about all the stuff they'd said and done, about coming over here and implying that I'd get fired. They were so proud of themselves I couldn't believe it. Oh, they thought it was a *big* old barrel of laughs. But George Bishop didn't think it was so funny."

I just looked at him; my mouth opened and closed, but no sound came out.

My father grinned. "Well, aren't you going to say anything?"

"You mean you got Shelton and Larry to tell the superintendent *themselves*?"

"Yeah."

"In a sports bar."

"Yeah."

"With the Laker game on."

His grin got wider. "Yeah."

I shook my head and asked, "Are you sure?"

My father and Claudia both laughed. "Yes, I'm sure," he said.

I turned all this new information over in my mind, and my mouth twitched a little, as if it couldn't decide whether or not to smile. The meaning of what he'd told me hadn't really sunk in. "That's great, Dad," I said cautiously. Then something occurred to me. "But how come you didn't go to the superintendent before the end of the semester?"

My father shook his head now, and looked down at the table. "I don't know," he said. "I think I was just hoping the whole situation would go away, and not get to the point that it did." He was silent for a moment, and then looked up again. "I couldn't believe it, you know? I couldn't believe that they would do this. I thought it was just a nightmare, and I kept expecting to wake up."

Claudia leaned forward, smiling at him in a way that she hadn't in what seemed like forever. "And when you realized you wouldn't . . ."

"I took action," he said.

Then I thought of something else. "So all those nights you were out with Larry . . ."

"I was laying the groundwork," my father said. He shook his head. "You can't imagine how awful it was to sit there and listen to that man spout bullshit. I'd go to the men's room every half an hour or so just to get away from the sound of his voice."

I laughed at the image of my father hiding in a bathroom stall; the news was gradually becoming more real. Then I remembered all the mean things I'd thought and said about him, and wished I could find a way to apologize. "Holy shit," I said, shaking my head. "Holy shit. So they're out, and you're in, and now you can do whatever you want with the team."

His face, which had been moving toward a smile, stopped now, as if it had caught on something. "Actually," he said, his voice a bit lower, "I'm going to be leaving, too."

I just stared at him for a moment. *"What?"*

"I'm leaving Hawthorne, too, at the end of the school year. I turned in my resignation today."

I continued to look at him, confused. "What are you talkin about? Why?"

He held his beer bottle by the neck and picked at the label, his eyes still fixed on my face. "There'll be too much bad blood now, even with Dr. Shelton and Larry out of the picture. I don't want to profit from turning them in."

"But what about the kids?" I asked.

My father sighed. "That's the only regret I have about leaving. But I'm not sure at this point that my staying would be good for them, the tension there is getting so bad." He paused. "Besides, if the kids knew I ever gave in to those jerks, I wouldn't be able to look them in the eye. Most of the guys I like the best will be gone in another year, anyway. And if they need me, they know my door is always open."

"But what about Eddie? What's gonna happen to him? I saw him outside, by the way."

Now my father smiled, looking happy again. "Eddie will be fine," he said. "Just fine. The guy who *is* taking over is Marcus

Shaw, the JV coach, and he's been a big fan of Eddie's since he coached him as a freshman." He paused. "Eddie's the only kid who knows at this point that Larry and I are leaving. I told him about it tonight. And since Eric Henderson really *did* fail my class, I also told him he'd be the quarterback next year."

Although I was glad to hear about Eddie, I was at a loss for what to say. "Wait a minute," I finally managed. "What are *you* gonna do next year?"

He shrugged his shoulders. "I don't know. Start looking for other teaching jobs, I guess. At first I thought about just giving up the coaching job and continuing to teach at Hawthorne, but then I realized that I really didn't want to have anything more to do with the place. I've outlasted my welcome there. It's time to go."

I looked at him, not sure, yet, how I felt about all of this. There was too much information to digest all at once. I didn't know what aspect of the situation to respond to first, so I settled on the simplest piece of news. "But you took care of Larry and Shelton," I said.

He smiled. "I took care of Larry and Shelton."

I smiled back, and our eyes met, and I suddenly felt better about my dad than I had in months. I went over and offered my hand, which he slapped like one of my teammates. We grinned at each other, palms stinging. "Congratulations," I said.

With that, I went upstairs, and got ready for bed, pondering all the things I'd just heard. It was still confusing; I didn't know what to think, especially about the fact that my father would be leaving his job. Now everything made sense, though—the phone calls, the secrecy, the appearance of Eddie Nuñez. And then, as I brushed my teeth, I realized I was glad that my father was quitting—even if he didn't know where he'd be the next fall, even if he floated around for a while. The school had treated him badly, and there was no reason for him to stay there—but he wouldn't be fleeing with his tail between his legs. He had made an act of resistance, which compensated, at least somewhat, for his initial giving in. I wasn't ashamed of him anymore, and I wanted to let him know that, if only by saying something nice to him before I went to bed. But when I got halfway down the stairs, I saw that he and Claudia were in the living room, sitting on the couch, his head resting on her lap and her fingers moving in his hair. I stopped where I was and watched them. Her palm was flat against the top of his head and her fingers rubbed up and down softly. It was such a soothing, loving gesture that I closed my eyes for a moment, as if Claudia were also doing it for me. And as I stood there looking at them—Claudia rocking a little and my father completely surrendered to her hands—I felt something I later recognized as envy. I'm sure that Claudia had been deeply disappointed in my father, as I had been, as he had been as well. But she had stayed with him, supported him, in his moment of failure, and it was only later, after I had failed a few times myself, that I understood how rare and wonderful that was.

CHAPTER 20

Normally, March was my favorite month of the year. The NCAA tournament was the biggest reason for this, and in the last few years, the networks had been showing the women's games as well as the men's. Also, March was the month the city heated up again—we went from the rains and cool temperatures of January and February to the hot, sunny days of March, straight to summer with no real spring to speak of. That year, I did my usual March activities—hoops outside, the beach on some late afternoons, hours in front of the TV set on weekends—but they weren't as enjoyable as they'd been in the past. Despite my half-choice regarding Washington, I was constantly tense—I wanted desperately to know what Raina was going to do.

As of mid-March, she hadn't picked a college yet. She was under a lot of pressure to make up her mind—each day, she sat down with her three piles of information from the corresponding schools, and each night, she received a call from at least one of the coaches. Claudia tried to get her to talk about the situation, but suddenly Raina was acting like me, keeping quiet and evading all our questions.

One evening, though, as we were shooting around in the driveway, Raina rebounded one of my misses, dribbled the ball for a second, and then looked at me. "So you made up your mind yet?" she asked.

"Nope," I said, and then waited for a moment, like I always did when I lied, to be struck by a bolt of lightning.

"I can't decide what to do," she said, shooting a lay-up. There was a small strip of sunlight reflected off the top of the backboard, and as I watched it, it grew thinner and then vanished. "At Virginia, I'd get less playing time, but they got a great team. Besides, it's near D.C., so I could go hang out there sometimes on weekends. At Michigan I think I'd play more, but I ain't sure about those winters. Washington's cool—good team, nice place—but there's water right in the middle of the city, and that's weird, you know, it throws me; it's like it can't decide whether it's ocean or land. They're all good schools, though, so I don't know what to do. What do *you* think I should do?"

"I don't know," I said. I looked out into the street, where some junior high school kids were playing a loud game of stickball. It was warm, and still light out, although the sun was now beneath the horizon. The breeze was strong and pleasant; I spread my arms, closed my eyes, and leaned into it. Raina rebounded her own miss and passed me the ball when I turned back to face her. I faked left, shook my imaginary defender, took a dribble to the right and sank the jumper.

"Well, what do you think of all those places?" she asked as she threw the ball back out to me. "And what're *you* gonna do?"

I heard excited shouts in the street as one of the kids connected with the ball for a good hit. I dribbled a couple of times, breathed deeply, didn't look at her. "Well, I'm definitely more into Washington and Virginia than UNLV and Arizona." It seemed safe to reveal at least a little. "They're both cool places. I think it's between those two now, for me."

I glanced up, found Raina looking at me with interest. "But you don't know which one you gonna go to?"

"No," I said. "Not yet."

"You'll tell me when you decide, right?"

"Yeah, of course."

"You *better* tell me. I'll kick your ass if you don't." She raised an eyebrow. "Although you ain't really got that much of an ass to *kick*."

I flicked her off, and then made a lay-up. She took the ball out past the free throw line and drilled a jumper. Her shot was beautiful to watch—high, arching, with the perfect touch of backspin; it found the net as cleanly as if it had been drawn there by a magnet. I threw the ball back to her, and she hit another. I kept passing to her, and she kept making them, from all up and down the driveway, hesitating when there was a gust of breeze so it wouldn't disrupt her shot. Then, after she'd hit about ten, we switched, and I did my little shooting circuit while she rebounded for me. We were both on that day, but neither of us suggested a game. I realized, suddenly, as I kept drilling jumpers, that we hadn't played any kind of game—not Horse, not Twenty-one, not Around-the-World—since our meeting two weeks earlier in the playoffs. This struck me as odd, but also, somehow, logical. It occurred to me that all of our little contests and struggles throughout the year, all of our games and challenges, had been, in essence, the posing of a single question. But by that evening in March, as we shot around in the fading light, the question, it appeared, had been settled. We had received an answer, and, in truth, it was not the answer that either of us had expected. But perhaps that wasn't the problem at all. Perhaps we hadn't really wanted an answer.

In late March, two things happened that tipped the scale of my emotions towards joy. The first occurred on a smoggy afternoon when I came home from school. A great wave of loss had hit me, as predicted, once the playoffs were over. Feeling sad and certain that my best days were behind me, I popped in a tape of our game against Raina's team. It always made me nervous to watch tapes of old games, as if the outcome hadn't already been decided; as if something new might happen by virtue of my letting the game, as it were, be replayed. This game was particularly excruciating to watch, of course, for several reasons, and so it would be that much more exciting when we finally won. The whole game seemed to go by in about two minutes. As I sat on the floor yelling at the tiny figures of my teammates and me on the screen, Raina came home from school and plopped down on the couch behind me.

"What's this?" she asked.

"Our game against you guys." I thought that maybe she wouldn't want to see it, and felt bad that I hadn't finished watching the tape before she'd gotten home. She didn't move, though, so I let the tape roll, fast-forwarding over time-outs and breaks in the action. I watched with the eyes of a coach, and cursed us. No one picked up help-side when Keisha drove to the baseline, and so she had a clear path to the hoop once she beat her defender. I felt the urge to write this down so I could tell my teammates about it later, but then I remembered that it no longer mattered, and that they were no longer my teammates.

The game was late in the fourth quarter, and Raina's horrible in-bounds pass was coming up. I wanted to fast-forward over it, so she wouldn't have to watch it again, but that would have drawn more attention to her mistake. So I just let the tape run, and held my breath as I saw myself knock the ball away from Keisha. Then I saw myself go up for the shot. "Shit," I said aloud, hands going instinctively to my calves. There on the screen it happened again, just like I remembered. I went down, rolled onto my back, grabbed a calf in each hand and stuck my feet in the air. I could hear my swearing and howling even through the static of the tape. I saw my coach run out and turn me into a sitting position; I saw him frantically massaging my legs.

Then I noticed something. While everyone else on both teams went back to their benches, one other person remained in the frame. It was Raina. She sat there on the court next to me, her hand on my shoulder, watching. Her little blue-and-yellow figure stayed there the whole three or four minutes it took for my cramps to loosen, and I didn't look up at her once. I hadn't even known she was there.

After the game had started up again, I turned and looked at Raina on the couch. She kept her eyes down, as if embarrassed. "I didn't know you were out there with me," I said.

She smiled, almost shyly. "You were occupied."

I turned back to the screen, then back to her again. "Well, shit, Raina. I mean . . . thanks."

She lifted her head and our eyes met. We looked at each other for several moments. For the first time it occurred to me that maybe I did mean something to her, that maybe I wasn't just a part of the landscape. "You would have done the same for me," she said.

The second thing that tipped the scale was that Toni was jealous. This came to light a few days after the videotape incident, on an afternoon when Toni had actually spent an entire hour or so in our house. I was just going out to shoot some hoops when I ran into her by the door.

"Wassup, Toni?" I offered as greeting. She didn't answer. Instead she turned with a quick, challenging lift of the chin, and gave me what I suppose was a glare but what felt more like she was poking me with her eyes. I was confused by this and drew back, and by the time I recovered wits enough to speak, Toni was already out the door. I went into the living room and looked at Raina, who was standing next to the piano. "Who pissed in *her* Wheaties this morning?"

Raina sighed. "Nobody. Well, actually, you kind of did. Or, I don't know, I guess *we* kind of did."

"What do you mean?" I asked. I had no idea what Toni was mad about, but I liked the sound of being included in Raina's "we."

"She doesn't really like the living situation."

Silence.

"What?"

"She doesn't approve of this . . . arrangement."

"You mean you and your mom living with me and my dad?"

"Yeah."

"Well, why not?" I started to ask, but then I knew.

"She thinks I spend too much time with you. She thinks that I . . . that *we* . . . talk to each other too much."

"You gotta be kidding."

"No."

Pause. I could hear the sound of her breathing.

"Well, that's stupid. I mean, it almost sounds like she's . . ." I couldn't say the word "jealous"; it was unthinkable.

"Yeah," said Raina. "Yeah." As if the concept were as strange and new to her as it was to me.

We were standing in the living room maybe five feet apart. I felt the air between us like a solid entity which lay still when we were still, and which moved when we moved it. Raina had not looked at me once.

My reactions to Toni's "disapproval" rolled in one after another. The first was anger, as in, how dare she be jealous of me in the context of a situation where she was clearly, despite the "living arrangement," the winner? The second was a curious spite—if Toni didn't want me hanging out with her girlfriend, then maybe she should try spending more time with the woman. The third was a minor thrill at Toni's marking my existence. And the fourth was a huge and sudden rush of guilt, of all things—guilt for creating this problem between them, and causing Raina yet more undeserved pain. This reaction, for some reason, was what won out in the end. "Jesus, Raina, I'm sorry," I blurted. I couldn't help it. It just fell out of my mouth.

"Why should you be sorry? You didn't do nothin wrong." She looked at me, just for a moment, and then looked away. For that one moment, though, the air in the room lifted like a layer of morning fog, and there was no space left between us.

"I know. But I mean, it's not like you ain't got enough to deal with already, without me bein an issue, too."

"Maybe, but that ain't your fault."

"What's she gonna do? Forbid you to spend time with us? Stop you from talkin to me?" My voice was getting higher.

"She *can't* stop me from talkin to you. I *like* talkin to you. I mean, you *listen* to me. You . . ." She cut herself off and pressed her lips together. She ran her fingers along the surface of the piano, just to the right of where the keys ended, and stared at the back of her hand as if something were written there.

"Just forget it," she said suddenly, turning. I stood there in the middle of the living room floor and watched her disappear up the stairs.

It didn't take long for me to become happy about all of this. Toni's anger, it seemed to me, was like a coded message, although it wasn't really her anger so much as what it suggested that pleased me. Ah, jealousy, that emotion that can be more unbearable than pain, but which makes you giddy with power when it's directed at you. The discovery of Toni's jealousy, and Raina's awkwardness afterwards, told me that I played a bigger role in Raina's thoughts than I'd known. She liked talking to me. I meant something to her. I provided her with something Toni didn't.

The significance of this jealousy, or at least my perception of it, grew and grew. I'd always been worried about the impression I was making on Raina, but now I was convinced that I'd been doing the right thing all along. All I had to do was be myself, and be there. And things got better between us. She noticed me more. Even the tension, and her pain at having lost to me, seemed to have faded considerably. This had already begun to happen as soon as the playoffs were over, but then Raina and I had played in separate senior all-star games. And while I had put on merely an average performance in my game, Raina, in hers, driven by the memory of her failure against us, had scored twenty-nine points and dished out thirteen assists. She'd reasserted herself in basketball, which made her happier in life, and some of the balance that had shifted between us, shifted back. I wasn't the least bit unhappy about this. I wanted her to feel better, because it made our relationship easier; we were actually beginning to get closer. The day after the scene at the piano, she kidded with me all through dinner, using a voice more familiar than she'd used with me before, like an arm thrown across my shoulder during the telling of a private joke. The next morning at breakfast she launched Frosted Flakes at me, grinning, while our parents read the paper obliviously. A few days later during *Oprah,* we chatted happily away at each other like old and intimate friends, and at one point Raina turned and fixed me with a broad smile, as if to say, "Isn't it great that we're together?" Something had changed between us; we were on firmer ground. Even the problems of December now seemed like events of a different life—just temporary setbacks, minor obstacles, which had been overcome successfully and which had quickly spiraled into the past. We never talked about the night we'd spent asleep on the floor together—we were both pretending, I think, that we had been too drunk to remember—but I knew she *did* remember, I knew by the way she looked at me, her eyes holding the weight of the things that her words couldn't say.

I was on a high that was getting higher. My joy about Raina affected my perception of everything—food tasted better, schoolwork got easier, our drabby neighborhood wasn't quite so gray and sad. Even the future seemed a little less daunting, although the signing period was only a week away. We'd have to announce our decisions within the next few days, and I was certain that Raina would choose one of the schools we had in common. She'd pick Washington or Virginia—I knew it. And then of course I'd go to the same place, and we'd be teammates, and maybe we'd live together for another four years. And we'd travel around the country together on road trips, and talk all night in the dorms or the library or in big hotel rooms in different cities. We'd get closer, and maybe one day she'd open her eyes and really see me, and then our friendship would blossom into the romance it had always been trying to be.

I was feeling so good that one Friday night I suggested we go out to a club. As a rule, I didn't like clubs, because the prospect of being trapped in a pulsating mass of sweaty strangers did not exactly appeal to me. But every once in a while, when I was feeling particularly happy and when I could go with the right group of people, I went to a club to drink and dance and generally let loose a little. I never picked anyone up, of course, but it was just nice to go to a place where I could be myself without the danger of being ogled at, or jumped. Raina didn't get out that much either, although she liked clubs a little better than I did. The whole thing was more of Toni's scene, I think.

We took my dad's car, and collected Stacy, Telisa, and Shavon on the way. Toni was visiting her mother that night and couldn't come, which caused me no great sorrow. The five of us went to the Executive Suite in Long Beach. I liked the Suite because it was big enough to get some serious dancing done, but not overwhelmingly huge and anonymous. The crowd was mixed, composed of roughly equal numbers of black, Latina, and white women. There were usually a few scattered Asian women, and also a few gay men. It depended. That night there were even two straight couples doing it up on the dance floor. In terms of dress, it ran the spectrum—some women were wearing heels, lots of makeup, and sexy dresses so tight it must have taken hours to shoehorn into them. Some were in jeans and T-shirts. We were in the middle. I wore a sleeveless blue dress, and Telisa, Shavon, and Stacy all wore nice pants and tight, flattering shirts. Raina wore jeans and a loose green short-sleeve blouse. Simple, but she looked sexier in this outfit than all the divas in their tight black dresses.

We'd had some beers in the parking lot, so we were feeling pretty good by the time we finally got inside. "I'm gonna go do some window shoppin," said Stacy, and so she, Shavon, and Telisa went off to watch the dancers. Raina and I got drinks from the bar and took a table near the edge of the dance floor. Soon the other three were back with reports of their findings—who they knew and who Stacy wanted to know. They asked if we wanted to go take a look. "I know enough people already," Raina said, and smiled at me from behind her glass.

Stacy went over to talk to someone she recognized, and the rest of us took to the floor. We danced in a loose square, drunk and laughing, almost falling into each other. People were getting mad at us for bumping into them, but we didn't care. Everything was funny that night—the guy behind us who danced (Telisa said) like he had a stick up his ass, the very butch waitress who kept winking at me as she passed by to deliver someone's drink, the strange colors we all turned because of the strobe light. Raina laughed at all of this delightedly, more relaxed than I'd ever seen her, and halfway through the fourth song she grabbed my hand. So we danced like that, sides of a square, hands and shoulders touching. Finally the other two went off to get some drinks, and Raina and I were left out on the floor alone. I took a step away from her, not trusting my feelings or my self-control under the power of the three beers I'd consumed. But God, it felt good to be carried along in that music, with Raina just inches away. We were seventeen then, the perfect age—no job, responsibility, or other trapping of adulthood stood between us and the living of our lives. I looked at Raina, my chest bursting with love. It felt like a sea full of thunderous waves; like a huge flock of majestic birds rising from the ground and taking flight; like a thousand voices were shouting joyfully in my heart. She was smiling, her smile so warm and open that I knew I'd finally touched her, and I thought to myself that this was it, this was happiness—and it was, until Toni showed up.

I don't know where she came from. She just materialized right there next to us on the dance floor, as permanent and inevitable as a rock. And I don't know whether she'd heard we were going to be there and had come to meet us, or had just happened to show up at the Suite that night by chance. What I do know is that Raina's face changed the moment she saw her. It was as if she'd been wearing a mask, so skillfully made and genuine that it was impossible to identify as a mask until it was lifted to reveal the face beneath it, a face recognizable but not quite familiar, which at this moment was filled with confusion, desire, love. I knew she'd forgotten me, just like that. I might not have even existed.

Without either of them noticing, I slipped off the dance floor and went back to our table. Our friends were nowhere in sight. I ordered another drink, a whiskey, and although everything else in my vision was blurry, Toni and Raina were clear. I sat there holding on to that drink like it was my only friend, and forced myself to watch them.

I should say that whenever I thought of Raina, I imagined her alone. For some reason I never pictured her on the basketball court, although that was the place where we both spent most of our time. I don't know why this was so. But the fact was that when she appeared in my memory, she did so by herself, with no one else around or even possible. She was usually staring out at something—those ducks in the green reeds at Blue Star, or the ocean that night in December—totally unaware that anyone else existed. I remembered watching her at the beach that night, thinking that she seemed so profoundly alone, and that I understood her then, because I felt that way myself. And I remembered wondering if I could reach her somehow, if she would ever let me in, and thinking that maybe by easing *her* loneliness and pain, I could do something about my own.

The thing that had made me so much less jealous than I might have been was that I just couldn't imagine Raina with someone else. But now she was, with Toni, and I couldn't escape it. The only times I'd ever seen them together were at basketball games, and for a few seconds at a time at my house. Never someplace so open as a club, never someplace where their relationship was laid out for all to see.

What can I say about watching them? They were like one person, so completely together that I couldn't tell where one of them ended and the other began. I mean this not just in the sense that they were physically close, but in that together they seemed to form a third being which contained them both. They danced just barely apart, eyes engaged in some ancient dialogue, each movement of their bodies like a sweet song sung only for the other. It was clear that they were no longer in a crowded dance club in Long Beach, but totally alone somewhere, on a deserted beach or on the path of some wooded mountain. For the first time I could see how much Toni loved Raina, see it in the way she negotiated the air, like it was a toy she'd just invented for Raina's pleasure. I saw all the pain they'd caused each other and would continue to cause each other, and I saw the overwhelming beauty of that pain. And sitting there, I knew that no matter what I'd thought, I didn't know Raina in the least, and I couldn't even begin to understand her. I remembered the joy I'd felt only moments before and was overcome with shame. I meant no more to Raina, I realized, than any other friend would, or any housemate. Or maybe I had never been her friend at all, but only, in truth, her witness. This realization didn't hit me suddenly so much as it grew, like a tumor, in my stomach. I was paralyzed with pain. In all the months I'd lived with Raina and in the two years before, I'd felt that because of her some kind of bottom had dropped away; that I'd punctured through; that I no longer skimmed the surface of life but had plunged into it. And where had it gotten me? To a hard chair in a noisy club, watching her with someone else. But I could not look away from her. I could not turn my eyes away. And as she moved there in front of me all I knew, despite everything, was the love, the inevitable love, which was deepening by the moment, which did not exist in me but in which I existed.

Half an hour later they left the floor. Raina disappeared down the staircase, and Toni headed straight for my table. I felt the hair on my arms bristle as she sat down beside me. She ordered a beer, and although I didn't look at her directly, I could feel her smiling. The drink arrived, and she sat there gulping, very self-satisfied, as I turned my own glass around and around in my hands.

"So what do you think, kiddo?" she asked finally.

"Of what?"

"Of Raina's deciding to go to Michigan?"

I didn't move. She sat there smiling. She knew I hadn't known. I gripped my glass very tightly and tried to stop my hands from shaking.

"Michigan's cold," I managed, and Toni grinned. All right, I wanted to say to her. You won. I didn't know what upset me more—Raina's going to the other side of the universe, or the fact that she hadn't told me about it. There were too many things to feel. Why hadn't she told me? She'd probably known for days, maybe even weeks, but had kept it a secret. Worse than that, though, we were going to be separated. This year would be all I ever had of her. I felt we'd reached the end, that very night—the end of the world as we knew it. It was as if I'd been walking for months with my head down, and had finally looked up to discover that none of the landscape was familiar—that I was a stranger to it, and I was alone.

Just then Raina appeared at the top of the stairs. She looked from Toni to me and back to Toni again, and she must have known that something had happened between us, because she hesitated there for a moment. Then she took a deep breath and straightened her back and walked purposefully across the floor to our table. She sat down in the empty chair and fixed her eyes on me.

If I had known when I was seventeen what the next ten years would bring, I would have held on to my last year of high school even more tightly than I did. Raina would go on to have a brilliant four years at Michigan—breaking all of their scoring records, doing well academically, eventually becoming an assistant editor at a political journal in Detroit. I would have a solid career at Washington. I'd start for my last three years, and have a few great moments, but not transcendent ones; I needed Raina for that. Somehow the game wasn't life and death for me anymore; I had proven what I needed to; I had won the only game that really mattered to me. I finally buckled down with my schoolwork, though, and did well enough to land a job with the Community Development Department here in Seattle—a job I like, but don't put all of myself into, the way I had hoped I would.

Over the years, my relationship with Raina became a watered-down version of what it already was—a complicated friendship where the stakes were not clearly defined, where the same events held different and undetermined significance for each of the people involved. Raina and I would go out for drinks when we came home for Christmas—at least on the years when we didn't bring our lovers—and she'd tell me, in one sitting, a year's worth of her thoughts on her girlfriend, her job, and the state of the world. Then, with this unloaded, she'd step back into her life. It wasn't even close to enough.

What I could never tell Raina during our Christmas talks was how much I missed her, and how much her absence had affected my life. Without her around to compete against, I simply don't demand as much of myself as I used to. Raina pushed herself relentlessly because that was the only way she knew how to live, but I lacked that kind of engagement, that expansiveness of spirit; I needed her presence to spur me on to excellence. Raina did occasionally compete against people, but she didn't really need them; her struggle was with herself, and not with others. And unlike me, who cringed at the possibility of failure, Raina used each of her failures to make her stronger. Seeing this showed me that I had been right all along; that Raina was purer and better than me. I could never live up to her, and in beating her once, I'd only given her the impetus to try harder. If Raina were still as much a part of my life as she had been in high school, the sheer proximity of *her* commitment and will might reawaken some of my own. But we move in separate worlds now, which never converge. There is no one else I really care to impress.

I miss the way I felt for Raina when we were teenagers. It was a clear, consuming, uncomplicated passion, the kind which may only be possible at that age. I never let her know about my feelings, though, because I couldn't face the possibility of rejection. And I also thought, stupidly, that if I ever told Raina about my love for her, it would somehow touch the feeling, and change it, the way that light distorts cells beneath a microscope. It seemed like the better thing to do, the more noble thing, was not to mention it at all, but I know now that I should have told her. I should have told her a lot of things.

When Raina sat down at the table in the club that night, I was sure she had forsaken me. I was sure she had made the choice she did so that I would not be able to follow. But then she gave Toni the most angry, piercing look I'd ever seen from her, and turned back to me with a pained expression on her face.

"I *had* to sign with Michigan, Nancy," she said. "I kept waiting for you to make up your mind, and then Virginia and Washington both filled their guard spots with other people."

I just stared at her. I couldn't believe it. And when the significance of this information finally began to sink in, I felt my heart clench up as painfully as my calves had a few weeks before.

"Well, have you decided where *you're* going?" Raina asked, voice high and distressed. "Where you gonna go?"

"Washington," I said.

"Have you talked to the coach already? When did you make up your mind?"

"About three weeks ago," I said, and I was almost crying now.

Raina looked at me, and in her face I saw all the hurt and betrayal that must have been in my own face just moments before. "Nancy," she said, "why didn't you *tell* me?"

Her voice was thick, and filled with loss, and it seemed that she wasn't just asking this in relation to my decision about school, but also about me, about us, about my feelings for her. And the answer, although I never explained this to her, was that I was afraid—afraid in the same way that I'd been afraid to pick a college. In the darkest corners of my mind, I feared that I didn't really have what it took for success in any realm; that I had tricked everyone, including myself, into thinking I was more than I was. Holding back had become the only thing I knew how to do. And I saw now that I had always hovered at the periphery of experience—everyone's, including my own. If I didn't try, I couldn't fail, and in the potential future, anything is possible. But what I realized as we sat there, with music pulsing all around us and Raina's soon-to-be-former girlfriend being mercifully, unusually silent, was that not trying had been a failure in itself. I should have at least made the attempt to see what opportunities might exist; I should have acted in terms of the things that really mattered to me—Raina, college, my friendships, my 'hood, and so many other things in my life since then. But I failed to engage these situations for fear that they would vanish, or that somehow, by stepping into them, I'd ruin everything. And sitting there, with the distance between Raina and me increasing already, I knew that I had lost her. In that one moment she'd become a part of my past. I felt betrayed by my own choices, as if I'd been waiting for something monumental to come along but had closed my eyes for a moment, and it was then that it had passed in front of me, unseen. I wondered what Raina was thinking, just then, as she stared at me across the table. I know what *I* was thinking. I was thinking of how strange it was, the love I felt for her, how odd that it could so easily alter the shape of that room, my life, the entire world, as if *it* had existed first, and all else after. And as I stared back at her I wondered, with the kind of questioning that is its own answer, if I'd ever care like that about anything again.

ABOUT THE AUTHOR

Nina Revoyr was born in Japan, and raised in Tokyo and Los Angeles. She is of Japanese and Polish-American descent. Ms. Revoyr received her M.F.A. from Cornell University, where she is currently a lecturer.